THE DEAD WIZARD'S HAND

Thurid shook his head. 'What is the object, witch? Is it of any real value to me?'

Svanlaug untied a pouch from her saddle. 'It's valuable. It belonged to a wizard before Djofull destroyed him.'

She tossed the bag to Thurid, who opened it and peered in. Then he gave a bellow of fright and flung the bag away. The troll hounds pounced on it, and one gave the bag a shake. Out tumbled a cut-off hand, to scuttle away with its fingers like a crab into the shelter of a rock. A red stone in the ring it wore twinkled like an intelligent eye. It lunged out at the snapping hounds, making a gesture with its fingers. They retreated with startled yelps, pawing their muzzles. Leifr took a long step toward it.

A wave of fear hit him, freezing him. He had never been gripped by such dread – and he knew it emanated from the hand.

Also by Elizabeth H. Boyer

THE SWORD AND THE SATCHEL
THE ELVES AND THE OTTERSKIN
THE THRALL AND THE DRAGON'S HEART
THE WIZARD AND THE WARLORD
THE TROLL'S GRINDSTONE

and published by Corgi Books

THE CURSE OF SLAGFID

Elizabeth H. Boyer

CORGI BOOKS

THE CURSE OF SLAGFID
A CORGI BOOK 0 552 13568 2

First publication in Great Britain
This edition published by arrangement with
Ballantine Books, a division of Random House Inc.

PRINTING HISTORY
Corgi edition published 1990

Copyright © 1989 by Elizabeth H. Boyer

This book is set in 10/11pt Plantin by
County Typesetters, Margate, Kent

Corgi Books are published by Transworld Publishers Ltd.,
61–63 Uxbridge Road, Ealing, London W5 5SA, in Australia by
Transworld Publishers (Australia) Pty. Ltd., 15–23 Helles
Avenue, Moorebank, NSW 2170, and in New Zealand by
Transworld Publishers (N.Z.) Ltd., Cnr. Moselle and
Waipareira Avenues, Henderson, Auckland.

Reproduced, printed and bound in Great Britain by
BPCC Hazell Books
Aylesbury, Bucks, England
Member of BPCC Ltd.

SOME HINTS ON PRONUNCIATION

Scipling and Alfar words sometimes look forbidding, but most are easy to pronounce, if a few simple rules are observed.

The consonants are mostly like those in English. G is always hard, as in Get or Go. The biggest difference is that J is always pronounced like English Y, as in Yes or midYear. Final -R (as in FridmundR or JolfR) is equivalent to -ER in undER or offER. HL and HR are sounds not found in English. Try sounding H while saying L or R; if you find that difficult, simply skip the H – Sciplings would understand.

Vowels are like those in Italian or Latin generally. A as in bAth or fAther; E as in wEt or wEigh; I as in sIt or machIne; O as in Obey or nOte; U like OO in bOOk or dOOm. AI as in AIsle; EI as in nEIghbor or wEIght; AU like OU in OUt or hOUse. Y is always a vowel and should be pronounced like I above. (The sound in Old Norse was slightly different, but the I sound is close enough.)

Longer words are usually combinations of shorter ones; thus, 'Thorljotsson' is simply 'Thorljot's son' run together without the apostrophe.

Of course, none of this is mandatory in reading the story; any pronunciation that works for the reader is the right one!

CHAPTER 1

No amount of cleaning and airing could clear Gliruhals of the cold and gloomy atmosphere which Leifr associated with Sorkvir. Unable to tolerate a long dark winter in a place where the fires refused to burn properly, he took up residence at Dallir where the memories were more pleasant. The troll-hounds cleared out the trolls in short order, and Thurid instilled in them a healthy fear by setting up insulting poles to ward them away from Dallir's boundaries. By midwinter, Dallir seemed almost comfortable. The old servants, including Snagi, had returned, with the addition of Snagi's young nephew, called Young Snagi. He was a grave, thin little fellow who studied and emulated Snagi's every action with an eye one day to inheriting his uncle's lofty position at Dallir. Even Gunnhild, the old dragon of a housekeeper, hobbled around in her customary bad temper as if nothing had changed, and they would all go about scratching their existence from the harsh landscape as they always had done.

Leifr finally gave in and allowed them to call him the young master. He was aware that some of them still regarded him as Fridmarr or the next best thing, in spite of the fact that he had removed the carbuncle from his neck, and kept it in a small pouch in a warm place under the hearthstone.

During the long days of twilight and darkness, Leifr increasingly left the dogs in the house and walked out alone, knowing that he would not be alone for long. As he worked at his outdoor chores, a small gray shadow would materialize silently at a watchful distance – a small gray cat with amber eyes. It followed him noiselessly as he carried peat to the house or perched on a beam in the barn as he fed the cows and horses, never close enough to come within reach, but he knew she was there watching him. She never uttered a sound or came around begging for fresh, steaming milk, as the other Dallir cats did. They were fat, confident cats, certain of a handout and a back scratch, but the gray cat hugged the shadows like a thin little wraith while the other cats lapped up the milk poured out for them. When he tried to approach her, she melted away into the rocks and shadows, not reappearing until he wasn't looking directly, slipping along in the tail of his sight to take up a watchful position. If others were near, she hid, so Leifr never mentioned her to anyone else.

Only once he tentatively mentioned to Thurid the fact that he had seen a cat's form shooting away from Sorkvir's fiery immolation when Ljosa thrust the hawthorn staff into the bear-fylgja's jaws.

'Cat? I saw no cat. She couldn't possibly have had time or enough power left for shape-shifting after dragging you away from Sorkvir. Some schools of thought would have it that a life form can't be taken from a realm without replacing or exchanging it for another form, but I don't hold with that notion. She's simply gone, Leifr, but we'll get her back when the rogue star Fantur is gone. By midwinter it will start to decline. Now stop worrying about things your Scipling mind cannot grasp. Leave the study of magic to the wizards.'

Since the cleansing of the Pentacle and the breaking of the alog on steel, Thurid had enjoyed a splendid revival of popularity among the settlements of Solvorfirth. The unaccustomed and heady infusion of self-confidence, complicated by the needful confinement of the winter months, was making Thurid's company almost insufferable.

The autumn equinox was near at hand when the late summer routine was suddenly shattered, causing all the minor irritations of harvest preparations suddenly to diminish vastly in importance. The brief growing season was ended, with the dull dark months of winter to look forward to, so the inhabitants of Dallir were savoring a brief respite from their labors. As was his old habit, Thurid delivered his nightly list of complaints, suggestions, and opinions regarding the most minute details of managing the farm and the dairy and the livestock. The small homestead was more prosperous than it had been in many years, as grateful neighbors brought tributes in the form of sheep, calves, colts, and fowls. Prosperity was a vexation to Thurid, whose shoulders seemed to sag under a perpetual weight of responsibility. Hence, the tone of his nightly natterings was sharp and worried.

On the evening when it all ended, scarcely anyone was listening to him except perhaps Kraftig, Farlig, and Frimodig. They lay on the hearth with their long sharp noses on their paws, their hairy ears alert. Suddenly they all raised their heads, listening suspiciously, growling deep in their chests.

Thurid glared at them. 'Hush, you flea-ridden brutes. Now as I was going to say, with the extra wool we can get from shearing the lambs this fall before we sell them—'

Raudbjorn added his own suspicious rumbling to the dogs' chorus of growling and reached for his halberd. 'Somebody coming,' he grunted and strode to the door to look outside. He whistled, astonished and wary. 'Six strangers,' he reported over one shoulder.

Leifr joined him on the front stoop of the hall. The strangers halted their horses on a knoll overlooking the house and outbuildings, as if they were trying to judge the strength of Dallir's defenses. They conferred a moment, then their spokesman rode forward, an elder Alfar with a long white beard tucked under his belt and a fine gray cloak worn over one shoulder. The rest of his garb was similarly fine and subdued, with a few glimmers of gold ornaments to bespeak his importance. He carried no weapons except a gnarled staff, which trailed a faint plume of smoke. Thurid inhaled a quick breath at the sight of it.

'Is this the abode of one known as Thurid of Dallir?' the stranger called in a civil and dignified tone, his stern eye sweeping over the small group assembling at the doorway of the hall.

Thurid stepped forward, likewise drawing himself up tall and straight with hauteur. 'Yes, this is Dallir and I am Thurid. I bid you welcome to our hospitality, if you have come in peace.'

The spokesman moved his horse nearer, and the other five joined him, similar to their leader in appearance and stately mien. None of them carried weapons, except for staffs, carven with various devices.

'We have come for a peaceful purpose. Allow me to mention our names. I am Fodur, and these others are Einkenni, Berjast, Sveinn, Skyldur, and Varkar. You may not have heard of us, but we have heard of your exploits concerning Sorkvir. We come from the Fire Wizards' Guild, and we were all extremely gratified to hear of Sorkvir's destruction and the lifting of the Solvorfirth alog. It is in regard to that event that we have come to speak with you.'

Thurid bowed slightly. 'As it happens, I have heard of your fame. Alight and share our roof and provender. You have traveled a long way.'

Leifr glanced at him in surprise, startled at his cold, clipped tone of voice, when a more expansive manner was Thurid's usual response to inquiries about their adventures. He followed Thurid into the hall, while Raudbjorn beamed at the strangers benevolently as they dismounted.

'Thurid, what does the Wizards' Guild want with you?' Leifr asked in a low tone.

Thurid's nervous glance swept the room, and small objects jittered under the force of his discomposure. He harrowed up his hair with his fingers. 'You'll soon find out!' he muttered.

Thurid composed himself hastily as their guests entered the hall and bid them to be seated with all the gracious aplomb he could muster. Surreptitiously, he smothered the excess energies that rattled the cups on their shelves and tweaked at the cloaks on the pegs. Leifr watched Thurid wonderingly, feeling a rising presentiment of doom.

When the social amenities were taken care of and the food and drink mostly dispatched, the servants retreated to the kitchen at Thurid's direction. Fodur lit his pipe in a preoccupied manner and leaned slightly forward in his seat to address matters more serious in nature.

'Perhaps you are wondering what has brought us so far from the Guildhall,' he began, his eyes resting appraisingly upon Thurid, who had succeeded quite well in quelling his nervous outbursts of energy.

Thurid stiffened, managing to nod slightly. 'I can guess why you have come. Everyone who has ever aspired to the higher crafts of magic knows and dreads the Wizards' Guild Inquisitors.'

'Inquisitors!' Leifr eyed them suspiciously, not liking the sound of the word, nor the way they studied Thurid with their pale, unblinking eyes, as if they wanted to keep him under their surveillance every moment, trying to detect him in some technical aberration.

Fodur inclined his head. 'There is nothing to fear, if you are truly practicing our art in its most pure forms, uncolored by alien philosophies borrowed, perhaps, from unapproved sources. It is our responsibility to protect our craft from mutations, slipshod shortcuts, and distortions, as well as malfeasance and misfeasance. Only the corrupt and maladroit need fear the Inquisitors. We merely wish to inspect your methods and ask you some questions — very probing and exact questions, to be sure, but certainly you will have no objection, since you have performed so nearly in accord with the specifications of the Guild, so far. You must surely realize that the Guild is always highly curious when an unknown wizard suddenly appears and performs so spectacularly, without benefit of a proper Guild education and apprenticeship and authorization to practice as a fire wizard. The practice of magic must be

11

controlled by someone, and if not the Inquisitors, then who could be more capable of unprejudiced and impartial judgment? Now then, we may as well proceed. The Masters have reviewed their records, and the records show that you were rejected for further training after your basic courses were completed, at the First Examination. The Guild is always interested in what becomes of the aspirants it rejects. We observed you carefully to make certain that your sensibilities were not overwhelmed by temptations from the other side which you might not be able to resist, with a view to practicing some sort of magic, at least, even if it were not fire magic. It seems that you resisted the temptations and became instead a diviner by – mechanical methods.' The slightest elevation of one bristly brow was sufficient to indicate enough distaste to wither Thurid's haughty composure, and he coughed to conceal his embarrassment.

'Much of the time I was reasonably correct,' Thurid said with aplomb. 'I did no harm, at least.'

'That will be a point in your favor,' Fodur replied. 'One of many I hope to discover during our inquiry. I hope it won't take long to investigate your practices and pro-nounce them in accord with Guild standards—'

'Or at variance,' added the wizard Berjast in a rasping tone, scowling as if there were not much hope.

Leifr rose slowly to his feet, incredulously surveying the impassive features of each wizard Inquisitor. 'Do I understand that you hold Thurid in suspicion of misusing his magic and that he might possibly be punished for what he has done to save Solvorfirth? Do you mean to say he has done something wrong by driving out Sorkvir, the Dokkalfar, and the trolls and saving a great many innocent lives?'

Fodur shook his head. 'To begin with, it is not his magic. It is our magic, and we are particular about who uses it, how they use it, and for what benefit to which persons. If there were no controls, thousands of rival factions would spring up almost instantly, and instead of

12

fighting the Dokkur Lavardur, we'd be fighting among ourselves. We have no wish to punish Thurid and we will almost certainly send him back safely to Dallir when we are through questioning him at the Guildhall. You have every reason to expect that he will benefit from the experience. If he is truly aligned with Guild policy, it will be an easy matter to have him instated as an adept fire wizard. Perhaps there is knowledge that we can share with him, if he has somehow missed something in the studies that have brought him to this truly amazing and inexplicable level of magical ability.'

They all gazed at Thurid for a silent moment, some stern, a few sympathetic. One of the hopeful ones was Skyldur, weather-reddened and wrinkled as a winter apple, whose features were softened by a wise and gentle smile.

'Tell us, Thurid,' Skyldur said, 'where did you learn the skills? We know it could not have been an evil or corrupt source, or you would not have been able to do so much good.'

Thurid closed his eys, inwardly shuddering, as if looking for the resolution to continue. With a deep sigh, he replied, 'My sources will not be approved by the Guild, I fear, but you have no reason to suspect that I will offer any resistance to whatever forms of correction I may expect at your hands. I will go to my fate with dignity. The staff and satchel I used were brought to me from a barrow in Bjartur, and I studied the rune sticks I found in the satchel until I learned to control the ancient lines of force once used by the Rhbus. I practiced at the old sites and learned how to use the stones to channel the energy of the earth and sky and how to store the power in stones so it could be used later. It seemed such a beneficial influence, when used properly.'

The Inquisitors exchanged glances, and Skyldur's expression was sorrowful. Fodur drew a deep breath, his tone regretful. 'Rhbu magic, or earth magic, is not recognized as reliable and safe by the Guild. In fact, it's regarded as an archaic and frequently dangerous usage. You will be required to surrender your satchel and staff, and your memory will undergo purging of all Rhbu spells. You are yet an unskilled practitioner, and the longer you continue, the more liable you are to gain acolytes, not to mention the discovery of knowledge that may in time pollute the fountains of fire magic everywhere. I truly regret what must be done, but it is for the protection of the powers of the Guild. Any corruption will weaken our knowledge and slow our progress toward the perfect understanding of the powers of the mind. Rhbu, or earth powers, were our ancient beginnings, but they are better left behind in our search for the mental and astral powers we use today.'

Leifr reeled with the shock, glancing at Thurid, who slumped in his seat, trembling at the bitterness of his defeat. 'You can't do this,' Leifr stated with cold fury. 'Rhbu magic is surely as good as your fire magic. I was there, I saw Thurid's spells. You can't possibly find fault with his power. It seems to me that your Fire Wizards' Guild is overly strict and narrow in its interpretations of what magic can be used and who is to practice it. If your fire magic is so superior, then why was it Rhbu magic that was Sorkvir's bane?'

Raudbjorn nodded and grunted in approval, his blissful innocence gradually becoming marred by a sinister scowl as he perceived the situation degenerating around him. Hopefully his eyes darted from Leifr to his halberd standing against the wall, where he could grab it at an instant's notice.

Fodur folded his hands patiently. 'There is a very simple answer to that question,' he said quietly. 'Rhbu magic was the source for Dokkalfar magic, the High Road and the Low Road of the same powers. This is why we deem it wise to eradicate Rhbu magic whenever it crops up among our wizards, quite by accident, usually. One is always discovering some forgotten standing stone or circle or holy hill with astonishing powers. The Pentacle will be investigated also, and changes may be made if anything irregular is discovered, as I fear it will be. It is difficult to eradicate the old beliefs among the Ljosalfar. Not all the fire wizards share the progressive viewpoint of the Inquisitors, I'm ashamed to say. A great many of them knowingly perpetrate a great deal of this archaic muck.'

'That archaic muck, as you call it, destroyed Sorkvir,' Leifr interjected. 'I saw no Guild wizards attempting to relieve the suffering of Solvorfirth, and none were there when we faced Sorkvir for the last time.'

'It may interest you to know that the situation with Sorkvir is not ended yet,' Fodur answered with asperity. 'Djofull, his overlord and teacher, has gathered Sorkvir's ashes and will restore Sorkvir to life at some time in the future. You see how your Rhbu powers can be reversed by the Dokkalfar. Their close similarity was the fatal flaw of the Rhbus and led to their destruction. With the fire magic of the Wizards' Guild, there is no need for Rhbu magic. Now I propose we proceed by having a look at this Rhbu satchel and staff, Thurid. Would you be so kind as to submit them for our inspection? We shall keep them in our custody until we arrive at the Guildhall.'

Thurid bestirred himself from his misery and rose to his feet. 'Sorkvir resurrected! After all we went through! After everything Fridmarr suffered! What is the Guild doing to prevent Djofull from doing this?'

The Inquisitors maintained their carefully prepared blank expressions. Fodur answered, 'Be assured the Guild will deal with Djofull in the way it sees fit.'

Thurid's shoulders drooped. 'The staff and satchel are in my laboratory, on the other side of the pasture. I shall fetch them, if you'll spare me a moment. Alone. I wish to say farewell to the life I once aspired to.'

The silence that followed his departure was loaded with hostility and tension. Leifr glared at the six wizards in helpless fury, and Raudbjorn's features were contorted by rage and disbelief.

The Inquisitors were not intimidated by Raudbjorn's

growlings and angry huffings. Fodur turned his scrutiny upon Leifr. 'We are rather curious about you, Leifr Thorljotsson, although Sciplings are beyond the realm of our control. What are the origins of that sword you used against Sorkvir?'

'It came from Bjartur with the satchel and staff,' Leifr answered truculently. 'Are you going to try to take it to the Guildhall, too?'

Fodur studied him a moment. 'It poses no immediate threat. You will shortly be returning to your own realm, and you cannot take that sword with you. We will take possession of it when you go.'

'I don't know that I'm ready to leave the Alfar realm,' Leifr answered. 'I have some unfinished business here.'

'You'd best conclude it quickly or forget it,' Fodur said. 'You've been a channel for Rhbu powers, although you're unable to summon and use them yourself. It would be wise for you to leave, before worse powers get hold of you for worse purposes.'

'That will never happen,' Leifr said coldly. 'As long as you're holding Thurid, I don't intend to leave.'

'As you wish – for now,' Fodur said. 'But you might live to regret it bitterly.'

Berjast glowered at Leifr with mounting displeasure. 'These Sciplings,' he muttered hoarsely to Varkar, 'are certainly a troublesome and argumentative lot.'

Conversation lapsed into silence and unfriendly stares on both sides. Presently it occurred to Leifr that Thurid had been gone quite a long time. The Inquisitors arrived at the same decision at nearly the same moment. They suddenly eyed Leifr with more suspicion than hitherto.

Coldly Fodur inquired, 'Where has Thurid gone? I had understood that he would not take long. I wouldn't like to think that he had taken flight to avoid his inquisition. I fear that might compound his crimes.'

'If he has, then I applaud him,' Leifr answered. With a sudden surge of hope, he pictured an image of Thurid flying at top speed along one of the ley lines, putting miles

16

between himself and the Inquisitors. 'If you wish, I'll send someone to his cave to see what is taking him so long. No doubt he's merely saying farewell to the life that has been denied him once more by the Wizards' Guild.'

'That won't be necessary,' quavered the voice of Snagi the Elder, stepping nervously into the room with Young Snagi reluctantly in tow. 'Thurid is gone. He took the boy to his cave with him, then sent him back with a message.' He pushed the lad forward.

Snagi the Younger gazed around the solemn assembly with frightened awe, mustering his courage. Opening his mouth, he spoke in the clear, flowing cadence of Thurid's speech as he repeated, 'This is farewell, Leifr, and goodbye. I leave you in the hands of the all-wise and dexterous Rhbus until we meet again. I could not shame Fridmarr's memory by surrendering my powers so easily. Let the Inquisitors come after me at their own peril, and we shall see which powers are the most fit to govern the Alfar realm and the Wizards' Guild.'

Thurid made his way to his cave, instinctively following all the steps of his complicated formula of ritual actions. When he at last reached the cave, he gazed around at its beloved clutter in anguish.

'Doomed!' Thurid whispered. 'Doomed! Oh, Fridmarr! After all we've done! After the horrors of that wretched Pentacle! Then I am told that it was all for naught! That my powers are suspect! And merely because of some snobbish prejudice of the Fire Wizards' Guild. The idea that my Rhbu magic is not as good as theirs – not entirely untainted by the dark powers of the underworld!'

Thurid strode up and down, lashing his cloak aside at each turn so he wouldn't tread upon it in his growing wrath. So great was his preoccupation that he didn't observe Young Snagi creeping down the passage and taking refuge behind a large chair. Young Snagi kept his wide and frightened eyes upon him, cowering away from the fiery glare of his gaze, lest a stray glance suddenly cause him to burst into flame, like a pine knot on the hearth.

'Does the Guild really suppose I will submit so easily to their judgment?' Thurid demanded of his image in a reflective glass hanging on the wall, his choler rising with each turn up and down the cluttered length of his cave. The fire on the hearth leaped in sympathy each time he strode past it. 'Shall I go cringing and crawling, begging for some small scrap of compassion? Begging to retain some small portion of my despised powers? Is that what those – buffoons from the Guild think?'

He whirled upon Young Snagi suddenly to pose the question to the empty chair at point-blank range, with the hairs of his beard and head standing on end and crackling with the fury of his pent-up indignation. Young Snagi withdrew his neck further into the ragged cowl of his hood, scarcely daring to blink lest the wizard suddenly see him and interpret it as a scurrilous insult to his dignity and retaliate with most unwonted fury.

Thurid turned his back and faced the hearth, his peaked shoulders hunched as he stared into the shifting scenes of the dancing flames, seeing jeering faces, mocking mouths, and riotous laughter in the conflagration.

'No!' Thurid swore in reply to the mirth of the flames. He turned toward the staff standing against the wall, its orb glowing with quickening light at his approach. 'No. By all that I've come to hold dear – by all the powers that are contained in that satchel from Bjartur – Fridmarr's memory – Bodmarr – Ljosa – I refuse to submit to their inquisition of powers.' His hand closed with gathering resolve over the blackened wood of the Rhbu staff, and the alf-light burst into glorious rays, disturbing the distant shadows high above in the vaulted arch of the roof, where papery clusters of bats rustled and squeaked and sent a few scouts diving angrily at the unwelcome glare.

Young Snagi flung up his arm to shield his eyes, unable to resist staring at the manifestation of power, although his eyes felt like searing egg yolks. Thurid stood transfixed, as if the light were flowing from within his body outward to the tip of each finger and glowing hair. As Young Snagi stared, spellbound, Thurid turned and slowly raised one long finger to point at him sternly, causing Young Snagi to slither downward further as the dread hand rose.

'Come forth, listener. You must take them a message,' Thurid commanded, his eyes boring into Young Snagi like bright twin daggers. 'You will tell them this, in my own voice. This is farewell, Leifr, and good-bye. I leave you in the hands of the all-wise and dexterous Rhbus until we meet again. I could not shame Fridmarr's memory by surrendering my powers so easily. Let the Inquisitors come after me at their own peril, and we shall see which powers are the most fit to govern the Alfar realm and the Wizards' Guild.'

Thurid gestured with one hand, riveting Young Snagi with terror. Cocking his head toward the door, he commanded, 'You may leave now. By the time you reach the hall, I shall be gone. You may also tell them there is little point in pursuit. They shall never find me unless I desire a confrontation with them.'

Young Snagi crept toward the door, unable to believe he was escaping unscathed. A quick inspection of his hands and visible clothing assured him that he hadn't been burned or his shape shifted without his realizing it, all of which afforded him limitless relief. He scuttled into the shadows near the doorway, where many of the disturbed bats were swooping and chittering in their irritation. Emboldened by his unexpected reprieve, he crouched down behind a pile of driftwood to watch Thurid's further activities, with a view of telling his marvelous exploits for years to come beside the kitchen fires.

After sweeping clear the table with one banishing motion of his arm, Thurid spread the contents of his ragged old satchel on the table and sat down to scowl over the rune wands one by one. At last he selected the one he was searching for, greeting it with a dry chuckle as he held it up and studied it. Gathering up the rune sticks, he circled the room once, selecting an armful of objects, which he dropped one at a time into the sagging satchel. To Young Snagi's astonishment, large volumes of sheepskin parchment vanished into the satchel, along with map cases, a large bag of provisions that went in starting at one corner, some odd-shaped instruments for measuring the heights of stars, and other things that were incomprehensible to the young thrall. The satchel devoured it all and looked no different. Thurid lifted it experimentally, then stuffed in an assortment of the random objects he kept underfoot for throwing purposes.

Satisfied at last, he took one last look around at his beloved cave. Then he fastened on his cloak more securely and gripped his satchel under one arm, holding the rune wand in his other hand. Speaking slowly and clearly, he began reading the runes. By the time he reached the third repetition, his cloak was billowing around him, and the air in the cave was full of random objects leaping and hurling themselves around with heedless abandon, as if all laws governing the conduct of solid objects had been revoked.

Young Snagi's resolve snapped when the massive table with tree limbs for legs began to curvet and clatter across the rough floor like some large four-square pony seized by an unaccustomed fit of friskiness. He plunged for the door and tore it open to escape the maelstrom behind him. Unable to resist one final glance over his shoulder, he saw the wizard in a column of flames, his clothing and hair glowing brilliant white, standing rigidly a moment before suddenly whisking upward toward the smoke hole with a scream of howling wind, taking Thurid with it and an accompanying storm of papers, sticks, bird nests, leaves, stray items of clothing, and hundreds of protesting bats.

Young Snagi's knees suddenly went watery as he gaped skyward, watching the column of fire streaking away like a comet into the night sky. Sinking down on the wizard's doorstep to gasp and tremble, he observed the furious activity of the random objects slowly winding down, until nothing remained of the manifestation except an occasional crackle and sputter from the fire and the odd spoon or knife or buckle suddenly hopping into the air like a beached fish and falling back with a startling clatter. Whimpering a little, Young Snagi at last managed to get his legs under him, staggering toward the hall and the awaiting Inquisitors. The news he had for them would not be welcomed gladly. His trembling of awe soon turned into the more commonly felt trembling of fear.

He returned and delivered his message.

Fodur glowered, livid with rage, as he rose to his feet with grim purpose etched in his brow. 'Fetch our horses immediately,' he commanded. 'The renegade must be found and brought back with no further delays.' He gazed at Leifr challengingly a moment, then turned away to conceal his temper, glancing over Raudbjorn with a shudder of disgust.

Raudbjorn grumbled under Leifr's restraint until the wizards had taken their departure into the night, galloping into the upper pasture like the wild hunt of the night-riding Myrkriddir, and vanishing with a rumble of thunder and a flash of lurid flames.

Old Snagi stifled a whimper, dabbing at his nose with the end of his sleeve. 'They've all gone and left me now. Fridmundr, Bodmarr, Fridmarr, Ljosa, and Thurid. I know you're not long for Dallir either, young master. When will anyone ever come back to Dallir?' Grieving, he limped away into the kitchen, shadowed by a self-important Young Snagi.

Raudbjorn and the troll-hounds gazed at Leifr in a fever of impatience, anxious to shake off the lethargy of winter and the domestic routine of farm life. Raudbjorn hopefully tested the sharpness of his halberd with his thumb, making an almost musical note.

'We go in the morning,' Leifr said. 'As Fridmarr once said to me when I knew him as Gotiskolker, we're on a turning wheel and we have no choice but to travel with it, wherever the Rhbus wish it to take us.'

Leifr spent most of the night getting his equipment

21

ready for the journey, sleeping only a short while. Shortly before dawn he awakened with a peculiar noise in his ears. The sound came from the main hall, so he stepped over Raudbjorn's snoring bulk and walked through the passage toward the hall.

The coals on the great hearth still glowed, casting a ruddy light on the ancient rafters. It seemed to gather in a pool in the center of the room. Leifr stepped from his concealing shadow, his eyes upon the solitary figure in the firelight, bending over his work. It was the Rhbu and the grindstone. Seemingly oblivious, the Rhbu finished sharpening the tool he was working on and put it down carefully on a sheep fleece. Then he selected his next project, which was Leifr's Rhbu sword, and put it to the stone with a metallic shriek that should have awakened the entire household. The metal glowed red-hot, spraying a shower of sparks on the floor, resisting the skill of the smith and the whirling stone. Leifr crept nearer, half-blinded by the sparks and gleaming metal. Even without the carbuncle, he knew that powerful magic was being wrought into the sword once more by the hand of the Rhbus, and it would be his duty to carry the sword and do with it what was required.

When the sword was sharpened, the Rhbu presented it to him with a slight nod, and at once the firelight began to fade. Leifr clutched the still-hot metal, protesting, 'No, wait! Don't leave! Tell me what to do! How do I find Thurid? And Ljosa—'

The hall was empty. Once more the Rhbu had brought his message and departed.

CHAPTER 2

Thurid's precipitate flight soon slowed until he was skimming just above the ancient ley lines. The marking stones glowed in the night, reaching ahead of him in a straight line of red beacons. Where several lines intersected, the beacons shone like the spokes of a wheel. This was not like the tumbling escape from Gliru-hals, with Leifr half-flying, half-running; this was flight. Exulting in his escape, Thurid thrust out his staff before him, with a flaring knob of alf-light peeling away ribbons of flame in the wind of his passage.

'Hreidurholl! May the goodness and power of the Rhbus take me to Hreidurholl!' Thurid breathed through his clenched teeth, feeling the power surge from the staff into his hands. Never before had his ancestors' settling place seemed like such a welcome retreat. Nor had he ever imagined as a restless youth that he would one day be hastening toward Hreidurholl with such eager haste to bury himself in the inauspicious homesteads and green hills of that little-known settlement on the inland tip of the little-known Slyddafjord. Due east it lay, toward the rising sun, beyond a stretch of shining lakes and dark clumps of stunted trees. The house where Thurid had come into existence long ago no doubt still stood there, occupied by Thurid's elder brother and sundry relatives upon whom Thurid had not bestowed a kindly thought in several decades. The notion that the arrival of the errant son would not be greeted with cries of rejoicing and gratitude was an idea that found no foothold in Thurid's plans.

As he was gathering comfort from his thoughts upon the isolation and smallness of Hreidurholl and the extreme unlikeliness that the Inquisitors would find him there, Thurid's course suddenly faltered, veering southward. Cursing and muttering, Thurid gripped the staff as it dipped dangerously near the surface of the earth, alternately skimming him along so near that he thought his nose was going to drag and tossing him aloft like a leaf. Before he could restore the faltering powers, he somersaulted into a patch of gorse and came to rest against a mossy standing stone. Shaking out his cloak and gown, he climbed out of the gorse and bestowed a glower upon the stone. A cursory scrutiny of the surrounding terrain assured him that no Alfar foot had trod upon this particular section of Skarpsey since the ley lines were built by the unknown Rhbus. The white mark stones stood out plainly against the black lava, pointing out the safe tracks across the hostile earth.

Thurid shivered suddenly, not liking the desolation of inland Skarpsey. He had reached Gliru-hals by the usual means of travel, which meant sailing around the coast of the island by boat. No one traveled overland, particularly alone. Now his capricious powers had abandoned him where he was most likely to meet up with Dokkalfar, trolls, jotuns, and all the other undesirable creatures that lurked beyond the borders of civilized laws. Here were things with no names; hence, no laws could govern them.

Uneasily Thurid sat down next to the stone, which was still warm from its glowing of the previous night. Regretfully he thought about the fine breakfast old Gunnhild was now preparing for the household at Dallir. Fresh eggs, clotted cream, new bread, huckleberries from the hill behind the spring house – he closed his eyes, suddenly astonished at the strange vehemence that had taken him away from all that. He closed his eyes, allowing himself the luxury of some much-deserved self-pity. In the midst of his pitying, he nodded off to sleep, more weary than he knew from his endeavors to channel the powers of the leys.

When he awakened, it was with the assurance that he

was no longer alone. His eyes opened instantly, their focus sharpened by suspicion as he warily raised his head and peered out from beneath his hood. Some voice had spoken, he was certain. He saw nothing but the barren landscape of skarps, stunted grasses, and shrubs, long-shadowed with approaching dusk. His eyes traveled southward, discerning a hill which he had not noticed before, spiky with the ruins of a hill fort. As he gazed, his flesh crawled with the cold certain breath of earth powers assuring him that the source of the unknown voice was there.

For a moment he dared wrestle with the idea that no power on earth could drag him into that old hill fort. Yet the harder he tried to turn his back on it and walk away, the more persistent was the feeling that some force was compelling him toward the ruins. It was a summons he was feeling, he suddenly realized with awe, and not a little pride – his first summons as a wizard. It could be the Rhbus themselves, wanting to speak to him at last about the powers over which he was custodian. Straightening his shoulders, he gripped his staff in one hand and strode toward the ruins.

What was once a fortress was now nothing but mossy heaps of stones, jumbles of fallen stone blocks, sunken pits that used to be cellars, and remnants of stone walls which Thurid marveled at. Inhabitants of Skarpsey now built with turf and wood. The Rhbus had built with stone, and their sacred places on the leys were marked with massive bluish quartz stone that had not come from Skarpsey's black and molten heart, but from some far-off location, raised upright by unknown means.

Thurid climbed to the highest point of the ruins, where the summons seemed to be the strongest. On the other side was a steep, jumbled slope, ending in a courtyard surrounded by high crumbling walls. A single central pillar still stood within a ring of broken stumps and heaps of shattered rock. Thurid's gaze fastened upon the central stone and his breath wheezed to a halt in his throat. A lone figure stood pressed against the stone, barely visible in the silver twilight. From that figure emanated a powerful wave of despair and fear and hopeless pleading for deliverance.

Something in the shadows stirred, where once stables had stood. A dark form moved forward into the courtyard, uttering a low and menacing groaning sound. It was a huge bull, flayed of its hide, its naked flesh gleaming with blood. A more horrible object in wizard lore was not to be found. Thurid crouched behind a rock, his palms sweating and his heart racing. An icy wind of pure evil fanned at him gently, inquisitively, until he drove it back fiercely with some muttered words and the brandishing of some potent amulets. The image of the flayed bull was a form taken by only the most powerful and adept of Dokkalfar wizards. Thurid also knew that the bull was strengthened by the letting of blood and the ritual taking of lives. The hapless creature clinging to the pillar below was no doubt intended as a sacrifice to strengthen the flayed bull's powers.

Again the victim's summons for help poured over him, making him shudder with the horror of his situation. A Ljosalfar wizard was bound to use his powers to assist when called upon or the penalty was a desertion of powers. He stood up slowly, gripping his staff and telling himself he was no fire wizard. Perhaps Rhbu wizards were not bound by the same oath, which was taken at the Final Investiture in a solemn assembly at the Guildhall. He wanted desperately to slink away, but his feet seemed rooted where he stood.

The bull suddenly scented him. It threw up its awful head and inhaled the scent of him, snorting and burbling with increasing menace, rolling its glaring eyes in his direction. The creature's horns curved in a lyre shape above his head, gleaming with a sinister blue light. Lowering its head, the bull repeatedly gouged its horns into the earth, flinging up clods of moss and grass, and pawed sprays of dirt over its back with its huge cloven hooves.

The figure tied to the pillar lifted its head, with long dark hair spilling down past shoulder-long. A woman's voice called out with desperate eagerness, 'Is someone there? Can you hear me? Help me, if you have a grain of pity!'

Thurid stepped from his hiding place, allowing his cloak to surge masterfully around him. His staff's orb glowed with brilliant alf-light.

'I hear you!' he called, moving warily down the slope.

'Please don't let me die like this,' the woman quavered. 'The bull is vulnerable only to iron and fire. If you can't kill him, then kill me and spare me death by the bull's horns.'

'Fire and iron are two elements at my disposal,' Thurid answered gallantly, approaching the edge of the court-yard.

The bull snorted and pawed, eyeing his approach with rocklike impassivity. It tossed its glowing horns and trotted forward, head held high and watchful. Suddenly it charged straight at Thurid, driving a wall of cold air and icy hatred before it. Thurid raised his staff with a hasty rebuffing spell and the bull plowed to a halt. Surveying Thurid for a long chilling moment, the bull swung its head around to look at the woman. It lowered its horns and turned toward her. Thurid conjured a fireball, which rolled and bounced across the ground like a great hot spark, straight at the bull. It slewed around with a snort and sprang out of the way with uncanny speed. Its eyes flashed, and a bolt of ice hurtled toward Thurid. Swiftly he countered it with a shield of fire, which exploded the ice with a crack of thunder, and he followed it up with a burst of pure flame that blackened the ground where the bull had stood a moment before. It was standing on the far side of the circle now, lashing its tail in rage and snorting frosty breaths that writhed around its legs like tendrils of fog. The fog twisted into the shapes of white wolves, which came at Thurid in a howling pack. He picked them off with darts of flame and sent a bolt arching high above

27

the circle, where it burst into a shower of sparks. The bull bellowed and plunged into the shelter of the old stables, its mottled hide burning in several places.

Thurid moved swiftly into the circle. With a thin jet of flame he seared the prisoner's ropes, but before she could run to safety, the bull rushed from the shadows, its eyes darting ice bolts. A roaring bellow nearly paralyzed Thurid on the spot, but he countered the compelling voice, staggering back under the force of the bull's attack. A wave of life-destroying abnegation swept over Thurid, but he protected himself with a whispered spell which enveloped him in bright flame without charring a single thread or hair.

The bull snorted and stared at this phenomenon, backing away as Thurid stepped forward, a living torch. Rolling its eyes, the bull snorted blasts of fog again, directing them toward Thurid. The moment the fog touched the flame, it ignited with a crackling roar, leaping back to its source like a bolt of lightning. The bull had no time to defend itself; its form ignited with a fiery roar. With a sizzling and crackling it melted down to a black puddle, leaving only the glowing horns intact.

Thurid drew a deep breath and beckoned to the woman hiding behind the stone. She crept out of its shadow and stood gazing a moment at the remains of the bull, still weak with fear and trembling, or so he supposed.

'That was very well done,' she said with composure. 'Allow me to present you with a suitable reward.'

She lifted a gold chain from her neck.

'No reward is necessary,' Thurid replied with unseemly haste, then he realized that refusing a gift was an unforgivable mistake. Yet he had learned a degree of caution from his past experiences with Alof and Finna, and he had an instinctive dread of this woman putting her chain around his neck.

So he hesitated a moment; in that moment the woman lifted one hand to her lips and blew a cloud of dust into his face, with an unpleasant chuckle.

'But I insist, you must have a reward,' she said in a mocking tone. 'Although I daresay it won't be a satisfactory one in your opinion.'

Thurid gasped and choked as the cloud of dust encircled him, filling his nose and throat with bitterness. An ominous weakness pervaded his limbs and his head swam so dizzily that his arm holding his staff seemed to be miles away, and the memory of the Rhbu spells was impossibly distant. Vaguely he was aware of the woman dropping the chain around his neck, making the binding complete. He could not lift a hand or stir a foot. The gold chain was nothing less than a thinly glamorized cord of mistletoe.

The woman turned away and spoke to the shadows. 'It is done, Meistari Djofull. He's trussed up like a rabbit, and it was as simple as child's play. Are you certain this is the one?'

Another figure moved out of the gloom and approached at a hobbling gait, leaning upon a staff still spewing clouds of fog. A warped and wizened Dokkalfar peered up at Thurid with a satisfied grin twisting his features, which were unpleasant to behold even in the half-light. His high-domed head was hairless and blotched with scars, discolorations, and slick oozing patches, the signs of wizardly tampering with the earth's forbidden secrets. His eyes burned with a fanatic gleam, and the hands that clutched the staff were knotted claws – at least one of them was a claw. To Thurid's distant surprise and discomfiture, the other hand was strong and healthy-looking, and actively trying to signal him with one finger. He could see that it was rather crudely sewn to the withered stump of arm with coarse black thread.

'Well met at last, Thurid of Dallir,' said the Dokkalfar wizard Djofull. 'You can't think how I've yearned to meet you in person, since I learned what you had done to my acolyte Sorkvir. A truly gifted apprentice is hard to come by, and Sorkvir especially is dearly bought. Six times I've bargained with Hela to release him from Hel, and she's not going to be pleased when I petition her again. Some ancient promises will be broken.'

Thurid could only stare, stiff as a stockfish, while Djofull beckoned with one hand, summoning a vehicle from the direction of the stables. It crept out, drawn by three skinny horses, a tall lumbering thing made of whale ribs and stretched skins sewn together, looking like the carapace of some monstrous and unsavory beetle.

A number of armed Dokkalfar swarmed around it, their insignia of Spider and Bat glowing redly. A pair of them tipped Thurid backward and carried him to the coach, still gripping his staff, and deposited him inside on the floor, like firewood. Djofull took his seat and propped his feet on Thurid's chest with a weary sigh.

'You performed satisfactorily, Svanlaug,' he said in his dry, rasping voice. 'But you weren't subtle enough with the mistletoe cord. He was suspicious of you at once. I don't know why he didn't blast you or escape. It must have been a touch of his ridiculous chivalry that made him hesitate. You would have missed him if he'd been any other wizard.'

'I should have used the alfbane dust first,' Svanlaug replied. 'I thought about ichor, but it works too slowly to stop a wizard.'

'Exactly. What else could you have done if he'd shied away, intead of standing like a stalled ox?'

'Shifted shapes and flown after him.'

'You haven't progressed far enough in shape-shifting. It would have been far too risky.' His tone was chastising.

'I could have used a song spell—'

'Your lesson is finished for tonight,' Djofull said curtly, and Svanlaug fell silent.

Thurid jounced on the floorboards of the coach, aware of the shadow of a large gate passing overhead and the sweet smell of flowers. Grofblomur, the white flowers said to bloom on the graves of the forgotten dead.

The coach halted inside some high walls, and when Thurid was unloaded by the Dokkalfar, he could see they were the walls of a ruin, with watch fires burning in the remains of alcoves and windows. The once-magnificent fortress now lay with its halls open to the sky, its walls crumbling into mounds of mossy rubble, but enough of its subterranean structure remained to form a refuge for the Dokkalfar and trolls and whatever night-faring creatures that preferred the damp and dark of underground. As they carried him down a long and winding flight of stairs, Thurid noted the gleam of trolls' eyes flitting in cross tunnels and smelled the unsavory smells of scavengers that had set up housekeeping in the dank underground grottos.

By the time Thurid was deposited in a clammy chamber that served as a main hall, the paralysis was beginning to wear off. He was unable to prevent his staff being extracted from his frozen grip by a swarthy, sooty smith with a huge pair of tongs and thick blackened gloves. The staff hissed formidably, and the smith gritted his broken yellow teeth against the heat as he carried it to a stone box designated by Djofull. The satchel was similarly carried away and safely deposited, and a heavy lid slid into place.

Thurid rose unsteadily to his feet and gripped the back of a chair made of bulls' horns to steady himself. 'I hope you have a reasonable explanation for this abduction,' he said haughtily. 'You've delayed me from some very important business.'

'Tut, tut, my business with you is more important,' Djofull replied, perching in another chair made of bones and skulls, no doubt of old enemies or recalcitrant servants. 'I have the Rhbu satchel and staff. Now all I require is the sword. You will summon your Scipling warrior and bring him to this place to return the property he has no entitlement to. You'll rue the day Fridmarr brought these tokens up from Bjartur. No Ljosalfar will ever be able to turn Rhbu magic to Ljosalfar purposes. Rhbu magic is too closely aligned with the Dokkalfar.'

'So it is said,' Thurid replied gloomily, thinking of the Inquisitors. 'But Sorkvir might not agree with you from his place in Hel. Is it true you intend to restore him to life, as soon as you drive your unsavory bargain with Hela?'

31

'Gossip travels quickly, it seems.'

'You were seen in the Grindstone Hall gathering ashes.'

'Was I? That shouldn't surprise those hoary old relics in the Wizards' Guild. They can't bear the idea that I have solved the riddle of death, and they haven't. It's a tempting idea, is it not? Unlike your Guild wizards, who hoard up their secrets and parcel them out only to a select few, I am willing to share my knowledge with anyone who will pay the price. You, Thurid, could be as deathless as Sorkvir. A tempting idea, eh?'

Thurid shuddered. 'No. And you can forget about Leifr. I won't summon him into your trap.'

'You're stubborn, Thurid.' Djofull shook his head with a sly smirk. 'Perhaps you'll change your mind. I'm rather famous for my powers of persuasion. No one is able to resist – and live to tell about it.' He pointed upward and lifted the sputtering whale-oil lamp to illuminate dimly the rocky roof of the cavern.

Thurid started nervously, staring upward in horrified fascination at a half-dozen human figures, dangling from wires. They were not alive; they had been preserved somehow in lifelike poses, clutching staffs and gesturing magnificently, as if frozen in the midst of casting a conjuration.

'My wizard collection,' Djofull said, with pride. 'They're all Guild wizards. You'll be the first renegade wizard to join them. I daresay you'd enjoy my hero collection, which hangs in my main chamber at Djofullhol. There's over thirty of them. Heroes are somewhat easier to catch than wizards – or far more expendable, as far as the wizards are concerned. You shouldn't feel too badly about turning over one Scipling to me. There's plenty more where he came from.'

'I am appalled,' Thurid replied, drawing himself up with dignity, 'that you believe I would succumb to such low temptations, or be frightened by such inept threats. It's clear you don't appreciate the value of the wizard you are dealing with.'

'And the Inquisitors do?' Djofull inquired with a rat's grin. 'You're alone, Thurid, and defenseless. You have no choices before you. But if you wish to think about your fate, I can allow you a few days to make up your mind.' He signaled to the waiting Dokkalfar outside the chamber. 'Tell the warlord Stjornarr that Meistari Thurid will be visiting at Ulfskrittinn for a fortnight or so, with his permission. Prepare for him a room with a charming view – the Upper Chamber, I believe, would suit him quite well.'

The Upper Chamber, as Thurid soon discovered, was a pit with slimy walls too steep for anything to climb out. A gallery with viewing platforms ran all the way around the pit, designed for the viewing pleasure of those seated on the platforms. Thurid did not need to peer over the edge to know what entertainments the place was intended for. The smells and noises rising from the pit were ample evidence to his delicate senses that he'd fallen into a very foul place indeed. He affected lofty unconcern, but all the while his mind was racing frantically, searching for some way out.

A pair of grunting Dokkalfar hauled Djofull into the chamber in a sedan chair, depositing him on the ground with a relieved jolt. He crept out and surveyed the scene with a withered smirk and turned to Thurid.

'How do you like your accommodations?' he inquired. 'I hope it's not too crowded for you?' He gestured into the pit, then swatted at the alien hand as it came climbing up his clothes, heading for his throat.

Thurid casually stepped to the railing and glanced down. A host of hairy faces peered up at him, gray trolls, great trolls, and degenerate trolls that seemed almost human, all quarreling and snarling over a scanty supply of well-chewed bloody bones.

'Tut tut,' Thurid said. 'Your pets are in dreadful condition, Djofull.'

'I feed them every chance I get,' Djofull answered. 'If they get too hungry, they'll eat themselves. You'll be

33

privileged to observe them at close hand. Their antics are most amusing, especially when they're hungry.'

Thurid's attention was distracted from the trolls by an ominous squeaking and grating sound. Five Dokkalfar were dragging a large iron basket contraption over the edge of the pit. It was a cage with an opening on the top side and it was moored with a large chain that disappeared in the blackness overhead.

'And what is this?' Thurid inquired interestedly. 'Your method of feeding them?'

Djofull wheezed and chuckled. 'You might say that. Very often it is. But for now, since we're limited on suitable accommodations for a wizard of your importance, the cage will be your berth, until more suitable lodgings are provided.'

'You shouldn't have given your own room,' Thurid protested. 'It was really too good of you.'

Thurid was hoisted aloft in the cage and swung into the center, overhanging the pit at a height just beyond the reach of the trolls. They leaped up at the cage, drooling and gibbering, their eyes glancing avariciously, while Djofull and the Dokkalfar watched from the gallery. In a rare act of cooperation, six trolls formed a pyramid by standing on each other's backs, but as the topmost troll was fighting Thurid for a handhold on the side of the cage, one of the trolls on the bottom of the heap bit the foot that was clawing him in the back, and the entire pyramid fell down in a scratching, snarling heap, leaving one still dangling from the cage. Regretfully Thurid trod upon its fingers until it fell, landing upon a particularly large and savage troll who thrashed him severely for his impudence.

The watching Dokkalfar found it highly amusing. Their numbers increased as time passed and word of the diversion spread through the fortress. To enrage the trolls further, food was sent out to Thurid by way of a rope and basket. The trolls went into a frenzy trying to reach him, and he diverted them by throwing down bits of food, which caused ferocious battles and much biting of ears and chewing of tails.

On the fifth or sixth day, Djofull hailed Thurid from the side of the pit. 'You'll be glad to know you won't be required to send for your Scipling,' he said with an unpleasant suggestion of a grin around his mouth.

'Indeed, I had no intention of it,' Thurid answered.

'You won't have to, because the Scipling is coming this way on his own initiative. He must have some sort of guidance to lead him into trouble so unerringly.'

Thurid groaned inwardly. Fridmarr's carbuncle had to be the cause. Even in death, Fridmarr's bad advice was unmistakable.

CHAPTER 3

Leifr and Raudbjorn camped in a notch high on the side of
a fell, overlooking the fortress below. A cloud of mist hung
over it continually, obscuring much of it from view, but
the mist shifted around, showing now a high jagged wall
with the tiny winks of watch fires burning in the empty
windows and crumbling stairways, or they would glimpse
the earthworks encircling the fortress, filled with slowly
crawling fog, reaching out like tentacles.

Raudbjorn leaned on his halberd and gazed down at the
fort with a scowl furrowing up his head. He looked at
Leifr querulously several times, puzzled and uneasy.

Leifr held Fridmarr's carbuncle in his fist, eyes closed,
striving vainly to form closer mental contact with Fridmarr. So far in their quest for Thurid, he had received
only nudges to advise him, scarcely more than strong
presentiments which were almost indistinguishable from
his own inborn fears and suspicions. Fridmarr's presentiments, however, were accompanied by a faint warm glow
from the carbuncle. Now there was nothing. The stone
remained cold, although he held it and breathed upon it
and silently cursed it. How like Fridmarr to bring them
this far, and leave them with no further instructions on
getting inside the fort and getting Thurid out – if indeed
Thurid was within.

At last he gave it up and put the carbuncle back in its
pouch, which he hung around his neck inside his shirt.

'We go in?' Raudbjorn rumbled.

Leifr shrugged. 'Not just yet. We'll wait awhile and see
if Fridmarr has any ideas.'

Raudbjorn looked around their campsite uneasily. He

did not approve of dead men offering advice to the living through the medium of a twinkling red stone. He seemed to expect to see a draug or a wraith fluttering dismally over his shoulder at any moment.

The day darkened into sullen twilight, and still Leifr had no clue as to how to proceed. The troll-hounds whimpered uneasily, turning their ears intently toward the fortress. Presently Leifr was able to hear what their keener hearing had detected; it was the distant howling of wolves, and it came from the fortress.

'Fylgjur-wolves!' Leifr said grimly. They had heard sporadic howling since leaving the safe boundaries of the last homestead in Solvofirth to enter the unknown and unnamed terrain inland. Leifr was nervous enough, knowing he was getting farther from the familiar sea element than any seafaring Scipling liked to get, without listening to the voices of the fylgjur-wolves that seemed to be tracking them across the waste. If they had been attacked, it might have been more reassuring than the suspicion that someone was watching their progress with cunning approval.

Leifr made his decision to retreat for a while and continue to observe the fortress, while there was yet light to withdraw further into the hills. They had not gone far when a burst of very close howling stopped them short, sending them quickly into the cover of a brushy ravine. As they watched warily, a lone figure dashed from the shelter of a thicket, coming toward them. There was enough light for them to realize it was a woman running for her life. Loping along behind her with the casual assurance of catching an easy prey were four large black wolves.

The woman glanced over her shoulder, tossing her streaming black hair. The wolves were closing the gap with ease, and one sounded a long howl, possibly to summon others to the kill. By unspoken consent, Leifr and Raudbjorn moved out of the ravine, and Leifr sent the troll-hounds forward to meet the wolves. The wolves plowed to a halt, stiff-legged and suspicious. While the hounds and the wolves edged around each other in snarling half-circles, the woman came gasping to within speaking range of Leifr and Raudbjorn.

'I beg your protection!' she panted, clutching her cloak around her shoulders. 'I came here with my brother, and Djofull's fylgjur-wolves have killed him. Don't let me meet a similar fate, I beg you! Give me into the hands of my enemies, or sell me as a thrall, but spare me the fate of being torn by wolves!' She was slight in stature, but her carriage was proud even when begging for help, and she spoke with the accent of the high-born Alfar, though with a curious inflection. The man's clothing she wore was ragged, but at one time it had been finely embroidered and trimmed with furs and gold stitching, of which only unsalable shreds remained. Even in distress, she had a haughty demeanor, as if born to better things.

'You have our protection,' Leifr said warily, yet perceiving very little threat about her, 'since you are no friend of Djofull's either.'

'Friend!' She spat upon the ground. 'He killed my brother with his cursed wolves. I intend to shed his blood with my own hand, if he has any blood in that dried carcass. I've waited a long time to get near enough to kill him. Tonight I nearly made it inside the walls.'

The wolves and hounds suddenly launched a ferocious battle, snapping, snarling, and whirling, until the wolves suddenly broke and ran, with the hounds in pursuit.

'Tonight you nearly died, you mean,' Leifr said. 'If we hadn't been here by some mischance to save you, I fear you'd be dead now. You must have a lie-up somewhere nearby. We'll take you there before more wolves come to see what the disturbance is about.'

'No need. I'm a gypsying sort, and my lie-up is wherever I see fit.' She was studying Leifr and Raudbjorn with increasing interest. 'Now warrior sorts such as yourselves could get into Ulfskrittinn with ease. I think I know what you've come for. It's that wizard Thurid, whom Djofull is holding captive, is it not? I skulk about

38

with the scavengers and wanderers that hang around the gates, and they know what goes on inside almost as well as Djofull.'

Leifr expressed a small, polite grunt of interest, not wanting to betray too much curiosity. 'That may be, or it may not,' he said noncommittally.

'Never mind, I understand. We'll neither of us ask any questions. We all want to get inside those walls, for one reason or another, but our purpose is the same. We can be of mutual benefit to each other, if we go together against Djofull.' She came closer, her voice dropping conspiratorially. 'I know from the scavengers that one of the small gates stands unguarded at this time of night for a short while only. The guards there turn to wolves at sundown and run away to hunt in the fells a few hours, then they come back before their replacements arrive. Those wolves your dogs chased away are the ones. Fylgjur-wolves are not allowed to hunt without Djofull's orders. These guards are young and reckless, and if we have any luck at all, we can walk right into Ulfskrittinn. This would be a good place to stake your horses until you return. It's a Dokkalfar burial ground, so no one comes here.'

Raudbjorn peered around in consternation at the green mounds rising from the earth, but he made no objection when Leifr directed him to stake the horses out to graze.

'We'll go and look at the gate,' Leifr said to him. 'If it is unguarded, as she says, then we'll go in to look for Thurid.'

'Smells like Dokkalfar trick to Raudbjorn,' grumbled the thief-taker, shouldering his halberd. 'Time to squash some Dokkalfar, eh, Leifr?' His small eyes gleamed hopefully at the prospect.

'I hope so,' Leifr said, running his hand along Jolfr's shaggy black neck under his thick mane. After all he and the old horse had been through together, he hated to leave him so undefended. 'I'm not going to trust this woman either, but we can take care of ourselves once we get inside Ulfskrittinn. Let's hope our horses can

39

fend for themselves while we're gone.'

'Alfar horses,' Raudbjorn grunted, giving Jolfr's hip a whack and narrowly avoiding a sharp nip in return. 'Tough.'

When they returned from staking their horses, the woman introduced herself, as a gesture of trust. 'My name is Svanlaug,' she said. 'You can't think how I've yearned for someone such as yourselves to come along to strike at Djofull. I've followed him around a very long time, from hill fort to hill fort. I hope this is the last time he begs Stjornarr's hospitality.'

The small gate was found exactly as she had promised. No guard stood outside, and no one made any objection when they shouldered open the gate and slipped inside. Leifr knew that Kraftig, Frimodig, and Farlig would keep the four Dokkalfar guards occupied, if not held at bay, until dawn.

Warily he surveyed the scene before him. It was an abandoned courtyard choked with shoulder-high weeds of the rankest sort, leaving only a narrow path twisting among them to approach the inner walls of the fortress, within which he could hear quite a number of horses and men moving about. As they threaded their way among the weedy heaps of rubble, he noticed what a sweet smell came from the large white blooms just opening on the weeds. It was almost too strong and too sweet to be truly pleasant.

Beyond the weedy courtyard was a warren of narrow passages, where the defenders of the fort could safely slaughter almost any number of attackers from the tops of the walls, though no one now seemed to be watching from above. The main activity of the fortress, as Leifr discovered, was the trade of scavenging, the buying, selling, or stealing of objects ranging from bleached bones, cartloads of rags, weapons, and foodstuffs from questionable sources, to hopeless-looking thralls, kidnapped children, and all the sinister objects important in working magic, sold in very small quantities by the most desperate and scruffy-looking of all the scavengers. From adjoining vendors, one could buy meat for the pot, a shirt stolen from a corpse, or dead men's fingernails for a necromantic spell.

'The Thieves' Market,' Svanlaug informed them. 'We can lose ourselves among the vendors, if that hulking Villimadur will stoop down a bit.'

'Not Villimadur!' Raudbjorn growled. 'Thief-taker, killer, warrior for hire, but not savage!'

Scarcely anyone in the Thieves' Market gave them a second glance. Every character there was more unsavory, more bizarre than Leifr and Raudbjorn. There were other thief-takers with their swords thrust into the ground, lounging against walls in their blood-blackened, reeking attire, who eyed Raudbjorn with professional interest. Wizards waiting for hire signaled their unemployed status by standing up their staffs to trickle inviting banners of mist among the throng of people populating the market. Other wares were offered from horse-drawn carts, hand-carts, or ragged bundles slung over shoulders.

If anything was to be sold, traded, or hired, it was available in the Thieves' Market, and the buyers were scarcely less appealing than the sellers. Most of them were Dokkalfar, recognized by their black hair and pale skin, frequently blotched by exposure to the sun. Plenty of dwarfs swaggered along at their rolling gait, some glittering with a wealth of gold and jewels, some sooty and black from their forges. A few trolls lurked about warily, clad in human clothes and speaking human speech in rough, growling voices. Leifr tried not to stare at them and at other races of people he could lay no name to. Some were almost the size of Raudbjorn, and some reminded Leifr strongly of Sciplings, but he knew better than to approach them with the bonhomie of foreign travelers. There were others who looked to Leifr like Ljosalfar, pale of hair and beard and threatening of mien indeed to command fear in the realm of Dokkalfar. Most of these were wizards who seemed to have fallen into evil paths, exactly the sort of malpracticing fellows Fodur and the Inquisitors wanted to prevent.

Those who could neither buy nor sell lurked about in the shadows, sharp-eyed as hungry rats, for a chance to steal. A sudden outburst of fighting and cursing usually heralded such an attempt, and the culprit either scuttled away into the dark with his prize, or was beaten on the spot without mercy. The skulkers and thieves were even lower than the lowest of the vendors of unearthed barrow metal.

'They'll cut your throat for a loaf of bread,' Svanlaug murmured, as a pack of the desperate creatures scuttled away furtively into the darkness. 'They'll do almost anything in exchange for food or silver.'

'They can't help us get Thurid out of there,' Leifr said, nodding toward Djofull's domain, where heavily armed Dokkalfar stood guard beside a tall double door leading further into the fortress.

'Don't be too certain of that,' Svanlaug replied, leading them into a narrow dark alley, where dark figures melted away like smoke at their approach. Raudbjorn grumbled uneasily under his breath, and Leifr kept his hand ready upon his sword hilt.

Ragged figures of men and women crouched over tiny fires, looking up with feral eyes as they passed. Dark, weasel-like children followed them for short distances, vanishing when Leifr turned to look at them. In Scipling settlements, there were always a few who preferred to live on the edge of death, surviving by their cunning and stealth instead of commerce and farming. Here, it seemed that a large portion of the population lived by such harsh rules.

Svanlaug's circuitous course twisted among the alleys and hovels until Leifr could no longer safely say which way was out. His suspicions were extreme, but he had enough confidence in his abilities to fight his way out that he said nothing. Presently she arrived at the ruins of a round tower, where a knot of the beggar people rose warily to their feet, clutching weapons under their ragged cloaks.

Svanlaug whistled a chirping signal, and they relaxed to

a small degree, but their eyes were fastened upon Leifr and Raudbjorn.

'They're friends, Nogur,' Svanlaug called, and one of them stepped forward warily, an individual of almost spectre thinness.

'Have you brought a gift for the family?' Nogur rasped, and Svanlaug put something into his hand. He examined it by the moonlight, holding up a slice of a silver coin. Then he gave it to one of the other three skulking at his heels. 'That will do,' he went on in his dry voice. 'What is it you wish this time?'

'I want to get these strangers inside Ulfskrittinn,' Svanlaug said, without elaborating further.

Nogur turned his gaze upon Leifr and Raudbjorn, assessing their equipment and garb. 'We can do it, but it will cost you more than an eighth of a mark. Two marks in silver.'

'You're a robber, as well as a thief,' Svanlaug replied. 'I'll give you one mark now, and one after we get in. Perhaps more, if we require your aid to get out.'

Nogur shrugged. 'You might not live long enough to get out. I want two marks now.'

'Get us inside, and then I'll pay you,' Svanlaug said. 'I have other friends who might not demand so much.'

Nogur growled and hitched one shoulder in assent. 'You're less willing to part with your silver than with your lives,' he growled. 'It's a dangerous game you're playing with Djofull.'

'Let me be the judge of that,' Svanlaug retorted sharply. 'My concerns are none of your business.'

The scavengers led them away from the noisy market, past two more guarded entrances, to a squalid area where hovels and livestock were clustered against the inner wall. Scavengers waited eagerly to bargain for the cartloads of trash and leavings that came out of the fortress, and tradesmen with carts waited for their wares to be chosen and taken inside.

'The kitchens?' Svanlaug queried in disdain. 'They

43

search those carts every time, Nogur. You'll have to try harder than that to trick me.'

Nogur sighed irritably, considering. Then he motioned, leading them away from the kitchen entrance, along a particularly dark and festering passageway. They emerged into a courtyard near one of the guarded entrances, where a contingent of ten Dokkalfar warriors spied them almost instantly, and raised a challenging shout. Nogur and his three companions melted away into the dark, but Svanlaug stood her ground as if she intended to brazen it out somehow. Leifr drew his sword when the warriors advanced with obviously warlike intentions, as if they recognized Leifr and Raudbjorn for enemies without questioning.

'The warlord Stjornarr has sent out word for your capture,' announced the burly leader of the warriors, whose helmet boasted a Fox insignia. 'A Scipling and a Villimadur traveling in company is not a commonplace sight, so we know you're the ones we want. Come along peacefully, unless you prefer to bleed while Meistari Djofull questions you.'

With one hand he motioned Svanlaug to move out of harm's way, as if he had expected to see her there, too. In a rush of suspicions confirmed, Leifr knew he had been tricked and trapped. He darted Svanlaug a baleful glare.

'It was all a clever hoax, wasn't it?' he demanded. 'The wolves, the unguarded gate, and now this.'

'It's a way of getting inside, isn't it?' she replied with a nonchalant shrug. 'And you said you wanted to get inside the fort. I suggest you sheath your sword, and order the Villimadur to drop his weapon. It will do you no good to fight, the result will be the same. Meistari Djofull has been waiting for this night with much anticipation.'

'Norskur, not Villimadur!' Raudbjorn rumbled.

Leifr glanced at Raudbjorn. 'Do you want to fight or surrender like sheep to whatever slaughter Djofull has in mind for us?'

44

For an answer, Raudbjorn whirled his halberd around his head with a roar and charged at the Dokkalfar. Leifr had no choice but to follow suit. In short order two Dokkalfar perished at the touch of *Endalaus Daudi*, dissolving in explosions of smoky red flames. The remaining Dokkalfar pressed their attack more warily, and an alarm was raised to summon more warriors as the door guard set up a loud braying on a horn. In short order there were too many sword points surrounding Leifr and Raudbjorn, and they were brought to a standoff, their backs pressed together, surrounded by at least twenty grim Dokkalfar warriors, predominantly seasoned Foxes and Wolves.

One gray-bearded Wolf flourished his sword and moved to confront Leifr directly. 'If you've no stomach for dying here and now, sheath your sword and command the Villimadur to put down his weapon. We have orders to capture you alive, if possible, and bring you to Meistari Djofull – as guests of Ulfskrittinn Stjornarr.'

Surveying the ring of sinister Dokkalfar faces around him, Leifr slowly sheathed his sword and kept his hands at his sides. Under his shirt, the carbuncle felt as cold as ice.

'Guests are always escorted inside by twenty armed warriors?' Leifr questioned grimly.

The ranking Dokkalfar lifted his shoulders in a shrug. 'It's better than being carried in dead, is it not? Keep your weapon sheathed and your Villimadur under control, and the Meistari can take your weapons from you if he wishes.'

Raudbjorn snarled at the mention of Villimadur, but he reluctantly lowered the halberd to a position of defeat at Leifr's suggestion. The ring of Dokkalfar and gaping spectators parted to form a corridor up to the gate, which grated open. Leifr scanned the crowd scowlingly, seeing mostly cynical curiosity in the warped faces. He also saw Svanlaug vanish into the open doorway ahead of him with a cursory hand gesture to the guard, as if flashing a ring to identify herself as one who belonged. Furious with himself for his gross underestimation of her threat, he advanced toward the door warily, with Raudbjorn ready to defend his back.

Once inside, they followed a long tunnel into the heart of the fortress, which was hollowed from the hill by a skill more developed than anything the current Dokkalfar inhabitants could boast. It was not Rhbu, Leifr realized with a cold chill, as his eye caught the details of the scenes carved into stone and wood. Never before had he sensed the sinister as well as aesthetic implications possible with art. The symbols and scenes filled him with a feeling of doom, futility, and darkness.

Djofull's presence inspired the same negative sensations. In a chamber lit by guttering torches reeking of rancid grease, Djofull awaited his so-called guests in a huge ugly chair made of blackened bones and skulls. He was a wizened, spiderlike creature with a pursed-up mouth and eyes that glared from their sockets, but Leifr felt a curious sense of relief to realize that the wizard was as alive and vulnerable to death as he, instead of the horrific combination of corruption and spiritual essence that was Sorkvir.

Beside him stood the warlord, who more aptly fit the chair, a scowling individual decked in well-used armor and the trophies of vanquished enemies.

'Welcome to Ulfskrittinn,' Djofull greeted him ceremoniously. 'You needn't have taken such a roundabout course to enter here. I would have gladly admitted you if you had approached my gate freely.'

'No doubt,' Leifr replied, 'as gladly as you admitted our companion and friend Thurid.'

'Ah. And you as his friends have come to inquire into his safety and well-being as my guest?'

'We've come to get him out of here,' Leifr answered. 'He's being held by you against his will.'

'No more than he deserves. He came looking for me, with the intent of stealing something very precious from me – the last remains of my dear friend and acolyte Sorkvir. It gave me a genuine pain to kill Sorkvir, that first

46

time. He was the most promising of all my pupils, and I could not guess whether or not I would be able to reclaim him from Hela. If my conjurations had not worked so excellently, I would have been truly grieved at his loss – for a while. You see I have worked most of my life to defeat the bonds of death, so any threat to Sorkvir's ashes must be looked upon as a serious offense.'

'What did you do with your guest, as you insist on calling him, who has committed such a grave offense?' Leifr asked suspiciously, offended by Djofull's reasonable, even amiable tone. Such politeness was nothing short of condescension to one in his dubious position.

'You shall see him shortly. First I wish to question you about that admirable sword of yours. Stjornarr, the warlord of Ulfskrittinn, informs me that several of his men were charred beyond all reclamation, so irretrievably dispersed that there's nothing even for rag-pickers to claim. Not even the escape spell could have saved them. This makes my position as his guest extremely awkward, you realize. Stjornarr's men are numbered and highly valued, and I shall have to pay wergild for them, so I urge you to restrain its use before the pressure of economics makes it more feasible for me to destroy you. Wizards have never been known to make monetary gain from their skills. This sword sounds like a most unfriendly weapon. Where did you get it, if I may be so bold as to inquire?'

Leifr scowled, his hand straying to the hilt of the sword, which occasioned a ripple of tension in the warriors who surrounded him on three sides. 'It was an inheritance,' he said. 'From the hands of the Rhbus themselves. Only death will make me relinquish it.'

'Of that I have no doubt,' Djofull said readily.

To Leifr's discomfiture, Djofull's left hand suddenly waved one finger to him in jaunty salutation and pulled itself from concealment along a fold of cloak. A large red stone glittered in an elaborate gold ring setting. The right hand, withered as a claw, seized the other hand and shoved it out of sight.

'Where is Thurid?' Leifr demanded, still determined to brazen it out with as much ill temper as possible. 'I'm not here to answer your questions.'

Djofull chuckled humorlessly. 'It would surprise you to know that you have no entitlement to that sword. No Ljosalfar, and especially no Scipling, can rightfully claim the war spoils of the Dokkalfar. That sword came from Bjartur, which was captured and destroyed by Dokkalfar long ago. Whatever is there belongs to us.'

'Not this sword. One touch of it and you'd wither like a dry leaf. Its metal is inimical to all night-farers.'

Unable to assail such an obvious truth, Djofull scowled and tapped one dark finger against his wrist, where Leifr could see large black stitches holding the healthy hand to a shriveled stump. A shiver of dread passed through him.

'Would you stake your life and Thurid's upon it?' Djofull suddenly demanded, with a cunning gleam in his eye.

'I would,' Leifr replied without hesitation.

'I could have these warriors destroy you now,' Djofull went on, 'but the fact remains, I could do nothing with this sword except keep it out of the hands of the Rhbus. A worthy enough purpose, but one can always do better. I have a bargain to propose to you, Scipling. I will give you a test of valor. If you succeed in the geas I shall lay upon you, you'll be a free Scipling. If you fail to accomplish your task in the allotted time, you'll spend the rest of your mortal days – and well beyond – in my service, using that sword against my enemies.'

'What is the nature of the test?' Leifr asked warily.

'You made the boast that the Rhbu sword will kill any night-farer it touches. In Hraedsla-dalur there is a species of night-farer I wish to see destroyed. If you can do it, you'll be free of my geas, and so will Thurid. I do love a contest of skills, don't you?'

'Thurid must accompany me,' Leifr said.

'That is impossible. He shall stay here as a surety that you will go to Hraedsla-dalur and kill the night-farers.'

'You're afraid Thurid will defeat your geas.'

'Not at all. The terms of the geas will be between the two of us. A simple matter, really, with a sword such as that. You simply kill the creatures.'

'Then you're already certain to lose our wager.'

'No. The night-farers could easily kill you first. Better them than me, or my warriors.'

'And if I win? Aren't you afraid that I'll come looking for you one day?'

'You're not so stupid as that. When two evenly matched foes have clashed, they usually avoid another possibly fatal confrontation. Besides, you'd hate to die with that unfinished business of Hroaldsdottir.'

'Don't speak lightly of Hroaldsdottir,' Leifr warned.

'But I could help,' Djofull said, and his healthy hand escaped his grip once more and climbed up the arm of the chair, appropriately made of arm bones. He tugged it free from its perch and smothered it once more in his sleeve.

'Then if I kill your night-farers, you will bring Ljosa back,' Leifr said, half a question, half a challenge.

'Done,' Djofull said immediately, 'and these warriors are our witness. The spoken word is enough, but I will record the geas on a rune wand, which you will signify with your mark.'

He motioned to one of his acolytes, who produced a smooth wand and a knife and commenced carving while Djofull dictated strange-sounding words. When he was done, he held it up for Leifr's inspection.

'Is that satisfactory? If it is, then you must prick your finger and dye these runes with your blood.'

'I don't know what they say,' Leifr answered. 'I don't read runic, and I won't commit my blood to something that could be completely different than our agreement.'

Djofull sighed and bit at his knuckle, while the pink hand climbed unnoticed up the chair arm again and signaled frantically to Leifr.

'Your lack of trust is understandable. I shall send for Thurid to verify the runes.'

'And Thurid will be freed along with me?' Leifr asked.

'Thurid will go with you only if he agrees to be bound by the same geas.'

Thurid was duly sent for. In the interval, Leifr and the warlord Stjornarr exchanged an unfriendly scrutiny. Like most Dokkalfar whose profession involved a great deal of killing, he wore trophies of his conquests as ornaments. Locks of braided hair dangled from the rim of his helmet to his shoulders, and his tunic was sewn with teeth and claws and more tassels of hair, attached with finger bones of dead foes, some of which dangled to make clicking noises when he moved. Much decorative stitching and embroidering denoted the attention of admiring women, and Leifr wondered uneasily if the Dokkalfar women took as fierce a delight as the warriors did in the gruesome display of their battle souvenirs. Thinking blackly of the perfidious Svanlaug, Leifr wondered if they weren't even more bloodthirsty and devious.

CHAPTER 4

Leifr had never seen Thurid looking so disheveled and distraught when he was brought under heavy guard into the warlord's hall. The wizard glowered at Djofull in silent fury, then turned his accusing and incredulous glare upon Leifr and Raudbjorn.

'What do you think you're doing here?' he demanded furiously. 'If I had never seen either of you again, it would still be too soon.'

'We came to get you out of here,' Leifr said.

'A pretty job you've done of it, too, getting yourself captured in the process,' Thurid retorted. 'Or was that part of your plan? I suppose every Dokkalfar between here and Solvorfirth knows my whereabouts now, since you've left a trail a mile wide behind you. Mightn't you have left well enough alone, for once?'

'This doesn't look like well enough to me,' Leifr said, surveying Thurid appraisingly. 'You smell like trolls and look like you've been kept in a cage with a dozen of them.'

'Exactly!' Thurid flared, bending a scowl upon Djofull. 'For the crude amusement of unspeakable persons. Most likely all three of us will become part of that entertainment now, until something worse comes along.'

'Your suspicions are completely unfounded,' Djofull said pleasantly. 'Your friend here has negotiated your release. You ought to be grateful to him.'

'Release?' Thurid shifted his outraged glare back to Leifr. His tone was suddenly cautious. 'What have you done, Scipling? Negotiated my release, without my advice?'

'Show him the rune stick,' Leifr said to Djofull, and the

acolyte extended the wand at arm's length toward Thurid, as if he wanted to risk no accidental physical contact.

Thurid snatched the wand and read the runes, growling under his breath. Then he hoisted one eyebrow and read them again, more slowly.

Djofull's pursed mouth stretched in something like a grin, or a sack getting ready to spill something. 'You see, my fellow wizard? The Scipling has made a deal with me. A rather good deal, I might add, especially considering that the position of Fantur is stronger with each passing day. Oh, I could easily command all of you to be put to death, or thrown into cells until you rotted, but we wizards are all gamblers at heart, are we not? There's nothing quite so fascinating as the working of a clever geas.'

'Such as the Pentacle?' Thurid interjected with a hostile flicker in his eye. He tapped the rune wand on his palm, scowling portentously and pretending to weigh the matter doubtfully in his mind.

'A noble experiment,' Djofull replied. 'Although it did cost me Sorkvir. However, it is only a small part of the entire scheme of ice wizard against fire wizard – the eternal conflict of two mighty natural forces, night versus day, cold versus heat, underground versus upper ground—'

'Life versus death,' Thurid added. 'Freedom versus slavery. Tell us more about these night-farers you want destroyed. Enemies of yours, I suppose?'

Djofull shook his head. 'Part of an old punishment for which I have no further use. The one I wanted to punish is long dead, and his descendants show no signs of any interesting reprisals or resistance. I've won my battle in Hraedsla-dalur a hundred times over. It's time to put an end to it and tie off the messy remainders. So I'll introduce a new element into the old spell, and give you a chance at your freedom and cause some disruption at the same time. As I said, I'm a gambler and a hunter, and both are always on the lookout for new prey.' He rolled his eyes upward at the grisly display dangling overhead.

'Yes, mere destruction gets so tiresome, doesn't it?' Thurid answered testily. 'And look what you'll have to toy with if we fail – a Rhbu wizard and a Rhbu sword. Of course you'll find a way to use us against the fire wizards.'

'Of course,' Djofull replied. 'What's the point in keeping you alive, otherwise? Inflicting death is a thousandfold art. Fascinating, yes; but even more fascinating and volatile is this interesting combination of Rhbu, Scipling, Villimadur, and Ljosalfar. I sense incipient disaster. If I can harness such a force against my enemies, they will rue the day our friend Fridmarr brought this primitive outlander into our realm.'

'And if the threat is turned against yourself?' Leifr inquired ominously.

'I will be protected by my geas, of course,' Djofull answered, a shade petulantly. 'Come now, Thurid, you've had long enough to study those runes. It's all perfectly straightforward. If you destroy the night-farers, you'll get your freedom. Seal it with your blood and you'll be on your way with my blessing.'

Thurid turned to Leifr. 'You're willing to agree to this binding?' he demanded.

'I think we've got a sporting chance,' Leifr said, with a sidelong glance at Djofull, whose strange hand was gesturing at him again.

'Yes, Djofull is certainly a sport, if nothing else,' Thurid replied sardonically. 'And if we can't kill those creatures he wants killed, we'll be in his power forever.'

'What is there that *Endalaus Daudi* can't destroy?' Leifr asked, putting his hand on its hilt.

'I don't know, but Djofull knows something that will work to our disadvantage,' Thurid replied, 'or he wouldn't have suggested this arrangement.'

'It's a gamble,' Djofull said. 'Merely a game of chance, my friends. Not heavily weighted on your side, I will confess, but if there weren't some opposition, there wouldn't be a contest, would there? Don't be such an old woman about this, Thurid. Or would you like to go back

53

to your previous accommodations?'

'This is a momentous decision,' Thurid retorted. 'You shouldn't wonder if we hesitate, when our lives and freedom are the stakes. Leifr, we can beat him. Stick your finger and let's get out of this vile place.'

Leifr pulled out his small eating knife and with its point pierced the ball of his thumb and applied his blood to the rune wand. Thurid followed suit.

'And the Villimadur,' Djofull said pleasantly. 'He'd look well in Djofullhol, hanging over the guest table in the Heroes' Hall.'

When the rune wand was suitably marked and sealed with their blood, Djofull dropped it in his satchel.

'Are we free to go now?' Leifr inquired suspiciously, unable to believe, somehow, that it was quite that simple.

'As far as I am concerned, your lives are now your own. For a year, at best.' Djofull waved one hand expansively and proposed a drink to confirm their bargain.

'A year is ample time,' Thurid replied boastfully, much of his former arrogance returning. 'With Leifr's sword, there is nothing we can't kill, and your geas will be broken as easily as a pastry shell.'

Djofull's thin lips wrinkled. 'We shall see. Sometimes there are interferences with the best of plans.'

Serving women brought gold cups of wondrous manufacture and design and a heavy stone flask, from which was poured out a dark red liquid that hissed slightly, exuding a faint cloud of fragrant mist. Leifr sniffed it cautiously, tempted by the sweet smell, but resolved only to taste the stuff.

'We'll drink to games of chance,' Djofull said, raising his cup. 'And to gamblers who risk all.'

Leifr wondered what Djofull was risking, and he watched narrowly over the rim of the cup before tasting the drink while Djofull drained his cup. No one had put anything into it that he had seen, but he remembered the sweet smell of Sorkvir's eitur. Doubtless it was a brew that had come from Djofull's laboratory.

He intended only a small taste of the red drink, but after one sip he couldn't stop himself from downing the entire cup, unable to believe that anything which tasted so tantalizing could be very harmful. He was even casting a longing glance at the flagon when suddenly he felt as if the floor had vanished beneath his feet, like an undulating wave, and something struck the back of his head like a half-filled sack of grain, soft and heavy at the same time. His view of the room dimmed and narrowed, and the last thing he saw was Thurid's face looming over him after he had somehow made his way to the floor, then the aperture of his vision narrowed to nothingness.

When he regained consciousness, he found that someone had considerately pillowed his head on Raudbjorn's belly, and Thurid was sprawled over his legs, snoring loudly. Inside his head was an ominous thumping sound, which jolted his brains painfully at each reverberation.

In a moment, however, he recognized the pounding as the measured clomping of Dokkalfar boots coming down the echoing corridor. With an uneasy and familiar presentiment of trouble to come, he lifted his head and looked around. A barred slice of light cast a faint illumination in the narrow cell, and a layer of dirty straw offered scant padding against the damp stone. He groaned and shoved at Thurid, not needing more than an instant to realize they had been drugged, disarmed, and imprisoned.

'Thurid, wake up!' he urged, giving the wizard a shake by the shoulder. Thurid groaned and raised a trembling hand to his forehead.

'What happened? Where are we?' he muttered thickly, propping himself up against Raudbjorn's bulk.

'In a dungeon, of course,' Leifr snapped. 'Did you really think Djofull would give us a fighting chance to break that geas? I thought you wizards had ways of knowing when someone is lying to them.'

'I claim no responsibility. You're the one that was so anxious to agree to the geas, merely to excape from Ulfskrittinn.'

'I thought I detected a slight degree of desperation from your quarter,' Leifr retorted. 'You were leaping at the chance to get away.'

'I certainly was not leaping,' Thurid snarled.

The Dokkalfar halted outside the cell and unlocked the door. There were six of them, high-ranking Wolves, by the look of their devices glinting coldly in the guttering red light of the torches they held. The symbol emblazoned upon the breasts of their hauberks was the skull of a wolf, with eyes that glowed red in the dark. The warlord's symbol stood below, a monster of some sort contorted in death throes, skewered by a lance. Their cloaks were long enough to cover their knees. Society members of lesser rank wore short cloaks, above the knee.

'This is a great honor to be hailed by Wolves,' Thurid greeted them. 'It's gratifying to see that I seem to be rising in Djofull's esteem.'

'Esteem has nothing to do with it,' growled their leader, a burly Dokkalfar carrying a standard ornamented with trophies taken from many fallen enemies – teeth, hair locks, finger bones, and scraps of clothing. 'Your worthless wizard carcass is required by our lord Djofull in the Hall of Swords. It seems there is someone who has come to bargain for your freedom.'

Leifr's heart gave a great bound. Immediately he thought of the Rhbus and his expectations of freedom swelled to rapturous proportions.

'You see the value of having friends in high places,' Thurid said arrogantly. 'Our friends will doubtless be gravely displeased at the treatment which my companions and I have received at your hands.'

'Displeased, perhaps, but not surprised.' The leader snorted incredulously. 'How could anybody expect anything else when they fall prey to the natural inheritors of the earth?' He motioned the prisoners to line up outside the cell. 'Your friends, as you call them, will be glad merely to find you alive at all. But if I were you, wizard, I would look back on these days at Ulfskrittinn with fond memories, once you see what's in store for you.'

'Fond memories!' Thurid repeated. 'You Dokkalfar are more perverse than ever I had imagined, if you think rotting in a dark hole and dangling in a cage over a pit of hungry trolls are my idea of fond memories. Dokkalfar have strange notions of hospitality.'

They brought their prisoners into the Hall of Swords, where Djofull sat in a great black chair, with a pair of fierce warriors dangling overhead. To one side of his throne stood a heavy table, its top barren of any object. Djofull turned to look at Leifr with his slanting, sunken eyes. He kept a grip on his grafted wrist, but the hand waved a finger to Leifr and made scratching movements as if it wanted to crawl away from Djofull's grip.

'Some old friends of yours here to bargain for your release,' Djofull greeted Thurid, with a small twisting of his withered lips that may have been a sardonic smile.

'I'm glad to hear of it,' Thurid replied. 'I trust that Leifr and Raudbjorn also will be released? And what about our weapons, which were somehow abstracted from us after we were drugged insensible?'

'All part of the package,' Djofull said. 'Although why they want the witling Villimadur is beyond my comprehension. Taking that cursed sword I can understand, but it will cost them dearly. And I do fear this is going to interrupt your search for the night-farers of Hraedsladalur – if not curtail it completely.'

He beckoned without turning his head, and a powerfully built Dokkalfar smith entered the hall, carrying *Endalaus Daudi* with a heavy pair of long-handled tongs. His hands were protected by thick leather gauntlets and he wore a leather apron. Sweat rolled down the bare hairy chest of the smith, and down his broad face, scarred and blotched by much exposure to the harsh influences of hostile metals. His eyes were fastened upon the sword he carried, not blinking once despite the acrid clouds of smoke roiling from the gleaming metal. With a gritting of his yellowed teeth, the smith placed the sword upon the table, where it burned a perfect outline of itself in the wood. With a sigh of relief the smith transferred the tongs to one hand and mopped his forehead with the cuff of one gauntlet. The assembled Dokkalfar in the hall seemed to breathe a collective sigh, and rustled as they relaxed their tense attitudes.

Next came Djofull's advisors, all old long-beards wearing the Owl insignia denoting the oldest and most learned of ranks among Dokkalfar. Their cloaks were fairly brushing the ground, also denoting great status, and the hoods of their cloaks were heavily encrusted with embroidery. Two of them bore Raudbjorn's halberd between them, another carried Thurid's satchel, and another carried the staff with his hand protected by a blackened gauntlet.

Djofull laced his hands together and surveyed the scene with satisfaction. To Leifr's mingled horror and amusement, the grafted hand struggled to free itself of the clasp of the other fingers, then shook itself with great distaste, as if resentful of such familiarity. Djofull nodded to the chief of his advisors who stepped forward and bound Thurid's hands behind him with a deceptively small cord.

Thurid winced at its touch. Once bound with elder cords, he stood with dignity beside Leifr, striking a haughty pose, but Leifr could tell from the too-bright gleam of his eyes that he was not as confident inwardly as he pretended.

'You might have dispensed with the elder fibres, Djofull. I have no intention of escaping now, when deliverance is at hand.'

'Wait and see from what quarter your salvation is coming,' Djofull said, showing his teeth in a ratlike grin.

Raudbjorn swung his head from side to side, squinting around the hall suspiciously and upward at the preserved warriors hanging overhead.

'Kalinn Grimson,' he muttered, rolling his eyes around. 'Nafar Red-Hand.'

'You recognize your old friends, I see,' Djofull purred.

'I preserved them as trophies for my friend the warlord Stjornarr, as a token of our friendship. They were particular enemies of his. Would you care to join your old friends in my collection?' Djofull sneered in Stjornarr's direction, and the warlord chuckled, raising his sword.

Raudbjorn shook his head. 'Not friends. Old enemies. Raudbjorn stay alive.'

'Only if your friends will pay a high enough price for the three of you,' Djofull said. 'They may have no use for you, and leave you here.' He motioned upward to his collection. Then he added, 'Ura, send in our guests.'

The main hall doors opened and the deliverers presented themselves in an orderly fashion. Thurid's eyes started wide when he recognized Fodur and the other Inquisitors, who gazed at him with stern disapproval as they came in and seated themselves in the provided chairs. Fodur alone remained standing. After gazing witheringly at Thurid for a moment he turned his attention to Djofull, whose strange hand was capering around almost uncontrollably. Djofull had to grip it securely with his other hand to preserve his dignity.

'I am Fodur, Inquisitor for the Fire Wizards' Guild. Your captives are fugitives from the judgment of the Guild, and it is our purpose to take this wizard Thurid to the Guildhall for examination of his practices. I am empowered by the Guild to negotiate a captive price for your prisoners.'

Djofull's left eyebrow hitched itself upward in amazement. He swept his gaze appraisingly over Thurid and Raudbjorn and Leifr.

Fodur continued, 'We knew that you had taken these prisoners, so we hastened to claim them. A young acolyte sorceress who claims loyalty to Djofullhol brought us the news, and hinted that you might be interested in considerably enriching your coffers and in ridding your future of certain complications.'

Djofull nodded slowly and turned his eyes in the direction of Svanlaug standing among the low-ranking Bat warriors. Leifr glared at her. Twice betrayed by a woman. He was as daft and trusting as Thurid.

Djofull chuckled drily. 'I never suspected they would be worth much in fangelsi-gild. Ofttimes it is better to rid oneself of troublesome guests, as well as prisoners. I don't know what they could have done to have aroused the ire of the Guild to this extent, but it must be worth quite a bit for you to get them back.'

'Five hundred marks in silver for each,' Fodur said.

Thurid snorted profoundly. 'Absurd! The Guild will expect to pay that much and twice over to free a wizard of my stature. And my companion Leifr is the only one who can use that sword, which makes his fangelsi-gild as much as mine.'

Djofull smiled. 'Then you are saying you'd rather take your chances with me and my geas than with the Inquisitors. That is a great deal of silver, and I am sorely tempted. I am not wealthy, and I am forced to depend upon the hospitality of sympathetic friends to shelter my head from the elements – in exchange for the aid of my powers against their enemies, of course, so the benefit is mutual. Fifteen hundred marks each for these two, and for the Villimadur—'

Raudbjorn strained against his bonds, baring his teeth in a menacing snarl. 'Not Villimadur,' he growled. 'Norskur. Warrior. Thief-taker. Not Villimadur.'

'If you have no use for him,' Djofull went on, 'I could hang him to good advantage here over the door in the Hall of Death. He would look well there, I think.' He spoke this last bit thoughtfully to Stjornarr, who rubbed his chin and nodded in agreement. 'It strikes a bit of awe into Stjornarr's enemies to see what might befall them.'

'We must have them all,' Fodur replied. 'We will pay the price you name.'

'This will take some talk,' Djofull said. 'Things besides silver can be exchanged. We shall discuss this in a more private place.'

Fodur bowed slightly. 'The name of Djofull is well

60

respected in the Guildhall. We may be enemies, but you have always dealt straightforwardly. We shall talk.'

Djofull motioned to his chief advisor. 'Beittur, take the prisoners back to the Upper Chamber. We won't risk an escape attempt now.'

'Not the Upper Chamber! You're not putting me into that cage again!' Thurid lunged forward, his eyes glaring wildly. He leaped toward the table where his staff lay, plowed aside a couple of guards and dived onto the table like a ship running aground in a storm. He fastened his teeth on his staff, mouthing the words of a spell as best he could, and burst the elder cords with a puff of smoke. With a roar of triumph he leaped to his feet, brandishing his staff, and the Dokkalfar and Inquisitors alike flattened themselves on the ground as a firebolt raked the hall, igniting one of the dangling corpses like a dry haystack. Raudbjorn seized his halberd and Leifr his sword, and they faced the roomful of warriors and wizards, menacing anyone who moved.

Fodur rose to a cautious crouch. 'Thurid, you ought to know that resisting the Inquisitors is not going to reflect favorably upon your record.'

'I've got a geas to break!' Thurid exclaimed. 'When I'm done with that, I'll turn myself in!'

Fodur shook his head. 'You aren't allowed to practice any more sorcery until you've been purged of all evil influences.'

'And what am I to do in the meantime, already up to my ears in evil influences?'

'Let's discuss it calmly, Thurid. There's no need for this unseemly display of disunity among friendly wizards.'

'I find nothing friendly in your intentions to divest me of my powers!' Thurid retorted. 'You can discuss it calmly with yourselves, after we are long gone!' Motioning to Leifr, he began edging toward the door, his staff flaring with hissing sparks, which the Dokkalfar made haste to avoid.

Djofull alone sat calmly in his chair, uncorking a small bottle.

'These are my captives, until you bargain for them,' he said to the Inquisitors. 'I hope you keep them confined for quite a long time, and keep them from interfering with any geas of mine until Fantur returns again next year.'

With a casting gesture, he waved the bottle and spewed its contents into the air. It settled over their heads in a fragrant mist reminiscent of the drugged wine. Raudbjorn inhaled deep sniffs and his halberd began to waver in its bellicose slashing and flourishing. To Leifr it seemed that the mist was crushing him down, lightly at first, then with irresistible force. The sword sagged out of his grasp, and the air still smelled wondrously sweet when he lost consciousness.

There was little light when his awareness came swimming sluggishly back to him, and he was still dizzy. Unable to rid himself of an unpleasant floating, swinging sensation, he closed his eyes and opened them again. His legs were almost numb, due to a deadweight sprawled over them. It was Thurid, using him for a cushion. Impatiently he began to shove at Thurid's inert bulk, wondering how long they had been asleep on the floor of Djofull's hall. It was an uncomfortable floor, and the place was noisier and smellier than he'd remembered. The smell didn't help his uneasy stomach.

His vertigo seemed to increase with his every move. As his eyes accustomed themselves to the gloom, he began to realize he wasn't in the main hall any longer. The walls of a pit rose around him, and there were bars. He reached out to touch them to be certain. Raudbjorn groaned and shifted, and the whole scene jiggled and swung alarmingly. From below came a sinister chorus of growling, and for an instant Leifr thought the troll-hounds had somehow found him.

But it wasn't troll-hounds; it was trolls who leered up at him, baring their broken yellow fangs, their green eyes narrowed with hatred and cunning, as well as hunger.

Some of them were dreadfully scarred and chewed, with ears and parts of noses missing, held together with scarcely more than scabs and scars. The creatures crouched in an expectant circle directly below, twitching their ratty tails and scratching their infested and scruffy hides with exasperated grimaces. Whatever lice were encountered in the process were immediately eaten.

Looking up, Leifr could see that they were suspended in a large cage, swinging gently at the end of a long chain that vanished above, where there was a distant, less dark opening and part of some large winding apparatus.

Their weapons, of course, were gone again.

'Thurid!' Leifr cried urgently, shifting his legs to disturb Thurid, who groaned in misery and groped about freely, feeling the bars of the cage.

Thurid sat up, opening his eyes a thready crack.

'No,' he whispered. 'This has to be a bad dream. It can't be the pit and the trolls again.'

'If it's a dream, I'm having the same one,' Leifr said grimly. 'What is this place? It looks as if they come and watch the trolls tear up people.'

'They do, and I've scarcely slept for seven days,' Thurid moaned. 'I wish I were dead instead of in here again!'

One of the trolls suddenly decided he had waited long enough, and leaped up at the cage, snagging a claw in Raudbjorn's breeches where they sagged through the meshes of the cage. Raudbjorn awakened with a startled bellow and leaped to his feet, causing the cage to gyrate and tip wildly as his weight shifted. It also caused the mechanism above to drop the cage another foot or so with a bouncing jolt that sent the trolls underneath it scuttling and screeching. The end of the cage occupied by Raudbjorn tipped dangerously low, an observation not missed by the trolls. They gathered on that side, bounding and gibbering in nervous anticipation.

Raudbjorn groaned as he took stock of the situation. He looked at Leifr lugubriously and gently rubbed the back of his head. 'Part of the geas, Leifr?' he asked mournfully.

'Part of Djofull's plan, yes,' Leifr replied bitterly. 'If we can't get out, we can't get to Hraedsla-dalur. All that talk about taking a gamble was just blather! He planned to trick us from the start!'

'You're learning fast,' Thurid said acidly. 'You should have known better than to make any agreements with an ice wizard.'

'You agreed to it as readily as I did,' Leifr retorted. 'You're the wizard; you should have known better what his ideas of sport would be. Give us impossible odds against an indestructible enemy, with everything to lose.'

'I'd have agreed to anything to get out of this cage,' Thurid groaned.

The trolls made a sudden concerted rush at Raudbjorn's sagging end of the cage, and four of them fastened their claws in the mesh and started to climb up. Raudbjorn seized the claws of two of them, yanking their legs inside the cage and stomping on them until the shrieking trolls scrambled out of his grasp and fell to the ground below. The remaining two thought better of their plan to jump inside the cage through the top opening. They scuttled around on the top, with Raudbjorn snatching at them from below with murder glinting in his eyes.

The cage dropped another grating foot.

'Raudbjorn!' roared Thurid. 'Sit down and hold still! In another minute we'll be on the ground with them, and you'll have more trolls than you know what to do with!'

'Raudbjorn knows,' he growled, sitting down reluctantly, his eyes still on the trolls. 'Tear legs off. Bash skull in. Squeeze necks till eyes pop.' With gruesome relish he vengefully demonstrated all these maneuvers for the watching trolls. They cowered back, snarling, shoving each other forward.

From the direction of the viewing platforms came the sound of faint applause. Djofull's hunched form sat among the shadows, making sounds of rusty mirth.

Thurid leaped up incautiously and shook his fist, bellowed in apoplectic fury, 'If it's a contest you want,

64

you grave-robbing corpse eater, give me my staff and satchel and come down here in this pit and we'll see who survives to walk or crawl out of it! You call yourself sporting? You'd shoot arrows at fish in a barrel!'

'Get out of it if you can,' Djofull called back, with a cackle. 'Then you'll have the Inquisitors to deal with. They won't let you escape from them again. I'd like to see you try.'

'When I do, it's your throat I'll be coming for,' Thurid raved, sitting down hastily in the wildly jolting cage. It descended another click, and the trolls could scarcely contain themselves in their hideous glee.

'We can hold them off, as long as they drop in on us one at a time,' Leifr estimated. 'Of course, it depends on how fast they drop in.'

Thurid glared at him. 'And what do we use for weapons? Our teeth? They've got teeth too, as well as claws!'

Leifr was about to form some cutting reply when the cage gave a sudden lurch upward. They all peered up in disbelief. A large counterweight dangled above, and creaking and grinding sounds were coming from the apparatus, as if someone were trying to turn it.

'Another of Djofull's wicked tricks,' Leifr growled, turning to glower at the wizard. To his surprise, Djofull was on his feet, staring upward at the opening and beckoning frantically to his attendants with the sedan chair.

'Someone's up there turning the hoist!' he exclaimed wrathfully. 'Get up there and bring him to me – alive, if you can, and dead if he resists! There will be no traitors in Ulfskrittinn!'

65

CHAPTER 5

Leifr peered upward with intense interest, unaware that any of them possessed friends in Ulfskrittinn.

'More of Djofull's trickery?' he queried Thurid.

'We're bound to find out,' Thurid replied glumly, but a light of desperate hope gleamed in his eye as the cage took another painful lurch. 'But at this rate, it will be hours, and Djofull's men will be up there. I wish I had my staff, and I'd do some levitation. Leifr, what are you doing? This is hardly the time for getting comfortable!'

Leifr sat down and took off his boots and slung them by their strings around his neck. Then he levered himself to the top of the cage and gripped the heavy chain. The links were wide enough to offer needed toeholds, but he would hoist himself up mainly by arm strength alone.

'I'm going to see if I can help whoever is up there,' he said, 'before it's too late.'

As he climbed, he heard Djofull cursing and muttering below, so he was not startled when an ice bolt tore past him, wide of its mark. A gust of icy wind threatened him the most, numbing his hands and bare feet, but he was so nearly out of Djofull's range that he was able to keep climbing, while bolts fizzled wildly around him. Concentrating on the opening above, he saw several indistinguishable figures straining to turn the windlass that raised the cage. When he was within reaching distance, he was surprised to see Nogur the scavenger reaching out a hand to him. Six other scavengers were trying to turn a capstan, puffing and grunting.

'Now it ought to come up,' Nogur said by way of greeting. 'We've got less weight and more pull.'

Leifr's eyes narrowed. 'The last time I saw you, you and Svanlaug had just led us into Djofull's hands. I'm not so sure I trust you now.'

'Svanlaug turns people to her own purposes,' Nogur answered. 'Helping you escape is our purpose.' He nodded his head to one side, where Svanlaug stood gazing at him with her vivid green eyes. She tore the confining net off her hair and shook it free.

'You?' Leifr demanded, incredulous and dismayed. 'What sort of trap do you have in mind this time? I've trusted you for the last time, witch. I'd rather go back down to that cage and entrust myself to the Inquisitors than have anything to do with any scheme of yours!'

'Would you indeed?' Svanlaug replied challengingly, her hair spilling around her shoulders like a horse's mane. 'I think not, Leifr Thorljotsson. My bargain will sound far more tempting to you, once we raise this cage.'

'You expect me to believe you're a traitor to Djofull?' Leifr demanded angrily. 'His prize acolyte? How stupid do you think I am?'

'Not to a completely unreasonable extent,' Svanlaug answered. 'But look around you at my allies. Would Djofull call upon the likes of these, when he has all of Stjornarr's trained warriors at his call?'

It seemed reasonable enough. Djofull had no use for scavengers, unless it was a double game Svanlaug was helping him play against Stjornarr.

'Djofull's sending men up to stop us,' Leifr said, bending his back to the capstan with a mighty heave. 'What do you propose to do when – and if – we escape from the Upper Chamber? You want us to do something for you, don't you? Something too dangerous for you to attempt alone.'

Svanlaug pushed beside him. 'I told you the truth before, about my brother and my father. Djofull stole something very precious from us, and I want to get it back. If you help me, I'll help you escape. That sounds fair enough, doesn't it?'

'It sounds fair, but you deceived us before. Why did you go after the Inquisitors? Was it because you realized there was no better way to destroy Thurid?'

'I didn't know he was at variance with them. I thought only that they would get you out of Ulfskrittinn. Djofull certainly has no intention of letting you get to Hraedsladular. I don't know what's there, but he wants you to fail. Once you are prey to his geas, he'll never have to worry about keeping you prisoners. Nothing and no one could ever free you then. Not even the Inquisitors and the Fire Wizards' Guild could stop him from claiming you and your weapons. You'll be hopelessly trapped.'

'Only if we fail,' Leifr answered grimly, 'but with Rhbu powers we won't fail. What is this property Djofull has stolen from your family?'

'You'll see, later. You agree, then?'

'Another deal with a Dokkalfar?'

'I've used no binding powers or spells, if that's what worries you. Only the threat that I'll leave you in Ulfskrittinn with Djofull and the Inquisitors. Believe me, it's a matter of simple theft. Once outside, you give me my property and we'll go on our separate ways.'

'I'd be insane to trust you,' Leifr growled.

'I had to bring you inside Ulfskrittinn somehow,' she said. 'There was no other way.'

'We won't leave without our weapons. You have to take us to them first. You should know where they are.'

'Agreed. The weapons, and then my property.'

'All right, it's a deal. But if you turn traitor against us, I'll let Raudbjorn comb your hair with his halberd.' He turned to Nogur and the slowly turning capstan. 'This is going too slow. It's barely crawling. Can't we increase the counterweight somehow?'

Without hesitation, six of the scavengers seized the chain one after the other, vanishing from view through the opening, and the cage began to rise steadily while Leifr and Nogur turned the capstan.

The cage arrived at the top with a crash, and Thurid and

Raudbjorn clambered out, none too soon to meet the rush of warriors that was pounding down the doors. Raudbjorn waited with open arms, and grabbed the first two that rushed in. He was so much larger and more powerful than the smaller Dokkalfar that he was able to smash them together headfirst and divest them of their weapons while they were still reeling from the concussion. Thurid and Nogur grabbed them and thrust them down into the cage.

Raudbjorn waded into the Dokkalfar like a berserker, using a broken timber like a scythe, smashing shields and flattening the Dokkalfar behind them. If his halberd had been in his hands, it would have been a bloody field day for the thief-taker. Unarmed as he was, he had to content himself with stunning and pounding as many Dokkalfar as he could, while Leifr guarded his back with a Dokkalfar sword and shield. In the space of a few ferocious minutes, the cage was full of Dokkalfar, the remaining few who were able to were escaping, and the cage was beginning to descend with its burden. With Raudbjorn to help push the capstan, the windlass speedily unreeled the chain with a deadly snarl. Nogur's companions clinging to the chain popped into view and were snatched to safety, adding to the velocity of the falling cage. The counterweight came hurtling up at them at a terrifying rate. Thurid shouted a warning. When the cage hit, the end of the chain wrapped around the capstan; the dizzying drop of the cage was halted just short of the ground, but the capstan assembly was smashed to splinters by the counterweight. After a few moments of grinding and splintering, it collapsed into the hole and the massive counterweight plummeted into the pit with yards of billowing chain following it down. It landed with a great thud near the cage, while the trolls cowered against the walls. The cage protected the Dokkalfar warriors from the lengths of falling chain that wreathed the cage. The trolls' nerves were too shattered by astonishment for them to look upon the situation as a culinary opportunity, and the Dokkalfar warriors were too amazed at surviving such a dizzying drop to do more than stir around faintly, groaning.

'Come!' whispered Nogur, beckoning.

He led them on a twisting route through the darkest and narrowest of tunnels, halting frequently as bands of Dokkalfar warriors clattered past in search of them. Several times they squeezed into narrow chimneys in the rock and worked themselves upward by bracing backs and feet against opposite sides. For Raudbjorn, it was a tight fit, with a couple of the scavengers pushing from below, but at last they emerged in a passage above ground level, with daylight showing behind barred doors.

'We're not leaving without our weapons,' Leifr said. 'Which way to Djofull's trophy hall?'

Svanlaug nodded and pointed straight ahead, where another dark figure rose out of the shadows and beckoned earnestly. On the ground lay a couple of guards, dead or unconscious. As Leifr approached he smelled a sickening wisp of smoke still rising from their watch fire, where a small bundle of herbs had nearly burned away. With a stick Svanlaug fished the herbs from the coals and trod on them.

'Very good, Vinur. They'll sleep a good long while yet. Long enough for us to take what we want and be gone.' Then she opened the door and led the group inside.

By the guttering light of whale oil and grass wick, Leifr saw the warlord's treasures hanging on the walls, and more were no doubt contained in the large carved chests flanking the great chair standing at the head of the table. It was set with gold and silver and jewels, designed to depict the skewered monster dying in the most spectacular and expensive of materials. Leifr did not waste time looking around; he bounded across the hall to the display of swords, where *Endalaus Daudi* hung gleaming among its rusty companions. Raudbjorn reclaimed his treasured halberd, looking it over anxiously for signs of abuse.

Thurid stood gazing around the hall. His eyes instantly settled upon a long carved chest standing in the center of a circle of runic writing. He walked around the circle, reading the runes. Making some signs with his hands, he strode to the carved chest and flung open the lid. As he removed his satchel and staff, a sudden clamor erupted from the walls around them. The captured weapons and shields clattered against the stone walls in a deafening chorus of alarm.

'Hurry!' Nogur shouted. 'They'll be here in moments!'

The doors at the other end of the room were flung open with a furious blast of cold air. A greenish bolt of ice came hurtling straight at them, whitening the ground where it passed. The thieves and scavengers hurled themselves aside. The dark figures of Djofull and Stjornarr moved into the room. The warlord's sword gleamed with a quivering lurid light, and green mist trailed from Djofull's staff like a nest of snakes to slither across the ground.

Thurid hastily composed himself in a warlike stance, holding his staff aloft with his cloak billowing around him. Leifr and Raudbjorn stood slightly behind him, dividing their attention between the two foes facing them. The scavengers melted into the shadows, waiting and watching, with traces of metal gleaming among them.

Djofull chuckled drily and tapped his staff on the ground. 'So, is this the way you want to end it, without the interference of the Inquisitors? I thought you'd come here. I'd give much to know who brought you this far, but I'll deal with that traitor later. Do you wish to surrender to the Inquisitors, Thurid, and entrust yourself to their safe-keeping, as is your right?'

'Surrender has never occurred to us,' Thurid replied. 'All we demand of you is safe conduct out of Ulfskrittinn to Hraedsla-dalur. Are you so afraid you'll lose – and lose Sorkvir's ashes in the bargain? Fainthearted cowards should never make wagers.'

'I never make wagers I can't win,' Djofull replied. 'Fairly or otherwise. Needless to say, I very seldom lose. Call it luck – or call it cheating, I don't care. I never hear any complaints from the losers.'

Stjornarr chuckled grimly and raised his sword. 'Better

to bring it to a swift end, Meistari. Rule them as draugar and you'll spare yourself the nuisance of claiming them later, when they fail in Hraedsla-dalur.'

'No, the Inquisitors may take them, for now,' Djofull said testily. 'I intend to have their silver, as well as these Rhbu weapons. This way we'll leave the good folks at Fangelsi-hofn in Hraedsla-dalur unmolested. It would be cruel to arouse their hopes, would it not?'

'Yours are the hopes doomed to disappointment,' Thurid replied. 'We're leaving Ulfskrittinn, and we're leaving without the Inquisitors.'

'Kill me if you wish, but the geas still stands,' Djofull said with a leer. 'I have no doubt that I'll soon return from Hel, even stronger and wiser than I am now.'

Leifr stepped forward with *Endalaus Daudi* in his hand. 'Taste death from this sword, and you won't return. There will be no one to gather your ashes and use your forbidden powers. You don't yet know if Sorkvir can be recalled. Do you wish to be another experiment?'

'I've nothing to fear from you,' Djofull replied, tightening his grip on his staff. As he suddenly spoke commanding words to his powers, Thurid raised his staff as a shield, and the forces collided with a rending shriek and a quivering of the earth underfoot.

'Use your spells on me,' Thurid said grimly. 'Let the warlord challenge the Scipling with the weapons they know best, if he dares. Then we'll fight our own battle with wizards' weapons.'

Stjornarr did not hesitate to step forward and touch swords with Leifr. A hot spark leaped from the Rhbu blade at the touch of Dokkalfar steel, but the warlord was undaunted. He swung a powerful two-handed blow at Leifr, who caught it on his shield and countered with a thrust at Stjornarr's helm. They battled, closely matched, exchanging stroke for stroke, until both were hot and winded and neither had given more than a foot or so of ground. *Endalaus Daudi* turned every blow with a shower of sparks and a ringing clangor. The two wizards and

Raudbjorn watched, their faces pale in the flickering light, each wizard surveying the other with distrust lest the other interfere in the fight undetected. Then Stjornarr called a halt to rest, and lowered his shield and leaned upon his sword. With relief, Leifr did likewise.

'A good fighter, for an outsider,' the warlord said with a grim smile, his eyes still deadly with resolve to destroy his opponent. 'Do you wish to call an end to it now while you can still escape alive?'

'Is it your own wish you're speaking?' Leifr returned. 'You must see your death over your shoulder, Stjornarr.'

'Not mine, but yours.' Stjornarr's hand flashed up and down, and a dagger flew toward Leifr's heart. He turned only slightly in the split second he had, and the dagger lodged in his right shoulder. He staggered back, his arm numbed, and Stjornarr surged forward with his sword.

Raudbjorn howled in rage and plunged forward with his halberd wound back for a deadly slice, but Thurid stopped him in his tracks with a word. Leifr seized his sword left-handed and closed with Stjornarr. Slightly overextended in his burst of confidence, Stjornarr left his right side unprotected for a moment, not expecting Leifr to remain standing much longer with a dagger in his heart. It was a favorite ploy of Stjornarr's, and he had never seen it fail; thus, he was greatly astonished when Leifr didn't drop. Not only did Leifr not drop, he knocked Stjornarr's sword aside and thrust at his unguarded side. With a deadly hiss *Endalaus Daudi* pierced Dokkalfar flesh. Stjornarr looked down at the smoking wound, his sword clattering from his grasp. With a wild imprecation he lunged in Djofull's direction, reaching out with a hand that glowed unnaturally, showing the shadow of bone beneath flesh. Collapsing with a despairing wail, he clawed the ground in a last enraged effort to reach Djofull, whitening and smoking like ash, dissolving at last to nothing but powder dusting a heap of armor and clothing.

Djofull recoiled, unnerved by the destruction of his ally. Suddenly he looked the part of the pinched and wary fugitive instead of the brazen predator. Holding his staff before him he began to retreat.

'Go your way, then,' he muttered. 'But after Hraedsla-dalur, you'll have no power to rise against me, remember that. You'll be in my control.'

Leifr swung around to follow, still clutching the sword. 'You won't live to see it,' he growled. 'We are all dead men, so it doesn't matter what time or place. Your time and place is now, you corpse-thief – murderer – liar!'

Raudbjorn roared an enthusiastic second and plunged forward like an avalanche. Djofull raised a hand as if to fend him off, and Thurid shouted a warning as he charged forward with his staff blazing to place himself foremost in the confrontation.

Djofull, however, stood frozen, one hand still upflung, and a dark shape suddenly hurled itself at Thurid, flapping in his face like a startled bird an instant before vanishing into the gloom of the Hall of Swords.

'He's gone!' Thurid brushed himself off disgustedly, lighting up his alf-light in a brilliant glare. Glistening bits of something slimy clung to his cloak. Djofull's body stood like a statue in a pose of retreat and fear. Only his strange hand was not frozen by the spell. It writhed and twisted around, beckoning frantically, as if reluctant to be attached to a nonliving body.

'He took the escape spell, and a very hasty one,' Thurid said disgustedly. 'He's left his carcass behind but his essence is fled. It'll do us no good to destroy what he left. He'd find another body soon enough, one we wouldn't recognize.'

Leifr lowered the sword reluctantly, his strength and fury rapidly draining. 'Svanlaug!' he shouted, and a shadow detached itself from the knot of lurking scavengers. She started to examine his wound, but he angrily fended her away. 'Conclude your business with him and take us out of here.'

Svanlaug's eyes were upon Thurid with sudden bright suspicion. The wizard approached Djofull and rifled through his pockets and pouches, suddenly falling upon a small black pouch with a triumphant cry.

'Sorkvir's ashes! I have them!' he gloated.

'Nogur, show them the way outside,' Svanlaug commanded. 'I'll catch you after I've regained my father's property. It will only take a moment, but I wish to be alone.'

They followed Nogur in a fast dash down the corridor and around some turns into narrower passages. Suddenly they burst into a lighted area where women and thralls were bending over messy-looking kitchen chores. Leifr briefly glimpsed a very unpleasant scullery area, where the floor was slimy underfoot and bad smells and unappealing sights assailed his senses. Greasy, suspicious faces stared at them as they raced through into a darker and smellier area where a vendor's cart and ponies stood. Nogur beckoned to the driver, who twitched back the covering, and Nogur motioned them to get inside. The covering was put back and the cart began to move, while the scavengers melted away with scarcely a patter of ragged boots.

The cart moved unhurriedly down a passage and stopped. Leifr heard the sound of voices, armor creaking and quivers of arrows rattling with feathery menace and the clink of swords. After a taut moment, the cart passed through a gate, turned and rumbled down a smelly alley outside the fortress. Leifr recognized the sounds of the Thieves' Market on all sides of them, then the sounds faded. The driver encouraged the ponies to a brisk trot. Leifr risked a look outside, and saw that they were approaching the main gates of Ulfskrittinn. He also saw that Nogur was riding ahead of them on horseback with a smoking torch in one hand. As he waved it, people on the road moved back in alarm, covering their mouths and noses.

The cart halted at the gates, and again Leifr heard the sounds of warrior garb and weapons moving nearby. 'Scavengers of the dead!' a muffled voice said in horror and disgust.

'Don't come near,' said the scavenger in a hoarse voice. 'It's plague! If you touch this cart, you'll be banished!'

The warriors fell back with an uneasy mutter. 'We've been ordered to search every cart that comes out,' one of them replied. 'Meistari Djofull's orders.'

'Do you want to lose your life following Djofull's orders? You know what this torch means, and you know what plague means. This cart will be burned, and this driver and I banished. Djofull's orders also.'

'Pass, then,' the guard said, falling back, his voice muffled under his hand.

The driver whipped up his horses and the cart rumbled out of the gate and continued on at a fast pace. People met on the road scattered in fear and loathing, with shouted warnings of the approaching plague wagon to those following.

When the cart stopped, they emerged warily, finding themselves in the familiar thicket region where they had left their horses. The driver waved and drove away into the thickening twilight, motioning toward Nogur's dark figure on horseback waiting for them not far ahead. Beckoning, he led them to a ravine, where a familiar outburst of barking greeted his appearance. Leifr whistled a signal, and in a few moments the white shapes of the troll-hounds burst over the rim of the ravine. They leaped around Leifr, smelling his injury and whining anxiously, then subjecting Raudbjorn and a most reluctant and indignant Thurid to a more boisterous greeting. Jolfr nickered Leifr a greeting, glossy of hide and well rested, not half-starved or stolen, as Leifr had feared many times during his captivity.

'Svanlaug's orders,' Nogur explained. 'We moved the pickets and tried not to get killed by your bloody dogs.'

The hounds bared their teeth and growled softly, eyeing Nogur with suspicion, as if barely restrained from flinging themselves at his throat.

Svanlaug came galloping after them, and insisted on

76

delaying their escape long enough to attend to Leifr's wound. 'I am more a healer than a sorceress,' she said, opening her satchel of herbs and cures. 'It won't take long to stop your bleeding, and there are spells to keep you from feeling the pain.'

'None of those,' Leifr growled between clenched teeth. 'I've had my share of Dokkalfar spells. I've seen worse hurts. Tie it up and we'll be on our way, and you'll be on your way. I trust you found your property.'

'I did indeed,' she said, 'but I'll ride with you for a short way to make sure you're well away from Ulfskrittinn. With Stjornarr dead, it will be rather lively around here until another warlord takes command.'

'No, we'll go on alone,' Thurid said. 'You've helped us escape, which is only our due since you got us captured, and you've got your father's property back from Djofull. I see no need to continue our comradeship a moment further.'

Svanlaug acquiesced with a slight bow, raising her hand in salute as they departed. As Leifr rode, eyeing Thurid's narrow shoulders, unpleasant doubts swirled in his mind. Then there was the matter of the geas. Leifr thought of that carved wand with their blood staining it. He knew that a geas extended beyond the limits of death, compelling draugar to endless and futile actions. Several times he opened his mouth to question Thurid about it, but Thurid seemed to read his thoughts and shook his head angrily, motioning for silence. Leifr could tell he was preoccupied with thoughts of his own, and from the looks and sounds of him, the thoughts were not pleasant. His staff's end smoldered, glowing like an angry red coal, and he kept his eyes upon the bristling landscape ahead and their trail behind. They rode along the ridge tops, picking their way carefully through the short dark night, continuing on into the silver hours preceding dawn. Frequently they paused, listening for sounds of pursuit and hearing nothing.

'Either we fooled them completely with the plague wagon,' Thurid said, 'or Djofull hasn't returned yet. If the Dokkalfar suspected there was no plague, they would have come after us by now.'

'They'll be occupied with fighting over Stjornarr's empty seat,' Leifr answered, his impatience augmented by the sharp edge of his pain. 'Our quarrel with Djofull isn't their quarrel, but I wouldn't be at all surprised if Stjornarr's favorites were ready to murder Djofull.'

Thurid made a sudden hiss for silence. With one hand he pointed toward a brushy ravine. 'We're being followed,' he said with an evil chuckle. 'One rider. I thought someone was behind us. One of Nogur's men, no doubt.'

They withdrew into a stand of thickets and dismounted, waiting crouched behind a skarp overhanging their trail. In due time the one who followed came trotting along, eagerly scanning the fells ahead. Though the morning was still twilight, he wore a Spider mask denoting one of the lowest of Dokkalfar warrior ranks, and a long black traveling cloak covered him from head to toe, protection against the unwelcome sun.

Thurid stepped from his hiding place to block the path, radiating a shimmering aura of power that billowed his cloak and dripped from the end of his staff. The stranger's horse shied violently backward and stood on its hind legs, dumping its rider on the ground. Then it galloped off, scenting the comforting presence of others of its kind behind nearby bushes.

Thurid pointed his staff at the Dokkalfar, who wisely did not attempt to rise. 'And now what about you, my fine fellow? You've come a long way with us, but now we must part. You've risked much, and we don't know even your name or how your face looks. If you are truly a friend to us, and have nothing to do with the fact that someone should have been pursuing us, you'll say your name and show your face to us now. Dokkalfar that you may be, there's not enough light to harm you.'

The Dokkalfar sidled away in sudden shyness, keeping his face averted and muttering gruffly, 'Names and faces

78

are not important. Not yet. I wish to travel with you awhile yet. They say Djofull put a geas upon you and commands you to go to Hraedsla-dalur. I wish to come with you and perhaps be of use to you. Though I am a Dokkalfar, I have no loyalty to Djofull.'

Thurid took a long step nearer, suddenly snatching away the Spider mask the fellow wore and pulling off his hood. A wealth of lustrous black hair escaped its confinement. It was Svanlaug, more pale than usual, her ice-green eyes flashing. She recovered her aplomb quickly and faced Thurid with the starch of defiance sharpening her voice.

'Well, I suppose you're thinking I'll lead you into another trap,' she said acidly as she got to her feet, keeping a wary eye upon Thurid. 'I tell you I'm done with Djofull. I've got what I wanted, and you've got Sorkvir's ashes.'

'The ashes are scarcely payment for one night in that cage with the trolls slavering and drooling below,' Thurid answered coldly, gripping his staff. 'You were part of Djofull's plot then, and you're probably part of his plot now, making it appear as if we escaped so you can attempt to steal the ashes and our weapons and make good your escape. You are no match for us, however. You'd better go back while you can.'

Svanlaug turned to Leifr, who scowled forbiddingly at the thought that she was attempting to appeal to him.

'Leifr, do you recall the words I said to you when we met?' she asked in a low tone. 'About my brother being killed by Djofull?'

'That's another lie, I assume,' Leifr said.

'No, it's the truth. I never lied once to you, Leifr. It was my friends who helped deliver you from Ulfskrittinn, was it not? Even Djofull with all his warlords and powers cannot command the loyalty of Nogur's band. My brother and I traveled with Nogur. He thought he could help my brother get inside Ulfskrittinn to take from Djofull what should have been ours by right. Instead, my brother was killed.'

'Indeed, a convenient story,' Thurid snorted. 'Calculated to sway our sympathies and lull us into a false pity for your homeless and kinless condition. Unfortunately for you, we're not so gullible as that. Once tricked, we never bestow our trust unwisely again. I suppose it was just a vicious coincidence that Djofull was training you as an acolyte.'

'I pretended to be a follower so I could get close enough to him to do him some harm, and find our property which he stole. And I succeeded. But as long as Djofull lives, the battle is not ended. I've got to destroy him, and I know I can count upon you to help me.'

'Absolutely not,' Thurid said. 'You have what you wanted, and we have the ashes. Go your way and don't come near us again.'

Svanlaug stood her ground. 'Nothing means more to me than the destruction of Djofull. You have enough powers to do it, Thurid. Why do you think he wants you to fail at his geas? If you'll destroy Djofull, I'll pay you. I came to Ulfskrittinn to get back a priceless object stolen from us by Djofull. I'll give it to you when Djofull is dead, with a hawthorn stake driven through him.'

Thurid shook his head slightly, but his eyes glinted as he inquired, 'What is the object? Is it of any real value to me? Jewels and gold mean nothing to a wizard.'

Svanlaug untied a pouch from her saddle. 'I think you'll agree it's valuable. It belonged to my father. He was a wizard before Djofull destroyed him.'

She tossed the bag to Thurid, who opened it and cautiously peered in. Then he gave a bellow of fright, flinging the bag away from him. The troll-hounds pounced on it, and one of them gave the bag a shake. Out tumbled Djofull's strange hand, scuttling with its fingers like an angry crab into the shelter of a rock. The red stone in the ring twinkled like an intelligent eye. It lunged out at the sniffing, snapping hounds, making a gesture with its fingers, and they retreated with startled yelps, shaking their heads and pawing their muzzles. Leifr took a long step forward, but a wave of fear hit him, freezing him to the spot. He had never before been gripped by such an unreasonable dread, and he knew it emanated from the hand.

CHAPTER 6

Thurid drew some deep breaths, also evidently in the grip of the hand's spellcasting. 'It preys upon the mind and the emotions. What is that thing?'

'All that remains of my father's potent devices,' Svanlaug replied. 'This hand belonged to a fire wizard my father destroyed, an old rival. Pabbi pirated his powers by saving his hand and ring. Djofull heard of it and killed Pabbi to get the hand of Gedvondur, and my brother also died in the fight over this hand. When I get finished with Djofull, not this much will be left. With your help, we can turn Djofull into nothing but dust.'

'A Ljosalfar helping a Dokkalfar? With family disputes? It's unheard of!' Thurid vociferated indignantly. 'Do you think I've nothing better to do than get involved in a broil like this? Important matters are awaiting my attention in Hraedsla-dalur.'

'Djofull won't be pleased by the theft of Sorkvir's ashes and Gedvondur's hand,' Svanlaug said. 'I doubt if he'll think it was his miserable little acolyte who dared steal them. He's going to think it was you and the Scipling. He's going to come after you. He has no intention of letting you get near Hraedsla-dalur, now that he has your blood on a rune stick.'

As they argued, Leifr suddenly noticed the hand crawling toward Thurid. Thurid saw it at the same instant and uttered a horrified scream.

'Great Hod, it's after me!' he exclaimed, seizing his staff. 'Get back, you filthy thing, or I'll fry you!'

'It means you no harm,' Svanlaug said, but it was clear to Leifr that she was in no hurry to approach it. The hand climbed deliberately onto a rock and faced them. 'It communicates through carbuncles or, if you touch it, directly. I fear it's an ungovernable thing sometimes.'

The hand pointed to Svanlaug and made an arrogant filliping motion with one finger. Uneasily she said, 'He's angry because I failed to find his ashes in Djofull's possession, so his body can be restored.'

'If Gedvondur was a fire wizard,' Thurid mused, 'then I suppose we share more in common than do you.'

The hand gestured, and Svanlaug translated. 'He says you are a buffoon and tainted by Dokkalfar powers. He also called you a dolt and a blowhard, but you must understand he's in a perfect fury about his ashes.'

Blinking in amazement and gathering fury, Thurid glared at the hand. 'I have been insulted by a disembodied hand,' Thurid said in outrage. 'Such a thing has never happened before. Svanlaug! This is your fault! Take this villainous little brute and go drown both yourselves, for all I care! Tell him he's nothing but a piece of carrion that ought to be fed to the crows, and his powers are nothing but swamp gas!'

Svanlaug looked at the hand in alarm. 'He understands what you're saying,' she warned. 'Don't offend him! You'd better apologize!'

Thurid glowered at the hand as it crouched on the rock, glaring back at him. 'If I have insulted him, it was because he insulted me first. I refuse to apologize to something that won't speak directly to me.'

The hand drew itself up on its fingertips, and the carbuncle ring glittered as if a light were passing through it. Thurid looked astonished, then he nodded his head. 'Very well, since you are capable of civility, I also apologize for my rudeness. We're all rather distraught, after what we've been through.'

'Well, it seems he's made a friend,' Leifr observed wryly, glancing at Raudbjorn. The thief-taker stared at the hand, his countenance pale with fear and loathing, as if he had never encountered such a horror in his lengthy career of mayhem and bloodshed.

Indeed, the hand climbed companionably onto Thurid's arm, and Thurid proceeded to introduce Leifr and Raudbjorn to it. Raudbjorn cringed away, baring his teeth in a savage growl of distrust. Leifr stood his ground, gazing into the twinkling carbuncle and feeling Fridmarr's carbuncle burning hotly against his chest, as if some heated communication were passing between the two stones which he was no part of. All he could sense was Fridmarr's vast displeasure.

'Thurid, what's happening?' he asked uneasily.

'Fridmarr is being his usual stubborn self. I'm trying to convince Gedvondur that you aren't Fridmarr, that you're something else.' His eyes blazed and his voice boomed, 'Gedvondur! Fridmarr, be silent! Leifr, touch Gedvondur's carbuncle so he can understand you. A Scipling with no carbuncle is as intelligible to him as a dead mackerel.'

Leifr gingerly touched the red stone with one finger, and received such a blaze of invasive presence in his mind that he staggered back a step, but not before the entire message was delivered:

'Who are you, and why don't you possess this carbuncle properly in your flesh, if you want to communicate with decent people? An outsider, a Scipling! Aha, I know you now and all about you. And Fridmarr, that renegade, you're not able to contact him much, are you? Just as well, he's a menace to everybody in the realm. Just listen to me, Scipling, and I won't lead you wrong. You're not afraid of an old dead hand, are you? Good, you're bold enough, if not too dreadfully smart, but you'll do all right with me to help you, once we get to Hraedsla-dalur. Then sooner or later you'll help me to get my ashes back from Djofull. No hard feelings, I hope, about the fright spell I used on you. It's my only defense. Shake hands, and let's be friends.'

The hand extended its index finger. Leifr glanced at Thurid, who regarded him with unhelpful blankness. Leifr extended his own index finger and gingerly touched it to the hand's finger. Instantly he felt a wave of friendly goodwill and cheerful bonhomie. The thought spoke in his mind, 'We can make great use of each other, Scipling.'

Svanlaug watched suspiciously. 'I beg to remind you all that the hand is my property,' she said coldly, 'and I shall be the one who uses his powers. He can be a tricky and disagreeable creature. I have a stout leather bag we can put him into. His only tricks are mind tricks, without a body to execute his will. Remember that once we have helped you break your geas in Hraedsla-dalur, you are obliged to help me destroy Djofull.'

The hand knotted into a fist, and Thurid said dubiously, 'He doesn't acknowledge your ownership. In fact, he says he'll melt you if you come near him. Your father did kill him once, so his dislike is understandable. I doubt if you have the strength to control a Ljosalfar carbuncle – especially one of wizard power.'

'Then you intend to steal him from me!' Svanlaug's veneer of good manners vanished instantly, and pure Dokkalfar fury transformed her features into a twisted mask of hatred. 'I should have realized what little honor there is to be had among Ljosalfar! You make much of your so-called superiority, but you're nothing but thieves and liars underneath! I've risked my life to regain this hand! A lone woman against Djofull, the greatest of the necromancers! I haven't come this far to be foiled by your trickery. You don't realize the danger in thwarting me. I don't accept disappointments or defeat, wizard!'

Even Raudbjorn was impressed by her malice, and one eyebrow crept upward in grudging admiration. The ring sparkled as the hand gripped Thurid's wrist, and Thurid calmed his own rising temper and spoke in a reasonable tone. 'Svanlaug, don't be angry. No one can own Gedvondur. A stronger foe may control him for a while, but you are not that strong. He wants to become our ally against Djofull, with the hope of regaining his form one day. He says you have valuable knowledge about Djofull and Dokkalfar matters, and you must be persuaded to join us. Personally, I couldn't see the last of you soon enough, but Gedvondur believes you will be useful. Your ambition of destroying Djofull will be realized in no other fashion, Svanlaug.'

Svanlaug glowered at the hand, and it beckoned to her to come closer. With trepidation, she eased nearer, eyeing it with suspicion. 'Since you request it, Gedvondur, I suppose I am obliged to follow,' she said bitterly. 'Fortunately, Pabbi bathed me in a vile concoction when I was a baby, so riding by daylight won't bother me too much.'

For a disembodied hand, it was monstrously particular about its traveling arrangements. It refused to ride inside a pouch where it could perceive nothing but darkness, and it disdained the offer of Thurid's pocket. It had a mortal fear of falling under the horses' hooves and getting trampled, so it refused to ride on the saddle behind someone. At last Leifr came up with an old boot which he tied to his saddle for the hand to ride in, and it was finally satisfied.

Throughout the day Leifr glanced down at the boot dangling beside his knee. The hand clung alertly to the top of the boot with the carbuncle ring sparkling in the intermittent sunlight, as if the carbuncle were indeed its sole organ of perception. The hand, he realized, was the mere vehicle of Gedvondur's carbuncle, all that remained of a once-powerful wizard. Musing upon the obvious power of a stone with the strength to cause mind spells, to communicate with living beings, and to command a dead hand to live, Leifr alternated between feelings of covetousness and fear. He wondered if such power could restore Ljosa to her true form.

Fridmarr, he knew, was not pleased. He could feel rather than hear a disapproving growl in the background of his thoughts. Once during the day, the hand extended one finger and cautiously tapped Leifr's knee, transmitting some kind of message that flashed through to Fridmarr before Leifr's slower consciousness could register on it. The reply was an instantanous crackling jolt that knocked the hand back into its boot. Leifr caught the gist of Fridmarr's remark, 'That should teach you to mind your own business!'

Later that night, after camp had been pitched and a hasty meal consumed, Leifr removed himself from Svanlaug's prying eyes and crouched in the lee of a standing stone to get out of the wind. He dropped Fridmarr's carbuncle from its pouch into his hand, searching mentally for the voice of Fridmarr. A sense of helpless frustration rose higher in him, realizing he was so lacking in vital Alfar abilities to communicate.

Yet the stone twinkling in his palm was a living thing, and he could sense Fridmarr's presence. Fridmarr could see and hear him perfectly, he realized.

'Fridmarr!' he whispered, and felt as if a hand were trying to part the heavy dark curtains of his mind, vainly attempting to speak. It was a warning, he was certain. Leifr put the carbuncle back into its resting place inside his shirt, startled and dismayed by the sudden revelation that both carbuncles wished to find a suitable host. It was an idea that tempted and repelled him – tempted him with the promise of unlimited power and knowledge, and repelled him when he considered the responsibility and the loss of his own singleness.

'I won't do it,' he said. 'Never. Not even for you, Fridmarr. I wouldn't like having your sharp wits under my skin. Traveling with you when you were alive was difficult enough.'

When he returned to the fire, he was conscious of the attentive scrutiny bestowed upon him by Svanlaug and Thurid and Gedvondur, perching on the top of a pack. They knew about his struggles and temptations and fears concerning the carbuncle. Different though they were from each other, their carbuncles united them with each other as well as generations of past knowledge, a unity of which Leifr could have no part in his lonely Sciplingness.

During the night, the troll-hounds leaped up with savage growls and bristled spines. Kraftig pawed at Leifr insistently, peering into his face as if trying to communicate with him in the simplest terms he knew how, still frustrated by the blockage in Leifr's understanding.

'Go,' Leifr said, and watched the three white forms vanish into the night.

Thurid stirred uneasily on the knoll above the camp, his smallest sounds audible to Leifr. Leifr checked the position of the stars overhead and decided it was close enough to the time for changing the guard. His shoulder was healing, thanks to Svanlaug's spells, but it ached annoyingly, making sleep difficult. He joined Thurid on the knoll, and they listened in silence, hearing a pack of hunting trolls two fells over challenging a rival pack, bellowing and grunting back and forth for a suitable period before starting to fight. It sounded like a dozen cat-fights combined, howling, screeching, and screaming. Finally one pack retreated with undignified yelps and whimpers, leaving the victors to growl themselves further away until all sounds of trolls vanished. Then at long last, they heard the troll-hounds fighting, far away, too far to tell what sort of creatures they battled.

'The realm is disturbed tonight,' Thurid whispered. 'It could be Djofull's fylgjur-wolves. He wouldn't stay away long in the escape spell – not while he's got that geas to look after.'

Leifr looked toward the bright star high in the heavens above them. Fantur the Rogue trailed a faint streak of light behind it. Its influence upon the earth was at its greatest and would not start to wane until after midwinter. Chief among its expected effects, Thurid had explained to him, was its detrimental influence upon the fire magic of the Ljosalfar. It would be helpful to discourage the Inquisitors somewhat from probing too deeply into Dokkalfar-held territory, where Hraedsla-dalur lay, but Thurid's own mixed powers also suffered certain aberrations. So far he had succeeded in setting a dozen small fires in unexpected places at unexpected times, and anything made of metal jittered nervously whenever Thurid came near, behaving most unaccountably. His alf-light was smaller and less bright, scarcely worth the great mental effort it cost him. His Rhbu powers, however, seemed untouched, and perhaps even stronger with Fantur's rise.

As they talked, Leifr noted Svanlaug's stealthy approach. When her foot crunched incautiously on a clump of frosty grass, she abandoned all pretense of slyness and approached openly.

'I simply cannot adjust myself to sleeping at night,' she greeted them. 'It still seems backward. After the troll fights and the dogs growling, there's no use in trying any longer. And Raudbjorn snores like a sty full of pigs.' To Leifr she said, 'If the pain of your wound is keeping you from sleeping, I have a powder which will help you. It's nothing you need fear, just a harmless little flower that blooms in the marshes.'

Thurid turned to glower at her, his breath gusting frostily. 'He has no need for your Dokkalfar quackery. You'd better keep your marsh flowers to yourself.'

Svanlaug tossed her head, freeing her hair of her hood. 'That's all I've got, since you've taken both the hand and the ashes of Sorkvir for yourself, without so much as blinking an eye. What do you intend to do with those ashes? Assay them for Djofull's secrets? Discover the secret of endless lives? You pretend a great innocence, Thurid, but I think your mind is revolving with ideas.'

'My only intention for those ashes is to ensure that Sorkvir and Djofull will never come together again long enough for Sorkvir to be restored to life,' Thurid retorted. 'How like the Dokkalfar mind to think of ways to turn everything to one's own advantage! I daresay there are ways to assay those ashes, but I certainly wouldn't stoop to it. My powers are the pure powers of the Rhbus, not the filthy practices of necromancy.'

Svanlaug gazed at him with no great amiability in her demeanor. 'High-and-mighty, aren't you, for an usurper? I've heard how you got that satchel and staff – through no merit of your own, I might add. The Rhbu powers made

89

you what you are – not that you were deserving of the honor. Although as a Dokkalfar, I must say you are a clever thief. I should know, from the way you took Gedvondur's hand away from me. It was my only hope of getting revenge upon Djofull for my father and my brother.'

Thurid cast a cold eye upon her and spoke in a curiously altered voice, gruff and menacing. 'You'll get your revenge a hundred times over, witch, before I'm done.'

With a frightened gasp, Svanlaug tossed her head, shaking her hair loose. 'That voice!' she whispered. 'I've heard it before, when Pabbi possessed the hand! It's Gedvondur speaking through Thurid!'

Thurid chuckled in an unfamiliar manner. 'Why should that bother you? You've said yourself that these fools need help, and I'm going to provide it.'

The hand sidled around Thurid's shoulder crab-fashion, and waved one finger jauntily to the others, then expressed an arrogant fillip in Svanlaug's direction.

'You'll destroy Thurid!' Svanlaug exclaimed. 'You're too powerful for such a minor practitioner!'

'Very well – for now.' Gedvondur departed from Thurid gradually, leaving Thurid sitting bolt upright, eyes wide and staring. Then he shook himself, gazing at his hands and flexing his fingers.

'Extraordinary!' he murmured rather shakily. 'What powers! And he's willing to share them with me!'

'You fool!' Svanlaug snapped. 'He'll burn you to a cinder, as he did the five wizards who tried to possess him after Pabbi. It takes more strength than you've got to control him. Even Djofull was afraid of Gedvondur.'

'He had cause to fear,' Thurid said. 'I don't. Gedvondur and I desire the same result, Djofull's death and the destruction of Sorkvir's ashes. Now take yourself away and quit nattering at me. It's quite useless, you know.'

'Yes. One taste of such power, and you're trapped, as if it were eitur in your veins.' Svanlaug tossed her hair and strode away, combing it with her fingers with irritated little jerks. Leifr gazed after her in consternation, then turned to Thurid.

Thurid returned his questioning stare with a smoldering glower. 'Mind your own business!' he growled, 'and I'll mind mine.'

'But Thurid, is this wise?' Leifr asked. 'You could lose yourself to that – to Gedvondur.' He wanted to use a more uncomplimentary epithet, but the hand was listening to him attentively from atop a stone.

'Don't worry,' Thurid said, suddenly looking very weary. 'This will be the best way to save us all from Djofull's geas. If we don't escape from the geas, how can we ever hope to recover Ljosa from her lost place? Don't you think I know enough about powers to know when I'm in danger of getting taken over?'

Leifr was not much reassured. Thurid retired to his pallet for a few hours of rest, much needed in his depleted condition. Leifr and Gedvondur's hand were left looking at each other speculatively, with Fridmarr's carbuncle grumbling warnings in the back of Leifr's mind. Leifr gazed at the hand uneasily, and it seemed to regard him with some sort of expectation.

'Eavesdropping on us, weren't you?' Leifr said, rather self-conscious at addressing a hand. 'If you've got such great powers, you'd better save us from Djofull's fylgjur-wolves, without damaging Thurid. Do that, and I'll try to think more kindly of you.'

The hand tumbled forward and touched him lightly on the foot, leaving him the message, 'Don't concern yourself about the fylgjur-wolves. Let me handle them.'

Leifr almost chuckled, but stopped himself in time. One bodiless hand against twenty or so powerful fylgjur-wolves was not a battle he wished to bet money upon. He nodded his head carefully, and the hand tapped him again. 'Svanlaug's the one eavesdropping. She's the one you ought to distrust. Her father was as evil an ice wizard as they make in Svartheim.'

The hand impelled Leifr to look toward Svanlaug's

hiding place. She stepped out from behind a rock, angry and arrogant. Gedvondur made an insolent gesture intended for Svanlaug and scuttled away at a tumbling gait that reminded Leifr of a leaf cartwheeling in the wind.

'Beware of him,' Svanlaug warned. 'He's looking for a body to possess. Thurid's just the weak and vainglorious sort he would prey upon, and you're a Scipling with no defenses to stop him.'

'I think you're jealous,' Leifr answered.

'Jealous! Not for a moment!'

'What would Gedvondur want with a short-lived Scipling carcass to carry him around?' Leifr demanded. 'It's more likely you who covets the powers he could give you, if you adopted that carbuncle of his.'

'It's you who are greedy for power, so you can save Ljosa Hroaldsdottir. The only way you'll do anything of importance in this realm is with carbuncle power. But you won't ever be the master of yourself again, once you do put one of those stones beneath your skin.'

'I don't intend to enslave myself to any carbuncle,' Leifr said testily. 'No matter what the powers.'

'Don't let Gedvondur change your mind. If possible.' She strode away with a tossing of her dark hair.

Leifr thought of Gedvondur's mind tricks uneasily. Throughout the next day he kept glancing down at the hand, remembering how it had created a sensation of terror and a sensation of fellowship and goodwill. If it wanted to, it could make him think almost anything it chose.

That night they made their encampment in a ruined hill fort and prepared for the attack of the fylgjur-wolves, but the peaceful calm of the night remained unbroken. An uneasy breeze filtered among the hollow-eyed walls and heaps of fallen masonry. Raudbjorn, Kraftig, Frimodig, and Farlig waited with their ears and eyes expectantly alert. They paced along the high wall of the battlements, but the desolate landscape waiting beyond betrayed no hostile presence.

Thurid was not reassured. 'They will come,' he said at midnight, clutching his staff and surveying the terrain. He ignited a small fire for tea and sat down with great aplomb to nibble some hard bread and cheese.

'They will come,' he remarked with certainty, turning a casual eye upon Svanlaug. 'When they do, I shall be ready.'

'Don't accuse me of anything,' she snapped. 'I can tell you're thinking that I warned them somehow, but I didn't. Djofull would be happy to hang me as a traitor, if he knew.'

Thurid swelled with indignation. 'Yet the fylgjur-wolves did not appear,' he said. 'Something must have alerted them to caution.'

Leifr thought uneasily of Gedvondur's hand and glanced in the direction of the boot, hoping the creature could not read his distrust. The hand was busy with a lump of soap and a basin of water, giving itself a wash. Twice it slipped in and thrashed about before crawling out again. The glittering carbuncle ring lay nearby. Leifr looked away, and caught Svanlaug eyeing the ring, the suspicion in her eyes evident even through the slits of the mask. Hastily she averted her gaze when she saw Leifr watching her.

Thurid also averted his eyes quickly from the carbuncle ring, scowling into his horn cup until the contents began to steam with heat. Surprised, he dumped out the tea with an oath, shaking his burned hand.

Leifr had never seen such worthless terrain as he saw during the next two days. Lava flows covered the earth like the seams of black scars, as if a massive clawed hand had ripped furrows in the tenuous green coat of wiry grasses and mosses. Between the flows were narrow green valleys, piercingly cold clear streams, and networks of troll trails. At night the wretched beasts lurked atop the flows, outlined against the silver twilight sky in garrulous troops. They roared and gibbered and fought among themselves with gestures curiously human. Once the companions heard the piteous crying of a baby in the wasteland of the lava flow above their camp. Svanlaug cursed Thurid for his callousness, but Thurid steadfastly refused to allow anyone to go in search.

'It's a common troll trick, and you know it,' he reprimanded her.

She leaped to her feet, hearing the heartrending little wail again. 'But what if it's not a trick this time?' she demanded. 'I know there's a child out there!'

'That's what they want you to think,' Thurid said. 'Who could resist such a helpless sound? But if you were to go in search of it, we'd find little left of you, come morning.'

Svanlaug heaved a sigh and sat down by the fire, her face livid in the reflected glow.

Leifr stroked Kraftig's silky ears to quiet his growling, not liking the idea of being completely surrounded by trolls any more than the troll-hounds did. These trolls were the great gray trolls, more intelligent and cunning than the small skulking creatures that haunted human habitations, waiting for an easy meal like the mean-natured little scavengers they were.

Suddenly Leifr heard a sound that almost stopped his heartbeat with fear and hope. The troll-hounds lifted their ears and listened curiously. It was the mewing of a cat, not far from their stronghold among the lava boulders.

Thurid turned a warning glare upon Leifr and extended one hand to bar his rising. 'You know it is a ploy.'

'But how could trolls know about Ljosa?' Leifr demanded. 'They wouldn't know she escaped in cat form. She must be following us, Thurid. She wouldn't stay at Dallir by herself, when we are her only hope. I saw her, Thurid. At Djofullhol.'

'You saw a cat. One cat is very hard to tell from another. They all have the same bloody disposition – teeth and claws and murder. If it's Ljosa yowling out there, you can bet she knows how to take care of herself. Cats are like Dokkalfar; they have nine lives.'

Raudbjorn grumbled to himself, holding his halberd across his knees and peering into the darkness. 'Dokkalfar,' he grunted, sniffing loudly with his finger pressed against one nostril.

'Dokkalfar and trolls united against us,' Leifr said. 'Djofull is still out there looking for us. He's not going to give up as long as we've still got the ashes and the hand. Thurid, something's got to be done, or we'll never find any sanctuary anywhere.'

'How very true,' Thurid mused, with a sardonic twist of his lips. 'The only solution, as you see it, is to stand and challenge him here and now and be done with it; am I correct?'

Svanlaug interjected, 'It's time you realized you've bitten off far more than you can chew.'

'We! You're the one that has done all the biting!' Thurid exclaimed, his eyes almost starting from his head. 'I wish I'd never set eyes upon you or pitied you in your captive state. Had I known then what I know now, I would have pitied Djofull. Surely if you'd stayed around him long enough, your mere presence alone would have destroyed him somehow, without your so much as raising a finger. Blast those ashes! And double blast Gedvondur's hand!'

The hand scuttled into the firelight and scratched some hasty runes. Thurid read them and spluttered, 'Inept amateur! Is that so? A mere hand is no judge of capability!'

An arrow suddenly hissed past Leifr's ear and struck the stone with a burst of sparks, the first of a volley approaching like a swarm of angry bees. Leifr dived to the earth along with Svanlaug. Raudbjorn crouched behind a rock nearby, with arrows shattering around him, rebounding with greenish sparks and smoking with dark powers.

The barrage stopped, and a voice called out, 'Surrender yourselves, thieves! You can go no further!'

Leifr replied, 'We have the ashes and the hand of Gedvondur. Approach and take them if you dare.'

The leader of the Dokkalfar moved his horse into view.

A long cloak hung almost to his heels, denoting a Dokkalfar of rank and power. About twenty others lurked in the rocks around him. Raising his arm, the Dokkalfar said some words, and at once a thick mist began to ooze out of the ground around his horse's feet, spreading in coils and tendrils until the Dokkalfar archers were obscured. It crept toward Leifr's position, bringing with it an icy breath that promised a deadly chill.

Leifr tried in vain to see Thurid, but there was no sign of him. Perhaps an arrow had caught him unsuspecting, as Leifr had nearly been caught.

A swath of blazing alf-light streaked through the gloom, searing the earth in its passage and setting the rocks to glowing and steaming.

He peered around anxiously for Thurid, tracing the blackened path of the fire bolt to a half circle of mortared stones. Thurid stood there with his staff extended and trembling, his cloak rippling and swirling in gusts of power emanating from his taut body. With the stiff wooden gait of a marionette, he advanced down the charred carpet toward the stronghold of the Dokkalfar. Their arrows exploded harmlessly when they reached an area a few feet beyond his staff's end, where glowed an impressive orb of alf-light. His clothing seemed to ripple with flames, even to the ends of his hair and beard trailing away in the wind with little tongues of flame. Thurid halted about midway, facing the Dokkalfar. The arrows had stopped, followed by a puzzled silence from the Dokkalfar as they peered out uneasily from their stronghold. Their leader moved cautiously into the fore, as if he intended to confront this flaming salamander that challenged him.

'Who are you?' he called warily. 'Our dealings are with the rogue wizard Thurid and the thieves who have stolen our lord's property. Stand aside and do not defend such vermin, lest your own name be tainted.'

'Kljufa, you great fool, do you fancy yourself as the warlord of Ulfskrittinn?' Thurid roared in the powerful, guttural voice of Gedvondur. 'Have you forgotten already what happened to Stjornarr? I will not be thwarted by such vermin as you. Take yourself out of my sight before my patience wears any thinner!'

He brandished his staff, and the Dokkalfar and fylgjur-wolves uneasily retreated a few paces, except for Kljufa, who urged his reluctant horse forward.

'I've come with a challenge,' he replied. 'You can fight Djofull with wizards' weapons, but I challenge the Scipling to exchange two strokes with warriors' weapons. If he is defeated, then you shall surrender yourselves to Djofull's judgment. You have an unknown traitor among you whom he is particularly eager to meet.'

Thurid cast his alf-light briefly in Leifr's direction. 'Scipling!' roared the voice of Gedvondur. 'You have heard the challenge of this flea-infested, maggot-brained viper of a Dokkalfar. What is your reply?'

Leifr unsheathed *Endalaus Daudi*, which gleamed in the night as he swung it around. 'Light down from your horse and come to meet your doom, Dokkalfar!' he answered.

Raudbjorn offered Leifr his massive shield. 'Take *Axi-Brotna*. No Dokkalfar get through it.'

Kljufa advanced on foot cautiously, cradling his weapon, which was a glinting broadaxe. His eyes gleamed with a fanatic light behind the slits of his helmet. He halted and regarded Leifr contemptuously for a moment, then shifted his shield from behind his back.

'Take your best swing,' he growled over the edge of the shield. 'Then it will be my turn.'

'Only if you live,' Leifr answered, taking a firm grip upon his sword hilt. Raising it aloft with a silent plea for the help of the Rhbus, he brought it down on the shield with all his might. *Endalaus Daudi* howled a shrill, brief note, and cleft the shield nearly in half with a jolting burst of force and a cloud of dust.

Stepping back, Leifr realized the shield was gone, replaced by a sizable boulder, shattered into fragments.

Kljufa staggered back, his armor whitened with dust.

'Warriors' weapons!' roared Gedvondur. 'No glamor spells! You forfeit the match, Kljufa! Djofull will nail you up by the ears for returning empty-handed!'

Kljufa replied in a vicious snarl, 'No Dokkalfar forfeits a match until he's stretched out dead! The Scipling failed to stop me! Now it's my turn!'

Winding his axe overhead with a wicked burring sound, he let it fly at Leifr. As it whirled, its form shifted from axe to deadly ice bolt. With a triumphant shout, the Dokkalfar surged forward, preceded by the fylgjur-wolves flocking to the battle with their eyes gleaming with blood lust. Raudbjorn plunged forward, swinging his halberd.

Gedvondur bellowed wrathfully, his shout ending with the words, '*Horfa undan! Afturkoma!* Leifr, get down!'

A sizzling ball of flame shrieked over Leifr's head as he flattened himself upon the ground, covered by Raudbjorn's shield. The forces of ice and fire collided nearly over his head, releasing a thousand rebuffed gusts and furies of ice fragments and sputtering sparks, as if an entire blacksmith's forge had fallen suddenly into a lake.

'Take that and tell Djofull about it!' bellowed Gedvondur, adding a mighty sheaf of blazing arrows which exploded over the heads of the astonished Dokkalfar and fylgjur-wolves. 'Thieves and murderers! When you have crawled back to Ulfskrittinn, you can tell him that Gedvondur sent you, with best regards to Djofull!'

A wave of invisible influence poured from the end of the staff, breaking over the scattering Dokkalfar and fylgjur-wolves with a roar of wind. They dropped their weapons, some falling to hands and knees, some attempting to flee. Shouts of terror gradually silenced, and the Dokkalfar gathered inexorably in a silent knot around Thurid's knoll, their hands dangling uselessly, their gait slow and stumbling.

Thurid chuckled in Gedvondur's thick voice, not a pleasant sound. 'They don't call me Gedvondur the Bad-Tempered for nothing,' he sneered. 'I control your wills and your fates. Your lives lie in the hollow of my hand. I could smite you all into the dust that you were created from and blow you back to Djofull on the wind. I could turn you all into pulverized jelly and grind your bones to powder. There are a thousand gruesome deaths for Dokkalfar. It would be amusing to watch the sun melt your flesh, very gradually, drop by drop. However, a dedicated wizard must put mere pleasures aside and attend to the business at hand. Take yourselves to Djofullhol as fast as hooves will carry you, and tell Djofull that Gedvondur has done this to you. Let Djofull be warned. If he attempts to meddle with this spell, he will regret it bitterly.'

He made a gesture, and instantly the Dokkalfar were transformed into a herd of wild pigs. They stuck their snouts into the air and sniffed warily, then broke and ran away with a savage grunting and squealing, leaving their weapons, equipment, and clothing scattered behind them.

Thurid doubled over and laughed, still in the voice of Gedvondur. Leifr and Svanlaug approached him with trepidation. His face seemed no longer the pale and aesthetic face of Thurid. His features seemed more coarse and ruddy, his eyes small and vicious.

'Thurid? Gedvondur? Who am I talking to?' Leifr asked suspiciously, halting at a safe distance, with Raudbjorn hovering behind him.

'That will teach Djofull to send a toady to do a wizard's job,' Thurid chuckled.

As Thurid spoke, the transformation faded. Gedvondur's hand released its grip on his right wrist and dropped to the ground, tumbling toward Leifr playfully. Thurid stood stock still a moment, breathing deeply, with his eyes unfocused. Then he toppled over as if he had been pole-axed.

CHAPTER 7

Thurid awakened the next morning little the worse for wear after his experience, although he had spent the night twitching and mumbling and thrashing, as if he were fighting Dokkalfar in his sleep. Raudbjorn killed a brace of hares that morning, and their bones and tender flesh simmered deliciously in a clear broth. Svanlaug spent several hours digging in certain spots in the wasteland and contributed some unfamiliar roots and herbs to the broth. Thurid ate most of it ravenously and, in an unaccustomed fit of generosity, inspired perhaps by his miraculous delivery from death, he ordered Leifr to pass around the small stone flagon he carried in his satchel. The stuff inside the flagon was a wondrous dark ale, which Leifr recognized immediately as the special vintage of Dallir. Its taste was sweet, but its memories were sad. Fridmundr and his sons were dead, and there was none other to bear the name and the bloodline. Part of his sadness, he knew, was the sadness of Fridmarr filtering through the carbuncle from the realms of the dead.

Thurid smacked his lips and lowered the flagon. 'A heady brew, but not so heady as the brew of Gedvondur's carbuncle. For a few moments there, I had in my possession the complete knowledge of centuries of Guild wizards. There was no vague thought which I could not bring to instant fruition, no destruction which I could not command. A few more moments of contemplating such power and I would have gone mad.'

'Do you recall any of it?' Svanlaug inquired, a bit too interestedly, her eyes shining with greed.

Thurid smiled secretively and tapped his beaky nose. 'I

feel as if my sight has been cleared somewhat,' was all he would say about the experience.

Leifr watched him closely thereafter and during the next two days he saw evidence enough to believe that the experience had changed Thurid in subtle ways. His temper was even shorter and more fiery than before, as if life were too short an experience to waste with patience and tolerance. He sought out the company of Gedvondur often and, without asking Leifr's permission, he took possession of the old boot that Gedvondur rode in, slinging it from his own saddle. Frequently he would take the hand and ride away out of sight of the others. When he returned, his manner seemed almost pixilated, and once his beard and hair were seared.

Despite it, he seemed to know with precise exactitude where they were going and how to get there, all without hours of poring over the maps. His dowsing had never been more precise and definitive.

'Gedvondur is the one leading us,' Svanlaug observed to Leifr as they sat on their horses watching Thurid dowsing. He strode ahead of them, all confidence and arrogance in his snapping cloak and glistening boot toes. 'I only hope it's Hraedsla-dalur he's taking us to and not someplace worse.'

Leifr took his eyes off Thurid a moment to glare at Svanlaug for her impertinence. 'Gedvondur! How could he be leading us anywhere? And why?'

'For Sorkvir's ashes, of course,' Svanlaug replied. 'Gedvondur is nothing but a hand and a carbuncle now, but if he had possession of those ashes, he would possess all of Djofull's secrets of necromancy. Gaining a new body is child's play to him. He could make one to suit him from dead parts. Or he could take one of us, any time he felt like it. You saw how he possessed Thurid.'

Raudbjorn grunted and shuddered, with a sound like a saddled horse shaking itself. 'Raudbjorn say burn that hand in the fire! Chop it to pieces! Evil thing!'

Leifr looked at Thurid prancing along in the full flower

of his confidence and groaned inwardly. Clearly Gedvondur was assisting him, lending him powers and teaching him new ones. Leifr knew the workings of magic well enough to know that for every reward there was a penalty, for every action an opposing reaction.

Echoing his thoughts, Svanlaug continued, 'One day Gedvondur will demand a price for all his help. What else do you have of value, except those ashes?'

Leifr waited until he knew Thurid was alone. The hand was bathing itself with its usual fastidiousness in a basin. Thurid was practicing something which required him to sit rigidly on a rock, eyes closed in utmost concentration as he inhaled deep breaths and slowly exhaled them.

Leifr knew he was interrupting, but it was an unavoidable intrusion. 'Thurid,' he said sharply, 'I don't like the way Gedvondur has taken over our expedition. He's going to want payment for all this one day, and what are you going to give him?'

Thurid's eyes glared yellow like a cat's when he opened them, and Leifr put his hand on his sword in surprise. The hideous yellow faded quickly to Thurid's usual pale blue color.

'Leifr, I am capable of dealing with Gedvondur,' Thurid replied haughtily. 'Your lack of trust is a betrayal of our friendship. I've made no deals with him, I assure you. He doesn't want to fall into the hands of the Dokkalfar any more than we do – or the Inquisitors either, for that matter. The Guild doesn't allow carbuncles to gallivant about in an unadopted condition, looking for a host.'

'No more than it will tolerate a rogue wizard,' Leifr added significantly. 'How do you know Gedvondur isn't an Inquisitor himself? He is – or was a member of the Guild. Where is he leading us, Thurid? Are you sure it's Hraedsla-dalur?'

'He's not leading us anywhere. I am leading us to Hraedsla-dalur!' Thurid's angry gaze raked over Leifr with a blast of heat, coming to rest upon a dry clump of furze, which burst into flame.

'He's teaching you fire skills,' Leifr said. 'Guild skills. Are you sure it's wise, at Fantur's position?'

Thurid lifted his head at an arrogant angle to look at Leifr directly. 'I am finding the skills myself. Gedvondur used me as a channel for his power, and it opened the gates and widened the ways in my own channels. All the blockages that once existed are now gone. I can become a Guild wizard, if I so desire, once I learn to control the power I possess. Gedvondur tells me I have marvelous potential.'

'Gedvondur!' Leifr looked around to make sure the hand was still washing itself in the basin beside the fire, with Raudbjorn looking on with a horrified sneer. 'Thurid, we can't trust him.'

'Leifr, he's not a Dokkalfar.'

'But he wants the ashes. And how long do you think he's going to be content to scuttle around as nothing but a hand and a carbuncle? He wants a body. He could take over anyone's he wanted.'

'He won't do that. He's got a great sense of honor. He is a Guild wizard, if you recall.'

'We're being pursued at this moment by Guild wizards. I fail to find that very reassuring.'

'Leifr, you don't need to worry about aspects of magic. I am the wizard and that is my domain. Kindly keep your ignorant nose in your own Scipling business, which is killing and maiming trolls and Dokkalfar and keeping us and Sorkvir's ashes safe. I regret speaking so harshly to you, Leifr, but you must learn not to question my judgment.'

Leifr said, 'It's Scipling nature to question everyone's judgment.' A shiver passed through him, and he realized that Fridmarr had managed to put the words into his thoughts.

Thurid gazed at him, evidently realizing it also. He sighed. 'I know it is, and it will be either the triumph or the downfall of your race someday. Be patient, Leifr.

Once we get to Hraedsla-dalur, I'll be able to start working on reversing the spell that holds Ljosa.'

'How much farther to Hraedsla-dalur?'

'We'll make a stop tomorrow at a settlement in Skollatur-jord to reprovision, then it's four days on to Hraedsla-dalur. I think of it as distance between myself and the Wizards' Guild.'

'The Bald Land.' Leifr mused over the dismal name. 'How do you know Djofull won't be there waiting for us?'

'The people of Skollatur-jord and Hraedsla-dalur are Ljosalfar in a Dokkalfar-held land. Believe me, they'll have potent protection against anything Dokkalfar. We'll be safer there than we are right now.'

'What's to stop the Inquisitors, though?'

'Fantur the Rogue. They won't risk Hraedsla-dalur with questionable stars.'

'And we will? I thought you said we'd be safe.'

'I'm relying on the Rhbu powers, which the Inquisitors don't have. Being questionable, Rhbu powers aren't affected by Fantur. We have no choice. We've got to break the geas.'

Toward midday they reached a landmark of significance, a raised mound and a spring, with a standing stone topping the mound. Thurid stopped to dowse and scowl over his maps and consult with Gedvondur. As he approached the upright stone on the mound with his pendulum swinging briskly, a force rebuffed him so violently that he staggered backward as if struck by a mighty blow. Gasping, he retreated, making signs to ward off evil influences.

'That settles it,' he panted, when Leifr and Raudbjorn came to meet him with their weapons in hand. 'We're lost. I suspected it the day before yesterday, but now I'm certain of it. This mound should have been half a day to the south, and not hostile. I've made a wrong turning somewhere. Skollatur-jord is well named the Bald Land. I think a bald head would have far more distinguishing features for travelers to navigate by.'

Thurid consulted his maps. Failing to find satisfaction therein, he started throwing things in random patterns, while Gedvondur looked on attentively. Svanlaug lurked nearby, spying upon Thurid until the hand made a stiff-legged dash at her, like a small, ill-tempered dog.

'Little beast!' she muttered, trying to salvage her dignity by holding her head high in disdain as she hurried away, keeping one eye upon the hand.

Raudbjorn was not happy with their stopping place. The hostile mound he avoided completely, but there were other stones scattered around the site, some half-standing, most lying flat. He prowled among these cautiously, keeping one eye upon Thurid and one upon Leifr. Betweentimes, he watched Gedvondur's hand skirmishing with Svanlaug, and his round countenance twisted with a grimace of revulsion.

'Dead hand not good,' he rumbled to Leifr as they passed on their wary patrolling of the site. 'Raudbjorn's hair stand up. Bad feelings. Something happen, Leifr.'

Svanlaug alternately stalked Thurid and Leifr. Now she appeared beside a tall stone, facing Leifr with defiance gleaming in her eyes. Raudbjorn clasped his halberd across his chest and glared down at her.

'The Dokkalfar are nearly upon our heels,' she whispered. 'If you want to escape, you've got to do it now. Djofull has brought us to this place. I felt his drawing powers, but Thurid would have none of my advice. You feel it, too, don't you?'

Uneasily Leifr scanned the stony landscape, where rocks looked like twisted forms of men and beasts, and the vegetation was bristly and stunted. A cold wind scoured the place, like clawed hands searching for life to blast.

Raudbjorn was nodding emphatically, but Leifr gouged him with an elbow. 'Your imagination is running away with you,' he said. 'This place is no different than any other. Unless, that is, you have cause to believe we've been drawn here – and what better lodestone for Djofull to draw upon than a Dokkalfar planted within our midst?'

Raudbjorn's features gradually darkened in a scowl as he figured out what Leifr had said.

Svanlaug tossed her head. 'Djofull knows well enough where you are without using me as a spy, just as a spider knows which portion of his web has been touched by prey. When you cross his ley lines and places like this, he knows. I don't think Gedvondur cares much about getting to Hraedsla-dalur. He'd like nothing better than to face Djofull, with Thurid for a vehicle. If you don't want Sorkvir's ashes to fall into Djofull's hands again, you ought to warn Thurid. It would be wiser if those ashes were in someone else's possession so, if he is taken, all won't be lost.'

Leifr disliked troubling Thurid again about the ashes, but he reluctantly admitted to himself that Svanlaug could be right. 'Your fears are entirely groundless,' he said. 'The ashes are safest with Thurid.'

'Fool! Thurid could be captured!' Svanlaug spat. 'Why do you think the Dokkalfar have stopped attacking us? It is because we are walking in the direction they want us to go, straight into a trap! One of us could escape. You and I could do it. As a Dokkalfar, I can hide you where Thurid cannot, which is among the Dokkalfar themselves. They would not look twice at me.'

'I wouldn't want to be the bearer of Sorkvir's ashes, and I certainly wouldn't entrust them to you,' Leifr replied and stalked away to further question Thurid.

Thurid's immediate response was to remove the pouch from his satchel and hang it around Leifr's neck. 'A splendid idea,' he said. 'I should have thought of it myself. Djofull won't expect you to carry the ashes. It's me he'll go for, and you can escape. No one is going to throw themselves on your sword. If worse comes to worst, and we get into a tight spot, that is.' He chuckled in rare good humor, and Gedvondur's carbuncle sparkled in reply.

'When are we going to leave this place, Thurid? It's rather strange here,' Leifr said uneasily, thinking of the spiderweb Svanlaug had mentioned, with Djofull watching them hungrily, like the spider.

'In due time, in due time. One can learn much by examining the enemy's forces.' He returned to his prowling and sampling of the atmosphere surrounding their stopping place, much like an adventurer who prods a hornet's nest until something comes out.

The day darkened as a storm rolled in from the direction of the sea, moving with uncanny speed and laden with the smells of the ancient brine and a sinister moldering smell Leifr had learned to associate with Dokkalfar. Wind buffeted at the raised mound, and thunders and lightnings crashed around in the swollen cloud mass as the threatening curtain of deep violet swept across the land. When it had engulfed their position, the day turned almost as dark as night.

Thurid leaned on his staff and watched. The wind did not tear at him as it did the others; he seemed to be standing in a protected dome, where his cloak billowed gently.

'Now it's too late!' Svanlaug exclaimed. 'Djofull is working this weather!'

This time the arrow that brushed Leifr's hair in passing struck Svanlaug in her arm. Leifr dived to the earth along with Svanlaug, who was cursing and wrenching at the arrow piercing her upper arm.

The sizzling volley of arrows slackened, then stopped. A voice called out, 'Surrender, thieves! You can go no further!'

Thurid maintained his lofty pose, striking the arrows out of the air with flashes of fire. He replied, 'We are not thieves. It is Djofull who has no right to the ashes and the hand of Gedvondur. Approach and take them if you dare risk everlasting death.'

The leader of the Dokkalfar moved his horse into view. A long cloak draped his figure – another Dokkalfar, with another twenty henchmen.

'A new warlord,' Leifr said. 'Ulfskrittinn can't very well be run by a pig.'

The large dark shape of a coach lumbered into view, with lamps made from human skulls glowing on each side of the driver's seat. Four high wheels jolted over the rocky earth, and whale ribs formed the cover, over which hides were stretched tightly. Three horses drew it, their eye shine gleaming in the light of the skull lanterns.

A cloaked form descended from the coach, carrying a staff, leaking phosphorescent mist as he advanced to confront the outlaws.

'Well then, Djofull!' roared the voice of Gedvondur, and Thurid swaggered forward. 'Again we meet! What folly has led you to believe I'm going to be captured and forced to perform your dastardly deeds again?'

'It isn't going to work, you know,' Djofull said, shaking his head. 'You're going to destroy Thurid, and then who will you be left with? The Scipling? The thief-taker? They won't last long, and you'll be out of friends once again. I am the only living being who can withstand your strength, Gedvondur, and you know it.'

Leifr heard Thurid's voice mutter, 'It was a near thing last time, you fool. He's not right, is he?'

Gedvondur's voice muttered back, 'Of course not. If I thought I were destroying my only hope, I'd be a fool to continue using you.' In a shout he continued, 'Go back, Djofull, or I won't answer for the consequences. You saw what we did to Kljufa.'

'It didn't last. You can't do anything to me that I can't undo, Gedvondur.'

'You've lost your chance at the Inquisitors' silver,' Thurid's voice broke in. 'You can't undo that.'

'They'll be back, come spring, if I send them word that their quarry is captured – if there is anything of you they want by then. You must know that hosting Gedvondur's carbuncle will leave you a hollow, rotted-out lunatic. And it won't take long, particularly since you must be already insane to attempt such a partnership.'

'Bah!' Gedvondur's voice retorted. 'You're envious, because you were afraid to try it.'

'I'm great enough with begging from you!'

Raising his arm, Djofull chanted some words, and a thick mist began to ooze out of the ground around his feet, spreading in coils and tendrils until the Dokkalfar archers were obscured. It crept toward Leifr's position, bringing with it a spirit of gloom and defeat, robbing Djofull's enemies of the strength to fight and resist. Even Raud-bjorn let his halberd sag to the ground, moaning helplessly with the burden of despair carried by the spell.

Svanlaug gasped, her teeth clenching in pain. 'We've lost our chance for escape. Once that fog touches warm-blooded flesh, we'll stay frozen like this forever. They say Djofull is building a wall in Djofullhol of nothing but his frozen enemies, and already it is a hundred feet long and shoulder high to a tall man.' Her voice faded as her consciousness slipped toward oblivion.

The cloud drifted gently around the hilltop until it was surrounded. Leifr tried in vain to see Thurid, but there was no sign of him.

'Fridmarr!' he whispered, listening for the voice of the carbuncle. He heard only a fateful silence, and the carbuncle was stone cold, as if Fridmarr had withdrawn completely.

The cloud formed a dome overhead, blotting out the light of the weak sun and turning the hilltop to premature twilight. The cold air seemed too thick to breathe. They covered their faces, but it brought scant relief. Raudbjorn slumped against a stone, rolling gradually like a landslide until he lay unconscious, breathing very faintly in small plumes of warm vapor.

Leifr struggled to his feet, gasping, unsheathing the sword. 'A brave warrior always dies sooner or later,' he panted, 'but he always takes at least one enemy with him when he goes.'

'Don't be a fool! You won't get near them before you die!' Svanlaug wheezed, clutching at his cloak. He stumbled out of her feeble grip, raising the glowing sword in challenge.

A fiery probe raked through the fog, melting holes and gaping pathways through it with the screaming hiss of red-hot iron tempering in cold water. One bolt passed over Leifr's position in a brief explosion of welcome heat and light, giving them untainted air to breathe and renewed hope for survival. Raudbjorn groped around for his halberd, his small eyes gleaming viciously at the insult that had been inflicted upon his pride. Leifr gripped the sword and looked around for Djofull's position.

'Stay down! Stay out of it! This is a duel for wizards!' The words burned in his mind like a swarm of angry bees, and Leifr recognized Fridmarr's voice. The carbuncle was hot to the touch, as if Fridmarr had managed briefly to bridge the gap between them. Leifr knew that the occasion that merited such effort must be fraught with peril indeed, so he left the battle to the wizards, watching with awe as vast illusions took form in the mist. Dragons, great snakes, frost giants, monsters, walls of flame, all combined in battle with each other until Leifr could not tell which manifestations belonged to which wizard.

'Thurid isn't going to last,' Svanlaug said. 'Djofull is throwing his most powerful spells at him, hoping Gedvondur's power will burn him out. Then he'll have us for the plucking.'

'It won't be easy for him,' Leifr said grimly, 'and only if Thurid fails. Thurid survived it once – and maybe more times than we know about.'

'But this is a duel,' Svanlaug said, wincing as a powerful illusion was exploded almost overhead. Flying creatures died in screaming spirals, trailing gouts of lurid flame and black smoke. For an illusion, it seemed a particularly potent one, scattering flaming debris over the earth below and sending the Dokkalfar scuttling for cover.

At last the roiling clouds of mist and smoke drifted away, and no new terrors took form. The night had passed, and the sun showed a pale golden eye over the edge of the horizon, looking upon earth seared and blackened, or frozen stark and white, and now gradually thawing. Strange vapors still lingered, unwilling to dissipate, as if possessing unnatural life of their own. To any eye, it was obvious a battle had been hard fought, though combat between only two opponents did not warrant such devastation.

Warily Leifr led the way, hoping to find Thurid still alive, but dread pounded in his heart. Influences brushed at him, still felt but swiftly losing their threat.

'There he is,' whispered Svanlaug, pointing across the charred, churned battlefield, where a solitary, unmoving figure sat on a hilltop.

Thurid sat huddled wearily on a stone, his staff propped upright nearby, trickling a faint sooty stream of smoke. His shoulders were bent in abject resignation, and he did not so much as raise his head when Leifr hallooed at him.

'It's happened!' Svanlaug hissed. 'His mind is gone!'

Leifr rushed past her and scrambled up the hill.

'Thurid!' he gasped. 'Are you all right?'

Thurid raised his eyes to Leifr, deeply weary and haunted in their depths. He was himself, unaugmented by Gedvondur. 'Of course I'm all right, you dolt,' he growled. 'Would I be sitting here if I weren't? Would you be there asking me stupid questions? We'd all be in Djofull's possession if I weren't all right.'

Greatly comforted by Thurid's snappish temper, Leifr looked around for Gedvondur. 'Where's the hand?'

Thurid motioned to another rock, where Gedvondur's hand lay stretched out as if completely exhausted. One finger raised and waved faintly in salutation.

Leifr went on, 'After what he put you through last night, I'm surprised you're still on your feet. It took you three days to get over it when Kljufa attacked us.'

'Kljufa attacked less of a wizard,' Thurid answered with withering scorn, his eye kindling with fiery pride. 'If Djofull hadn't retreated because of daylight approaching, we would have cooked his goose for him. The world is not often privileged to see a partnership such as Gedvondur

111

and Thurid. Using me as a channel holds him back somewhat, but with practice, I could one day aspire to approach his strength, and then the Dokkalfar empire will reel to and fro and crumble into devastation and ruin.'

Svanlaug tossed her head. 'I think it will take more than just the two of you to knock down the Dokkur Lavardur and the Ulf-Hedin warriors. They make Djofull and his fylgjur-wolves look like apprentices to a dollmaker.'

'Bah,' Thurid said disagreeably. 'Leifr, find that flagon in my satchel. It's time for a small restorative.'

In the late afternoon they arrived at their destination in Skollatur-jord. Already the shadows were long across the barren land and the low valleys hidden in the early twilight of approaching winter. Small bands of shaggy sheep and goats scavenged among the rocks and straggling thickets, which stood on leggy bare trunks, gnawed by sheep for food and chopped at by men for firewood. The denizens of the settlement came out to stare at the travelers with scant hospitality evident in their ragged clothing and suspicious demeanor. Looking at them, Leifr had the feeling they were trying to decide whether the travelers were likely to kill them or whether they ought to kill the travelers.

It hardly looked like a propitious place for reprovisioning, but Thurid somehow managed to grease the appropriate palms with promises of certain magical interventions, and they found themselves comfortably accommodated in the house of one Tvofaldi and various of his relatives, who had come to the settlement to barter for hay. As they approached his homestead, Leifr observed symbols carved into upright stones and gateposts and forged into the metal of swords and amulets.

'Wards against Dokkalfar,' Svanlaug explained uneasily as Tvofaldi performed a spell to allow them to pass. 'The Ljosalfar of Skollatur-jord and Hraedsla-dalur are well-nigh wizards. They have to be if they are to survive.'

Leifr saw Tvofaldi and his brothers eyeing Svanlaug suspiciously. At the door of the house she stood still, unable to pass, until a bough of blackthorn was taken down from the lintel. Tvofaldi smiled unpleasantly at her and bowed with exaggerated courtesy, allowing her to pass before him. She held her head high, but Leifr noticed her eyes darting warily around the house for more hostile devices.

A hearth occupied each end of the house, with people on one side and animals on the other, and a front and a rear door offered passage straight through the center. No gracious tapestries covered the walls here; sheep fleeces were fastened to the turves, and the weaving was all of the most practical and sturdy design to combat the cold brought by the invasion of the Dokkalfar.

Svanlaug garnered the barest of courtesy and thinly veiled hatred from Tvofaldi's household. Thurid and Leifr and Raudbjorn fared slightly better, especially after Gedvondur emerged from Thurid's sleeve and strolled casually across the table to drag the ale flask to the visitors' end. The hard-bitten Ljosalfar around the table froze, watching. After that, their manner improved markedly, even extending to Svanlaug. A lone Dokkalfar among so many, and a woman at that, was nothing to be concerned about, after all.

After the repast, Tvofaldi even unbent so far as to bring out his harp to play for the entertainment of his guests, though his songs were of the most defiant and bloodthirsty sort, dealing with past injustices and battles with evil Dokkalfar.

On the following day, Thurid taught Tvofaldi how to employ stronger wards against the Dokkalfar, and reclaimed a particularly important mine shaft from Dokkalfar control by setting new wards around it. The dominion of the Dokkalfar warlord of Skollatur-jord was nothing Thurid and Gedvondur could do anything about, but they could make the oppression somewhat bearable for Tvofaldisstead.

The land had not borne a crop of wheat since the possession began many years ago, forcing the Ljosalfar to trade with the Dokkalfar warlord at exorbitant prices. To compensate, a thriving underground trade system had grown up among the Ljosalfar, carried by the scavenger-traders who roamed the wasteland with pack trains or pony carts, where roads existed. Under the most ideal circumstances the goods were stolen from the Dokkalfar hill forts by raiding the pony trains that brought their supplies, and then sold at reasonable prices to the Ljosalfar settlements. No loyal Ljosalfar was above raiding the Dokkalfar whenever possible, and Tvofaldi was one of the most adept of raiders. Absolute secrecy was essential; once the warlord suspected who had raided his supply train, another Ljosalfar settlement would be devastated, and the occupants never seen again.

Thurid taught him a spell for disguising himself and his men and horses, and one to throw confusion into the Dokkalfar. It was generous payment for the supplies given in exchange. Information as well as supplies were given. Tvofaldi marked Thurid's maps and told him all he knew of Hraedsla-dalur and its settlements.

'Fangelsi-hofn is one of the oldest farms in the land,' Tvofaldi said, sucking on his pipe and scowling. 'It's an unlucky place, as they say. Nothing ever seemed to prosper after Slagfid died – that's the man who settled there, but he wasn't the first by any means, if you get my meaning.'

'Ah. He built on an old site,' Thurid said.

'That he did, and they say he went mad at the end. After him, madness seems to run in the family. Of course, that might have been because of the jotuns. I doubt if jotuns would help anybody's sanity. The farming never prospers where there's jotuns or suchlike creatures of the dark side. It was a mistake to build there, and seven generations of Slagfid's heirs for seven hundred years have been paying for it.'

'Why don't they move off?' Leifr questioned. 'After seven hundred years, I'd think they'd be discouraged.'

'Nay, there's no sense in being hasty,' Tvofaldi replied,

114

shaking his head. He went on to discuss Slagfid and several generations of his descendants as if he had known them perfectly well. Leifr marveled silently; among Sciplings a man was forgotten almost as soon as he died.

'Then it's jotuns we're to kill,' Leifr said as soon as he could speak to Thurid alone. 'Djofull said they were remnants of an old spell. Probably one of his predecessors was responsible, and Djofull wants to get rid of any rival influences.' Leifr was rather proud of that bit of deduction. He felt as if he were getting quite knowledgeable about the Alfar realm.

Thurid shook his head. 'Djofull doesn't want those jotuns destroyed.'

'He doesn't? Then why did he send us out to find them?'

'He didn't, you fool. He put a geas on us, as impossible as he could think of. If we destroy those jotuns, then he will have failed. Djofull does not plan for failures. Why do you think he's trying to stop us?'

'Because he has no sense of honor. I thought it was more of a contest. He has no intention of letting us get to Hraedsla-dalur, does he?'

'No more than a cat has of letting the mouse go when he's playing with it. We stepped into that geas, and if we fail we are more securely trapped than if Djofull kept us in one of his darkest dungeons. From a dungeon there is always a chance of escape. If we fail at this geas, there is no escape. Ever.'

'But we've come farther than he expected,' Leifr said.

After a moment of thought, Thurid said, 'Yes. We have. And we will get even further.'

The day before leaving Tvofaldisstead, Leifr was going over his saddle in the stable when he felt a familiar ghostly chill. Looking up slowly, he saw a thin gray cat watching him. When he spoke to the creature, trying to coax it to come nearer, it arose in alarm and walked away to indicate that friendly advances were not going to be successful.

Reaching the doorway, it seemed to melt before his eyes, like gray mist.

'Ljosa!' he whispered, but the cat had vanished, leaving him with a heavy premonition of imminent danger.

CHAPTER 8

Leifr had enjoyed the brief return to a somewhat normal pattern of life, but now it seemed he could not get away from Tvofaldisstead fast enough. Their departure, however, was delayed by the arrival of a high-wheeled trader's cart drawn by a craggy-hipped old horse, accompanied by a wizened little man with a tall walking staff. The cart was loaded with goods from a merchant ship, which old Vidskipti intended to trade to the settlements for the odd bit of gold or silver. Thurid could never resist a trader's cart, and he swooped down upon it with a cackle of joy. In moments he was going through a chest of what Vidskipti optimistically called antiquities, gazing fondly through foggy seeing orbs and sniffing dubiously at dried specimens of animal and plant life.

The ladies of the household exclaimed over the bolts of red and blue cloth, woven of fine soft wool, the colored glass beads which they loved to string between their cloak brooches, and the horn combs for their hair. Tvofaldi bargained for wheat and corn, while Leifr looked over the other merchandise.

'You drive a hard bargain,' Vidskipti grumbled, at last striking palms with Tvofaldi in agreement. 'I could get more for that grain at another settlement.'

Tvofaldi grinned and replied, 'You could also lose it at the next river crossing, or thieves might steal it from you. I think you are satisfied with your bargain.'

'Are there many strangers on the road?' Leifr asked with feigned carelessness as he fingered a fine gray cloak.

'Strangers, aye,' Vidskipti answered with a scowl. 'Wizards too, by the look and feel of them.' He passed his

117

hand through the air as if testing for subtle currents.

Leifr pretended to be interested in some outlandish imported trousers, which used five times as much fabric as was needful. He couldn't imagine appearing in such garb, even if the color weren't a violent yellow. 'Wizards? I daresay they were only foreigners. It's hard to judge by appearances whether men are wizards or not.'

Vidskipti swelled with indignation and wounded pride. 'Oh, I suppose I'm no judge of men. Just because I travel the Barrens of Skarpsey from Quarter to Quarter might not mean I see all sorts and know what they are about by just looking at them.'

'What would wizards be doing so far from the Guildhall and the big settlements?' Leifr scoffed.

'Guildhall? Did I mention the Guildhall?' Vidskipti crowed. 'Perhaps it's Guild wizards I've seen, and perhaps it's the other kind, but this much I'll tell you. They were looking for someone.' Vidskipti tapped the side of his nose with a cunning grin.

Leifr merely snorted and moved away to the other side of the cart to demonstrate his lack of interest, all the while considering how to elicit more information from the old trader without arousing suspicion.

Suspicion, however, ranked only second to curiosity in the composition of Vidskipti's character. He sidled around to stand beside Leifr, his weaselish bright eyes darting over Leifr's garb and accouterments.

'As I said before, I'm a judge of men and their business,' he whispered in a loud whisper that carried much better than a spoken voice. 'I can see that you're the fox who flees, sniffing each breeze for his enemies.'

'If any man knew about fleas, it must be you,' Leifr retorted. 'How long have you been in the Barrens? They say it makes you crazy after a while.'

Vidskipti grinned slyly and rubbed his warty red nose. 'I've been walking the Barrens almost forever. The oldest man can't remember a time when I was not here. Be warned, young man. If I was the one running from those wizards, I'd not linger long in Skollatur-jord. Word of strangers passing through here has found its way past the Barrens to ears you'd never dream. These wizards were all mighty interested to hear about it.'

'Wizards!' Leifr snorted. 'Old scavenger, you've been in the Barrens too long for your own good.' He chose an antler-handled knife from Vidskipti's merchandise and held it up critically. 'This is almost acceptable as a knife. I suppose you want three prices for it.'

After haggling Vidskipti's outrageous price down, Leifr thrust it in his belt and sauntered away, looking for Thurid. He discovered the wizard at the kitchen annex talking to one of Tvofaldi's daughters, who was looking coy over a string of new glass beads. Leifr terminated the discussion unceremoniously and hustled Thurid away from the house to talk.

'The Inquisitors are on our trail,' Leifr said. 'Or more likely it's Djofull. If we leave here now, it won't be soon enough. Word travels across the Barrens faster than it does anyplace else.'

Thurid slapped his pockets impatiently. 'Of course it does. Gossip is swift in a war zone. Where's Gedvondur? He's got to tell us where to go next. Drat that piece of carrion, where's he gone to?'

The hand appeared on the edge of the barn roof and waved cheerily. Beside him, a small ragged figure dived into a hole and peeped out suspiciously, showing nothing but a tiny wizened face wreathed with a wisp of white beard.

'The house guardian,' Thurid whispered. 'Now that's something I'm glad to see. This place will be all right. Didn't I tell you things were strange in a war zone?'

Leifr glanced at Thurid incredulously to see if further explanation was forthcoming, then back toward the hollow on the barn roof. Nothing was there now, and Thurid was striding away impatiently barking orders, as if leaving were entirely his idea and everyone else were blundering obstacles in his path.

Not so coincidentally, Vidskipti was also about to depart. He ambled alongside Thurid's horse at his rolling gait and graciously suggested, 'My friends, since we seem to be going in the same direction, we might as well travel together until we reach the next settlement.'

Thurid eyed the bony-hipped old horse and dilapidated cart and agreed reluctantly, saying in a pompous tone, 'However, we won't be going to the next settlement. We're bound for a destination we don't care to disclose, lest that information somehow find its way to hostile ears.'

'Allow me to be your guide,' Vidskipti said with a raffish grin. 'I know this region as well as I know the warts on my nose. I know where you'll want to go, before you even think about going there.'

'I don't think so,' Leifr said. 'We prefer to travel alone, and unencumbered.'

Bestowing a suspicious glare upon Vidskipti, Thurid turned and said to Leifr, as if he had no knowledge of common courtesies, 'In Skarpsey, one does not refuse the offer of protection, nor does one refuse a plea for protection, from whatever the source.'

Leifr retorted, 'Your Skarpsey is not so different from mine, Thurid.'

'By anybody's standards, your manners were rather discourteous just now,' Thurid admonished. 'Perhaps he is a disreputable old beggar, but even so, you owe him a small degree of civility. Or are you afraid his motley appearance is going to embarrass you?' His disdainful eye ran over Leifr's stained and ragged garb. In a lower voice he added, 'It might not be politic to refuse his help, Leifr. This is the Barrens of Skollatur-jord, after all.' He tapped his staff significantly, hinting at unknown powers.

Svanlaug interjected, 'Are we going to stand about for the rest of the day? Since we are forced to travel with this lice-bag peddler, the least he can do is hurry his filthy carcass to keep up.'

Vidskipti only chuckled and flicked his horse lightly with his whip. 'Come on then, let us be off.'

120

The cart lumbered along at what seemed a snail's pace to Leifr, stopping once more that day at the next settlement, where they spent the night. The next day they stopped twice before rolling into the region called Hraedsla-dalur – translated by Svanlaug, not without relish, as the land of horror.

When the early twilight descended, the travelers took refuge in a ruin. Roofless though it was, it offered some protection from the icy wind interlaced with driving flakes of snow and ice pellets. Vidskipti pointed out a blackened corner in the angle of the walls where he had built many a fire on a cold night in early winter. As Leifr warmed himself by the protected flames, he gazed around at the lofty masonry walls still defying dissolution. Tall pointed windows framed nothing but the first stars, and the great arched doorways stood vacant, the wood of the protecting doors long ago burned for firewood by travelers. Symbols were etched upon the walls or scrawled in charcoal, and Leifr supposed they were the names of other travelers or messages left for those who followed.

Nudged by a whisper from Fridmarr's carbuncle, Leifr said half to himself, 'We are safe here. This is a Rhbu place.'

'So 'tis,' Vidskipti said, worrying at a piece of meat without glancing up. 'There's marks on the floor, almost grown over by grass now. The sun comes in those windows, certain times – or the moon or certain stars. They got their powers from the stars too, you know, those Rhbus. That's why they did their magic mostly at night. The fire wizards thought they were just more Dokkalfar, but it isn't so.'

He looked up from his avid gnawing of the bones to see Leifr and Thurid both gazing at him with grave interest.

Svanlaug hoisted one brow with aristocratic disdain. 'How would a vermin like you know about the Rhbus?' she inquired haughtily.

Vidskipti rubbed his red nose and winked. 'I've been traveling in these Barrens a long time. Too long, your

121

young friend says, and maybe he's right. I've seen as many ruins as any man and used some of them for shelter. There's some that welcome you, like this one – Gledi-hofn, it was called. Then there's others you don't want to get near. Call it a gift or a curse, but I can see into the past at certain times. I've seen beautiful ladies in long gowns dancing and men in fine cloaks shivering like rainbows, with gold helmets and gold on their shields. I've seen battles, with horses and riders flying through the air, carrying lances and banners, and I've seen frost giants and storm giants—'

'What were you drinking at the time?' Svanlaug interrupted impatiently. 'These places are as dead as the people who built them. Even if there were ghouls, a scrap-chaser such as you would not be shown them.'

Vidskipti cackled and rubbed his gnarled hands together. 'Envy is the best whetstone for a sharp tongue, my lady Dokkalfar. There are Rhbu spells that any Dokkalfar would lie, steal, murder, and even die for.'

'Envy! Indeed! The idea never occurred to me!' Svanlaug snarled. She was changing the dressing on her arm, and the discomfort was not improving to her temperament. 'Nor to any Dokkalfar, as far as Rhbu powers are concerned. They were inferior powers, and the Rhbu all perished.'

Vidskipti rose to his feet and hobbled away to look at his ancient horse, muttering something under his breath that sounded to Leifr like, 'Not all, not quite all, my fine lady.' But he was feeding something in a bucket to his horse, so Leifr could not tell which fine lady the old rogue was speaking to.

Lots were drawn for guard duty, and the first turn fell to Raudbjorn. Vidskipti watched in amusement as Raud-bjorn pulled a long face and hoisted his halberd to his shoulder with a grunt, lumbering away to find a suitable watching spot among the ruins.

'There's no need, no need at all,' Vidskipti said. 'This place is as safe as your mother's arms. Safer, in fact. In all my travels I have never met with disaster in one of these gracious halls. We have protection here.'

Svanlaug tossed her head. 'So do we, Raudbjorn. Old rascal, I think your wits are more than addled, if you don't take precautions for your own safety. Nothing but luck has protected you all these years.'

'It's been good luck, hasn't it?' Vidskipti chuckled, his eyes bright and sharp. Wrapping himself in his eider, he curled up like a cat between two smooth boulders and went to sleep at once, snoring with soft whistling exhalations, like a kettle simmering gently over a slow fire.

When Raudbjorn prodded Leifr awake for his turn at watching, Leifr noticed that Vidskipti's eider was vacant. Leifr even poked it to make certain. Then he walked all around their sheltered camp, certain the trader had not gone far. When he did not find Vidskipti, he awakened Thurid warily, not knowing whether a carelessly muttered spell or outflung hand was going to wreak havoc.

'Vidskipti is gone,' he whispered, when Thurid's eyes lost the maniacal glare of the sleeper disturbed.

'You woke me up to tell me that?' Thurid asked between his clenched teeth, his eyes retreating beneath his furrowed brows as an ominous scowl gathered.

'Come on, let's find him. Don't tell me you don't think he's a bit peculiar.'

'Everyone is peculiar if they walk the Barrens long enough,' Thurid retorted, stalking ahead of Leifr with an aggressive stab of his staff at each step.

'How long, exactly, has he been doing it?'

'How should I know? What does it matter?'

'Thurid, I think old Vidskipti is a—'

'Great gods of earth and sea! Look at that!' Thurid whispered excitedly, pointing with a shaking finger.

A doorway stood open in the ground, with steps leading below. A heavy slab of stone had been pushed aside to allow entrance to whatever lay below. A familiar cracked voice lifted in song drifted up from the black chasm.

'Thurid, now I know I'm right. Vidskipti—'

123

Thurid suddenly leaped in fright, causing a smoky bolt of flame to leap from the end of his staff. Gedvondur's hand had seized the hem of his cloak and was clambering up like a spider. Hastily Thurid thrust the hand into his satchel, his eyes still on the doorway. He fairly trembled with excitement.

'This could be a treasure mound. Not a word now. Above all, don't speak my name, or whatever powers lurk below will have a claim upon me. Or upon you, too, for that matter. Now follow.'

They descended a short flight of mossy steps. A faint light glowed below, revealing the form of Vidskipti seated on a stool, tapping his foot and nodding his head to the tune of music only his ears could hear. Heaps of rubble surrounded him, illuminated by the feeble light of one smoky lamp.

'My friend, what's the meaning of this?' Thurid spoke sternly, and Vidskipti left off his tuneless singing and tapping to look at his visitors.

'Shh! Don't let them see you!' the trader whispered. 'Can't you see them? Endlessly dividing their plunder. This was the jarl's treasure vault. The Dokkalfar chieftains who destroyed Gledi-hofn are taking what they believe to be their fair share. Watch now; the first blow is about to be struck in the battle of the chieftains.'

He gestured with one hand. The dim light trembling selfconsciously against the dank gloom of the vault suddenly flared, leaping to all quarters of the vault. Torches and sconces blazed with lurid red light, shining on the heaps of gold and silver and jewels, and on the scowling features of the armored Dokkalfar confronting each other with the treasure at their feet. Leifr could not understand their distant garbled voices, and their images seemed to float and waver whenever he blinked, but he understood well enough their intent. Their gestures were fierce and angry as they quarreled over the treasure, each asserting the greater right. Suddenly one chieftain drew his sword, menacing another. A third chieftain struck him

124

down with an axe, causing his men to leap forward with a ghostly cry. Before Leifr could see the outcome of the battle, the ghoul faded away once more into the dark.

'Go now!' whispered Vidskipti. 'Do not look back once or you'll never leave this place. Take this, but don't look at it until you're safely beyond the doorway. You are out of your realm now.'

Thurid felt something in his hand. It felt like nothing but a common rock.

'What is this, a joke?' Thurid blustered. 'It's only a rock, and you're making fools of us!'

'Come on, let's get out of here,' Leifr said, starting forward. 'Joke or no joke.'

'I won't be laughed at by anyone!' Thurid dropped the rock on the stairs and started up.

'Don't be a fool! Don't throw it away!' Vidskipti called, with an ironic chuckle. 'But you'd better hurry. In a few moments when the moon shifts, the door will close, with you inside.'

'Find what you dropped!' Leifr grabbed Thurid's cloak to stop him. He groped around on the floor, searching for the stone.

Above, the angle of the moonlight pouring through a high window fell directly upon the stairs, covering less than half of their width. The heavy stone slab creaked and grated slightly.

'We've got to get out! It was nothing but a rock!' Thurid exclaimed. 'No wait, here it is! Let's go!'

They hurried up the steps. Suddenly a thunderous voice bellowed out a challenge, followed by the sound of creaking armor and heavy footsteps thudding on the steps.

'Don't look back!' Thurid gasped.

Leifr pushed Thurid ahead of him, his neck hairs prickling, as if the ghostly warrior were breathing great foul breaths on the back of his neck. He felt overwhelming temptation to look back, but he resisted. The sounds ended abruptly. In the sudden silence, he heard the soft mew of a cat. He halted in his tracks, even as the stone slab gave another menacing creak.

'Thurid! It's Ljosa! We can't let her be locked in!' he whispered.

'My name! You fool!' Thurid reached back and grabbed Leifr, hauling him up the last few steps with superhuman strength and flinging him onto the mossy turf beyond. The stone door closed, catching Thurid's foot in its inexorable grasp. Thurid howled with pain and fright. Leifr bellowed for Raudbjorn in a voice that awakened every echo.

'It's no good! Nothing can move that slab!' Thurid gasped, and fell to cursing furiously as he jerked at his trapped foot.

'We'll have to move it somehow! We can't leave you here for the Inquisitors to find,' Leifr exclaimed. 'Or more likely, fylgjur-wolves.'

Thurid soundly cursed the Inquisitors and the fylgjur-wolves, slashing at the air with his staff with a shower of sparks. Raudbjorn lumbered into view, followed by Svanlaug. With unusual perceptivity, he grasped the situation at once. Seizing the edge of the slab, he shoved and groaned until his fingers were raw, but it did not stir a particle.

'It's no use,' Thurid declared impatiently. 'I can't escape.'

'The foot will have to be cut off,' Svanlaug said grimly. 'His chances of surviving under any circumstances are very slim.'

'No, we couldn't.' Leifr recoiled. 'We'll stay here and defend him.'

'Until the disease in his crushed foot kills him, bit by bit, like some animal in a trap?' Svanlaug inquired.

'This is my fault,' Leifr said bitterly. 'I called him by name. If I hadn't been so stupid—'

'There's nothing to be gained by such talk,' Svanlaug said sharply. 'What happened, happened. Now we've got to do something about it.'

'You'll have to leave me here,' Thurid said with a grand

flourish. 'I shall have to fend for myself. Go, and save yourselves!'

'Don't be stupid,' Svanlaug said sharply.

Listening to the deep gasping of Raudbjorn and the muttered curses of Thurid, they stood helplessly gazing at the stone slab, now fused into place as if it had never stirred. Then the silence was broken by the first distant howl of the fylgjur-wolves. They all froze, hearing triumph in the hideous sound.

'Leifr! You've got to do something!' Thurid cried, his eyes fairly blazing with the sudden fervor of his convictions. 'The sword, Leifr. What about Fridmarr's carbuncle? Where's Gedvondur, drat him, when I need him?'

A quick search revealed no sign of Gedvondur, nor of Vidskipti.

'I can't do anything without Gedvondur,' Thurid spat furiously. 'How like him to desert me in my hour of greatest need! And that cursed peddler! This is all his fault! He led us into that trap!'

'The foot will have to come off,' Svanlaug said inexorably. 'It's better to have a wooden foot than to die. If you hadn't been so inquisitive—'

Leifr's fingers ran unconsciously around and around some object in his pocket. It was a ring. Automatically, Leifr pushed the ring onto his finger to see if it would fit. Instantly he felt an invasion of influence, some outside force long pent up, and now exulting at its liberation. He felt it flow to the ends of his fingers, through the muscles of his legs, and up his spine. For an instant he felt his consciousness begin to slip, then Vidskipti's voice rebuked the invading power.

'That's far enough, Eign. You can't take him over entirely. Do as he bids you and withdraw.'

'You're a cruel one, Vitur-Einarr. It's been thousands of years since I've stretched myself, and there's a load of vengeance I want to get rid of.'

'In time, in time. Be patient, and don't get greedy, and we'll all gain much.'

Leifr jerked the ring off his finger and looked at it more closely in the moonlight. To his surprise, it shifted shape, appearing as nothing more than a lump of rock. He returned it to his pocket, and felt the smooth roundness of the ring again slipping over his finger. Pulling out his hand with sudden curiosity, he gazed at an unfamiliar ring, glinting darkly in the moonlight. It was the gift he had taken from the treasure room, a ring made of twisting figures like intertwined snakes. Two heads with tiny red eyes met at the top, their jaws locked in combat.

The voice of the ring spoke rather irritably. 'Well, tell the buffoon what to do or he's going to stand there all night staring at the ring. Where did you find this creature, my friend?'

'He's a Scipling. Leifr!' commanded Vidskipti's voice. 'Lift the slab and push it aside. You have assistance.'

CHAPTER 9

The ring twinkled in the moonlight, as if the two fighting snakes shared some secret between them. Leifr seized the edge of the slab and began to shove until he heard every nerve and sinew cry out in protest. The stone itself protested, giving way with a cracking sound and a reluctant grumble.

'It moved!' Svanlaug exclaimed in amazement.

'Not enough!' Thurid gasped. 'One more shove, Leifr!'

Raudbjorn collapsed to his knees, still wheezing, looking at his lacerated hands and back to Leifr with a pathetic expression of dismay. He flexed his muscles and winced.

Leifr closed his eyes and gave the slab another heave. The stone almost shrieked as it trembled between two powerful spells, then moved yet another inch. Thurid pulled his foot out and staggered away, leaning on his staff for support.

'It's probably crushed,' Svanlaug said with professional briskness. 'We'd better examine that foot and bandage what's left of it. Luckily it wasn't a hand. A wizard can get along with a wooden foot, but the hands are indispensable.'

'Stay away from me, you Dokkalfar witch!' Thurid spat. 'There's nothing wrong with my foot! It's going to be fine!'

Leifr sank to his knees in the frost-crisped grass and looked at the ring on his hand. The eyes no longer gleamed. He slipped it off his finger and into his belt pouch and turned his attention to the slab lying askew of its usual position, just in time to hear a soft scuttling and a clinking of metal. Gedvondur's hand heaved itself up over the top lip of the vault, dragging perhaps a dozen rings looped together on a string. Pausing to adjust its burden, it saluted Leifr with a jaunty wave, then staggered away toward camp.

The slab trembled again, groaning as its governing magic slid it slowly back into its rightful position. Within moments its outlines were once more blended with the rubbly earth, as if it had never been disturbed.

Leifr read Raudbjorn's doleful expression and clapped him encouragingly on the shoulder, as one might pat a horse to soothe it.

'Never mind, Raudbjorn,' he said. 'I was aided by magic. But if muscle and heart could have moved that slab, I'm sure you would have done it.'

Raudbjorn beamed gratefully and nodded. 'Magic, yes. Only magic stronger than Raudbjorn.'

When they returned to the camp they found a chaotic scene, with Thurid in the midst of it, soaking his damaged foot in a fragrantly steaming basin. The contents of his satchel were strewn everywhere, as if a cyclone had been looking impatiently for something. Svanlaug strode up and down, riffling her hair and tossing her head.

'Those cures are worse than nothing!' she was saying. 'You might as well rub dirt and pig spit on it!'

'At least it would be a Ljosalfar pig, and not a Dokkalfar one!' Thurid retorted fierily. 'Where's that bloody rogue Gedvondur when I need him?'

The hand scurried past him and dived into his boot with a clatter of gold artifacts. Thurid swelled with outrage.

'Doing some looting of your own while I was suffering ghastly agonies with my foot being crushed alive? You avaricious scoundrel! Pirate! Parasite! We are no longer friends, you little mercenary!'

He picked up the boot and flung it against a rock so hard that a seam burst. The gold clattered out. Gedvondur scuttled for shelter to one of the saddlebags. Leifr returned him his loot, saying, 'Pay no attention to him.

He'll be over his temper tomorrow. It was lucky for you he got his foot caught, or you'd still be down there, you thieving rogue. Is Vidskipti still trapped, or did he get out somehow?'

'Don't worry about him,' Gedvondur replied with a quick tap on Leifr's hand before diving into the depths of the boot.

Svanlaug turned her wrathful gaze upon Leifr, her hair surging around her head like a bushel of snakes. 'So there you are,' she greeted him. 'You might have asked me to go along with you on your escapade. Didn't you think that I might have wanted a gift from the treasure hoard?'

Leifr retorted, 'I had no idea of gifts at the time. And you might have been behind Thurid. I couldn't have opened that door another inch. Where would you have been then?' He stalked away, feeling that even the soulful eyes of the troll-hounds were gazing at him with reproach.

Incredibly, old Vidskipti was sleeping through it all, very soundly and much too innocently. Leifr scowled at him, letting the moonlight cast his shadow long and dark over the wizened trader. Vidskipti stirred uneasily and opened his eyes, bunching up his eider suddenly when he recognized Leifr looking down upon him with no great friendliness in his attitude.

'What were you doing tonight in that treasure vault?' Leifr demanded. 'Did you deliberately try to entrap us?'

Vidskipti's eyes widened and he sat up. 'You were in my dream,' he said. 'Yes, I saw you there, and your friend the wizard. I don't know how you got into my dream, but I'm pleased to see you got out again.'

'I know who you are, you old fox,' Leifr whispered. 'You're a Rhbu. You gave me a ring of force.'

'Rhbu! Me!' Vidskipti went into a fit of coughing. 'Do I look to you like a Rhbu, with spells and powers and great magic at my command? Would I be following this bone-sack of a pony on this old cart if I were a Rhbu?'

'What better place to hide from your enemies than in plain view?' Leifr smiled grimly. 'If the Dokkalfar suspected you, they'd have you in their clutches, extracting your powers from you. And the Wizards' Guild would send their Inquisitors after you as well.'

'Powers! I have nothing they could covet,' Vidskipti protested, his eyes darted nervously toward Svanlaug.

'Come now, I recognize you.' With a surge of inner affirmation, Leifr added, 'Fridmarr's carbuncle recognizes you. I've seen the Rhbu with the grindstone twice before, but he never spoke to me. Now I've got you and I want to ask some questions. How did you get out of that treasure vault? What am I to do with that ring? How are we to free Ljosa from her spell? How do we destroy the night-farers of Djofull's geas? Where can we go to escape the Inquisitors? How—'

'Tut, tut, tut! No questions!' Vidskipti interrupted. 'I cannot answer them. Now goodnight, if you please.' He pulled his eider up under his chin, screwing shut his eyes and pursing up his lips as tightly as the mouth of a miser's gold pouch.

'Please, Vidskipti, or whatever your real name is. I'm a Scipling, and not of this realm. I'm a fish out of water. All of you have your carbuncles with generations of wisdom and memories, but I have nothing except my wits and my sword to defend me. How can I do what the Rhbus seem to expect of me if no one will offer me any guidance?'

Vidskipti resisted a moment, but finally he heaved a resigned sigh and opened his eyes in reluctant slits. Gruffly he whispered, 'Keep that ring about you. Others will recognize it one day when you need more help than you do now. Beyond this I cannot speak. Now goodnight, please!'

In the morning, Thurid's foot was too swollen for a boot, and his temper was even more swollen and untouchable. With a great deal of cursing and muttering he got onto his horse and rode up and down, harrying the others as they packed to leave.

'Can't you hurry yourself?' he snarled to Vidskipti. 'Or are you afraid you'll wake up the bedbugs in your beard?

We've precious little time for traveling, and here you're wasting it by eating breakfast!'

'Thurid!' Leifr chastised him, when they were safely on the road. 'He was there in that treasure vault last night. Don't speak to him that way, or you might regret it. I think he's a Rhbu.'

Thurid looked at Leifr down the length of his nose, allowing the silence to say what he thought of such an observation.

'Treasure vault!' Thurid snorted at last. 'I have no idea what you're talking about. Have you got a brain fever? What would that old scavenger have to do with a treasure vault?'

'You have no recollection of injuring your foot last night?' Leifr asked warily.

'I put it down a hole of some sort following you on some harebrained scheme of yours,' Thurid retorted. 'The rock shifted and trapped my foot. What's there to remember? Except that bloody Gedvondur did something to make me angry. I can't remember what, but I'll get on to it—'

To his amazement, Leifr found through careful questioning that none of the others had any recollection of the events of the night previous. He looked sidelong at Vidskipti, who looked sidelong at him with his lips carefully pursed up again as if nothing could ever extract another word out of him. Gedvondur alone seemed to know something, scuffling happily around in his boot with his gold pieces.

Near sundown of the third day they came into view of a tall black stone, much scarred by runes old and new. Vidskipti drew his horse to a halt and pointed northward with his whip.

'That way lies a shortcut to the place you seek,' he said. 'You'll have to go over the bogs, but no one will be able to follow you. The next house you reach should be Fangelsihofn. My route takes me to the south, and perhaps those who follow you will follow me. Be cautious in the bogs. It is a boundary place, where what is real sometimes isn't,

133

and what isn't is. If you had a bit of a seeing glass you could find your way perfectly without a misstep.' He darted a glance at Thurid, who unconsciously tightened his grip on his satchel.

'Good-bye then,' Thurid said, turning his horse toward the dark line of the bogs. 'I can't say that it's been much of a pleasure.'

Leifr lingered behind the others. Vidskipti had dismounted from his cart to examine something which was unraveling from the harness.

'Don't worry. Your secret is safe with me,' Leifr said. 'I wish to thank you for your safe conduct – and for the ring. I hope we'll meet again someday, when your kind has no need of hiding and fear.'

Vidskipti grunted and shook his head. 'I don't know how likely that is, in Skarpsey as it is. Watch yourself, young Scipling. You don't know the weight that rests upon your shoulders. Be careful of that wizard. He's a skittish one, not one I would have picked. Tell him he's got a seeing glass and he'd better use it. Worse things are waiting for you. Now I want to give you a Name.'

'I have a name,' Leifr answered, puzzled.

Vidskipti shook his head impatiently, muttering, 'Only a Scipling would misunderstand! I'm giving you a weapon you can use when you get into difficulty, but you can only use it three times. The Name is Komast Undan. Now don't forget it. You'll need it, beyond there.' He nodded toward the bogs and Leifr turned to look also.

When Leifr turned back, Vidskipti and his cart were gone, simply vanished. Jolfr's nostrils flared with astonishment. Leifr quickly turned his back on the crossroads and galloped after the others, not wanting to remain alone in a suspicious border place. Nor did he want to mention what had just happened.

The path they followed turned from the rocky highlands down into a broad green valley. Steep black fells towered on either side, shedding the water from their glaciers down to create the boggy lowlands. A virtually unmoving river of sluggish mud and stagnant water crawled like some vast unclean monster toward a distant rendezvous with the sea. Ancient trees clawed for root hold where the soil was still firm, battling with each other for sky space until their limbs formed a tangled canopy over the narrow trail. The earth was moist and slippery, smelling of ancient decay.

The path led them to some water-filled pits where the tracks of ponies and sledges indicated that someone had been cutting peat. That person had piled up a cairn of stone and thoughtfully decorated it with several skulls of men and horses taken from the peat, as a warning.

Thurid barely glanced at the browned skulls, which were well preserved from their years in the peat.

'We'll go on,' he said. 'Those hills are not far beyond the bogs. I'd rather spend the night where the ground didn't quiver underfoot and picket pins don't sink out of sight when you pound them in.'

'Have you a seeing glass, Thurid?' Leifr asked levelly. 'It might be of benefit now.'

'Of course I have, and it's a fine one, too,' Thurid said, a shadow of annoyance crossing his face. 'When the need arises, I shall certainly consult it, but any fool could get across this little stretch of swamp. I can see the far side of it from here, can't you?'

'It's almost dark,' Svanlaug observed. 'A damp bed for one night is better than a cold one forever.'

Nothing could have served as a better spur for Thurid. Fuming, he charged ahead on the path, following the tracks of the peat cutters. The horses slipped on the knobbly knees of the trees, and branches raked at the riders, while the underbrush clawed unmercifully from the sides of the narrowing path. As the day darkened, the water-filled tracks of the ponies became harder to follow, and eventually the path dwindled away to nothing at the side of a large, scummy pool.

'We've made a wrong turning, that's all,' Thurid announced with false cheer. 'Turn back, we'll find the way. It's just around the next bend to the end of this mess.'

'There seems to be too many bends,' Svanlaug finally observed, drawing her horse to a halt. The twilight was deepening now in its gradual way toward darkness. 'I think we're lost. If you've got a seeing glass, I suggest you start using it now.'

'What a notion!' Thurid spluttered. 'Lost indeed! This bog isn't big enough to get lost in. You saw yourself that the dry hills were just beyond. All we need to do is keep going north and we'll be through it.'

'Use the glass,' Leifr said, 'and we'll be through it quicker. The horses are tired, Thurid, and so are we all.'

'One more bend and you'll see that I'm right,' Thurid said, riding ahead.

Much later the horses wallowed to a halt, hock deep in smelly water.

'Blast those peat cutters!' Thurid fumed. 'Couldn't they have left a decently marked path for strangers to follow? What's the matter with those hounds of yours, Leifr? Why can't they sniff out the way?'

Leifr glanced down at the dogs, belly deep in water. 'If they sniffed here, they'd drown themselves,' he said irately. 'They hunt by sight most of the time. They don't like hunting in mud. They have bad memories of bogs, and so should you, if you know what I mean.'

Thurid stiffened and turned to glare back at Leifr. 'If you're referring to Finna, I urge you to reconsider before you tempt me to lose my temper.'

'Finna, the niss?' Svanlaug questioned knowingly. 'Oh, I've heard of her. She's—'

'Enough!' Thurid roared, his voice startling the crickets into silence. 'Now let us proceed to the next bend, where I will prove to you that we are not lost.'

At the next bend, they all halted and stared bleakly at the black and tangled maze of bog lying ahead, with a few bright gleams of water at wide intervals between stretches of fen and brake.

'Lost,' Raudbjorn grunted with uncharacteristic gloom.

Thurid heaved a sigh. 'I can't understand it,' he said pensively. 'It looked so simple, several hours ago. This bog seems to expand the longer we're here. Boundary places simply can't be trusted to follow the usual rules of behavior.'

'Now it's time for the glass,' Leifr said.

'Look there!' Svanlaug said suddenly. 'I see a light!'

She pointed through the trees, where a light did glow faintly at a distance.

Thurid grunted suspiciously. 'Fox-fire. Corpse-light, perhaps, to lure us to share a watery grave with the restless dead of this place. Bog draugar are always eager for fresh life.'

'We can get a closer look, at least, before we flee in terror,' Svanlaug said acidly.

The light grew brighter, strained through the trunks of many trees and bushes. As they approached a dark pool, a dark shape suddenly lumbered out of the shadows with an explosive snort. Two others lurched from the underbrush, splashing through the water.

'It's only horses,' Svanlaug called excitedly. 'It must be the peat cutters, at last. We'll follow the horses right to their door.'

The horses trotted obligingly ahead of them, stopping to wait when they crossed a miry spot. A path appeared, leading them to a much-mended gate, composed mainly of sticks, rope, knots, and what looked like bones. Thurid opened the gate, and they came into view of the house, rising like a large hummock out of the ground. The light which they had faithfully followed issued from a pair of lamps outside the door – lamps made of two skulls with fire burning inside.

'People acquire strange tastes living in places like this,' Thurid said with a nervous chuckle, tapping with his staff on the window shutter.

The door opened a crack, shedding a narrow beam of red light on the travelers.

'Who is it, and what do you want?' croaked a hoarse voice suspiciously. A peat-colored eye was pressed to the crack, shifting up and down and around to survey the strangers standing outside.

'We're lost in the cursed bog,' Thurid said, a shade impatiently. 'I daresay that's happened frequently enough to innocent travelers, hasn't it? If it's not too much trouble, could we bother you for food and fire and a little hospitality, if you can spare it?'

The eye traveled around the circle of weary and hopeful faces. 'Well, I suppose you must come in.'

The door opened further, revealing an aged individual who might have done some of his aging under several feet of peat. His face was long and sad, like that of an ancient horse. Long locks of hair straggled from his temples and chin to his high, crouching shoulders. He wore an old-fashioned tunic that ended in ragged festoons around his knees, and his lower legs and feet were an indeterminable assortment of rags and knotted strings.

'I'll send a boy to look after your horses,' their host grumbled, then roared into the darkness, 'Skuggi, you lump of darkness, come and see to these beasts!'

A small dark figure, wearing at least as much mud as clothing, crept out of a hole beneath the house and sidled toward the horses. The troll-hounds pricked up their ears and sniffed eagerly at the creature's legs as it slunk past. They whined, puzzled, and licked their chops. Leifr spoke a word of warning to quiet them, but Kraftig's golden eyes and gleaming teeth yearned after Skuggi. To resolve the burning question of whether Skuggi was a troll in disguise or not, Kraftig opened up his gaping jaws and snapped at Skuggi's leg in passing. All he got for his trouble was a mouthful of rag, and a sharp reprimand from Leifr. Mouthing the rag for any lingering clues, Kraftig slunk contritely into the house at Leifr's heels.

Inside, the house consisted of one room with a hearth against one wall and a wall bed against the opposite wall. Sitting beside the hearth was the dame of the house, a lady

138

about the size of a large overstuffed straw tick, with the proportions of a stack of bulging grain bags. Her greenish hair was crammed untidily under a man's hat with earflaps and stuffed peaks and lurid embroidery, and the grin she turned upon the uninvited guests gleamed with madness. Her secret little eyes sparkled and she clasped her hands in rapture.

'What a surprise it is! Company! Halsi my pet, we must make them all welcome!' she crowed, giving a pot on the hearth such a vigorous stir with her stick that some of the stuff slopped out and began to burn. 'What a lonely little house it is, away in the middle of the bog. Halsi precious, make them welcome, the dear things!'

'Shut up your blaring, you daft thing,' Halsi precious growled furiously. 'Shut it or I'll bung it shut for you and bottle that empty head of yours until it rings like a bell.' To his guests he said gruffly, 'She's as crazy as a botfly in the springtime. Pay no heed to her.'

'What a silly old bear he is,' his wife crooned in a sweet falsetto, her eyes darting over the company, who were decidedly uneasy now. 'He doesn't mean a word of it. Sit you down, my fine ones, sit you down, sit you down—'

Halsi took a swing at her head with a stave of firewood, mercifully missing or her poor addled brains might have adorned the table instead of dinner.

'She rattles on like that until it drives a body to murder,' he grated between clenched teeth. 'Serve the food, woman, and keep your mouth quiet.'

As the bowls were handed around, Svanlaug muttered to Leifr, 'Any woman would go mad married to a man like that and living in a place like this.'

Leifr was inclined to agree. He kept one eye upon Halsi and one upon Nafli, his wife, not knowing which was the more dangerous. Nafli was clearly mad, but one never knew when a morose and inward individual like Halsi would calmly decide to stick his knife in somebody's heart for some offense, real or imagined. He sat at the table and glared at his wife with a smoldering eye, constantly

139

threatening to silence her merry babbling by violent means.

Sleeping arrangements were simple. The guests took the floor, and the married couple slept in the wall bed. Leifr could scarcely believe they could safely confine themselves to such a small space without a fight breaking out. He lay down uneasily, but, as tired as he was, sleep was a long time in coming.

It seemed he had scarcely shut his eyes before he was awakened by a gurgling scream from outside. The hair on his head lifted with horror at the sound of it and he was crouching on his feet with his hand on his knife before he was fully awake.

Svanlaug also sat bolt upright. Raudbjorn and Thurid, both hardened snorers and thus accustomed to a great deal of ungodly racket at night, slept on soundly.

The scream sounded again, filled with desperate terror, dying away to a watery wail.

'He's killing her!' Svanlaug gasped, seizing her knife and leaping to her feet. 'Leifr, we've got to help the poor creature!' She was out the door in her bare feet before Leifr's sputters of confusion and protest could stop her.

Leifr raced after her, down the path, stumbling over the tree roots in his bare feet and squelching through soft mud that made him shudder. He burst through a screen of bushes and saw Halsi and his wife struggling in the water of a pond. He had his hand buried in her streaming hair, shoving her head under the water. She bobbed to the surface, gasping, uttering her poor dumb beast's screams for help. Seeing Leifr she reached out her hands appealingly, but Halsi shoved her under the water again. Svanlaug leaped from the bank and clung to his back like a cat, pummeling him with her fists. After a moment of this abuse, Halsi shook her off into the water and shoved Nafli like a boat out to deeper water.

Leifr jumped into the water and grappled with Halsi. The slippery bottom of the pool receded as they thrashed their way into cold deep water. Nafli bobbed to the surface, grinning madly, and seized Leifr by the shoulders and shoved him down under the water in her efforts to save herself. He freed himself and returned to the surface, where she grabbed him again and thrust him under with such deliberate strength that it seemed intentional. This time she did not release her grip on him, her fingers digging into his shoulders like powerful claws. The bloated body that he battered against was scaly and hard, and a large fin slithered out of his grasping hands. His instincts for self-preservation took over, and he fought furiously for his next breath of air. Both Helsi and his wife struggled to drown him. Their strength was beyond normal. A feeling of powerful evil surged through him, adding impetus to his efforts to escape imminent death in the black water.

Between the splashing and Svanlaug's screaming, he heard the sharp voice of Fridmarr. Cold iron! He ripped the little knife from his belt, the one he reserved for eating, and slashed at the huge scaly belly blocking his access to the surface. Nafli let go of him and floundered away, shrieking. Leifr lashed out at Halsi, and found himself free. He struggled to the surface, gasping with fiery lungs and looking around warily for Halsi and Nafli. In the moonlight, the scummy pool rippled gently, betraying no sign of attack.

As Leifr hauled himself out on the slimy bank, Thurid burst through the underbrush, with Raudbjorn crashing behind him. Svanlaug reached down to offer him a hand, helping him crawl up the muddy incline to the turf above.

'A fine house you led us to, Svanlaug,' Leifr panted. 'I don't think much of their hospitality.'

'Halsi is a neck,' Svanlaug said grimly. 'And his wife Nafli is a nix. We should have known nobody would live in a boundary place, unless they had something to hide.'

'Mightn't you have told me you were going for a stroll in the moonlight?' Thurid demanded. 'Haven't you learned by now that you shouldn't wander around alone, especially at night, when you're in this realm?'

'I can take care of myself,' Leifr retorted. 'I don't need you for a nursemaid.'

Thurid replied mockingly, 'Certainly, you've done well for yourself. The neck didn't kill you, if that's what you mean by doing well.'

'That's exactly what I mean,' Leifr snapped. 'This may be your realm, and I may be Scipling, but that doesn't mean I'm completely helpless.'

At the house he found a bucket and a barrel of rainwater, and Raudbjorn poured the clean water over him to relieve him of his mossy smell and some of the mud. For the rest of the night they maintained a vigilant lookout, but Halsi and Nafli did not return.

In the morning as Leifr was saddling his horse, Thurid came limping out and sat down on a stone.

'Speaking of rude hospitality,' he said, 'your hounds have killed and eaten Skuggi.'

Leifr looked at the hounds. They wrinkled their lips in guilty grins and thumped their tails on the ground uneasily as he scrutinized them.

'He must have been a troll,' Leifr said.

'Let's hope so. We can't have your dogs eating children indiscriminately. It's frightfully bad manners.'

'Skuggi was nothing but a troll,' Leifr said. 'I suppose you could send condolences to his family.'

Thurid ignored his last remark. 'I suppose,' he began thoughtfully, 'that you don't think it strange that Svanlaug played such a part in your escapade last night? Didn't it enter your head that she might be a spy for Djofull?'

Leifr shrugged it off. 'If you hadn't been snoring the rafters down, you might have heard the screaming yourself. I had to go after her when she went out there. I didn't think old Halsi and Nafli could get the better of me. And they didn't, either.'

'You're getting overconfident. You should have awakened me, or at least Raudbjorn.'

'Why should I? A man can't hide behind the skirts of a wizard forever. If I'm going to stay in this realm for a while, it's going to be on my own merit, and not yours or someone else's. And that includes carbuncles,' he added, seeing Gedvondur's hand creeping out of his saddle pouch, stretching itself sleepily.

'You can't manage without either a carbuncle or a wizard,' Thurid declared. 'And that means you'll have to follow my instructions if you are to survive, Leifr.'

'With this sword, I can survive anywhere.'

Thurid glared at him a moment, then at the hand. 'So there you are at last. Leifr was almost killed last night and you slept through it. What's the sense in keeping you around if you don't do your share in protecting the rest of us?'

The hand tapped his hand with a brief message.

Thurid snorted. 'He says you needed the experience. Who needs the experience of getting drowned? Especially if you've got those ashes on you. I don't know how you could have been so foolish, Leifr, risking your life for that dreadful old creature, even if her husband was drowning her. I think she probably deserved it. You Sciplings have a dangerous streak of heroic altruism in you. This idea of helping people is what gets you into trouble.'

'And the Alfar realm makes use of it whenever it can,' Leifr added with a sardonic smile.

'I never asked anyone to come with me into exile,' Thurid promptly reminded.

'No, but it's a good thing we did,' Leifr answered. 'Either the Inquisitors or Djofull's fylgjur-wolves would have picked you off by now.'

'The lot of you just make it easier for them to follow me,' Thurid snapped, stalking away to maintain his dignity.

Leifr swung his saddle onto Jolfr's back. Then he prodded the saddle pouch where Gedvondur had taken refuge. Gedvondur lifted the flap inquiringly.

'Where were you last night?' Leifr demanded. 'You could have warned me, you know, and saved me swallowing a lot of muddy swill.'

Gedvondur crawled out and tapped the back of Leifr's hand where it rested upon the saddle skirt.

'You want to stand on your own as a man in this realm, don't you? Well then, you can't be looking to others for your protection, as you said.'

'But a simple warning wouldn't have hurt,' Leifr said.

'You will have to learn the delicate balance between independence and cooperation,' Gedvondur replied. 'Then you will become a real warrior in your own right. It is a good sign that you want to break your dependence upon Thurid – but you must go carefully. You may hurt yourself, not to mention the fact that he relishes his power over you. What wizard wouldn't? A Scipling warrior is free of the bonds and oaths of this realm – the perfect tool.'

'And I don't relish being anyone's tool,' Leifr said, tipping Gedvondur back into the saddle pouch and lacing it shut firmly. 'Especially not yours. I've done exactly as I was told since I entered this realm. Now I think I know enough to make some decisions for myself.'

Gedvondur scratched inside the pouch vigorously, and Leifr felt a wave of vehement denial through the leather.

'I'll show all of you,' Leifr retorted, swinging onto his horse.

CHAPTER 10

Thurid produced the seeing glass at Halsi's rickety gate and consulted it nonchalantly, as if it were his habitual practice.

'North by northeast will lead us out of here,' he observed briskly, holding out the milky stone at arm's length. Its center glowed with iridescent light when he held it facing the proper direction.

Svanlaug eyed the stone covetously. 'A seeing stone is well and good for traveling in boundary regions,' she said jealously, 'but nothing compares to the Dokkalfar ley lines and hills and mounds for true direction-finding.'

'Dokkalfar ley lines!' Thurid cried, his eyes blazing. 'Those lines were constructed by Rhbus, not Dokkalfar!'

'Tush, what nonsense,' Svanlaug retorted. 'Dokkalfar, Rhbu, what's the difference? They are all part of the same parcel. Perhaps they worked together, before the Rhbus rebelled and tried to go their own way.'

'Never! Rhbus and Dokkalfar were enemies from the beginning, vying for the same power source for different purposes. Dokkalfar designs were dark and manipulative. Rhbu designs were for freedom for all.'

'Freedom does not work for all,' Svanlaug snapped. 'Only the strongest and smartest have freedom. Why waste it upon the lowly and dull who cannot appreciate it? You Ljosalfar have no idea of governing people!'

The argument continued for the rest of the day, with varying degrees of temper and insult. The boggy terrain gave way gradually to grass and thickets as the land rose, and by late afternoon their way was across the spiny crest of a windswept fell.

Thurid dropped the seeing stone back into his satchel and snapped it shut.

'We won't be needing that anymore,' he said.

'Why not?' Leifr demanded. 'We're not at Fangelsi-hofn yet, are we?'

'I can find our way without such primitive devices,' Thurid answered loftily, unfurling a map and producing a small dowsing pendulum.

In a matter of hours they were lost. Where they should have spied the first small settlements of Hraedsla-dalur they saw wasteland, studded with black lava flows and struggling tufts of grass. The wind howled jubilantly across the scoured earth and lashed at the cloaks of the travelers and the ragged manes of the weary horses.

'This is almost as inviting as Skollatur-jord,' Svanlaug observed acidly, showing nothing of her face to the bitter wind except a small slit for her eyes. 'I can well imagine our skeletons gracing this rock pile in years to come – providing that our dead carcasses would ever unthaw long enough for the ravens and foxes to pick. For all we know, we're heading right back into Skollatur-jord – or even toward the Guildhall.'

Thurid brought his horse to an abrupt halt and started delving in his satchel for the seeing stone with stiff cold fingers. He held it up to the gray and sunless sky.

'We're off course!' he exclaimed with a note of genuine surprise. 'We're heading straight south! How could we have gotten turned completely around? How could my dowsing be so thoroughly inaccurate?' Still unconvinced, he faced the direction the stone indicated, then faced southward, his narrowed eyes watering in the wind. 'This way feels right. I feel a powerful drawing force coming from this direction. The stone must be some vile trick of that old scumbag Vidskipti. Whom shall I believe, my own impeccable instincts, or some gewgaw handed to me by a traveling rag and bone collector?' Thurid threw the stone into his satchel and snapped it shut with a vicious yank.

'What if it's a trick by the Inquisitors?' Leifr asked. 'I've heard of drawing spells. They might be pulling you in the direction of the Guildhall.'

'I think not,' Thurid said indignantly. 'I have enough strength left to interpret a drawing spell when I feel one, and this one has nothing to do with the Inquisitors. We shall continue south.'

The wind gusted at them ferociously, peppering them with pellets of snow. Svanlaug suddenly lifted her head and hissed, 'Listen! Did you hear something?'

Through the uncharacteristic gloom of the low-hanging clouds came a familiar, distant wail. Thurid glared in that direction, and began delving in his satchel for the stone.

'Fylgjur-wolves!' Leifr said.

'I thought this weather smacked of manipulation,' Svanlaug said triumphantly. 'Djofull isn't far behind us, wizard, thanks to your confused attempts to guide us with that map. If you hadn't got us lost, we'd be safe in Fangelsi-hofn tonight!'

'Don't start gloating yet, Svanlaug,' Thurid retorted. 'We're a long way from being captured yet.' He paused a moment, peering into the stone, then added in an inspired tone, 'We'll follow the directing of this stone. Djofull is probably using that drawing spell. Come along, we've had enough delays.'

The early twilight had descended into a threatening purple gloom, and the cries of the fylgjur-wolves were more insistent on their trail when they saw a light ahead.

'Just as I told you,' Thurid said. 'Breiskur! It's a small trading village on Breiskurfirth where the ships from north and south stop. I knew we'd come to it if we kept at it. My sense of direction is as keen as a cat's. There'll be a dozen houses here and a bright, roistering inn where we can stay. Soft beds, warm fires, and plenty of food and ale! How does that sound, Leifr? Raudbjorn?'

Raudbjorn shook a little snow off his shoulders and responded with a distant rumbling chuckle from somewhere in his frost-rimmed bulk. He hadn't moved or spoken for half the day, except to glance at Leifr in brute misery and heave a gusty sigh. A faint smile gleamed on his frozen countenance.

Gradually, however, the image of a dozen houses and the cozy inn disintegrated into one lonely house built like a small hill fort in the center of a wide valley. Its barns and walls were grouped around the main hall to form a square. A stout door in the center of the thick turf wall led directly into the main hall, and its companion door gave access to the stables beyond. Its aspect was defensive and unfriendly. As the travelers approached the place, protective wards were disturbed, warning the inhabitants of the homestead of their approach. Once a flock of birds exploded from under the horses' feet, circling away toward the house, screeling in alarm. Svanlaug gasped as if struck when they crossed a small stream. She halted her horse and made hasty gestures in defense before continuing.

'They'll know we're coming by the time we get there,' she said grimly. 'And they don't like Dokkalfar, which should be welcome news for you.'

When they reached the gate, they found it shut tight, and a pair of suspicious eyes peered out at them through a small portal. Thurid lit his alf-light with a splendid, sputtering flare and swept it over the gate, casting weird dancing shadows in the gusting of Djofull's storm.

'Halloa!' he called. 'Is there food and shelter to be had at this house for weary travelers?'

'There is,' came the cautious answer, 'if you can explain why you're traveling in the company of one of the Dokkalfar. The night-farers are not beloved in Hraedsladalur, and you bring with you unfavorable elements. I can see you are a wizard of one sort of another, so you'll understand if I'm slow to offer you our protection.'

'Djofull is pursuing us,' Thurid said. 'This does not look to be the kind of place where gates would be locked against Djofull's enemies. This Dokkalfar with us is also an enemy of Djofull, under temporary truce with us until we accomplish our mutual objective of destroying Djofull.'

The guardian of the gate whistled softly in amazement.

'Then you are a Ljosalfar wizard, of the Guild?' he asked.

'Ljosalfar wizard of the Rhbus,' Thurid replied. 'The only force that can destroy the Dokkur Lavardur and his legions. Djofull would not be so enraged against us otherwise. We have recently escaped his captivity in Ulfskrittinn. Doubtless you have heard of the death of Stjornarr at the hands of the Scipling, Leifr Thorljotsson, who carries the Rhbu sword of Endless Death.'

'You should have spoken your names earlier,' said the guard, sliding the bolts back on his side of the gate. 'If I had known who you were, I wouldn't have kept you standing so long in the storm. Welcome to the hospitality of Killbeck. The chieftain Jarnvard will be glad to greet you.'

Opening the door, he beckoned them to come inside, where they dismounted rather cautiously under the scrutiny of at least a dozen armed warriors. Jarnvard stood foremost, a young Alfar who had apparently just succeeded to the leadership of his chieftaincy.

'Welcome,' he said, surveying his visitors keenly, gazing with suspicion upon Svanlaug. 'We have heard of the events at the Pentacle, and the killing of Stjornarr. Anyone who causes this sort of disturbance among the enemy is our friend, or at least allied in our common purpose.'

Killbeck reminded Leifr more of a small warlord's hill fort the more he saw of it. An innocent farmer would have had no need for so many armed men under his roof, nor for the defenses they had witnessed earlier. Jarnvard's hall opened off the central passage to the right, where a bright fire burned invitingly, and a table was soon spread with finer food than the travelers had seen since Dallir. Since much was already known of the adventure of the Pentacle, few questions needed to be asked. Jarnvard and his warriors yearned to hear about Ulfskrittinn firsthand, so the tale was told with great effect by Thurid, pacing up and down, flinging his hands around with sparks and bright ribbons of colored light. By the time he was done, even the most suspicious and wary of the warriors was won over.

'So now you are come to Hraedsla-dalur,' Jarnvard said, by way of subtle questioning. His amber eyes glowed, flicking knowingly over his warriors with pride and expectation. 'The Dokkalfar have ruled here for six hundred years, since the death of Slagfid's sons. Our people have seen wizards come and go, but none as powerful as Djofull. Instead of twenty warring Dokkalfar warlords, he has them united in the oppression of the Ljosalfar.'

'Yes, we have come to Hraedsla-dalur,' Thurid intoned pompously, sipping at a horn cup of ale. 'There is a dark and ancient evil here, festering away like an old sore, which must be cauterized before this embattled land can heal itself. Do you know of a place called Fangelsi-hofn?'

Jarnvard stiffened, and his friendly demeanor suddenly disintegrated once more into wary suspicion. 'I know Fangelsi-hofn,' he said with a cold glint in his eye. 'What do you want in that place?'

'There is a geas concerning Fangelsi,' Thurid said with a heavy frown, as if pondering each word. 'Something very old and dark. Djofull has done everything under his power to prevent us from reaching Fangelsi and whatever awaits us there, so we suspect a powerful key to his hold upon Hraedsla-dalur lies therein.'

Jarvard stood up and paced the width of the room, his handsome features drawn into a threatening scowl. Leifr watched, his uneasiness growing. The atmosphere in the hall had changed dramatically, and he didn't relish the sensation of all those Alfar eyes turned upon him with suspicion.

At last Jarnvard turned to face Thurid. 'You can't go to Fangelsi-hofn,' he said. 'What you say about an important key to Dokkalfar power over Hraedsla-dalur is very likely true. But the descendants of Slagfid still live there. They have suffered much over the centuries and wish only to be left alone by Dokkalfar and other Ljosalfar alike. Slagfid had commerce with the Dark Realm to gain the powers that he held; although seven centuries have passed, the shame of it is still alive today for his heirs. For you to arrive at their gate, saying you're going to help them and rescue them from Slagfid's folly, would be a great insult to their pride.'

Thurid plucked at his ear thoughtfully. 'How many people remain at Fangelsi?'

'An old woman, Syrgja, and her brother Ketil, and three sons of her sister's child. Hryggd was the sister's name, and she drowned herself in the sea many years ago – the last of her generation, leaving her aunt her children. The history of these people is one of misfortune and misery. None of them live to peaceful old age. Some accident or disease always carries them off – if not death at their own hands. Leave these people alone, Thurid. After so many years of pain, it's too late to help them.'

'I understand,' Thurid answered. 'But there is a geas involved, as I said before, upon myself and these others. We will go forward as carefully as we can, but we must make the attempt and continue until we break this old enchantment, or die in the attempt. Our alternatives are not pleasant ones.'

'I realize I can't persuade you,' Jarnvard said with a sigh, still troubled. 'Nor can I be of much assistance to you, or the Dokkalfar warlord will come down hard on us. It's bad enough that you're here.'

Leifr spoke for the first time. 'Can you tell us what we're likely to find in Fangelsi? Djofull made mention of some night-farers that we are supposed to destroy. Somehow I suspect it's more than just the resident Dokkalfar warlord falling into Djofull's disfavor. That would be too easy for the geas he's laid on us.'

At the mention of the night-farers, a ripple of surprise went through the ranks of Jarnvard's warriors. He darted them a quelling glance, silencing their whispers and nudges. His eyes narrowed and he could scarcely conceal his own incredulity.

'There is truth in what you say. I believe you were sent here under geas from Djofull. Otherwise you would not know of the curse of Fangelsi-hofn. If I were in your position I would be seeking the powers to break that geas, but I would not go to Fangelsi to do it. Those night-farers you speak of are beyond the power of any sword or any spell. If you have come for the purpose of destroying them, then you have come to meet your own doom. The spell that binds these creatures is seven hundred years strong, woven in such hatred and vengeance that no wizard alive today can break it.' His gaze turned to Thurid. 'He will only break himself upon it. I strongly urge you to reconsider. As chieftain of this area, I would forbid you to go to Fangelsi, but I hesitate to draw a line which would be costly to defend.'

Thurid puffed energetically at his pipe, scowling. 'What manner of creature are the night-farers of Fangelsi?'

'Jotuns,' Jarnvard replied grimly. 'Tall as a man on horseback, armored with stone, and as crazy as wounded bears. They can smash down the door of a barn and carry away a yearling cow over one shoulder. Shepherds caught by night in the fells are mangled. You might have wondered at the structure of our house. It makes an excellent defense against the whims of occasional Dokkal-far mischief-makers, but the main reason is to save our necks from being broken by the Flayer, and others of his kind.' In response to Thurid's hoisted brow and question-ing look, Jarnvard continued, 'We call him the Flayer because he usually rips the hide off the beast he has killed before he carries it away, as easily as a man would skin a rabbit.'

'Has anyone hunted these jotuns before?' Leifr asked, glancing toward the troll-hounds stretched out before the fire.

Jarnvard nodded reluctantly. 'Foolish ones. They might as well have gone into the bear's den bare-handed. Not only is it useless, but the people of Fangelsi do not welcome it. They don't want strangers on their land.'

'How many jotuns are there?' Leifr asked.

'One, usually. A long time goes by with no jotun, and then suddenly one appears for no reason and rampages for a few years, then it is gone – for no apparent reason. I think the Fangelsi people must have a secret way of dealing with them. Hogni is the new master there, since his uncle Thorkell died, and, although Hogni is no trained wizard, you could call him very skillful.'

'Then they deal somehow with the jotuns individually, instead of getting at the root of the curse,' Thurid said. 'Perhaps they would welcome a wizard who could put an end to the jotuns forever.'

'The Grimssons don't welcome anyone,' Jarnvard replied grimly. 'Even travelers who stop there don't stay. Friendliness is one thing of which no one could ever accuse Hogni and his brother Horgull, or their aunt either. Old Thorkell and his brother Ketil were the best of them, but Thorkell died last winter, and now Ketil is going in the same direction. I bid you to be welcome at Killbeck as long as you wish to stay. We're likely to have an early winter this year, thanks to Fantur the Rogue. You're welcome to share our fires and shelter until spring, when it passes out of our skies.'

'Your offer is kindly and gratefully noted, but I fear we must make our attempt upon Fangelsi-hofn and whatever hospitality we discover there,' Thurid replied, with a sigh of regret. 'Fangelsi could not be as bad as a dungeon in Djofullhol.'

'It's not a pleasant choice,' Jarnvard replied. 'This may be the last comfortable night you spend, if you truly insist upon going to Fangelsi-hofn.'

There was plenty of room on the sleeping ledges around the walls for more warriors. Although Jarnvard did not claim to be a warlord, it was obvious to Leifr that he was very quietly gathering his forces for resistance to the occupying Dokkalfar. His men were not the brawling,

153

roistering sort of warriors who pounded on their own shields and bellowed arrogant challenges; they were the quiet and efficient sort who were capable of doing their work by the dark of night, if necessary, with complete secrecy. They had heard of *Endalaus Daudi* and the Scipling who wielded it. They had scant interest in wizards and jotuns; it was the sword they wanted to see and Sorkvir's death they wanted to hear about. Raudbjorn they viewed with admiration, as they would any highly efficient instrument of war and destruction.

When the attention turned to Leifr and the sword, Thurid seemed somewhat put out by the warriors' interest in the power of violence, rather than the power of knowledge.

Jarnvard's curiosity next extended to Svanlaug, who could not help appearing stiff and pale in the presence of so many of her erstwhile enemies.

'What do you hope to accomplish?' Jarnvard asked bluntly. 'Your life isn't worth cats' meat if your people catch you in this treachery. It's one thing to plot against your own kind, but when you join your hereditary enemies to do it, you've passed beyond ordinary Dokkalfar deceit.'

'Revenge has a way of making you forget the future,' Svanlaug replied. 'If Djofull perishes, that will be enough for me. I can get closer to him than any day-farer can — close enough for a fatal encounter, I hope.'

'Treachery is second nature to Dokkalfar,' Jarnvard said ironically. 'You could betray the Scipling more profitably, I daresay. This storm outside is one of Dokkalfar manufacture, is it not? Haven't you in truth been advising Djofull of the direction his quarry is taking?'

Svanlaug eyed him coolly. 'Djofull doesn't need me to tell him what he can easily see. You underestimate the extent of his powers.'

'I think not,' Jarnvard answered. 'Djofull uses people for tools whether they wish it or not. Thurid, you'd be

154

wise to look well to your defenses while you're in Hraedsla-dalur.' He glanced significantly at Svanlaug. 'And while I'm giving out warnings, there is one more. Hogni and Horgull have a younger sister, Ermingerd by name. She is bespoken by me, when the time comes that she decides to marry. That time is not yet, but the girl and I have an understanding. Do I make myself plain?'

'Perfectly,' Thurid replied, and Leifr nodded, thinking that twelve armed Ljosalfar were ample reinforcement for Jarnvard's warning.

The storm raged and prowled outside the thick turf walls, abating only at dawn. The travelers departed from Killbeck shortly thereafter, taking a little-used road that wound higher into the rugged fells, scarcely more than a sheep-track twisting among the black lava skarps. They passed an abandoned turf-cutter's hut, where the door had been smashed in with such violence that the wood was splintered like kindling, and a gloomy spirit of death lingered around the place. The hounds cast around with interested yelps and growls, and Leifr wondered if it were jotun they were smelling.

The clouds hovered close to the ground, promising the unseasonably early snows Jarnvard had predicted. In three hours, the rough track led them to the crest of a fell, looking down into a narrow dark valley. They were stopped by the sign of a carrion crow, which radiated such a feeling of forbidding doom and terror that they were unable to approach the standing stone where it was carved.

'The work of Hogni, the skillful amateur,' Thurid said, dismounting from his horse and lighting his alf-light with a disdainful snort. 'His wards may be strong enough to keep out the Dokkalfar, but they won't stand against the powers of the Rhbus.'

Waving his staff before him, he started forward. The etched figure of the bird glowed a threatening red, and again Thurid was stopped. Backing away, he glared at the stone and pulled a handful of rune sticks from his satchel.

'Very well, if that's the way you want to play it,' he

155

muttered angrily, scanning and discarding wands one by one. Selecting one with a dire chuckle, he studied it a moment and strode forward with his cloak surging importantly to the point where the bird-figure began to glow. Raising his arms, he shut his eyes and spoke commandingly. Fire encircled the stone and the bird, crackling fiercely, but the figure still glowed as brightly as ever, and worse yet, a high-pitched screaming suddenly burst from the bird. They all clapped their hands over their ears and hastily retreated, including a discomfited and irate Thurid.

'Ljosalfar warding spells are more complicated than you can imagine, wizard,' Svanlaug called, evidently enjoying his discomfiture. 'They've been keeping the Dokkalfar out for seven hundred years. You're not going to walk into Fangelsi until Hogni decides to allow it.'

'He has no choice in the matter,' growled Thurid. He rummaged in his satchel for a ball of dirty wax, and stuffed each ear full, muttering ferociously. Then he selected another rune wand and stalked toward the stone.

The screaming sound halted. The bird-figure flickered and abruptly turned dark. Thurid stared at it dubiously, then warily edged nearer, like a swimmer testing the coldness of the water with one toe before plunging in. When he was able to touch the stone and walk around it, he called back in a casual tone, 'Come ahead, it's done with its tricks now. My disarming spell must have been a bit slow in working.'

Svanlaug shook her head and laughed. 'It only means that Hogni is letting us through so he can take a closer look at us. These Ljosalfar are more clever than you know. They're either clever or dead Ljosalfar in Hraedsla-dalur.'

A faint rocky path led them down the fell into the valley, giving them a view of the settlement at last, a decayed house built in the midst of a lowering ruin. In dismay, the travelers stopped in the crumbling gateway, discerning the dismal view beyond. The second attempt at settling the site had been perhaps even less successful than the first. The once-secure and imposing hill fort was mostly crumbled away, its walls and embankments modified into the walls of barns and paddocks. One round tower remained, though at half its original height, and it had been roofed over with turf at one time, which now sagged in green billows over the top stones. Leifr noticed the signs of unsuccessful farming; the broken gates and fences, untenanted paddocks, the empty hay barn, the skins of sheep hanging to dry. The turf house had been built to utilize some of the ancient mortared stone walls, which created a rambling, blank-faced, brooding house with peculiar tall roof angles. One skinny dog came out to bark halfheartedly, as if he had little he cared about defending.

'Well,' Svanlaug said in a deadly calm tone, 'here we are. Fangelsi-hofn. This is an evil place.'

Thurid snorted without much assurance. 'Rumors of the place have been greatly exaggerated,' he said, nudging his horse forward. 'Yet, there's something about this place – I feel emanations of great power coming from somewhere very near. Great events and heroic deeds or disasters have taken place here. I think this is the place whence came the drawing spell.'

Gedvondur's hand suddenly scuttled out of his saddlebag and clambered up the snow-flecked slope of Thurid's shoulder, almost trembling. His voice boomed from Thurid's lips, 'That tower! We've got to get inside it. The power there is unimaginable!'

Thurid's voice sputtered in retort, 'Get back to your saddlebag, you carrion! I don't want you frightening these people by your tricks. Stay out of sight!'

Thurid leaned down from his horse and tapped at the shuttered window.

'Halloa!' he called. 'Is this the abode of one magician known as Hogni Grimsson?'

Not a sound came from within the house, although moments before they had heard the busy noises of kitchen activity. Then the door was unbarred, and it swung back slowly into the central passage. Beyond was the open door of a firelit kitchen, revealing a cloaked figure standing dark against the light. 'What is it you want?' a man's voice inquired suspiciously. 'There are better accommodations for travelers at Killbeck. Why do you insist on coming here?'

'We were sent,' Thurid replied with dignity.

The stranger surveyed Thurid's garb and his flaring staff. 'It's rather late for the Guild to send a wizard now. My ancestor Slagfid could have used your help, but such help was denied to him.'

'Those are old quarrels,' Thurid replied. 'It's time to begin anew.'

'Old quarrels, true, but they can never be forgotten.' The speaker came into the light, a narrow, dark-bearded Alfar of middle years, dressed in the garb of a scholarly man, rather than the rough attire of a landsman. His eye passed over Leifr and Raudbjorn with scant approval and came to rest upon Svanlaug, who wore her Dokkalfar mask against the pale and intermitten sunlight. 'No more than a truce can exist between night- and day-farers. The sole reason I permitted you to pass my wards was to see what nature of men you were to mingle freely with the enemy. No Guild wizard would brook such a tainting of his skills.'

'Svanlaug is sworn against Djofull, and we've thrown in our lot together, for a time,' Thurid replied, unruffled. 'The Guild influence does not extend all the way to the heart of Hraedsla-dalur and our doings here. I assume you are Hogni Grimsson, and your brother Horgull.'

Hogni was joined in his wary scrutiny of the strangers by a larger Alfar dressed in shepherd's clothing, who gazed out at them in stolid disapproval without speaking.

'Light down,' Hogni said at last, though his manner was not inviting. 'If you're not a Guild wizard sent from the Guildhall, I want to know who you are and who has sent you. My brother Horgull will attend to your horses.'

Horgull shuffled forward with manifest reluctance, and

Hogni escorted them into the house, which was divided in half by a dark passageway ending in another door. On one side a large door opened into the main hall, which once stood in grandeur for feasting and drinking and furnishing the quarters for thralls and warriors. Now it offered stalls for horses and lambing pens for the sheep, another token of the poverty that festered in Fangelsi-hofn.

The other end of the house still provided the kitchen area and the private quarters for the family of the ruling landholder, as it had in centuries past. A heavy scarred door opened with a grudging squeak into a cavernous kitchen. Wall beds with worn carving on the doors had taken the place of common sleeping platforms along one wall, almost large enough to be counted as small rooms in their own right. The enormous hearth nursed a small sullen fire of peat and a whale-oil lamp sputtered in the middle of a black and battered table, shedding the sole light in the overwhelming gloom. Entire carcasses could have hung from the beams, instead of the meager few smoked legs that hung there.

In the red light of the smoldering fire a craggy-shouldered old Alfar sat hunched in a tall black chair, oblivious to the intrusion. He moaned softly and rocked to and fro, his bandaged hands fluttering restlessly. His bright and feral eye swept over the strangers unseeing, coming to rest upon Hogni with a sudden flare of hatred. Though a cloak draped the old one, Leifr had the impression of mighty bulk and strength still lingering in the ruined frame. The face was startling and unpleasant; his brow was swollen and knotted until the hawkish eyes were sunken in pits, and his nose more like a gnarled beak. Baring his teeth, the old Alfar snarled at the sight of Hogni.

A gray-haired woman looked up from the pounding of some acrid concoction beside the fire. Her bone structure was more imposing than that of most Alfar women, hinting at hidden strength, though very little flesh covered the bones. Large and reddened hands gripped the mortar and pestle, and her eyes in their dark hollows flashed with displeasure. She folded her arms and scowled forbiddingly, raising one eyebrow in mute comment as Raudbjorn shambled into the room. For a moment her gaze locked with Hogni's in silent argument, causing a faint chilly breeze, then she nodded once in a curt acquiescence and turned back to the fire and shadows.

'Ermingerd,' she commanded in a grating voice, 'we'll fix our guests something to eat. Where's your useless brother? He can help see to their horses, and tell him to go sparingly on the corn.'

It was an inauspicious beginning. Leifr cast Thurid a menacing glower, seeing no help forthcoming from these suspicious and recalcitrant Alfar.

CHAPTER 11

A girl's soft voice replied, 'Starkad is in the hall with the sheep. I will fetch him.'

A slight figure rose from a chair near the firelight. She passed through the lamplight, drawing up her hood before entering the cold and unused portion of the house. Before the shadow obscured her face, Leifr glimpsed a soft pale cheek and one clear eye like a startled deer's. A wisp of silvery hair escaped the dark imprisonment of her coarse wool hood and gleamed in the firelight. In an instant her light step had carried her out of the gloomy kitchen, leaving behind some sense of relief from the darkness and oppression which Leifr had sensed in the older woman. As she departed the room, she tapped her two fingers lightly upon an icon hanging on the wall, a sword-shaped thing hidden by shadow.

'A pretty child!' Thurid said appreciatively, continuing to gaze in the direction Ermingerd had gone long after it was needful. 'Your sister's daughter, I presume? I think I detect a certain family resemblance, a similar lightness of foot, perhaps.'

The elder woman spoke sharply, arresting his attention.

'Save your empty compliments. There's little levity in this house,' she said uncompromisingly. 'My brothers and I have raised the four children of my sister's daughter from infancy, an unwelcome responsibility which has weighed heavily upon our aged shoulders. Their mother was a weakling and a coward. Killed herself because she couldn't bear the injustices life had dealt her – as if she were the only one. That wasn't such a bad idea, except she left me her four young whelps. If not for them, all this would be just about over.' She gestured impatiently with one hand to include the house, Fangelsi, and a lifetime of stored-up injustices.

'My aunt Syrgja does not believe in mincing words,' Hogni said in a dry tone, glancing at her warningly. 'Sit you down and be as comfortable as you can. Fangelsi-hofn has very few guests, except those we know who come for a purpose. We don't have much to do with outsiders or strangers, so our manners are rough and out of practice.'

As she prepared the simple meal, Syrgja's eyes traveled uneasily to the figure beside the meager fire. He moaned softly, making helpless pawing motions with his bandaged hands on his knees. When his face caught a gleam of firelight, it appeared furrowed and twisted by pain.

'What is his illness?' Svanlaug asked. 'I am a healer; perhaps I could be of help.'

'It concerns you not,' Syrgja replied quickly. 'Common herbs and remedies will do him no good. Ketil is my last remaining brother. You must pardon him if he offends you; he's not well.'

Ermingerd returned and built up the fire under a black kettle. Syrgja produced bread and cheese and ale in no great quantities and placed them before her guests without comment.

'A noble house, this,' Thurid said, in an effort to make conversation. 'I fear I haven't heard much of Fangelsi or your ancestor Slagfid who built it. Surely he was a great and famous jarl to have built such a house, with obvious hopes of a fine family to inherit it.'

'You won't hear it from me,' Syrgja replied with a bleak scowl. 'I don't gossip about my ancestors.'

Hogni chuckled ironically. 'A failure has a scant tale to tell. Best to leave Slagfid to rest in peace.'

His eyes traveled involuntarily to the icon Ermingerd had touched. It was indeed a sword hanging on the wall near the hearth. Leifr's interest sharpened, noting the gold hilt chased with silver designs and the guard which was ornamented with some sort of flying creature. From tip to hilt the gray metal was etched with blackened runes.

Syrgja divided her attention between keeping a close watch upon Ermingerd beside the fire and old Ketil, who pawed jerkily at his face, growling and snarling all the while and glaring at Hogni.

'He's in pain,' Svanlaug said, rising to approach him. 'There are many preparations that would give him ease. Surely you don't intend to allow him to suffer.'

Impatiently Syrgja stepped forward to block her, crossing her arms across her bony chest. 'Don't concern yourself about me or mine. I have plenty of the proper cures for him. You're strangers; and you'll be gone tomorrow.' Then in an undertone as she turned away, she added, 'For what ails him there is no cure, except people minding their own business and staying out of mine.'

Svanlaug's eyes widened, and she sat down, glancing at Leifr and Thurid, who was gazing at Ermingerd appreciatively as she served up the contents of the kettle in the firelight. Syrgja noticed where his attention had strayed and slapped down a platter forcefully at his elbow, causing him to jump nervously. His startlement caused a surge of energy to gust through the room like a cold breeze, jittering metal objects in their pegs and swinging the weights on the weaving loom in the corner. Syrgja whirled around to look at the cloaks flapping on their pegs, narrowly missing Gedvondur's hand as it scurried across the floor from Leifr's saddle pouch beside the door and dived into Thurid's pocket.

'Pardon me,' he said with freezing dignity, smothering the glowing knob of his staff with his sleeve. 'A little power escaped without my realizing it.'

'We have no need of a wizard here,' Syrgja snapped, glaring at the saddle pouch suspiciously. 'Meddling with the forces that be has been the bane of our forefathers. Your kind has caused nothing but trouble in the past. Tell that to your fine masters at the Guild.'

Hogni kept his shrewd eyes upon Thurid, saying nothing about the creature he had plainly seen scuttling

163

into Thurid's pocket. 'This is no Guild wizard,' he said.

Syrgja glowered. 'We have no use for any kind of wizards,' she snapped, then turned to Hogni. 'You're no better than Slagfid when it comes to temptation, are you?'

Hogni paid her no heed, addressing Thurid. 'Since we have not sent for any wizard, it stands to reason that you were sent by someone.'

'So it would appear,' Thurid replied, lighting his pipe rather ostentatiously by cupping his hands around it until a coal commenced to glow in the bowl. 'It also appears that you have no wish to let anyone inside your boundaries. I wonder what it is you're trying to protect – yourselves or Fangelsi-hofn's secret.' He puffed clouds of obscuring smoke, and peered through at Hogni with slitted eyes.

Hogni made no betraying move, but Syrgja stopped her work to listen, hovering like a vulture over Thurid's words.

'There is a curse here,' Thurid continued delicately. 'It is the source of festering rot that sustains the Dokkalfar influence in Hraedsla-dalur.'

Hogni nodded agreeably. 'And no respectable Guild wizard will venture to tamper with it – even if we would permit it. Part of the curse is the promise that the situation will worsen drastically if ever anyone attempts to break this spell. The Guild knows this. So I am curious to see what manner of wizard comes prowling around Fangelsi, asking questions about our curse and our past. Perhaps you have some dark spells of your own in that satchel.'

He showed a few of his teeth in a humorless smile, which Thurid returned with a similar lack of amusement.

'One evil can be mended with another, eh?' he inquired with seeming pleasantness, and Hogni's smile stretched a small bit further in tacit agreement.

'Never!' Syrgja retorted fiercely, looking from one to the other. 'Your uncle would not tolerate strangers meditating such an attack upon our heritage. You know it is forbidden – our fate inescapable. Send them on their way, nephew, and let us continue in our own wretched way.'

164

Hogni's cold, slate-colored eyes dwelt upon Leifr and Raudbjorn. 'Not just yet, Aunt. I'm still curious, and I will be until I know who has sent them here.'

'Fatally curious, as was Slagfid,' she muttered, swinging away with her elbows braced like weapons.

'We'll be pleased to stay as long as it takes to satisfy your curiosity,' Thurid said. 'Although it could take awhile.'

'We've had jotun hunters here before,' Hogni said bluntly, still eyeing Leifr and Raudbjorn. 'Most of them were killed – skulls smashed, necks broken, ribs crushed. Small loss they were, too – the sort who think to aggrandize themselves by killing a fiercer foe. This is the first time I've seen jotun hunters who have brought a wizard with them. That's dangerous. You might actually cause some damage.'

'The damage will be to us,' Syrgja added forcefully. 'These fools can kill themselves anywhere else but on Fangelsi soil. Interference will not be allowed.' Her head jerked meaningfully toward the door, and the direction of the leaning tower beyond.

At that moment someone knocked loudly upon the door. Old Ketil lifted his head in a wolfish howl, his eyes red-rimmed and glaring with fury. He cried out in a surprisingly strong voice, 'He's come for me! Let me go to my brother!' He lumbered to his feet and stood stooped and swaying unsteadily on bandaged feet.

'Hush! It's no one but Starkad!' Syrgja commanded. 'Thorkell is dead. He won't be coming for you.' She swept her gaze over her startled guests, then motioned to Ermingerd to unlock the door for Starkad.

Starkad stepped jauntily into the room, his eyes dwelling eagerly upon the strangers. He was a fox-faced youth of considerably less than twenty, largely unwashed and ungroomed, with an unruly thatch of curly straw-colored hair that appeared cowlicked in all directions. Throwing off into one corner a cloak pieced together from various pelts, he revealed a dashing costume – a ragged, loose-necked shirt belted about with an assortment of knives and pouches, and drooping pantaloons stuffed into worn, carelessly laced boots. He paused, reaching automatically to touch the sword hanging on the wall, as if he had been trained up from infancy to do so.

'I'm Starkad,' he announced proudly, sitting down next to Leifr and seizing a slab of bread and boiled meat. He commenced to wolf it down, his slightly slanted eyes never leaving Leifr for an instant. Their stare was direct and disconcerting, not untinged by amusement, and Leifr had the uneasy feeling the youth was using powers to pry at his thoughts.

Between mouthfuls he said, 'We almost never get travelers, except the ones Hogni lets through the wards. I've never been allowed to travel any further than the next settlement, but one day I'm going to go exploring the world. Beyond Skarpsey, even. Have you come from far? Are you going someplace exciting?'

'Starkad!' Syrgja reproved in a voice of thunder. 'Get yourself gone and quit troubling our guests with your ill manners and rude questions!'

Starkad wiped his mouth on his sleeve, ignoring her. 'I wager you were out on your own adventures when you were almost eighteen summers old, weren't you? No one kept you imprisoned away on a small desolate bit of earth.'

'Eighteen summers?' Leifr had to smile. 'It was the year I sharpened my father's old sword on his grindstone and went a-viking with a cousin of my mother's. She didn't want me to go, but what else is there for a younger and therefore unnecessary son?'

Starkad's eyes glowed. 'What else indeed!' he exclaimed with rabid enthusiasm. 'Did you hear, aunt?'

Syrgja favored Leifr with a chilling stare. 'Don't go putting notions in the boy's head,' she said. 'He's not going anyplace. This land is where he belongs, helping his brothers. One day it may be his inheritance.' Her lip curled bitterly, and she glanced toward the hearth where the sword hung, or perhaps it was old Ketil she looked at. He was lost again in his miseries, slowly shaking his head back and forth in self-absorbed abnegation of his fate.

'I meant no harm,' Leifr said. 'It's a restless age to be, and a restless realm to live in. I haven't explored it nearly well enough myself yet.'

'What's to explore?' Syrgja snapped. 'Trolls waiting behind every rock, the Dokkalfar holding every other settlement, and all the boundaries shifted until you scarcely know where it's safe to set foot. Time was when you knew where you were safe, but no more. Chaos is ruling the Alfar realm. We have lost the proper way of doing things. No one pays heed to the rules anymore.' She emphasized her point by cuffing Starkad on the side of the head, raising a cloud of dust. 'And you're a good example, you young beast. Sleeping out of doors, trekking across the barrens and marshes, prowling in barrows, messing with old spells. If there was another way for you to get into trouble, I'm sure you'd do it.'

'I would, too, to get away from this place!' Starkad retorted, leaping to his feet. 'And you and Hogni and Horgull! Fangelsi is a prison, as its name says, but I'm not going to rot here forever! I'm going with these jotun-hunters, and we're going to kill the Flayer!'

Syrgja made some hasty signs in the air. 'I won't hear such talk in my house,' she snapped. 'You're upsetting your uncle Ketil with such words.'

Ketil swung his head in Starkad's direction, glowering at him and muttering under his breath. He started to get to his feet, fists knotted, but another arrival distracted him. Hopefully, he grumbled. 'Thorkell? Is it you, brodir?'

The door swung open, and Horgull stepped into the room, hanging up his cloak on a peg and touching the sword on his way to sitting down in the dark end of the room, where he gazed at the strangers in his house with no welcome evident in his manner. For an Alfar he was burly and dark-haired, with a black beard and

167

beetling black brows meeting over a jutting nose. In age he seemed near to Leifr, but in surliness he exceeded even Syrgja.

'I should explain,' Thurid began bitingly, 'we don't regard ourselves as jotun-hunters, so you can stop hailing us by that derisive title. We come here seeking to fulfill a geas placed upon us.'

'Geas!' Hogni repeated. 'Who has sent you on this fool's errand to challenge our curse?'

'One whose name doesn't bear mentioning in such proximity to a site of such magnitude as that tower,' Thurid replied sharply. 'By merely calling his name, you could summon untold horrors past your wards. The entire settlement here is charged with emotions that linger yet, discernible to one of my prepossessing skill. Do you practice your own skills there?' His voice was tinged with contempt for this amateur practitioner.

'I attend to the needful spells of this house,' Hogni answered, raising his eyes to Thurid with a measuring look. 'But no one dares occupy that tower. Fangelsi was built around the tower before our ancestor Slagfid knew what ill luck it was.' Hogni spoke with a note of grim satisfaction. 'I doubt if its powers will be of interest to you, unless you are a Dvergar or Dokkalfar – or the one who sent you here is. Sent you here to meet your dooms, unless you wisely give up your hopeless quest now and accept the lesser consequences of your geas.'

'They go in the morning,' Syrgja rasped, and Horgull grunted in agreement. Leifr saw Starkad and Ermingerd exchange a charged glance, and a glint of resolve flashed in Starkad's eye. Quietly he left his seat and let himself out of the hall.

'At least you have consented to keep them one night,' Hogni said to his aunt. 'Your hospitality is twice what it was, aunt.'

With such an inauspicious beginning, Leifr's expectations for the night could not have sunk much lower, even when their sleeping accommodations were pointed

168

out to them – a cold stone shelf in the farthest corner from the warmth of the ungenerous fire. Horgull, the silent brother, sat in the shadows and watched them as if they were housebreakers.

Raudbjorn's expression gradually sagged into a disapproving scowl. He settled himself in a watchful heap beside the door with his eyes upon Horgull. The trollhounds crowded around him, resting their chins on his knees. Since neither Horgull nor Raudbjorn would give up their unfriendly surveillance first, Leifr ended the confrontation by suggesting that Raudbjorn and the hounds sleep in the hall to guard the horses. Syrgja nodded approvingly, and Raudbjorn willingly removed himself to a more suitable environment. The rest of the family took their places in their sleeping quarters, with Syrgja shutting herself into the wall bed nearest the hearth.

In the morning when Leifr awakened, he gazed around the gloomy cavern of the kitchen, wondering if he had dreamed it all. The blackened chair where Ketil had sat was now empty. Syrgja and Ermingerd were preparing the food in silence, and Hogni and Horgull were gone. They must have slipped out very quietly, taking elaborate care not to awaken their guests.

The door to the hall swung open with a noisy screech and banged against the wall behind it as Raudbjorn entered the kitchen, closely followed by Starkad, still with straw clinging to his hair and clothing.

'Good morning to you,' Starkad greeted Leifr, with enthusiasm and curiosity glowing in his amber eyes. 'Tell me,' he went on in a whisper, darting a respectful glance toward Raudbjorn, 'how did you come upon this great Norskur you travel with? I thought they were uncivilized and dangerous creatures.'

'So they are,' Thurid interjected venomously as he crawled stiffly from the sleeping shelf. 'He would have killed us all, but he decided it would be more detrimental to eat all our food and thus starve us to death, by slow degrees. One of these days he'll have our emaciated heads in his trophy bag and a fat reward waiting for him.'

'Then you are outlaws?' Starkad whispered, his voice almost squeaking with the enormity of his discovery.

Leifr shook his head. 'We've committed no crimes, except to escape from an unjust judgment. Raudbjorn was a thief-taker for Sorkvir, sent against us. His loyalties have shifted to our side, however.'

Starkad's eyes glowed. 'What sort of unjust judgment is it? Were you falsely accused? Who is following you?'

The voice of Syrgja cut across the torrent of questions, making him jump nervously. 'Starkad! It's work first and talk later, as well you know,' she barked. 'We have extra livestock to feed this morning.'

'I shall help you with that.' Leifr pulled on his boots and stood up to accompany Starkad. As they were leaving the house, Ermingerd came out behind them with a basket over one arm, her feet making scarcely any sound in her soft shoes. She turned and went in the opposite direction, going out at a broken gate into the meadow. Leifr gazed after her a moment, comparing her soft moonlight beauty to Ljosa's haughty wildness, mentally weighing the sleek and subdued manner of Ermingerd's dress against Ljosa's proud posture in her ragged shepherd's garb. His attention was momentarily diverted by the stealthy dark form of Svanlaug vanishing behind a heap of rubble, shadowing the unsuspecting Ermingerd. Leifr halted in his tracks, wondering what Svanlaug was up to.

Starkad's voice broke into his thoughts. 'If it's my sister you're gazing at, you'd best know there's another ahead of you – Jarnvard of Killbeck, and he's not likely to be disappointed, if my aunt and brothers ever give him their approval, which they won't so far; and there's no other man hereabouts with Jarnvard's ambitions.'

'Jarnvard warned us away himself and he's not one I'd care to pick a quarrel with. He's got the look of a warlord. Hraedsla-dalur needs more of his ilk to get rid of these Dokkalfar.'

'I'd join his warriors, but Hogni won't allow it,' Starkad

said bitterly. 'One day I'll do what I please, when I'm certain I can get away from his wards and binding spells. And when I can thrash Horgull.'

Looking at Starkad's slender build, Leifr thought it would take him awhile to equal the burly Horgull. He said, 'You'll get your freedom one day, never fear. It comes to all of us, sooner or later.'

'Not at Fangelsi,' Starkad answered. 'The only ones who have left this land are the ones who died or did away with themselves. I've heard tales of my relatives going hunting for members of the family who had escaped. They were always brought back. Anyone born here must die here and be buried here. And I'll tell you something else strange. All Ljosalfar value their children. Sons and daughters are the hope of the future. But in Fangelsi, the young ones are despised. Syrgja will tell you it would have been better if we had never been born to our mother. Is that not unnatural? Even trolls prize their offspring.'

Leifr was struck by the uncomfortable truth of what Starkad was saying. With a shiver he said, 'It must have something to do with your curse.'

Leifr took a better look at the desolate farm as they walked around the hall toward a long barn. Even if the farm had not been sited atop a ruined fortress, the location was gloomy enough. Tall black crags scowled down from two sides, cutting off the settlement from the others and funneling the green land steeply toward the sea. The waves beating restlessly against the rock kept up a ceaseless undertone of dismal groaning, and the mist hovered about with unrelenting clamminess, dulling the already pale sun and rendering the land bleak and drear. The tower reared up sullenly against the mist, its blackened stones chinked with moss. Merely looking at it gave Leifr an uneasy sensation that something, or someone, was watching him back.

'What was the purpose of that place?' he asked, nodding toward it, interrupting the flow of Starkad's endless chatter, which Leifr only partly listened to.

Starkad shrugged. 'No one knows for certain. There was an old fortess of some kind here when our ancestor Slagfid arrived on a ship. He built right over the ruins, since there was such a plentiful supply of cut stones. It was a bad choice, though. Fangelsi never prospered long. Which is why I'm anxious to leave it. You could take me with you when you leave. I'll work hard, and when it comes to a fight, there's nothing I like better.'

'You might not like our prospects when we leave here,' Leifr said grimly. 'It seems there's more to Fangelsi-hofn than killing the jotuns which plague you. And afterward, our troubles are not over. Nothing in this realm is ever straightforward.'

'I see no reason why the jotuns can't be killed,' Starkad declared. 'I've told Hogni and Syrgja thousands of times that they defeat themselves by refusing to try it, at least. Even if the jotuns were draugar, draugar can be destroyed, especially with a sword such as yours. I've heard of it from the traders and news-carriers. It's nothing short of fate that brings you and that sword to Fangelsi-hofn. You're destined to destroy those jotuns.'

Leifr dragged his eyes away from Starkad's fervent gaze, more uneasy than ever. Fridmarr's carbuncle was glowing hotly against his chest, as if seconding Starkad's interpretation.

'Time will tell,' he hedged. 'If your elders have no intention of allowing us to search out the cause of the jotun curse, then I won't get near any jotuns with the sword. At least, not without their permission.'

Starkad grinned cunningly. 'I daresay you'd get their forgiveness swiftly enough once you destroyed the jotuns. The two of us will do more with that sword and your hunting hounds than Hogni and Horgull and Thurid can do muddling around with their magic spells. But you can't let them know what we're planning, or they'd never allow it.'

Leifr opened his mouth to protest, but Starkad's agile mind had leaped ahead to the next set of questions, which related to the Scipling realm. Hoping Starkad would forget about hunting jotuns with the dogs, he replied to the questions and a lot of excited chatter. Normal speech seemed too slow for Starkad; his thoughts were always pushing at Leifr's mind, searching for a faster way in.

They reached the barn by a rather roundabout way, so Starkad could show Leifr more of the old ruins. As they approached, Hogni came around from the other side of the barn in a hasty manner, gazing up into the green fells towering over the valley.

'Starkad! You were the last to leave this barn yesterday eve,' he barked. 'You must have left the door unlocked. All the horses escaped last night.'

Starkad gazed inside the vacant barn with an amazed expression. 'I'm certain I locked the barn, and put wards on it, too. Something stronger than trolls opened that door.' He elevated his nose, sniffing suspiciously, and extended his hands to swirl the air, testing for influences.

'Bah! Don't bother,' Hogni snapped, his manner threatening. 'There's no trace. I think it was your forgetting to lock the door that lost us our horses. You're the one that has to go find them, little brodir, so you'd better get started now.' Casting a sharp glance at Leifr, he added, 'It seems you'll stay a little longer now, Scipling, and enjoy our Fangelsi hospitality. A pity you won't see any jotuns before you leave.'

'The pity's more yours than mine,' Leifr replied. 'Your fate can be averted, while mine can't.'

'You're certain of that?' Hogni queried, his gaze dropping a moment to Leifr's sword and the growling hounds crouching around his legs. 'Do you think it is simply a matter of killing the jotuns?'

'No,' said Leifr, 'but it could be a start.'

Hogni snorted. 'Sciplings! If they can't understand it, they kill it. I warn you, and you'd better pay heed. Don't ever attempt to kill one of those jotuns, however long you stay here. It will be your death.'

He stalked away to break the news to Syrgja, who was

173

feeding her geese and ducks on the doorstep, her fists on her angular hips, radiating displeasure.

Starkad turned to Leifr. 'You'll come with me to hunt the horses.' It was more a statement than a question. 'I have a feeling those horses went straight up into the fells, past the last pasture and gate, and into Skera-gil.'

'From the tracks, I'd say it appears they're heading toward the strand,' Leifr observed.

'My instincts tell me the horses went into the fells,' Starkad insisted. 'Mere tracks in the dirt can be so deceiving. We'll look in Skera-gil first and the strand second. If there's time.' Glancing around covertly, he whispered, 'Are those hounds of yours good hunters and fierce fighters?'

'The best and the fiercest,' Leifr answered. 'Bred especially for hunting the greater gray trolls of the mountains.'

'Have they hunted jotuns?'

Leifr considered Ognun at Bjartur a moment, then nodded. 'They'll track and hunt anything I set them onto.'

'Good. Then it's time they learned the smell of jotun.'

Starkad led the way up into the fells above Fangelsi-hofn, with the hounds leaping along in high spirits with a great deal of the intent sniffing and enthusiastic tail-wagging that indicated troll scent. At the end of the sixth and highest pasture, Starkad halted at a gate with two piles of stone for pylons. The carrior crow sign was burned into the top rail of the gate, and Leifr shrank away from its radiating waves of repulsion.

'We can go no further, for today,' Starkad said, leading the retreat, but he paused to point beyond the gate. 'That is Skera-gil, where the jotuns hide. One day we'll go in there and find where the Flayer lairs.'

Leifr gazed at the black walls of Skera-gil rising from the green sward of the high fells in a mighty gash, as if the wounded earth were spewing out its black heart in a hundred ravines and gullies. The glacier capping the fell issued dozens of streams that cascaded seaward, raising a cloud of mist that hovered over the black crenellations.

Looking at it, Leifr shivered. 'Why doesn't Hogni's ward face into Skera-gil to keep the jotun away?' he asked. 'With a jotun hiding in there, who would want to go in?'

'Treasure seekers. They say the jotuns guard a treasure,' Starkad answered, his eyes aglow with a wolfish light. 'Gold enough to pave the floor of Fangelsi's great hall, my grandfather used to say. Hogni's got wards to keep people out, and wards to keep the jotuns in – and everyone in Fangelsi. But I'm not going to stay here and die. I'm getting out of here, and you're going to help me.'

Leifr felt Fridmarr's carbuncle growing hot, distracting him from Starkad's compelling stare. 'Come on,' he said rather impatiently. 'This is all very interesting, but we've got to find those horses before dark, and before the trolls and jotuns find them.'

They found no horses, instead spending the day hunting for traces of the jotun. The sky was almost dark when Leifr and Starkad came slinking back to Fangelsi-hofn. They made a wide detour around the tower, where a strange light flickered through the slit windows. The house door opened, revealing Thurid waiting impatiently for their arrival.

'It's rather dark to be out prowling,' Thurid said.

The troll-hounds pressed against Leifr's legs and growled uneasily, as if agreeing with his judgment. Their back hair stood up in ridges and they held their necks stiffly as they scented the dank evening air. A clammy breath traveled from the north, insinuating its way into the valley.

Thurid halted in mid-stride, turning slowly to face the north. He raised his hand to read the influences, and Hogni likewise stopped with one hand on the door latch, arrested by the discernible breath of evil powers. Reluctantly their eyes met.

'A power,' Hogni said. 'Something has followed you.'

Thurid scanned the darkening peaks looming over Fangelsi. 'Drat! And we could have got out of this place

175

this morning, if not for those horses straying. They hold the heights now. There's no getting beyond the fells. Are there other people in this valley? Fighting men, perhaps?'

'A few shore people,' Hogni said with a shrug, as if they were of no great account. 'We buy their driftwood and whale fat and fish, but there's none of them that can wield a sword or axe. What sort of oppression have you brought upon us, wizard?'

Thurid folded his arms and nodded his head with bleak satisfaction toward the high peaks as a distant wailing howl was raised to the blood-red evening sky. Other voices joined in, making an insane chorus that chilled the heart with apprehensions of hopeless doom.

'Dokkalfar fylgjur-wolves!' Hogni said. 'Well then, we are trapped between the Dokkalfar in the highlands and the jotun in Skera-gil. This should prove to be a most entertaining winter. There's no question now of going over those passes to Killbeck, or anywhere, until Fantur the Rogue is no longer in our sky and the Dokkalfar return underground. I thought when I saw you, Thurid of Dallir, that misfortune was riding hard at your heels, and now I am sure of it. It's a nithling's deed to bring your enemies to the doorstep of your host.'

'This is your reward for taking strangers in!' Syrgja carked in gloomy triumph. 'You should have sent them on their way before they touched one foot to our ground.'

Thurid scanned the night air intently with his fingertips and staff. The orb glowed an unhealthy red color as he snorted and said grimly, 'It's well enough to look back now on what you might have done, but unless your wards are strengthened, we'll have fylgjur-wolves clawing at our doors tonight. That one was a scout for the others. They're all around Fangelsi in the fells, waiting for the order to attack.'

'I ought to have known you outlaws would bring something unsavory after you,' Hogni said angrily. 'My wards are not strong enough to hold out Djofull!'

'They will be after I tell you what to put into them,'

176

Thurid said. 'I fear that our decision to leave Fangelsi must be postponed for a while. It is worse than a nithling's deed to send guests out to certain death at the hands of their enemies.'

'Then you shall have to stay,' Hogni said with no great welcome in his tone. 'But only until the spring equinox, when Fantur sets and the fylgjur-wolves lose some of their strength – and only upon my conditions. You must not seek to harm any jotun, and no one must set foot in Skeragil. Too much knowledge of Fangelsi will make it impossible for you to leave. No one who knows the truth of it ever gets away.'

'Agreed,' Thurid said. 'We'll risk the knowledge.'

'The geas states we must destroy the jotuns,' Leifr protested. 'Are we going to wait here and do nothing all winter?'

'We'll look to the securing of Fangelsi first,' Thurid snapped. 'We may not be able to get out easily, but I intend to see to it Djofull won't get in.'

When Thurid and Hogni were gone in search of the ward-signs, Starkad observed ironically to Leifr, 'Now you're as much a prisoner of Fangelsi as we are. But with your help, this time we're going to escape.'

'There have been others?' Leifr questioned.

Starkad shrugged. 'Many others, but not in my lifetime. They all died searching for Slagfid's Ban.'

CHAPTER 12

Leifr and Starkad returned to the house, where Syrgja muttered and flustered in dismay, turning the sharp edge of her fear and fury against Svanlaug, who came out of hiding only after the excitement of the fylgjur-wolves was over.

'It was your doing that brought those filthy creatures here,' she spat. 'Like attracts like. You must have sent for them, hoping to destroy us all.'

'I'd be destroyed along with you,' Svanlaug retorted. 'As if you cared, or would believe me. It would surprise you to know that Dokkalfar have their rivalries and factions among them as well as with the Ljosalfar. In their eyes, I'm perhaps a worse traitor than these others. I could expect nothing but death at their hands.'

'The sooner the better, then,' Syrgja retorted. 'I don't want your kind prowling around my house, even if what you say is true.'

'Very well, I won't prowl where you can see me.' Svanlaug gathered her cloak around her and spoke some words. With a smoky whirling, she shifted shapes into that of a small unidentified flying creature that kited around the house like a bat before tilting out the smoke hole to vanish with a triumphant chittering sound.

Syrgja gasped, and turned an indignant glower upon Leifr and Raudbjorn, looming in the doorway. 'Why can't you leave us alone?' she demanded. 'Can't you see we don't want your help, as you call it? I wish you'd never come here!'

Leifr was inclined to agree until his eye caught Ermingerd's glance as she knelt at the hearth. For an

178

instant her glance burned with hope and desperation, then she demurely looked away, leaving Leifr to wonder if he had imagined her unspoken plea.

It was some hours later when Thurid and Hogni returned from mending the wards. 'Where were you today?' Thurid greeted Leifr indignantly when they returned. 'We found the horses hours ago down on the shores of the firth. I suspect you were off adventuring all day, instead of hunting horses.'

Starkad looked sheepish. 'Well, we got distracted by chasing trolls with the dogs, and we lost the hoofprints right off anyway, so we went roving.'

Hogni surveyed them both critically. 'You didn't go into Skera-gil, did you?' he demanded.

'No, indeed,' Starkad said virtuously.

Hogni snorted in disdain, and started setting up a chess game with Horgull.

'Fine jotun-hunters you've got,' he muttered to Thurid with a derisive smile. 'Off chasing trolls when there's fylgjur-wolves surrounding Fangelsi. I'd be worried about satisfying that geas, if I were you.'

Darkly Thurid glanced up from the pile of old vellums and rune sticks he was pulling from his satchel. He cast his eyes over Leifr and then over Raudbjorn, who had spent the day contentedly sleeping. 'They'll do well enough for the job at hand,' he said. 'They survived the Pentacle and purged it of Sorkvir's influence. Now we'll unravel Fangelsi's jotun spell, since Djofull has been clever enough to trap us here with nothing to do for the winter. It's going to be difficult for you to stop us, in fact, pervasive as the influences are here.' He gently fanned the air with one hand and a glowing trail followed his motions.

'I warned you what would happen. You'll either die, or be trapped here, in some unpleasant manner. I've half a mind to let you try, so I can watch what happens to you,' Hogni replied with a grim smile.

'Not if you value what wretched bit of life you've got left,' Syrgja snapped. 'You'd better let sleeping dogs lie, instead of stepping on their toes.'

'Sleeping dogs?' Thurid said. 'You mean sleeping jotuns, and I wouldn't let them sleep long if I had the opportunity to rid Fangelsi of all jotuns forever.'

Hogni held his gaze a moment, then turned to Syrgja. 'What if he could break the curse, aunt? We have nothing further to lose.'

'Don't be such a fool! Your uncles Thorkell and Ketil wouldn't have considered such risks, when they were the masters here!' Syrgja roused up the fire savagely, muttering angrily under her breath, 'No one touches the jotun spell as long as I live under this roof.'

Leifr was glad it was Ermingerd who served them their food that night, some rather scanty leavings, since Leifr and Starkad had missed the main meal. She sat down on the opposite side of the table with a small bit of sewing to keep them company while they ate. Most of her communication with Starkad was silent glances with a wealth of meaning behind them. Leifr watched the two young Alfar and slowly formed the conviction that the disappearance of the horses had not been mere coincidence. Ermingerd and Starkad both desired freedom from Fangelsi's bonds and saw possible deliverance in the arrival of these strangers.

Starkad turned to Leifr and said in a low tone, 'One day Ermingerd will have a fine enough dowry to marry her to a jarl or a king. We've long planned to sail away in a ship, far from Fangelsi, where no one can come for us.'

'Those were childish dreams, Starkad,' she said gently. 'You know it can never happen.'

Starkad raised startled eyes. 'Why not? It would be easy, once we have enough gold. We've found some bits, on the battlefields, and around old barrows. I thought this was our plan, Ermingerd.'

'There is not enough gold,' she answered, keeping her eyes upon her sewing. 'It was an amusing game, and no more. We'll never leave Fangelsi, and it's time we got used to the idea. We aren't children any longer.'

'You've given up?' Starkad asked incredulously, in an

injured tone. 'You can't give up! Listen, Ermingerd, there's something I've got to tell you. Remember the stories about the treasure in Slagfid's Ban?'

'It's just stories, Starkad,' Ermingerd answered.

Crestfallen, Starkad watched her cross the room to her loom. 'I won't give up,' he muttered to Leifr with a flicker of fiery resolution in his eye. 'If there's a treasure in Skeragil, we're going to find it.'

For two days an uneasy truce reigned in Fangelsi, with the fylgjur-wolves testing the barrier of wards, and the two wizards skirmishing around each other over the issue of Djofull's geas. By day Thurid studied the tower, drifting nearer to it despite Hogni's warnings to stay clear. Leifr knew by his reverent expression that Thurid was hopelessly fascinated by whatever mysteries lurked there. As for Leifr, he watched for signs of the jotuns, but so far, after three days, Fangelsi seemed a perfectly normal place, if a gloomy one.

It was the evening of the third day, when Fangelsi was most peaceful. Hogni and Horgull were bent over their chessboard and the women were sewing. Starkad sat at Leifr's feet, watching in open-mouthed admiration as he polished *Endalaus Daudi*, ever vigilant against flecks of rust in Fangelsi's dank climate. Thurid sat poring over his vellums and rune sticks, assisted by Gedvondur clamped to his wrist, the blood-red carbuncle glittering like an intelligent eye. Svanlaug lurked ominously in the shadows, watching Thurid.

A sudden savage baying of the hounds in the main hall startled them all with the rude intrusion of such noise. Uncle Ketil started up from his dozing beside the fire, his eyes glaring with ferocious eagerness below the bandage Syrgja had wrapped around his head. He listened intently, with one gnarled hand cupped behind a swollen ear. Outside the hall, something crunched upon some sticks of driftwood gathered for winter fires. No one in the hall moved, listening with a frozen rigidity that might have been a wizard's spell. Leifr felt their fear and tension

181

rising around him in a dark tide, making his own heart thud with anxiety. After a long interval of silence, Hogni relaxed and moved his piece on the gameboard, taking one of Horgull's. Ermingerd's poised needle descended to rest on her lap, but her eyes were still haunted. Ketil heaved a miserable sigh and shut his red-rimmed eyes.

A voice moaned under the one high window, securely shuttered. With a wordless muttering, Ketil lurched to his feet and staggered toward the door with his hands trailing streamers of bandage.

'Thorkell!' he rumbled thickly. 'He's come! Brodir, I'm coming!'

Syrgja leaped to her feet, terror in her eyes as she attempted to soothe him, saying, 'Hush now, brother. You know there's no one outside. It's not Thorkell. Thorkell is dead and gone.' She tried to hold Ketil back, but he shoved her roughly aside as if he did not hear her imploring voice. His eyes gleamed with a bestial light as they dwelt upon the door. No further sounds came from outside, but Leifr had the feeling something was out there, watching and waiting, and it was not a day-faring creature.

Ermingerd put one hand on Ketil's shoulder, trying to soothe him, but he shook her off with impatient energy and shuffled toward the door.

Ketil cried out, 'Thorkell! My brother! I'm here! I'm coming!'

More faintly, the thin voice whimpered outside, 'Come out! Open the door, Syrgja! It's so cold out here!'

'Brodir! Help me, I can't get out!' Ketil roared.

The voice faded away, soon lost in the uneasy blattering of the sheep penned outside and the growling of the trollhounds in the main hall across the passage. Ketil's energy seemed to ebb as the creature moved away, and he finally sank into his chair with a defeated grumble. He closed his eyes and pulled his ragged old cloak up to his ears, commencing a wracking shivering and moaning.

Thurid strode to the door and plunged into the passage, his alf-light blazing, and Leifr hastened to follow. They

182

both went outside the hall and stood in the snow, looking at the enormous tracks in the newly fallen skiff. Leifr's neck hairs bristled, and he was glad when they went back in and shut out the menacing dark behind the thick kitchen door.

'It's gone now,' Thurid reported. 'I presume we have just met the Flayer who terrorizes Hraedsla-dalur, murdering and plundering wherever he goes.'

Syrgja recovered her ill-tempered aplomb quickly. 'Yes, the Flayer,' she said, struggling to calm her voice to its normal toneless croak. 'A wretched, hapless creature who haunts these old ruins, calling out the names of the living and trying to lure them to destruction. People hereabouts call him the Flayer because of what he can do to a cow or a sheep.' Then she added with emphasis, 'And poor Ketil has the delusion that the jotun is his dead brother Thorkell. You should leave this place before you learn too much. You don't know the danger here.'

Thurid drew some deep breaths and composed his clothing more neatly. 'Jotuns and fylgjur-wolves and a hostile tower are not beyond my capabilities.' He quirked an eyebrow toward Syrgja as if to include her in his list of threats, and thought better of it.

Once the danger was past, Svanlaug's lizard-bird form dropped down from the roof beams, and she resumed her human shape with a black swirling of power and a few stray feathers. Syrgja made signs to ward off evil, scowling.

'Thurid,' Svanlaug said nervously, 'this influence is far too big and powerful for you to tamper with without risk of getting ensnared. It's Dvergar. Particularly old and evil Dvergar, too.'

Thurid cast her one withering glance. 'You can keep your beak closed until I want to hear from you,' he said acidly. Then he turned back to Hogni with a sharp, scrutinizing stare.

'Why do you cherish these nasty secrets so dearly?' he asked, almost in a whisper. 'Perhaps there is something else you prefer to hide besides the treasure of Slagfid. Or do you enjoy living with such miseries?'

Hogni met Thurid's challenge with a cold and level stare. 'Better to live with old miseries than to court new ones,' he said. 'Wizard, who is your co-walker? I've seen your dead hand, and since you've brought it into our house, I want to know if the spirit possessing you is good or ill.'

Thurid plucked Gedvondur off his wrist and thrust him into his satchel. 'You've nothing to fear from Gedvondur,' he said. 'You see that it doesn't possess me, but I it. We are partners in this endeavor. We both believe the source of your trouble with jotuns lies in that tower. I crave your permission to investigate it.'

Hogni and Horgull exchanged a glance, and Hogni said, 'As you wish, but the force inhabiting that tower has not allowed anyone access for many years. It won't let you in.'

'It doesn't know me,' Thurid said. 'Or Gedvondur.'

Syrgja made a growling sound of despair and disgust. She turned and climbed the steps to her bed and slammed the doors after herself, her departure signaling the end of the argument. After the others had retired to their beds, Thurid paced up and down the room a few times, scarcely able to contain his glee.

In the morning at the first hint of daylight, Thurid prodded Leifr awake. 'What a lot of useless sleeping you Sciplings do, when there's better things to be done. Come on, we're going to take a look at the tower,' he said, his eyes gleaming.

Grudgingly Leifr parted with his eider and followed Thurid through the frost toward the tower, which stood at a distance from the house. Thurid strolled around its base, trying to appear the casual explorer, but the nearer Leifr got the more difficult it seemed to approach. His steps slowed, and twice he actually turned away. The very look of the tower repulsed him, with a swollen lid of ancient turf spilling over its jagged top edges, as if something brownish had boiled up from within and was crawling out.

184

A pair of high, narrow, slit windows gazed down at him, emanating unfriendliness and an atmosphere of cold that made him shiver.

Thurid straightened up from his casual inspection of the door and the lock. With the end of his staff he pushed the door, and it fell open with a resentful squeal of rusted hinges. Thurid staggered back as some invisible force hit him in the chest, but it was only a disturbed owl flapping indignantly over his head.

Halfway overcoming his revulsion and unexplained fear, Leifr edged nearer the doorway, curious to look within. Thurid barred his way with his staff, breathing hard as if he had been running. The pupils of his eyes were dilated to almost complete blackness.

'Don't get too close,' he warned. 'There's something in there, and it's not at all friendly. This tower does not belong to the above-ground world.'

'What of those others?' Leifr nodded toward the house. 'Does Hogni belong entirely to the above-ground?'

Thurid's cloak fluttered as he retorted, 'Dear me, yes, they're regular Ljosalfar, but I fear they're tainted with something peculiar, even that lovely and precious Ermingerd. I don't know what it is, but this tower must have something to do with it.'

Leifr stepped forward, but Thurid extended one arm and barred him from stepping over the threshold, his eyes gleaming with fierce elation as he whispered, 'Can't you feel it, you nerveless lump? There's power coursing through these stones from the earth below. I couldn't be responsible for what might happen to you if you set one foot in this place before I consecrate it for my usage. This place is an unholy site.'

Leifr peered in at the narrow view of the interior of the tower. Straw littered the floor, as if it had been quarters for animals at one time. A hearth occupied one side, where a hole in the masonry perhaps allowed the smoke to trickle out. A second floor hung rather precariously overhead, where it hadn't already collapsed, and the dark area above smelled as if it harbored bats and pigeons. In the darkest portion of the tower, a pile of stones stood near one wall, not quite in the form of a table, but almost, and its appearance gave Leifr an uneasy feeling. It reminded him of an altar and associated dark rituals.

'This is a terrible place,' Leifr said, shivering suddenly. The tower seemed to nurture coldness within its walls, making its atmosphere even more forbidding.

'Ah, you do feel its importance then,' Thurid crooned. 'Even a Scipling recognizes a site of such magnitude. I'll wager that it rivals even Murad's bogs, and the Guildhall.'

'It needs cleaning up,' Leifr said, impressed with the sense of the uncleanness of the tower, a feeling which was not entirely due to its apparent filthiness, but to the entity that inhabited it.

Thurid declared, 'It's perfect the way it is. No one will touch a thing. I must study the random patterns existing here before anything is added or taken away.'

Thurid made some fine, impassioned passes with his hands about the doorway, then stepped inside. At once the power within rebuffed him, knocking him flat on his back across the threshold. He scrambled to safety and hastily composed his dignity, muttering, 'A frisky spirit, rather. A good sign that it fears my approach.'

Leifr took a step backward, not liking the sinister barrow smell welling up in the tower, as if the influence that lingered knew well that the smell of death made living men uneasy.

'And you think this tower has something to do with the Flayer's curse?' he asked.

Thurid folded his arms and gazed into the tower with magnificent contempt. 'I know it does,' he said darkly. 'I feel the same emanations I felt from the Flayer's presence. An ancient, black, murky hatefulness, twisted deep down by the remembrance of wrongs so far past that they must be as old as Ginnungagap and Muspell.' Thurid's eyes rolled upward rather alarmingly and he swayed slightly on his feet as he chanted the words that seemed to come from

186

some unknown well of knowledge. The voice he spoke in was Gedvondur's. 'A profound grudge, carried by the whole race of them against every living thing above on the surface. Such suspicion and revenge must surely be Dvergar. Dvergar. Yes, that's the essence here, the cold, the smell, the dark fury, the broken promises—'

With a gasp, Thurid broke out of his trance, and Gedvondur crawled out of his sleeve to perch on a worn post, waving jauntily at Leifr. Still swaying, Thurid gaped into the tower a moment, then began to edge away, his eyes glazed and staring.

'What a nasty place!' he muttered, flicking his cloak around him. 'I don't know what Gedvondur wants with it. I'm sure that crude chimney won't draw properly. I'm not staying in there, Gedvondur. Stay in there yourself if you like it so much. There's plenty of fleas and lice to keep you company, I'm sure.'

He started to leave, but Gedvondur waylaid him, bringing him up short and turning him around stiffly to face the dark opening. Raising his arms aloft suddenly, Gedvondur intoned, 'Hverfa, lostur! Ohugsanlegur, fara!'

The barrow smell of the tower vanished, taking with it all the foreboding emanations and fears.

With a devious chuckle, Thurid stepped over the threshold, taking possession of the tower by his very arrogance, albeit borrowed mostly from Gedvondur. He strode around, then beckoned to Leifr to come in. Reluctantly, Leifr approached the threshold and poked at it with some wary passes of his hands to make certain nothing was going to happen before he stepped over it. Once inside the tower, it suddenly seemed more commonplace, nothing more than a smelly old tower used for broken junk and a haven for bats. His confidence increased moment by moment, until he happened to notice that the walls glowed with dusky red runes where Thurid's influence brushed by, as if Thurid were a lantern in a dark room.

Gedvondur's voice chuckled. 'Lucky Scipling, you are

protected in so many ways. Perhaps it is better not to see as much as the elder races see.'

Leifr eyed the glowing runes suspiciously, wondering what else in the tower he was not seeing, which made him so lucky. 'I see enough to know I don't like this place,' he grunted. 'It's evil. Gedvondur, you shouldn't do this.'

'Don't be ridiculous,' Thurid answered. 'Gedvondur and I shall control this place and find some answers, shall we not, you lump of carrion?'

'We shall,' Gedvondur replied. 'Between the two of us.'

'I've had enough of this,' Leifr said. 'I'll wait for you outside.'

Leifr eased himself out the tower, lest a cowardly retreat be excuse for the tower entity to attack him. As he exited the place somewhat hastily, he met Ermingerd walking quickly along the path leading to the tower.

'You were inside the tower?' she said with a nervous gasp, halting abruptly. A heavy willow basket with a cover swung against her leg with a jolt. 'You mustn't go in there. It isn't a safe place.'

'I know that,' Leifr said. 'Gedvondur – ah, Thurid was there, so I was in no danger.'

'Don't say that,' Ermingerd whispered. 'Anyone who goes in there is in danger, I assure you. Even Thurid and Gedvondur are in danger. And you're not the way we are. You have no defenses. Hogni says you are a stranger from beyond the barriers of the realm. You possess a carbuncle, but you do not know magic.'

'I wish I did,' Leifr said, to his own surprise, and thought about Fridmarr's carbuncle, which would make him as Alfar as Thurid himself. Yet even as he spoke, the skittish Scipling in him shied away from the idea of giving up total control and total independence. 'That basket looks heavy. Can I carry it for you, wherever you're taking it?'

A shadow of alarm passed over Ermingerd's face. 'No, I'm not going far,' she said. 'Just to the shore people. My aunt is sending something for an old sick woman. It isn't heavy.'

'Then it's no bother for me at all, is it?'

'My aunt,' she said reluctantly, looking away from him, 'and my brothers would not look upon it with understanding.'

'Oh, I see,' Leifr said carefully, remembering that marriage had been forbidden her; thus, his attendance upon her would be greatly frowned upon by her guardians. Among Sciplings, a woman's brothers were her chief defenders throughout her life, even above her husband. If the brothers did not approve of the husband, they had the right to apply whatever punishment they thought suitable and bring her back to her mother's house. Leifr supposed it was also true among Alfar. 'I wouldn't wish to cross your brothers – particularly Starkad. What a loyal guardian he will make one day. But he tells me they won't allow you to take a husband and leave Fangelsi.'

A brief spark of joy in her eyes was almost immediately quenched. She looked down at her hands a moment. 'He's yet a child, and he doesn't know a great many things,' she murmured, sidestepping him and his question on the path as if she intended to go on about her errand.

'Wait, Ermingerd. There's so much we don't know. I want to help you. Can't you tell us anything to help break this curse?'

She hesitated, and hope burned in her eyes, but she shook her head. 'My brother Hogni is watching from the fell,' she said, making a covert sign in the air between them. 'He has powers of hearing from afar. You are here and you must see what needs to be done and do it, without any seeming help from me. I am loyal to my family and the heritage that binds us. Go now, and I beg you to stay out of that tower.' She turned, then seemed to relent. In a whisper she added over her shoulder. 'Tell Thurid that the number ninety-nine is significant.'

Then she turned and was gone, leaving Leifr more puzzled than before. 'Ninety-nine!' he muttered, feeling a chill of dread creeping up on him. 'Thurid!' he called impatiently. 'Come out of there!'

Thurid took his time, and Leifr did not relish the thoughts of going into the tower after him.

'What's the significance of the number ninety-nine?' Leifr asked, when Thurid finally emerged from the tower, trailing wisps of mist from his fingertips, with his beard crackling energetically.

'Ninety-nine!' Thurid halted as if he had run into a wall, and his eyes glazed over as his fingers winnowed the air. With a sly smile he muttered, 'Yes, that's getting nearer, isn't it? You don't care for that, do you? You're an old fox, whatever your name, but so am I. Perhaps you've met your match at last.'

'And perhaps not,' Leifr added, not liking Thurid's fanatic rapture. 'I don't see why you're so enthralled with that tower. You ought to be thinking about killing jotuns instead of resurrecting old evil spirits. How are we going to get the Flayer if Hogni won't allow us to go hunting him in Skera-gil?'

Thurid waved the questions away like troublesome gnats. 'Don't bother me about jotuns,' he snapped. 'This tower and its influence are the most important step in my progression. Jotuns can wait.'

'Not for long, Thurid,' Leifr retorted. 'The spring equinox is only four months away.'

'Plenty of time,' Thurid scoffed, turning on his heel to stalk back toward the tower. 'Just keep yourself out of trouble, Leifr,' he added. 'We're on thin ice with Hogni as it is. Don't do anything to rile up his temper, if you can possibly avoid it.'

Leifr stalked back to the house, simmering. Starkad was waiting for him with more plans for tracking the Flayer with the hounds. Leifr didn't think it safe to blatantly ignore Thurid's warnings so soon, so he rather curtly rebuffed Starkad's invitations for the next two days, choosing instead to put on the appearance of compliance.

On the morning of the third day, as Leifr was going out to feed the horses, he stopped and looked back at the ancient house, lowering in the mist and gloom. The feeling pervaded his awareness that someone was watching him, perhaps attempting to signal him. A pale shadow stirred beside the door and glided away, taking a devious route between the crumbling buildings as if to avoid anyone's notice. It was Ermingerd, hooded and cloaked for going outside, with a basket over her arm. Leift did not speak to her, allowing her to think he had not noticed her. She quickly crossed the outer wall, taking the path across the frozen hay meadows leading westward, toward the sea-coast. Leifr supposed she was taking something to the shore people, who were poor folk and really little better than scavengers upon the land. As he stood and watched from his vantage point, however, Ermingerd's course took a sudden bend northward as soon as she supposed she was out of sight of the house, and she hastened toward Skera-gil. Leifr started to parallel her course along the upper slope so he could watch without being seen. She left her basket on a pile of stone, which someone had set up as an offering place, perhaps to appease the jotun. Leifr sighed at the hopelessness of such a ritual gesture. She stood gazing northward for a long time, finally raising one arm to wave. Turning, Leifr saw a rider on a hilltop. It was the direction of Killbeck, and Leifr had no trouble forming the conclusion that it was Jarnvard, on the other side of Hogni's wards.

He returned to the homestead thoughtfully and found Starkad in the horse barn pitching soiled straw onto the steaming midden heap. Starkad threw down his pitchfork and looked at him expectantly.

'There's precious little being done about the Flayer and the fylgur-wolves,' Leifr said in a cautiously low tone. 'Thurid's more interested in that tower, and your brothers will never do anything. If we want to get rid of the jotuns, we're going to have to do it ourselves, without any help from Thurid and Gedvondur. It won't be a difficult matter to kill the Flayer. He's much like a great gray troll we killed in Bjartur. We know he'll be back to steal some meat, and we know where he dens.'

Starkad grinned conspiratorially. 'I knew from the start that you weren't one to mince around so carefully,' he said. 'These hounds have been begging to hunt the Flayer from their first smell of him, and so has Raudbjorn.'

'So has *Endalaus Daudi*,' Leifr added, placing his hand on his sword hilt. 'This will be for Ermingerd. I can't bear to see her become old and sour like Syrgja. She deserves a chance to live free.'

'Aye! That's the talk!' Starkad agreed. 'We'll hunt the Flayer to earth and kill him with your Rhbu sword and put an end to all this disagreement. These old cautious ones are making this far more difficult than it need be. The Flayer always comes after the sheep on moonlight nights. He'll be here again tonight, since he didn't get away with anything last time he was here.'

On the pretext of defending the hall against the Flayer's attack, Leifr, Starkad, and Raudbjorn bedded down for the night in the main hall with the sheep, but not to sleep. They listened in the darkness for the first sounds of the Flayer coming down from Skera-gil. The troll-hounds heard him first and commenced growling and wagging their tails in eager anticipation. Quietly the three jotun-stalkers let themselves out of the hall. When the dark bulk of the Flayer appeared against the snow of the fell, they silently glided forward to meet him. He was large and indistinct in form, and Leifr's heart pounded when the great creature spied them and stopped short, crouching defensively. He was the size of Ognun, but differently shaped. Grumbling, the Flayer swung his massive arms pugnaciously, as if daring them to attack. The hounds charged in to attack first, with a ferocious snarling blur of snapping teeth and driving paws. The Flayer clouted them aside, scarcely faltering in his determined advance upon Fangelsi.

'You aren't going to attack Fangelsi tonight,' Leifr said, flourishing the gleaming sword, which left faint arcs of light in the air as he moved it. 'It's time your mischief was put to an end, jotun.'

The Flayer replied with a derisive sound that might have been a distorted laugh and flailed about challengingly with his huge arms, stepping forward without fear. Leifr thrust at him with the sword, not near enough to do any damage. Also cautious, the Flayer swatted at the sword, and conflicting powers thrust at each other with an ominous buzzing sound, like angry bees. Leifr stepped back, wondering if the position of Fantur the Rogue also affected his Rhbu sword.

With a challenging roar Raudbjorn lurched forward, scything the air with his halberd, his little eyes gleaming murderously. Winding the halberd around and around, he let it fly to bounce off the Flayer's chest with a loud clang, as if it had struck solid rock. Growling, the Flayer advanced to place one foot on the halberd. Raudbjorn lowered his head, returning the Flayer's snarl with a nasty one of his own. Without further warning he lowered his head behind his shield and charged like a bull, smiting the Flayer with a resounding crash, carrying the Flayer backward several steps with his impetus. The Flayer dealt him some heavy blows with his fist, but Raudbjorn deflected them with his shield and pressed forward enough to retrieve the halberd. Then he dealt the jotun some tremendous blows, showering them both with sparks. The jotun hammered Raudbjorn back with a mighty smashing against his shield, but Raudbjorn returned the offensive, and so the battle swayed back and forth, favoring first one then the other.

Leifr and Starkad and the dogs skirmished at the edge of the titanic struggle, virtually unnoticed by the principal combatants. The sheer force of numbers and the grim determination of the defenders of Fangelsi eventually won them the grudging retreat of the Flayer. Slowly at first, he withdrew. As his opponents allowed him the space, he moved more quickly, until finally he turned and made for Skera-gil as fast as he could go. The hounds yammered and worried at his heels, often taking a determined grip and swinging clear of the ground until the Flayer paused to club them half-senseless with his fist.

They chased him as far as the entrance to Skera-gil, where Leifr called the dogs back and they halted to catch their wind and reconsider. Raudbjorn and the hounds were more than eager to pursue the jotun right up to the mouth of his hiding place, but Leifr was a little more cautious, thinking of the desperation of a cornered bear. Listening to the angry roars of the Flayer echoing through Skera-gil, he was even more reminded of the folly of pursuing a dangerous creature into its own domain.

'We've taught him a lesson for tonight,' Leifr said. 'If he knows that Fangelsi will fight him, he won't be so anxious to come here for his next meal.'

'This isn't enough,' Starkad replied. 'We've got to destroy the Flayer before Fangelsi will be free.'

'Aye, kill Flayer,' Raudbjorn puffed. 'Next time.'

CHAPTER 13

When they returned to Fangelsi, they found lights lit and people waiting for their return – and waiting with no goodwill in their hearts.

'What you have done is forbidden!' Hogni blazed, after the doors were closed and barred. Everyone glowered at the jotun-hunters, including Thurid and Svanlaug. Even Ermingerd turned her face away.

'But it worked,' Starkad protested. 'We drove the Flayer back to Skera-gil. He didn't come down and smash things and kill our sheep. We taught him a lesson he won't be forgetting soon.'

'You may get a lesson yourself, which you won't forget soon,' Syrgja retorted. 'We may all be punished for upsetting the natural course of this spell. There is a balance which must be maintained.'

'Balance?' Leifr repeated. 'What sort of balance is there when the people of Fangelsi lose every time and the jotun wins? Nothing will ever change until you act. Jotuns will haunt Fangelsi until there are no people left.'

Hogni chuckled humorlessly. 'That is the plan, Scipling, and no one must interfere with it. The balance of the spell was upset the day you set foot on our soil.'

'See here, we'd be glad to leave, if we could,' Thurid answered with a flare of temper. 'A geas binds us to this place until the jotun curse is broken or until we die.'

'I'd rejoice to have you gone,' Syrgja said.

Hogni darted her a significant glance. 'Some time must pass before it's safe to let them go. Who knows what rumors they would spread? Already they have knowledge.' He turned and raked Leifr with a scathing glance. 'What I now demand of you is to stay away from Skera-gil with your hunting hounds, and away from the Flayer. There can be no jotun-hunting, or it gets worse for all of us.'

'What could be worse than this?' Starkad demanded bitterly. 'I won't cringe and cower before my supposed destiny, which seems to be ending up in the gullet of some jotun. From now on, I shall deal with the jotun in my own way, and trolls take you and your way, Hogni.'

'You'll have to do it from the inside of the granary then,' Hogni said. 'We'll lock you in if you can't be controlled. And you, wizard,' he added, rounding upon Thurid suddenly, 'you'd better control your warriors, or I shan't speak for the consequences.'

'Consider it done,' Thurid said with freezing dignity, bending a savage scowl upon Leifr and Raudbjorn. 'Usually they don't proceed without my express instructions. It won't happen again.'

'Instructions!' snorted Leifr. 'I'm accustomed to following my own instructions. What harm was there?'

'For every action there is a counter-action,' Hogni answered with a sharp little smile. 'Especially when you're dealing with a curse such as this one.'

For two days the Flayer stayed away. The oppressive atmosphere of Fangelsi was in no wise lightened by his absence; on the contrary Leifr felt a heavier burden of suspense, wondering if he had indeed done something to cause the jotun curse to worsen. To add further to his unease and guilt, Hogni spent much of his evenings gazing into a seeing sphere, his expression grim and intent.

'It begins,' he said quietly, on the second night. 'The Flayer preys upon Killbeck tonight.'

Ermingerd pricked her finger at her sewing. Leifr saw her face turn white and bloodless. It was Jarnvard she feared for, he realized.

'Something must be done,' Syrgja said in her harsh voice. 'Someone may recognize him – as coming from Fangelsi. We might be held to blame.'

'I tried to do something,' Starkad muttered resentfully.

'Getting rid of the jotun is the only idea that makes any sense.'

'Hush, little brodir,' Hogni said sharply. 'You don't know yet what good sense is. When the Flayer was here, at least we knew he wasn't beyond the bounds stirring up the settlements against him – and us.'

Leifr found he had no ready answer to hurl against the bristling powers arrayed against him. After returning Hogni's dark stare in a silent battle of wills, Leifr retreated into his own corner to brood upon the injustices being heaped upon him. Thurid was still angry and short-tempered and too abstracted by his study of the tower and the entity that inhabited it. His only ally in his disgrace was Starkad.

On the third night the Flayer returned in full fury, starting his wrathful howling in the pastures above the house. Leifr unsheathed his sword and laid it across the table in readiness.

The jotun paused to tear a gate from its moorings, heaving it aside with a crash, before approaching the window to pound on the shutters in a rude parody of the usual Skarpsey manner of saluting a house.

'It's so cold, Syrgja,' a faint voice called. 'Let me in, Syrgja. The sheep have frozen to death.'

Ketil flung up his head to listen, then buried his face in his bandaged hands a moment, rocking to and fro in some private misery of his own.

'Brodir is dead,' he whispered, breathing huge breaths that rattled deep in his chest.

Then with a bellowing scream the jotun attacked the front door of the passage, smashing at it as if each fist were a mighty hammer. Grunting with dissatisfaction when it wouldn't give way, the creature moved around the house, clawing at each door or window he encountered. The troll-hounds answered with vociferous barking when he shook the doors at the other end of the passage, which were nearer to the main hall. Then he returned to assault the front door with a loud growl, battering at it determinedly,

197

each heavy blow causing Ermingerd to shrink and flinch against Syrgja's comfortless shoulder.

Thurid arose to his full height and moved toward the door, his cloak surging behind him. Leifr took up the sword and followed. Hogni and Horgull stubbornly blocked their approach.

In a stern voice Leifr commanded, 'Move aside, and allow me to confront this night-faring creature! If it's the Flayer, I'm geas-bound to destroy him!'

'Don't be a fool,' Hogni answered, his eyes rather wild and distracted, shifting abruptly as Starkad flung open a chest and emerged with a great rusty axe in his hands. 'You, Starkad! Put that weapon back! Is the door secured into the great hall?'

'As well as possible, but Raudbjorn will have to stop him if he knocks it down one of these nights,' Starkad replied excitedly, brandishing the axe. 'Why don't we kill the Flayer and be rid of him?'

'Put down that weapon, you fool!' Hogni thundered. 'We can't kill him!'

Ketil rose to his feet, rattling the chain that bound him to the hearth, and raised a soul-chilling howl, echoed by the jotun outside the door. The heavy single knocking became a faint scratching and tapping. A pleading voice called out, 'Ketil! Come out! It's time! You'll miss the Skylaus fairing!'

'Brodir!' Ketil whispered, his eyes glowing. 'He's come for me, Syrgja! Open the door and let me out!'

'Hush, Ketil,' she answered. 'It's not brodir, it's only the Flayer, wanting to pick your bones. Sit down, you don't want to go out.'

Ketil shook his head, unconvinced, and thrust away her restraining hands, muttering about the fair.

'They've come for him a dozen times,' Hogni muttered. 'Your same old tales won't fool him any longer. We'll have to open the door and let him go out if we're to save ourselves!'

'No! We can't!' Syrgja twisted her hands helplessly.

'He's my brother! The last, next to me!'

'He's got to go or we die,' Horgull added gloomily.

'No! No! Not like this!' Syrgja gasped.

Thurid and Leifr exchanged a mystified glance. The occupants of Fangelsi were so completely absorbed in their own agonies that the visitors were forgotten.

Starkad glowered from one of his relatives to the other. 'As long as I live, you're not going to turn our poor old uncle Ketil out on the fell to die at the hands of jotuns, are you, just because his wits are gone and he can work no longer? What sort of kinship is that?'

'Silence, upstart!' Hogni commanded, and his eyes flickered over Leifr and Thurid, recalling him to his proper reticence. 'There are strangers about. We'll not talk of our problems before listening ears.' He flung out one hand in a quelling gesture, and Starkad lost his defiance and slunk away.

Holding their breath, still standing in confrontation, they all listened for the jotun's next move. Another heavy knock shook the door outside, this time with sounds of incipient collapse.

Thurid strode forward to the door and extended one hand commandingly. Gedvondur's hand perched on his shoulder, pointing his forefinger with the glittering carbuncle ring.

'Move aside, you buffoons,' Gedvondur's voice commanded, his influence altering Thurid's face in the usual ugly manner, 'or you're going to be fried in your own fat. This is not a matter to be settled with blood and steel. I see now what must be done. The key lies in the tower, not in mindless killing.'

Hogni and Horgull gazed at Thurid's face and backed away a few paces; even Syrgja's wrath was momentarily quelled.

'Thurid! It's jotuns we've come here to kill,' Leifr protested angrily. 'So let's begin with this one!' Starkad seconded him heartily, swinging his rusty axe in anticipation.

199

'There's no need to kill the jotun,' Hogni said, making signs with one hand. 'All he wants is the eldest member of the family, and he'll be satisfied for several years.'

Syrgja made a strangling sound behind a handful of her apron. 'No! Don't, Hogni!' she whimpered.

With a series of rending crashes, the outer door was finally breached, falling into the passage mostly in splinters. Growling triumphantly, the jotun lumbered forward, pausing to claw at the kitchen door, still breathing in hoarse, heavy gasps from the exertion of tearing down the stout door.

'Wizard!' rumbled a thick, guttural voice. 'Come out!'

Thurid extended his glowing staff's orb and advanced to the door, parting the tense knot of combatants poised there.

'Leifr, open the door,' he whispered, still in Gedvondur's voice, and Leifr was only too glad to do so. He flung the bar down and leaped to one side, with his sword drawn as the door crept open of its own accord.

A lumpish, towering figure shrank back from the firelight encroaching into the dark passage, flinging up one misshapen and massive arm. Two reddish eyes glared over the gnarled forearm, which could not hide all the swollen dark masses encrusting the creature's skull. Rags fluttered in a crude parody of dress, and a soiled dark cloak was flung over the stooped shoulders. The jotun bared a mouthful of distorted fangs in a hideous snarl, venturing a tentative swat at the glowing end of Thurid's staff which held him at bay. He didn't come too close to it, and shuffled a step backward as Thurid moved closer.

'Get out of Fangelsi, wizard,' the Flayer growled. 'I will destroy you!'

Raudbjorn's vast bulk suddenly lurched into the passage from the main hall, his eyes fixed on the jotun. The Flayer turned with a furious snarl to face this new enemy. Slowly Raudbjorn scythed his halberd through the air, baring his teeth in an anticipatory smile.

'Time to die, jotun!' Raudbjorn rumbled, taking another step forward.

Leifr saw their opportunity, with the jotun trapped in the passage between them. He twisted past Thurid and plunged into the passageway.

'We can take him, Raudbjorn,' he called. 'Don't let him back away. We'll keep him between us.'

'You'll do nothing of the kind!' retorted Gedvondur's voice, and a burst of repelling force caused Leifr to stagger backward, through the doorway.

The Flayer sized up Raudbjorn and the snarling troll-hounds a moment, then turned and charged for the open door, rushing past Leifr so near that he was almost knocked off his feet.

'Blast it, Thurid!' Leifr raged. 'Why didn't you let us have a chance at him? I didn't know you were such a faint-hearted old woman! You can do all the pottering and mumbling around that wretched tower you like, but you won't allow us to fight the Flayer!'

'Our investigations come first,' Gedvondur's voice replied. 'You can wait for your part!' Thurid shoved Leifr back into the kitchen by raising one hand and impelling him with an invisible force.

Hogni and Horgull slammed shut the door, bolted it, and barred it with their bodies. Scowling silently at Leifr and Thurid, they stood and panted like trapped animals.

Gedvondur's hand slipped inside Thurid's sleeve and crawled out underneath his cloak. Gedvondur's mask vanished, leaving Thurid swaying on his feet, like a tree about to topple. Thurid's eyes rolled, then he blinked several times and shook his head.

'Incredible,' he gasped in his own voice, speaking more to himself than the others, as if his mind were racing far ahead. 'I've never seen such a creature. I'd swear it was human from its voice and manner.'

'It's not human,' Hogni said. 'It's a jotun.'

Thurid sifted the air with his fingers, his eyes alight with a questing gleam. 'Yes, there are traces of the human

201

in its influence, but those traces are almost subverted by something else more ancient and evil. This is a creature possessed, and that thing in the tower is to blame. Hogni, you must tell me all you know about the curse.'

Hogni almost smiled. 'If I told you, you would be bound here by the curse of Slagfid as much as we are. Leave that tower alone, wizard.'

'I agree!' Leifr snapped. 'Let's go after the Flayer! You do remember Djofull's geas, don't you?'

'Hang the geas!' Thurid flared. 'This curse is far more important! An unknown force has issued me a direct challenge, and I intend to respond. I'm going to break this curse, without slaying any jotuns, and without sending poor Ketil to his doom. You're a nithling to tolerate such an unreasonable demand, Hogni – and a murderer if you go through with it.' He glowered around the silent kitchen, his eyes coming to rest upon Ketil, who moaned and rocked miserably in his chair. Syrgja moved in front of him protectively, folding her arms across her chest as a bulwark.

'All your fine talk is worthless,' she spat. 'No one has been able to rid us of that curse for seven hundred years. What makes you think you can?'

'I feel lucky,' Thurid replied loftily.

Leifr was so angry he could barely sleep before the house was stirring again for the morning round of chores. Thurid's high-handedness infuriated him to an almost unendurable degree. Fortunately, Thurid was occupied with sounding out the tower once again that morning and thus was unavailable for argument. As Leifr worked at his share of the morning chores he glowered frequently at the crumbling tower. Mist was creeping out the open door, adding to the unsavory gloom of Fangelsi. The spirit of oppression lay heavily over the homestead. Perhaps it was the overhanging cloud which always hovered over Skera-gil, sealing Fangelsi's narrow valley like a gray lid. Impatiently he thought of the time Thurid was wasting, when he should be searching for jotuns, or finding a way back for Ljosa.

202

His concentration was cut short by the appearance of Hogni and Horgull, coming around a corner of a ruin, and they had Svanlaug with them, walking before them with her head held arrogantly high.

Starkad stepped from the cow byre with a pail of steaming milk and gaped at them in astonishment. Sensing an incipient dispute, he put down the pail and hurried after his brothers. They ignored his questions; their expressions were hard and angry.

'Halloa, wizard!' Hogni's voice bore not the slightest trace of friendliness. 'If you're to stay here meddling with the balance of the elements, you'll have to keep this Dokkalfar witch confined to the house. I won't have any Dokkalfar prowling at will over Fangelsi. I don't know that she isn't a channel for Dokkalfar attacks and blights and more misfortune.'

'I was doing nothing of the sort,' Svanlaug snapped, keeping her face covered. 'I was just getting some exercise. The Dokkalfar of Hraedsla-dalur are as much my enemies as yours. You can't expect to keep me as a prisoner here!'

'We must do as our gracious hosts wish,' Thurid said.

Horgull grunted suspiciously, 'She was in that nasty flying lizard shape. Spying us out, she was.'

'I was trying to be of assistance to Thurid,' she retorted. 'If he succeeds, it will only help you.'

Hogni replied, 'If he succeeds, he'll do it without Dokkalfar help, or not at all. She might well have gone to Djofull to tattle.'

They all stared at her a moment with unfriendly suspicion. Indignantly she blustered, 'I did nothing of the sort. Why would I wish to hurt my own cause and further Djofull's? I want him destroyed.'

'You aren't bound by their geas,' Hogni observed shrewdly. 'Perhaps you were only making sure of your own future. No one likes to be a homeless, lordless wanderer.'

In a cold tone Thurid stated, 'Henceforth, Svanlaug, you will stay in the house where someone can watch you.

203

You shall not venture outside alone.'

'And not at night,' Hogni added, 'especially in her fylgja shape.'

'You'd just as well chain me up like a sheep-killing dog, then!' Svanlaug flared.

'Nay,' Horgull grunted. 'We kill sheep-killers.'

Starkad protested furiously, 'Hogni, she's our guest and you can't treat her that way! There's no harm in her, or she wouldn't be with a Ljosalfar wizard.'

Hogni glowered at Starkad menacingly. 'Be silent, you young fool. I'm the master here, in case you've forgotten, and I'll determine who or what is harmful. Now stop your blathering and get back to the cattle. There's work to be done before breakfast, even as poor as you do it.'

Starkad's spine stiffened challengingly as he faced his brother. 'I'll be along,' he said arrogantly, 'when I'm ready.'

Hogni's eyes narrowed and he spat upon the ground before he turned to leave. 'We'll see about that,' he said over one shoulder.

Starkad bestowed an admiring look upon Svanlaug. 'You can go anywhere on Fangelsi you wish and I'll accompany you,' he said. 'The hospitality of Fangelsi and all within it is yours. I, at least, bid you welcome. You won't hear it from anyone else, I fear.'

'You poor lubber,' Svanlaug said, 'you're going to catch it from your brothers. Hadn't you better be careful before you get the thrashing of your life?'

Starkad shrugged with elaborate unconcern. 'I'm used to it,' he said. 'They treat Ermingerd and me like thralls. Worse than thralls, because thralls cost money to replace. I'm nothing but a dog to eat the scraps and catch the kick in the ribs.'

'I'm beginning to understand how you feel about this place,' Svanlaug said, still glaring after Hogni and Horgull venomously. 'Those two are up to some evil, or they wouldn't be so particular about being spied upon. They took a sledge up Skera-gil this morning, Leifr. I saw them coming back.'

'What of it?' Leifr asked, still suspicious of her.

She shrugged her shoulders. 'Maybe nothing. But their manner was strange, as if they were guilty of something. They were certainly angry when they caught me watching.'

Leifr looked at Starkad. 'What business would they have in Skera-gil?'

Starkad's brow puckered in puzzled thought. 'Nothing that I can think of. There's nothing in Skera-gil except trolls and the Flayer.'

Leifr thought of Ermingerd's ritual offering to the jotun, wondering if perhaps Hogni and Horgull had made a similar conciliatory offering.

Midway through the rather silent and gloomy breakfast, Starkad suddenly put down the spoon he had been wielding with such gusto and looked toward the chimney corner. Ketil's old black chair stood empty.

'Where's Uncle Ketil?' Starkad demanded sharply.

Syrgja did not hesitate in her service of the porridge, and Hogni and Horgull kept their eyes lowered, not pausing in their steady pace with knife and fork. Ermingerd flashed Starkad one mute glance, her eyes bright with danger, making Leifr think of a wary deer stalked by hunters.

'Gone,' Syrgja said in a guarded tone.

'Gone where?' Starkad demanded suspiciously. 'He can't go anywhere. What have you done with him?'

Hogni raised his eyes, loaded with menace. 'Nothing that's not for his own good, and the good of us all.'

Starkad shoved back his chair and stood up. 'What have you done with Uncle Ketil?' he repeated, his eyes blazing. 'Have you taken him off in the fells and abandoned him to die at the hands of the jotuns? It would be something like your cowardly hearts would enjoy!'

'Mind your tongue, you!' Syrgja exclaimed.

Ignoring her, Starkad flung himself away from the table and crossed the room in three long strides to seize his cloak. 'I know you've been planning to get rid of him, so you'll be the undisputed master here, but I won't allow you to do this. I'm going to find him!'

'Sit down, you young fool!' Hogni thundered, rising to his feet. 'We haven't given Uncle Ketil to the jotuns! If not for these strangers, I'd make you smart for that accusation!'

'Where is he then?' Starkad still held his cloak ready.

Hogni growled, 'We've locked him up in a place he can't get out of. If we don't, he'll take himself into the fells and die. He's in the granary. If you don't mend your ways and watch your tongue, you'll spend some more time there yourself.'

Syrgja raised her head. 'It might be a good idea,' she said acidly, 'the way he's been making himself a fool over that Dokkalfar woman. Bah! That I should live to see the day one of our enemies eats at my table!' She darted a venomous look toward Svanlaug.

'Then you won't,' Svanlaug said, rising and stalking away. 'I've never cared for enmity as a sauce for my food.'

Starkad glowered. 'Now you're insulting guests at your table, as well as keeping your own brother in the granary like a prisoner.'

Syrgja spoke bitterly. 'This is what comes of taking strangers in. I was never in favor of it!'

'Worse luck might have come from turning them away,' Hogni said. 'Particularly when you're dealing with a wizard.'

Thurid inclined his head in a dignified nod. Both his own hands were occupied with knife and cup, and Gedvondur's hand was striking a natural pose, holding a fold of cloth across his chest. To all appearances, Thurid possessed three hands. In Gedvondur's voice he replied, 'And turning away two wizards is worse luck yet.'

'What about Uncle Ketil?' Starkad demanded. 'You shouldn't lock him up like an animal.'

'You should be treating him for his dementia as well as his disease,' Svanlaug volunteered, 'not locking him away out of your sight. I'm a healer, and I've offered to help you. His misery is your fault, old woman.'

They surveyed each other in taut silence. Then Syrgja said, 'I don't want your unclean Dokkalfar magic touching my brother. I'm sure he'd rather suffer than be cured by you – as if there were a cure for his disease.'

'Dementia is often caused by harmful influences,' Svanlaug said, 'and I can feel rivers of evil influence flowing through Fangelsi. Some of it even comes from you, the blackest and most hopeless of despair. And look at your hands, how swollen they are. You're suffering from the same strange disease as Ketil, in its early stages.'

'No, I'm not!' Syrgja exclaimed, hastily covering her knuckles with her shawl. 'You're poking and prying where you're not wanted, you Dokkalfar witch! You've got no business seeing these things! People are entitled to their secrets, without everyone meddling around and offering useless advice! This is my house, and I'll run it as I see fit, without your help!'

'Very well,' Svanlaug said with asperity. 'Let your mistakes be on your head and not mine.'

Syrgja's breast rose and fell in ragged gasps as she turned to Hogni once more, with pleading in her eyes. 'You'll look after Ketil well, won't you? He may be ill, but he's still clever. You can't take your eyes off him for a moment, or he's out the door. One day he's going to escape and go into those fells. You've put a good stout lock on the granary door?'

'Hush, aunt,' Hogni warned. 'All is well with your brother. He's more content where there's no disturbance. We'll bring him out, once these strangers are gone. He isn't the best of company.'

'You won't let him escape?' Syrgja demanded.

'Even if it means keeping him locked up in the granary until the last,' Hogni said soothingly.

Horgull grunted, 'We couldn't stop Uncle Thorkell.'

His words produced a frozen silence, with Starkad standing in the middle of it, looking in confusion from one

207

of his relatives to the next. None, not even Ermingerd, met his puzzled gaze. Leifr suddenly felt a powerful negative surge of influence surrounding the table, as if many of those present were silently willing Starkad to be silent and sit down. Subsiding into his seat once more, Starkad fell to eating and remained silent for the rest of the meal.

After Hogni and Horgull disappeared with a pony and sledge, Starkad's spirits expanded noticeably, inducing him to abandon all thoughts of his regular work.

'There's a den of trolls in the fourth pasture we've been trying to get rid of for years,' he said to Leifr, his eyes shining with anticipation. 'Could those hounds of yours dig them out? We've tried smoke, water, rocks, and spells, but nothing discourages them. If anything, our attempts make them all the more insolent.' Seeing Leifr's glance in Syrgja's direction, Starkad added hastily, 'I won't get into trouble. Getting rid of the trolls will be a good job of work for the day.' Then he added hopefully, 'And perhaps Raudbjorn could come with us. I'd like to see him use that halberd on some trolls.'

Leifr was glad enough to leave the house, although Svanlaug glowered at him with betrayal in her eyes.

Of Thurid there was no sign, except clouds of mist seeping from the windows of the tower, so they departed without disturbing him. Starkad insisted on carrying along an assortment of shovels and prying bars, taken rather furtively from the disused main hall.

As they departed, taking a circuitous course to avoid surveillance from the house, they passed the granary where Ketil was confined. Starkad's expression darkened as he paused outside the door and examined the lock.

'Uncle Ketil!' he called, rattling the door slightly. 'It's Starkad. Is there anything you want? I put a candle on the beam by the window last time I was here. You won't have to sit in the dark, at least. Uncle Ketil, can you hear me?' He tapped at the door but he was unable to elicit any response. 'He's probably asleep,' he said to Leifr. 'He's hard of hearing since the disease took over. The growths are over his ears.'

'He might not appreciate being disturbed,' Leifr said warily. Ketil was one of the worst curmudgeons he had seen, but Starkad's concern over his uncle was indeed touching. If Hogni had possessed a grain of such concern, there would have been no thought of turning Ketil over to the jotun.

The fourth pasture was a rocky one, and mostly taken up with barrow mounds and ship rings around the graves of vikings. Raudbjorn gazed around and grumbled uneasily as he trudged along in the rear.

'Thief-taker legs made for horse-riding,' he grunted, puffing and pop-eyed from the long climb uphill. 'Not walking.'

'This is a barrow field, Starkad,' Leifr protested at last, when they had proceeded into the thick of barrows. 'You can't go digging up your ancestors' graves just to get at some trolls.'

'The trolls have been digging around here for years,' Starkad said, 'and nothing dreadful has happened to them, as luck would have it. See that big mound? That's where they are. All we have to do is climb down into the first room, and open the way far enough to let the hounds into the next room, and that's the end of the trolls. We'll kill the ones that get past them, and the sun will kill the ones that get past us.'

It seemed reasonable to Leifr, so they set to work opening the barrow. The trolls had found a narrow way past the fallen lintels that obstructed the opening, which the three troll-hunters sought to widen with their implements. The hounds assisted the digging by excitedly scratching shallow holes in useless places, shoving their noses into the holes and sniffing and snorting as if they had found something important.

Several times Starkad halted his feverish digging to grope around in the loose dirt for some small artifact. Once he found a gold coin and held it up with a triumphant cry. 'This is Fangelsi gold,' he said, resuming his enthusiastic digging, 'and it's going to help me escape from Fangelsi.'

Leifr leaned on his shovel a moment. 'Are we hunting trolls, or are we robbing a barrow?' he asked guardedly, wondering if Starkad's enthusiasm was rubbing off on him.

'Hunting trolls, of course,' Starkad replied, his voice muffled in the tunnel they were digging. 'It's against the law to rob barrows, but anybody can kill trolls whenever they feel like it. Whatever you find by way of valuables, you can keep. This grave has already been dug up by trolls anyway.'

By the time they reached the first room, they had a small pile of gold and silver coins, ornaments, rings with stones, and glass beads.

'But no bones,' Leifr observed, suddenly aware of the lack of skulls and skeletal fragments. 'I wonder what happened to them. Nobody would take bones, not even trolls.'

Starkad could not have been less interested in the question of the bones. He was the first into the burial vault. The first room reeked of troll occupation, and the trolls had trampled the floor to an almost glassy smoothness. Neither the intended occupant of the barrow, nor his skeleton or his treasures was anywhere in evidence, but his chairs, chests, weapons, and tools had all been put to good use. Smelly raw hides adorned the walls, where ends of horns and antlers had been thrust in to form pegs and hooks for some ragged cloaks and the odd bits of human clothing some trolls liked to flatter themselves with. A crude wooden door about as tall as a man's knees led to the room beyond. When Leifr rapped at it warily, the trolls beyond responded with sinister growls and whimpering voices that sounded enough like human speech to raise gooseflesh.

Starkad ignored the trolls completely and commenced ransacking the room, dumping out the chests and boxes of

210

troll plunder, most of which nobody else would want, but occasionally among the bones and rocks and teeth, Starkad fell upon a piece of gold or silver. His eye glared with the mad light of the treasure seeker, and he even dug up sections of the floor in his search.

'There's nothing here,' he finally announced. 'We'll have to go on to the next rooms.'

Leifr leaned on his shovel. 'Starkad, it's the barrow gold you're after, and not trolls, isn't it?'

'The trolls will certainly suffer for it,' Starkad replied with a raffish grin. 'No one will ever know the difference. If we find some gold while we're digging out trolls, that's no fault of ours. It's Fangelsi gold. It's not like I'm stealing somebody else's gold. We belong together, this gold and I, until I find the means to get myself and Ermingerd away from Skarpsey entirely.'

'What about Jarnvard?' Leifr asked. 'Your plan for taking Ermingerd away might have worked before, but now she might not want to leave.'

Starkad shrugged, his joy fading slightly. 'Well, a jarl or a prince will make her forget Jarnvard soon enough, once we're established as rich people somewhere.' Impatiently he continued, 'Let's get these trolls out of here, or it'll be dark soon and all their friends and relatives are going to come to help them.'

The troll-hounds charged willingly into the next den, resulting in a horrible snarling and screeching. The sounds diminished, and the troll-hounds came out, panting and waving their tails. Kraftig pawed at Leifr, whining expressively, his manner clearly distressed and disappointed. Leifr thrust his lantern cautiously into the next room and saw furnishings similar to the first, and no trolls. A round dark hole in the floor echoed with the faint sounds of troll voices and troll feet scritching on the rock.

'They've got a bolt hole,' Leifr said uneasily. 'It could lead to other dens, and more trolls could be coming up here. I don't see any signs of more barrow loot, Starkad. The trolls probably took it long ago, or perhaps other people did. I think we'd better get out of here.'

Starkad made a hasty sweep of the room and found nothing for his trouble. 'Robbers! Thieves!' he muttered darkly. 'Nothing worth taking is left! I wonder who has our ancestral gold now? Some fat troll king or some of the fine neighbors at Killbeck and Ness and Perlastrond?'

'Better that barrow robbing be kept in the family, I suppose,' Leifr answered wryly.

'All my life I've heard tales of our ancestors' wealth,' Starkad said, 'such as the gold-plated doorposts brought back from a voyage by Hreidarr, one of Slagfid's sons. And there was a silver-covered chair of Slagfid's, and drinking horns made of gold, and bowls and pitchers and urns, all of gold or silver. Saddles and harness covered with silver and gold and jewels. Nothing like that is here now. There's scarcely one gold nail left.'

'No,' Leifr admitted with growing unease. 'Starkad, I hear a lot of trolls down there, and I don't want to be here when they come up. This barrow is robbed already, and I can't say I'm sorry not to claim the privilege.'

The angry mutter of approaching trolls was louder. Leifr and Starkad retreated to the surface and hastily began replacing the stones they had dislodged. Raudbjorn shoved some large boulders into the hole, and Starkad carefully concealed the fresh dirt.

'No sense in announcing what we've done,' he said. 'Even if it was a failure.' He surveyed the small pile of findings with a discouraged sigh.

'Great failure,' Raudbjorn agreed, exchanging a commiserating glance with Kraftig. 'No trolls killed.'

On the way back to Fangelsi, Starkad again chose a devious course to avoid detection. As they passed through a roofless stable near the granary, Starkad stopped and turned around to look at the granary with a curious expression. Dropping his purloined implements, he raced back to the granary, followed by Leifr.

'There's no one in there!' Starkad pounced upon the lock dangling uselessly. Tearing open the granary door he plunged into its darkness and yelled his uncle's name until the house door opened below and a yellow beam of light sliced the twilight.

'Starkad, silence that racket!' Hogni's voice ordered.

'Where's Uncle Ketil?' Starkad bellowed back. 'You've taken him into Skera-gil! You've given him to the jotuns! You've murdered him!'

CHAPTER 14

'Someone left the lock off,' was Hogni's grim verdict, after silencing Starkad and briefly inspecting the granary.

'I brought him his food this morning,' Syrgja said in a shaken voice. 'I made certain I put the lock back on. He's so likely to wander away, imagining things. I wouldn't have left it off.'

Scowling, Horgull scratched his scalp and said in his gloomy voice, 'I brought him more straw for his bed. Maybe I left it off, but I doubt it.'

'We've got to search for him!' Syrgja demanded. 'He might have gone into Skera-gil! Either trolls or jotuns will have him before dawn!'

'You took a sledge up Skera-gil this morning!' Starkad declared furiously, the awful revelation dawning upon him. 'Svanlaug saw you in her fylgja form. Leifr and I saw sledge runner marks at the granary. You've taken him into Skera-gil and abandoned him to die!'

'You must have taken him early this morning,' Syrgja said in a voice that shook with fury. She twisted her reddened hands in her apron. 'Then you returned for breakfast, like black-hearted demons, as if nothing had happened. It's not his time yet. He's not ready to give up this life. We've got to go find him and bring him back. He won't be far, walking on such poor swollen feet. Starkad! You'll go with me to find your uncle. No one else seems to care about the fate of a sick old man.'

'I'll help,' Leifr added with a defiant glower at Hogni and Horgull. 'Locked in a granary is no place for an aged relative, no matter how his wits have strayed.'

'This is a family matter,' Syrgja said. 'Starkad, you

know the direction he takes when he escapes.'

'Aye. Skera-gil,' Starkad said reluctantly.

'Fetch a lantern, it's darkening.'

Hogni glared at his aunt. 'It's a fool's mission,' he said. 'You'll regret it if you bring him back. What is, must be, and you can't go against nature.'

'I can, for a while,' Syrgja replied coldly.

Silently the Grimssons led the way back to the house, leaving Syrgja to stand outside waiting. Thurid scowled like a judge as he seated himself before the fire, his brow knotted with incredulity and wrath. 'I'm straining to believe you didn't have such evil intentions as the youth accuses you of. We shall investigate, and if it appears a crime of this nature has been committed, serious steps will have to be considered. If this is true, your chieftain will receive a complaint against you.'

'You have no proof of any crime,' Hogni said. 'The lock is off, but it wasn't intentional. We took the sledge up Skera-gil this morning to rebuild a gate. There's much you don't know, wizard. Leave it be the way it is.'

'It's the curse of Slagfid,' Horgull said, his voice hoarse and unexpected. 'Skera-gil always draws the old ones to their doom.'

'He wants to go out,' Hogni said. 'Is that worth nothing? Does not a man have that final choice?'

Thurid responded, 'Not when his sanity is in question. If Ketil were in his right mind, he might not want to die. It is something the chieftain judges at the Althing must decide, not us.'

Hogni's eye flashed over Thurid and Leifr and Raud-bjorn. 'You meddle where you have no business,' he said in a deadly tone. 'You don't know what you do, interfering with powers you neither understand nor control.'

By the time Starkad returned to the house with Ketil, it was dark outside and the trolls and fylgjur-wolves had started their nightly chorus. Syrgja and Ermingerd claimed Ketil and led him stumbling into the kitchen, with gratitude and relief in their eyes. Ketil moaned, shaking his head stubbornly, trying to shield his eyes from the light with his hands.

'Skera-gil again,' Starkad said grimly, rubbing the side of his head, where his ear glowed a painful red, 'and he didn't want to come back, not even with the Flayer howling and growling up in the gil.'

Clearly Ketil was in a nasty humor again, clouting at Syrgja and shaking his head when she attempted to poultice his boils. Leifr averted his eyes uneasily; the disease had progressed alarmingly. His hands and face were red and bloated and his manner was more distracted than before. The very sight of strangers so enraged Ketil that Syrgja directed that he be taken to a small storage room in the passageway.

'He's still got his pride,' Syrgja sniffed. 'He doesn't want to be stared at or pitied.'

'The only pity,' Svanlaug replied acidly, 'is the lack of proper healing treatment. That cold and drafty granary is wreaking havoc upon his swollen joints.'

'I'll thank you to mind your own business,' Syrgja snapped, and Ermingerd darted Svanlaug a veiled look of silent apology.

Thurid stood warming himself beside the fire when they gathered for the long-delayed evening meal. Leifr looked at him curiously, noting how the firelight accentuated the thin boniness of Thurid's hands and the raddled appearance of his features. Something seemed to be devouring him from within. Leifr recalled uneasily that Hogni had warned him about being drawn into the Fangelsi curse.

Starkad lowered sullenly from his place at the end of the table when his brothers sat down and began to eat. When the food was placed before him, he stood up and stalked away angrily.

'I can't eat with murderers,' he said defiantly.

Syrgja looked quickly at Hogni and Horgull. 'Be silent, Starkad. You don't know enough to judge your brothers, and you should keep your jaws shut until you do.'

'But I do,' Starkad insisted. 'And so do my friends.

They saw what I saw.' He looked to Leifr for support.

'These outlaws, you mean?' Hogni said, jabbing his knife in Thurid and Leifr's direction. 'Sit down, boy. Their word won't be worth much against the Grimssons. Our ancestor was Slagfid, a man of war and power. I may not be known as a warrior, but word has spread of my power. No one will get through my wards until I'm ready to allow it.' He gazed at Thurid with raptorial intensity.

'Do not attempt to insinuate yourself into my thoughts,' Thurid warned, clipping each syllable. 'My powers are not ordinary Ljosalfar powers. You could unwittingly spring upon yourself some hideous transformation spell, or curse that would travel down the lines of your descendants for centuries to come.'

'Bah!' Hogni said, his challenge vanishing suddenly in a burst of harsh laughter. Syrgja darted him a frightened glance. 'It's too late to frighten me with such talk as that. I have no future to worry about.'

'That may be true, but tomorrow you will release those wards on your borders so Leifr may pass,' Thurid said commandingly.

'Is that a challenge?' Hogni demanded.

'Make of it what you will,' Thurid answered, returning Hogni's angry glower. Thurid turned to Leifr and continued, 'As soon as it's daylight, you're going to ride to Killbeck and tell Jarnvard that I wish to complain against Hogni and Horgull Grimsson, who are plotting the untimely death of their aged and infirm relative. He will be warned that in the event of Ketil's death, he is to suspect the working of Ketil's nephews.'

Leifr nodded, and Hogni responded with a thin smile.

'You're forgetting my wards,' he said. 'No one gets through them without my permission.'

'I think I can break your wards easily enough,' Thurid replied disdainfully.

'And I think not,' Hogni answered. 'I'll let you go out gladly, but you won't get into Fangelsi again. Perhaps you don't mind trading the penalties of Djofull's geas for the

217

satisfaction of saving Ketil from the jotuns. It would also be childishly simple to summon him to take you off our hands. I don't want to do that, but be careful not to force my hand, Thurid. You see before you a desperate Alfar who has absolutely nothing to lose. But you have much to lose in a battle over such a small matter.'

Thurid stared back at him a moment, then conceded the battle with an impatient toss of his hand. 'I suppose it's true we have nothing but the suspicion of your guilt, so far,' he admitted grudgingly.

'That lock didn't come off by accident,' Syrgja added to the argument, her bony arms crossed defensively as her bleak scowl dwelt upon Hogni.

'Make of it what you will,' Hogni said coldly, and began setting up the pieces for a chess game.

Svanlaug swooped out of the shadows, abandoning her eavesdropping for a direct attack. 'Thurid, you aren't going to let him frighten you, are you?' she demanded. 'If you don't do something, he's going to murder his poor old uncle! Are you as coldhearted as he is?'

'It may surprise you to learn that we are not on particularly firm ground,' Thurid said pompously, after a moment of silent conferral with Gedvondur, perching on his shoulder. 'I shall allow this attempt to pass this time. But if there is another, I fear we shall be forced to act.'

He strode up and down the room a few times, ignoring the smoldering stares fixed upon him from Leifr and Svanlaug both.

Leifr glowered in particular at Gedvondur, wishing Svanlaug had never brought the hand out of Ulfskrittinn. The old Thurid at best was often a blustering fool, but Gedvondur's powers lent him an ominous aura of authority which Leifr despised. Thurid consulted with no one except Gedvondur. All Leifr's instincts revolted against the idea of Gedvondur whispering words and ideas and spells into Thurid and compelling him to act as Gedvondur wished.

'I shall retire to the tower,' Thurid said at last.

'Gedvondur tells me we have some interesting work to do. Don't expect me to return very soon.'

'I'll walk out with you,' Leifr said, reaching for his cloak. 'And I want to talk to you, not Gedvondur, so put him in your pocket or your satchel.'

'I shan't do that,' Thurid answered as he closed the door behind them and followed Leifr into the chilly center hall, lit by one dim oil lamp. 'You can talk to me. He doesn't always involve himself in my conversations. I find him a great source of confidence and inspiration.'

Leifr followed Thurid to the tower, where he entered with great suspicion, peering around at the dank, cluttered interior as Thurid lit a fire and some lamps.

'Now what is it you wish to speak to me about?' Thurid seated himself in an old chair, with Gedvondur crawling around the back, seeming to peer at Leifr slyly over one or the other of the wizard's shoulders.

'Didn't we come here to kill jotuns?' Leifr demanded. 'Have you forgotten the geas completely? We should be plotting how to kill the Flayer, instead of your mumbling around in this tower while the rest of us do nothing. You should worry about Ketil, and what his relatives are trying to do to him. And what about Ljosa? I don't think anything you're doing in here has the least relation to solving the spell that's holding her.'

Thurid was making a masterful attempt to conceal his temper, and the forces it might release. 'I am dealing with these matters in the way I see best fit.' He spat each word with elaborate emphasis. 'I've warned you, Leifr, we must go slowly here and very cautiously. You must stop haranguing me about everything you suppose I'm doing wrong. It's true, I've diverged somewhat from our original purpose, but it's dreadfully essential right now that I do so. Gedvondur has discovered astonishing things already about Fangelsi and Slagfid's heirs. There's a terrible power lurking here, Leifr, worse than any jotun.'

'But that's not what we're at Fangelsi for,' Leifr protested. 'Gedvondur's led you off on a wild-goose chase.

If you weren't so greedy for power, you'd know I'm right, Thurid. Since you started listening to him most of the time, you've changed. You're getting as stubborn and bad-tempered as he is.'

'Why can't you just be quiet like Raudbjorn and stay out of my way?' demanded Thurid, rapidly losing his temper. 'Your grasp of this matter is so slight as to be almost nil! Yet you persist in pestering and interfering!'

'Unlike Raudbjorn, I can think,' Leifr retorted furiously, 'and I can see you're making mistakes. You're going too slow, Thurid. It's going to be spring equinox before you know it, and Djofull will have us. Look at yourself, and see what Gedvondur is doing to you. You don't sleep, you eat very little, you look like a corpse, and you're completely obsessed with this filthy curse, which makes you absolutely useless to us. If you don't do something about the geas, I will.'

'You'll mind your business, which is staying out of my business, and I'll mind mine, which is breaking Slagfid's curse,' Thurid replied, with an ominous billowing of his cloak. 'Now if you're finished, why don't you leave so Gedvondur and I can get to work?'

'One moment more,' Leifr said. 'I want to talk to Gedvondur.'

The hand settled itself companionably on Thurid's shoulder, and Thurid's countenance altered to the smirking lines of Gedvondur's. Gedvondur's voice inquired, 'What is it, Leifr? You're worrying too much about this, you know.'

'I'm concerned about my life and freedom,' Leifr answered in a seething tone, 'and right now you're the biggest obstacle to breaking Djofull's geas. You don't seem to care what your presence does to Thurid's body, nor what Djofull will do if we don't kill the night-farers of Fangelsi. Get out of Thurid and leave him alone, Gedvondur, and let us deal with the jotuns as we ought.'

'Don't force me to lose my patience with you, Leifr,' Gedvondur's harsh voice responded. 'It's bad enough that you require so much of Thurid's attention to keep you out of trouble, but when you go looking for trouble, it's almost more than I can endure. I warn you, don't go digging up any more barrows, and stay away from Skera-gil and the Flayer until you know what you are tampering with. You could destroy what I'm seeking.'

'So you'll do nothing about the geas?' Leifr asked. 'Nor the Flayer? Nor Hogni and Horgull? And Ljosa is to be forgotten entirely?'

'Yes, for the time being,' Gedvondur spat. 'Just wait, Scipling, until your betters tell you what to do!'

Leifr's eyes narrowed as a cold and rising rage gripped him, showing him with merciless clarity what he must do. He nodded, apparently acquiescing to Gedvondur's commands, and pretended to turn toward the door. Then like a cat he whirled and pounced on Thurid's shoulder. In one fluid move he hurled the hand into the fire.

Thurid rose up with a screech and would have plunged into the coals with his hands if Leifr had not blocked him. However, in the scuffling and swearing that ensued, Gedvondur scuttled out of the coals before Leifr could stop him. Belatedly he grabbed a stave of wood and tried to thrust the hand back into the fire, but Thurid swelled up for a mighty effort and rebuffed him with a shout, sending him stumbling across the room. Fortunately he found the door at his back, in case he needed it.

Gedvondur scuttled up Thurid's arm to his shoulder, looking quite singed and blackened. Thurid glared at Leifr in speechless rage, one half-extended hand twitching as if he struggled with his baser desires for retaliation.

'Leifr!' Thurid gasped, turning his attention to Gedvondur and brushing some of the soot off him gently. 'Do you know what you've done?'

'Less than I'd hoped,' Leifr grunted, eyeing Gedvondur rather apprehensively nonetheless.

'You'd better get out of here while you can!' Thurid said. 'He's going to be furious!'

'It's all right,' Gedvondur's voice said with surprising

calm. 'It's what you might expect. I don't blame you for trying to destroy me, Leifr. Your crude methods were ineffectual, but I was able to discern your intent.'

'All I intend is to kill the jotuns,' Leifr replied in a low and deadly tone. 'Then I want Ljosa brought back.'

'All in good time!' Gedvondur said impatiently. 'You and I are working for the same goals from different directions, with different methods. Don't flummox up what Thurid and I are trying to do, Leifr. Even if you don't understand it, you must do as we ask.'

Leifr shook his head. 'I won't talk to you any longer, Gedvondur. Let Thurid come back.'

Gedvondur's expression vanished, and Thurid gazed back at Leifr in great disapproval. 'Leifr, don't draw battle lines between us,' he warned. 'You can't win against Gedvondur, and I have no desire to turn my back on him. Why can't you just cooperate, you miserable outlaw?'

'Why can't you tell me what you're doing?' Leifr countered suspiciously. 'If it had anything to do with the jotuns or Ljosa, I'd understand it. But you and Gedvondur both know it doesn't. Thurid, I can't sit here and do nothing all winter, counting the final days of my freedom. I understand hunting and killing night-farers, and that's what I'm going to do, with or without your help.'

He whirled and stalked away from the tower, with a final admonitory glower over one shoulder. Thurid glared after him, his arms folded across his chest.

'Then you're on your own,' Thurid declared. 'See what will happen without me to advise you. Just don't get yourself killed right away. I'm going to need someone to use that sword.'

Leifr did not speak to Thurid for the next two days – not that Thurid noticed or cared. He was spending long hours in the tower, and longer hours in the evening engrossed in his vellums, manuscripts, and a growing disorderly heap of random objects in the far end of the kitchen, which Syrgja eyed with barely concealed loathing.

Leifr hated the long hours of confinement after sun-down, with Thurid and Gedvondur rummaging and mumbling over their incomprehensible junk while Hogni and Horgull buried themselves in a game of chess. Ermingerd usually sat by the light, sewing, or often gazing into the fire with her clear gray eyes, miles away. Syrgja bathed Ketil's swollen red hands in a basin of some reeking infusion, re-bandaged his feet, and applied compresses to the sores on his face when he would allow it. Svanlaug watched her efforts with critical disdain.

'She's got no more notion of healing than a cow does of dancing,' she muttered angrily to Leifr, pausing in her restless catlike prowling of the house.

Thurid was occupied as usual with his vellums, rune wands, scrolls, and moldering books, poring over them attentively, with Gedvondur dragging things forward or shoving them impatiently away and pointing out lines of interesting script.

Syrgja glared at Gedvondur, shivering with indignation and disgust. At last she declared, 'You may defame my house with your spells and your influences, but I'll thank you not to allow that dead hand to prance around on my table. There are limits to hospitality, and dead hands are well beyond them!'

Thurid glanced up, disoriented and disconcerted for a moment, then his choler started rising. 'You're frightfully particular, considering your situation,' he said frigidly. 'I'm doing my best to relieve your life of this dreadful burden of jotuns, and you deny me the use of your kitchen table. I've suffered insults and abuse at many finer houses than this, my good woman. After tomorrow I won't trouble you with my presence any longer.'

'You're leaving?' Syrgja asked hopefully.

'No, I'm establishing my laboratory in the tower. The only personages I'll disturb there are the ones who have been disturbing Fangelsi for seven centuries.'

'Not the tower,' Syrgja said. 'You'll go mad if you stay in there long.'

'Why not the tower?' Hogni interjected calmly, not taking his eyes off his game. 'A good wizard should be able to control those influences. If he can't, then we're better off without him. By all means, yes, the tower.'

'Thank you for your kindness,' Thurid said witheringly, gathering up his possessions and stuffing them into his satchel. 'Your faith in your deliverance is inspiring. You'll eat those words one day.'

'And you'll break yourself on the Fangelsi curse,' Hogni said companionably. 'All your arrogance will dissipate like gas, and you'll become one of the lesser-known entities haunting that tower. You'll likely take the rest of us down with you, but none of us here have any prospects for long and happy lives anyway, so we shouldn't mind. If there's any assistance you require, by all means call upon me to aid you, Thurid. After all, I was once a bright and hopeful student of magic, when I thought this curse could be broken. I don't know that I've harmed it any, and perhaps I've made it worse in unknown convoluted ways, but there's no one who knows more about it than I do.'

Thurid snapped his satchel shut, his gaze smoldering. 'I shall let you know if I need your help,' he replied in a tone that implied such a remote probability as to render the idea stillborn.

In the morning, after the usual sullen breakfast, Thurid retreated to the tower with specific orders not to disturb him, and the Fangelsi family separated for their various duties. Leifr elected to accompany Starkad on a hopeless search for the sheep the Flayer had scattered in his last attack. They trudged across the frozen dooryard toward the outbuildings. Crossing through the falling walls of a roofless stable, Starkad approached a small square structure which leaned despondently against the cow byre. A thin wisp of smoke from an ungenerous fire inside crept out of a hole in the roof. Starkad looked at the small building with loathing.

'The granary. They put Uncle Ketil in here this morning,' Starkad said angrily, giving the lock a shake.

224

'With a different lock this time, to keep the rest of us out. Just like Uncle Thorkell, and the jotuns took him, too, or so they said.'

Leifr approached the door and listened while Starkad knocked and called out to his uncle. 'There's a candle on the beam over the window, uncle,' he called. His answer was a loud, angry bellow of wrath and a restless rumbling of some heavy object like a chair. A large rusty lock held the bar down against intruders, and the door showed signs of recent patching.

Leifr asked, 'What happened to your uncle Thorkell?'

'He was sick, like Ketil,' Starkad replied. 'It's a disease that happens from generation to generation in our family, with swellings and knots and lumps. It's painful, and toward the end whoever has got it goes mad. Uncle Thorkell got it. He suffered with it for years. Each year he got more twisted and more crazy. Then last year he broke out of the house and disappeared. It was the last we saw of him. It was about the same time as the Flayer started plaguing the settlements hereabout. That beast must have killed my uncle, and yet my aunt and brothers won't hear of my going after it and killing it. Did you ever hear of such foolishness? I suppose they don't think I'm able enough.'

'Perhaps they fear for your safety,' Leifr said.

'You're mistaken,' Starkad said, his eyes flashing. 'There's no love lost in this family. They'd soon I'd never been born. Many's the time my aunt has told me that. I think they fear I'll find out the truth about Uncle Thorkell. I think they took him away into the fells and murdered him themselves and blamed it on the jotuns, so he'd be no further bother to them. That's what they plan to do with Uncle Ketil, and anyone else who gets in their way. I think they know where that gold of Slagfid's is hidden, and they want it all for themselves. Syrgja, Ermingerd, and I might all be killed to satisfy their greed.'

'That's a serious accusation,' Leifr said uneasily. 'One which we all may be happier if we don't prove.'

225

'Do you think I like coming from a family of murderers?' Starkad cried. 'If I don't do something about it, then I'm no better than they are. I don't want to share their guilty secrets. It's not a burden I wish to carry with me for the rest of my life. I don't want to be tainted by my family's secrets.'

Leifr touched Fridmarr's carbuncle, as was his uneasy habit. 'I don't blame you for that. If I had brothers like Hogni and Horgull, I'd want to get away, too. Thurid's no better when it comes to allowing me any freedom. I don't know why everyone insists upon being so cautious, when the way is straightforward ahead. Kill the jotuns, and all our troubles will be ended. You'd think these old fools could see that.'

'That I can attest to,' Starkad said, with a crooked, irrepressible grin. 'Say now, wouldn't you like to go with me in the fell to look for the sheep? I daresay it would be better than staying down here and looking at my aunt Syrgja. Her name means "sorrow," you know, and she tries to live up to it by making everybody miserable.'

Leifr agreed heartily.

Starkad and Leifr found the strayed sheep and penned them at the little shepherd's hut near the top of the fell. It was a lonely and barren area. The wind coming down from the top of the fell gusted with a wintery breath and carried with it weird echoes from the icy caverns of the glaciers of Skera-gil above.

'Now I will show you something,' Starkad said, pointing his chin toward a faint path running southward. They followed the path to a rock cairn, where it abruptly ended. The skull of a horse stood upon a post in grim warning.

'Beyond this mark we cannot go,' Starkad said. 'Nor can the fylgjur-wolves on the other side pass this mark into our lands. This is the farthest ward of Fangelsi. From here you can get a better look at Skera-gil.'

Skera-gil was a great, deep gorge splitting the side of the fell, as if a giant axe had cloven it to its roots. The runoff from the glaciers glazed the jagged black sides of the gorge with frozen waterfalls. Even at midday, Leifr could hear the distant grunts and growls of trolls among the gloomy crags, particularly where the mist hung in defiance of the wind and pale sun, like banners of an undefeated enemy. The troll-hounds pricked their ears and licked their chops, stretching out their forepaws and prancing around Leifr eagerly, waiting for the command to hunt.

Starkad gazed into the deep maw of the great ravine, gripped with the endless fascination of youth for the forbidden.

'My uncle Thorkell once told me there's a cave down there called Slagfid's Ban. He said that's where Slagfid and his six sons are buried with chests of gold and silver and jewels. Why do you suppose they were buried in a cave instead of a barrow mound? Caves are border places – neither above nor below the earth. I wonder if the dead rest quiet there. Perhaps that is why they called the place forbidden.' He shivered with pleasurable dread.

'More likely it was to protect the gold in the graves,' Leifr replied. 'Draugar guard their treasures jealously.'

Nothing could have whetted Starkad's curiosity better than Leifr's cautionary tone.

'I'm not afraid of a lot of dead draugar,' he said with a boastful swelling of his chest. An avaricious gleam fired his eyes as he added in an undertone, 'Do you know what gold and jewels and treasure there must be in that cave? More than enough to get me on a ship away from Skarpsey – and Ermingerd, too. She'd have no lack of dowry then.'

'You'd rob the graves of your own ancestors?'

Starkad shrugged, suddenly becoming sullen. 'You're not going to tell anyone I said such a thing, are you?' he asked suspiciously. 'I was only talking wild. I wouldn't really do such a thing. If I was to, I wouldn't tell anybody, especially those who consider themselves my elders.'

'I'm not on the side of your aunt and brothers,' Leifr said. 'I think you should be allowed to leave Fangelsi and make your fortune how and where you will, as I did, and you should be allowed to waste it, too, as I did.'

Leifr paused a moment to consider that he had not yet reached his twenty-fifth year mark, and all he had to show for it was a Rhbu sword, a bag of ashes from his fallen enemy, Fridmarr's carbuncle, and Gedvondur's hand. Hardly a fortune, in anyone's estimation.

Leifr turned away from his study of the ravine. Something about it did seem to draw him toward its darkness and secrets. Starkad also tore himself away reluctantly.

'We'd better get the sheep started back,' he said with a dreary sigh. He looked at the hounds and back at Leifr with a sudden burst of cunning insight. 'There's even a reward for the Flayer. He gets past Hogni's wards sometimes and over into the other settlements and rips around like a mad thing. They've been trying to get him, and he's killed a few of them. Jarnvard's the one putting up the reward. A hundred marks in silver and a pile of red cloth. Wouldn't Ermingerd in a red cloak and a red hood turn their heads around? All I'd take would be enough to buy our passage, and a little more besides. We could catch the Flayer, I'm sure of it, with these hounds. The jotun's lair is up there somewhere,' Starkad whispered. 'I've hunted for it a thousand times. I know those hounds of yours can follow his scent right to the cave, with all that treasure.'

Kraftig, Frimodig, and Farlig caught his enthusiasm, as if they knew when their prowess was being discussed. They wrinkled up their lips in appealing grins, capering around Leifr in ecstasy. As if on cue, they all threw back their heads and howled, an eerie cry that echoed through Skera-gil, silencing the rumblings of the trolls. After a stunned moment, the trolls began to bellow and grunt questioningly across the gil.

'If we don't catch the Flayer, I don't think anyone else ever will,' Leifr said bitterly. 'No one at Fangelsi dares stir beyond their doorstep – or that tower. I came here to hunt jotuns, and that's what I'm going to do. What would your

228

'family say to such an undertaking?' Leifr asked guardedly, trying to resist Starkad's contagious enthusiasm, which was not unassisted by subtle compelling Alfar powers, he was certain.

'They wouldn't approve it,' Starkad answered. 'They seem to believe it's their fate to be persecuted, but I'm with you, Leifr. We'll stride up to Jarnvard's hall tomorrow and throw the Flayer's head on his doorstep. Ha, wouldn't that prove to the settlements of Hraedsla-dalur that Starkad of Fangelsi-hofn is a man!'

Leifr followed Starkad's gaze to the dark ravine that cleft the white fell. The cloud of mist oozing over the face of the fell perpetually obscured much of it from the rays of the sun, thus enhancing its mystery.

'We'll do it,' Leifr said, his resolve not unmixed with a certain degree of spite against Thurid and all his precautions.

'And what will Thurid say?' Starkad asked delicately. 'He seemed as opposed to hunting the Flayer as Hogni.'

'Thurid and I have come to an understanding, of sorts,' Leifr answered with a wry grimace. 'He'll go after the curse in his own roundabout way, while I deal with the jotuns. Hogni's not going to be pleased, but Hogni's standing in the way of both of us. I daresay he can't watch us both at the same time, particularly since he's gone to Killbeck right now.'

CHAPTER 15

By midday they reached the highest gate in the last pasture of Fangelsi, and passed beyond into the wild land unbounded by Hogni's wards. At the bottom of Skera-gil, a gate was formed between two upright pillars of stone, and Hogni's mark was emblazoned on the gate. The carrion crow warned them back with sensations of danger and fear. Leifr halted in dismay, but Starkad pulled a rune stick from his belt pouch. Reading it over several times, he spoke the prescribed words for lifting the ward.

'I stole this from Hogni's satchel long ago,' Starkad explained with an ingenuous smile. 'Going into Skera-gil is strictly forbidden, but I've managed to get around Hogni since I was quite small. You won't mention it when we get back?'

'I'm no fool, Starkad,' Leifr replied. The enticement of curiosity and the spice of the forbidden were strong in his blood as he stood looking ahead at the sheer black cliffs and skarps of Skera-gil. The troll-hounds' ears pricked eagerly, catching the faint sounds of trolls grumbling among the crags.

In the gloomy twilight of Skera-gil, they found a path at the bottom, running alongside a rocky stream bed. Starkad viewed the surrounding crags with interest, pointing out several small caves.

'But none of them is Slagfid's Ban,' he said. 'I believe it will be much larger. Perhaps it is what this path leads to. It seems a well-beaten path. That's a sign that the Flayer uses it, perhaps.' Much of the bravado had left his tone, and his eyes traveled around nervously.

Leifr looked around uneasily at the towering crags and

long black shadows, where the odd troll flitted just at the tail of his glance. The Flayer could be hiding almost anywhere, watching them. It was a flesh-crawling thought.

A rough trail led them into the upper end of Skera-gil, where an icy stream plunged over a fall, casting up a screen of mist and giving the earth and rocks a wet sheen. The higher they climbed into the gorge, the steeper were the walls, the narrower the way, and the less the light that filtered down to the bottom. High above, the wind moaned through the skarps, and rocks fell bouncing from ledge to ledge, while the trolls snickered from their hiding places. The path they followed was well traveled, scored with myriads of three-toed-troll tracks. The troll-hounds panted and whined with desperate eagerness to go hunting their natural prey, which was in so much abundance around them, but Leifr commanded them to stay close, where they could cause no disturbances. He had never felt such oppressive gloom; the farther they went, the heavier his legs seemed, and the more reluctant he was to continue. The oppression grew to a condition of panicky fear, which he had trouble concealing.

'You feel it, too,' Starkad said, looking around with a shaky laugh. 'We're not wanted here. The nearer you get, the worse it feels. I think it's a spell of Hogni's. The treasure cave is up here somewhere. I feel it. I've never been this near to it.'

'It could be the jotun warning us away from his cave,' Leifr growled. 'Starkad, let's go back. You can see where the ravine ends up ahead. I don't think there is any treasure cave in Skera-gil. It's just the jotun, trying to keep us out. Look how the dogs are tracking. It's a fresh scent – too fresh for just the two of us. We need Raudbjorn, if it comes to a fight.'

'Let the dogs go. If they can't find the jotun's scent, we'll go back.'

The hounds loped ahead eagerly. A rockfall plugged the gorge with a jagged jumble of broken rock, but, to Leifr's astonishment, the hounds did not stop for it, nor did they go over it. They simply plunged into it and vanished.

'It's only an illusion of Hogni's!' Starkad exclaimed. He hurled himself at the rockfall, and immediately stumbled and slithered down again, rebuffed.

'If it's an illusion, why does it look and feel so real?' Leifr inquired uneasily. 'And how did the dogs run through it as if it weren't there?'

'Animal minds are almost impossible to work spells upon. They can't reason themselves into believing something that isn't real, as people can. We'll climb over this thing,' Starkad said determinedly.

'That would take all day,' Leifr objected, 'and it'll get dark early in Skera-gil. We'd better go back and wait at the mouth for the jotun to appear.'

'Forget the jotun. It's gold we're after,' Starkad said, starting up the steep side of the rockfall, and Leifr had no choice but to follow. The rocks felt more like solid ice to his touch, and they began to steam where he stood. Backing away, he watched in awe as the rocks were gradually engulfed in tendrils of creeping vapor. Groaning, grinding sounds came from deep within as the rocks creaked and shifted.

'I knew it was a concealing spell,' Starkad whispered, pulling Leifr backward. 'Hogni's illusion can't bear the touch of a Scipling foot. You must have iron nails in the soles of your boots. What else do you have that's iron?'

'A table knife – and this.' Leifr drew his old Scipling sword from its sheath at his back, and its metal glowed with a sinister blue light. 'It has no powers, but the iron itself is often enough to discourage attackers.'

Starkad drew back, making defensive signs that glowed in midair, his fascinated stare fixed upon the sword. 'So dross in so many ways, you Sciplings,' he murmured, 'yet you handle that cursed metal without harm. Few are the Ljosalfar smiths who deal with iron, and even the Dvergar avoid it. I wonder what it will cost you, as a people, one day in the future. They say it makes men more warlike.'

'Not that I've noticed,' Leifr said, his attention upon the rockfall. The rocks were crumbling now, slithering down in heaps of steaming slush mixed with sand.

Starkad chuckled. 'A clever spell, Hogni, but we've broken it. Now I know we're very near to Slagfid's Ban. My brothers thought to have all the treasure to themselves. Won't they be angry when they have to share it with us?'

Beyond the rockfall, the dark narrow way had nearly reached the heart of the fell, and the cliffs towered overhead, blotting out the light of the sky. In the silent, perpetual twilight loomed the dark maw of the cave. Leifr and Starkad crouched behind a boulder, scarcely breathing as they stared at it. Though it was a natural opening, there were signs that man and his tools had worked upon it to alter it to his purposes. A massive sill and lintels still stood firm, but the heavy door lay on the ground, torn from its hinges with a violence that still seemed to linger in the gloomy atmosphere. Shreds of pulverized wood littered the ground, whitened with years of exposure, and some desolate splinters still clung to the useless hinges, now corroded with green crystals.

Standing sentinel beside the door was a stout post crowned with a human skull, as a warning to any imprudent enough to approach.

'It's the jotun's cave!' Leifr said, the realization suddenly bursting upon him. 'What better way to defend a treasure than to hide it where the jotuns are!'

Starkad nudged Leifr and rose to a crouching posture to creep up on the mouth of the cave. Long past making a prudent judgment, Leifr followed. His heart no longer thumped with fear and excitement; a calm resignation to his fate had overtaken him and he was determined to push ahead as long as his luck held out. With curiosity and awe, he touched the battered door frame and examined the fallen door, trying to picture what had caused those thousands of frayed dents in the wood. It came to him with an unpleasant shock that the pounding had been done from the inside of the door. Something, or someone, had been trying to get out. From the looks of the door, they had succeeded altogether too well.

'We've found it!' Starkad breathed. 'Slagfid's Ban!'

'The lair of the Flayer,' Leifr murmured, resting his hand upon his sword hilt. 'Today may see the end of your curse and my geas, Starkad.'

'Perhaps so,' Starkad answered in a voice that trembled with fear and eagerness, 'and the beginning of my escape from Fangelsi with Ermingerd, rich as a jarl.'

Starkad paused in the doorway to fumble with one of his belt pouches, withdrawing at last a small purple vial. Uncorking the stopper, he held up the little bottle and said, 'Here's something else I looted from Hogni's satchel.'

Leifr scowled at the vial suspiciously. 'It looks like something a wizard would possess,' he said. 'We don't need that sort of help, Starkad.'

'It's only seeing-drops,' Starkad said. 'You put them into your eyes to see in the dark. Now don't worry about it, it's perfectly safe and much better than candles or dips.'

'This is probably a mistake,' Leifr grumbled, 'but go ahead. Alfar magic might not work on a Scipling.'

Starkad shook a couple of drops in Leifr's eyes, whereupon a ferocious stinging and burning commenced. Leifr shook his head, blinking and rubbing at his running eyes. When he could open them again, he peered into the darkness of the cave and discovered that he could indeed see, just like a cat.

Starkad applied the drops to his eyes, gritting his teeth against the stinging until he could open his eyes and look around. To Leifr's astonishment, his eyes glowed red, and he supposed his own glowed red also.

'No, green,' Starkad replied. 'Because you're not an Alfar, I imagine.'

Leifr and Starkad stepped into the earthy, reeking darkness beyond the threshold, followed by the troll-hounds. Leifr paused to pick up a fresh rib bone, well gnawed – whether human or animal he could not tell. The breath of the cave was fetid and rank with the smell of bones old and new. With the aid of the seeing-drops he noted the green glow of his eyes traveling across the oozing walls and damp floor, well beaten into a descending path. Imagining the feet of the Flayer wearing the path, Leifr touched the sword and found it humming softly beneath his palm.

At his signal, Kraftig, Farlig, and Frimodig took the lead, not straying far ahead, not giving voice to their usual joyous hunting chorus, but trotting along with their ears pricked alertly, heads carried low. Several times they paused at cross tunnels, scenting the faint cave breath, then choosing the way that must lead to the jotun's lair. Underfoot the path became steeper and rougher with a curious regularity that reminded Leifr of stairs, clogged by years of dirt and fallen rock.

Leifr had even more cause to wonder what sort of place this cave was when the hounds paused beside a tall doorway, faced with carven wood, where intricate figures of men and strange beasts looped through one another to form a delicate design like twining vines. The door stood half-open, jammed by detritus and its own rotten swelling. After seeing the underground ruined splendor of Bjartur, Leifr thought he knew what to expect, but he stood aghast, with gooseflesh washing over him as his jumping gaze erratically illuminated the scene beyond.

'A burial chamber!' Starkad whispered, and edged himself forward for a better look around the edge of the door, making shaky signs with his hand against the evil of the restless dead.

Leifr stood his ground, looking within. The green light of his gaze glimmered on dusty gold objects, the rim of a drinking cup, a helm etched with figures, arm rings, and so much more that the eye reeled in confusion. Seven heaps of treasure and dust, Leifr belatedly realized. He stepped further into the room for a closer look, discerning bones among the treasures, skeletal hands still bearing rings, rib cages displaying golden chains, and dusty skulls wreathed in matted hair and golden helms and coronets.

Starkad recovered swiftly from his fright. Crowding behind Leifr he peered around the shadowy room with avarice gleaming in his eyes. 'Look at the gold in here,' he whispered hoarsely. 'This is the fabled wealth of Fangelsi-hofn. I recognize some of these things from old stories. There's the chair and the doorposts, moldering away and waiting for thieves to break in and steal them. I've searched for this place for years.'

'We're not those thieves, Starkad,' Leifr retorted. 'You know what ill luck follows barrow robbers.' But his own heart thrilled with avarice. 'Think of the curses of the dead. Fylgja-draugar will follow you. Whatever you take could be possessed by the draug of its past owner.'

'But these treasures belonged to my ancestors,' Starkad protested. 'It belongs to Fangelsi-hofn. These skeletons belong to ancestors of mine. They wouldn't care if we shared their wealth, would they?'

Leifr took another look around the room. At one time it had been a hall, hung with tapestries and banners, which still hung in dark festoons, preserved from decay by the darkness and the slow-moving air of the underground. None of the designs were familiar Ljosalfar symbols of birds, animals, and other above-ground devices.

Starkad suddenly paused, his hand upon a sledge draped with harness. 'What's this doing here? This is Uncle Thorkell's. This must be one of Hogni and Horgull's secrets. They said Uncle Thorkell was taken and killed by jotuns. But they must have put his burial goods here instead of the barrow mounds. They used his sledge. I'd recognize those harness hames anywhere. His father made them. Gold, they are, and the last precious thing our house possessed.'

Leifr moved a few steps nearer to the sledge, where the gold harness hames twinkled invitingly, among other needful items for the journey to Hel's realm. A bier was made in the sledge, as if a body once had lain there.

'There's no corpse,' he said uneasily.

'Of course not. He was eaten. This is proof of my brothers' evil intentions,' Starkad replied. 'They let the jotuns kill my uncle Thorkell, and they're the ones who robbed the barrows and brought all the valuable things here, hoping to have it all for themselves one day.'

'That's why the barrow we dug up was empty,' Leifr said. 'Didn't you notice there were no bones?'

'I noticed there were no burial goods,' Starkad said, still gazing around the burial vault. 'There, look!' he whispered, his eyes feverishly brilliant as he pointed toward the largest bier, occupying a central position in the vault. Draperies, once sumptuous, now hung in dusty tatters on either side of a large burnished shield, emblazoned with the familiar symbol of the carrion crow. 'It's my ancestor Slagfid, the one who named this cave Slagfid's Ban – Slagfid's Curse. He was as rich as a jarl, they say. Let's see what's on his bier.'

Leifr reached out to detain Starkad, but the youth glided past him with an elusive twist of his shoulders, and Leifr had the uneasy feeling that intervening Alfar magic had prevented him from stopping Starkad.

'Starkad! Wait a moment!' he said in alarm, picking his way after the young Alfar, sidestepping a few scattered bones and rags of grave clothing. He heard Starkad's quick intake of breath and the sound of metal and jewels clattering musically.

'Look at this, Leifr!' Starkad urged in a low tone that vibrated with excitement, and Starkad held up a long jewel-encrusted sword sheath. 'This goes with the sword on our wall, Slagfid's sword. I ought to take it back.'

'You can't! Put it down!' Leifr commanded, loud enough to awaken a faint echo. 'Let's get out of here! Starkad, this is all too strange. You can't even think about taking any of these things.'

Starkad hesitated, a rebellious shadow crossing his face, but Leifr was spared a confrontation with him. The troll-hounds braced themselves in the doorway, growling and bristling, their muzzles pointing down the dark corridor,

237

away from the outer door. Distantly, they heard a groaning, grumbling sound that raised the hair on their necks.

'The Flayer!' Leifr cried, momentarily frozen between the necessity for flight and the lure of the treasure.

The troll-hounds wrinkled back their lips and snarled, with their tails curling against their bellies, fearful, where they had not feared Ognum. A powerful desire to escape overwhelmed Leifr, as if the cave itself were hastily expelling them. He moved toward the passage, followed by Starkad scuffling along with careless clatters of disturbed bones and jingling of gold. When they reached the hallway, they both broke away into ignominious retreat at the same moment, racing as fast as they could go toward the distant doorway, which soon appeared as a less-dark square in the darkness.

Breathless, they burst out of the cave and did not stop to look back until they were well down the ravine and their unaccountable fears had subsided somewhat. Starkad laughed uncertainly and said, 'The Flayer won't be coming out in the daylight to chase us. We found it, Leifr. What do you want to do now?'

'Get back to Fangelsi before someone gets suspicious,' Leifr replied curtly.

'We found Slagfid's treasure,' Starkad went on, his eyes glowing. 'This will be our secret, will it not, Leifr? And there's something else.' He rummaged in his pockets, producing a cascade of small glittering objects – rings with twinkling stones, short chains of gold and silver, medallions, a string of amber and carnelian beads.

Leifr said nothing, feeling the dawning horror of the sight of that forbidden treasure spilled out on the mossy stones, exposed to the pale winter light of day for the first time in seven hundred years. 'This is wrong, Starkad,' he murmured. 'There are going to be consequences.'

'Not if we keep our mouths shut about it.' Starkad gathered it up quickly and stuffed it into his pockets and pouches. Looking at Leifr searchingly, he asked almost wistfully, 'I can count on you to keep this secret, can't I, Leifr? You understand why I'm doing this, don't you?'

Leifr sighed and nodded. 'You have my word, Starkad.'

As they returned to Fangelsi, Leifr battled against the feeling that he had done something dreadfully wrong and that he felt a need to slink past the old tower. To prove his own courage, he deliberately turned out of the path to pass closer to it. Just looking at it filled him with uneasy revulsion, and Starkad must have felt the same, suddenly halting and staring back at the tower. Gazing at it with the traces of Hogni's seeing-drops still in his eyes, Leifr could see rippling, colorless waves of something coming off it, shimmering as did hot rocks on a summer day.

Thurid came out of the tower suddenly, striding along at an impetuous gait with frequent glances over his shoulder at the tower. Relieved to see no signs of Gedvondur, Leifr waited to speak to Thurid, with the idea of magnanimously forgiving him for his past behavior.

'Something's happened,' Thurid greeted him curtly, his features drawn into a worried scowl. His clothing was disheveled and dusty. 'One moment I was there, poking and prying at the influences in the tower, then suddenly the creature became enraged and blew me around the room awhile and then threw me out. As if he didn't know I won't be discouraged by such tactics!' He turned and spoke to the tower, his cloak gusting with the force of his indignation. Then his nose began to twitch and he turned sharply back to Leifr. 'Where have you been? There's an odd dusty smell about you – like a barrow.'

'There's plenty of barrows in the fourth pasture,' Leifr replied evasively, 'with trolls for hunting.'

Thurid grunted, his eyes going back to the tower. 'Well, clean your boots before you go into the house, or you might lead a draug straight to our door. Drat, I wonder what disturbed the influences. I've conjured some excellent ghouls of old Slagfid himself, and his sons too. There's a shadowy character I can never quite catch in the image somehow – as if someone is trying to hide him from me. He's the one I'm stalking.'

Leifr shook his head, his old impatience again reaching the boiling point. 'You're chasing shadows, and I'm chasing jotuns,' he said bitingly. 'Perhaps when you get your hands on that shadow, you'll be ready to help with the real work, which is killing the jotuns.'

Thurid's abstracted gaze sharpened into a glare. 'This is the real work, Leifr,' he snapped. 'The more I see of it, the more I'm convinced we've got to get at the root of the jotun curse. What's the matter with your eyes, Leifr? They look peculiar.'

'No more than usual,' Leifr retorted, turning away hastily and silently cursing Hogni's seeing-drops. 'Starkad, come along. You're stopping Thurid from chasing his shadows. Valuable work is being hindered.'

Starkad followed Leifr reluctantly, glancing back at Thurid with a yearning even Leifr could not mistake.

'I wish I could be a wizard,' Starkad finally burst out, while they were attending to the horses. 'Do you think I have any natural ability in magic, Leifr? If I could but get away from Fangelsi and my brothers, perhaps I could apprentice myself to a wizard in exchange for ten years of servitude, or twenty, or whatever it would take.'

'You'd do that?' Leifr inquired, leaning on his hay fork. 'Give up your freedom for that sort of bondage?'

'I would,' Starkad answered earnestly. 'And you're the one who's going to help me become something besides a useless younger brother, Leifr. I know it, I feel it in every one of my bones.'

'I can't argue with bones,' Leifr said, then added uneasily, 'How long does this seeing stuff last, Starkad?'

Starkad shrugged. 'I've never used it before. Are you seeing things that aren't there?'

Leifr darted a swift glance at the doorway of the barn. Shadowy images had been going in and out since they had started working, but he was determined to ignore them. In an offhand tone he answered, 'I suppose you could say that.'

'It's nothing but old images,' Starkad said, looking around. 'I can see myself from days ago – even years ago when I was a small lad. Every action makes an impression in the influences surrounding us. Shadows, and nothing more. Usually they can't be seen, unless something awful has happened, like a murder or a crime. Thurid's got a great job of work, if he's trying to sift them out.'

Leifr began to feel positively haunted, crowded about by the images of the past, and was relieved when the pictures began to fade. It was nearly dark when they finished their work outdoors and returned to the house. As Leifr was reaching for the latch, a ghostly hand inter-posed. Leifr leaped back from the shadowy ghoul image standing before him on the threshold, knowing it was absurd even while he was doing it. The shadow wore a ragged cloak, as a wanderer might, and one shoulder was higher than the other. Leifr's heart stood still as he suddenly understood the recent vague uneasiness the carbuncle had given him. It had seen Fangelsi before. He would have recognized the twisted form of Fridmarr from even less of a shadow.

'Fridmarr!' he whispered, and the ghoul vanished like a puff of smoke once he had named it.

Four dismal days followed, with blowing wind and drifting snow that spelled death for any creature unwise enough to venture forth. It was possible to get lost between the space of house and barn without a rope for a guide. The sheep were brought into the old barn, but the horses and cows remained apart in their stables. Twice daily Leifr groped his way through the storm to feed them. Raudbjorn faithfully accompanied him, interposing his towering bulk between Leifr and the brunt of the storm.

Denied access to the tower, Thurid did his work at the table once more, under the unfriendly eye of Syrgja. The cold weather aggravated her reddened hands, but she wouldn't allow anyone else to make the trek to the granary with Ketil's meals.

During one of her absences, Leifr sat down facing

Thurid across the untidy heap of wands and vellums.

'Gedvondur, I want to talk to Thurid,' Leifr said in a low voice, conscious of Hogni lounging across the room apparently engrossed in a carving he was making.

Gedvondur obligingly crawled down from Thurid's shoulder, and Thurid gazed at Leifr impatiently, tapping a wand on the table to encourage Leifr's temper to fray.

'Thurid, Fridmarr has been here,' Leifr said.

Thurid greeted the news with a sigh, rubbing his eyes wearily. 'Yes, I know that,' he said, 'and I don't dare to ask how you came by that information.'

'Do you know why he was here?' Leifr asked.

'No. He wasn't here for long. I've seen only a few shadows of him. It won't surprise you, perhaps, that he spent considerable time around the tower.'

'Can't you find out more?' Leifr asked.

'Out of mere curiosity? I should think not. Obviously he was prowling where he shouldn't have been, being Fridmarr. Perhaps his addiction to the eitur was another way Sorkvir kept him from venturing too far. Or too near, I should say.' Thurid's voice dropped to a whisper, thus spoiling Hogni's obvious eavesdropping. 'Be on your guard, Leifr, against everyone in this house. I'm on the brink of discovering something which they don't want anyone to know. There's something of value here at Fangelsi. Djofull covets it, Hogni and his family know what it is, and I'll wager money that these jotuns protect it. Why else would he want us to destroy them?'

Leifr avoided Thurid's piercing gaze, swallowing a sudden surge of uneasy guilt. He knew perfectly well what Thurid was driving at, and he wished he didn't.

When the storm passed, the supply of wood and hay had grown perilously low. A freezing period followed, forming a crust on the snow thick enough for a horse to walk on, drawing a sledge with ease. Hogni and Horgull harnessed a team and departed for the settlements of the shore people, who gathered driftwood from the sea and raised a few skinny sheep. Then they would travel onward across the frozen sound to trade some of the firewood for hay, expecting to return in two or three days.

Their sledge was scarcely out of sight when Syrgja took command and ordered the return of Uncle Ketil to the house from the granary. To Leifr's surprise, Ketil seemed almost compliant when they brought him into the house. He sat in his chair in a dark and drafty alcove, contented to grumble away for hours over some interminable internal dialog.

At the first opportunity, Starkad called Leifr outside on one pretext or another and outlined his plans for his brothers' absence.

'I've thought of nothing else but Slagfid's Ban since we went there.' Starkad's words tumbled out in a feverish torrent. 'You saw the amount of gold just lying there. That fortune belongs in the hands of the living, not with the bones of the dead. With a small fraction of it, and your help, I can get Ermingerd away from Fangelsi-hofn and our brothers. We can buy land someplace else and start a wealthy holding. We'll be neighbors, you and I and Ermingerd. We'll celebrate our feast days together and we'll cradle-promise our children to each other. Fangelsi and its jotun curse will be left far behind and forgotten. Plenty of wealthy men have gained their start with a bit of help from the family barrow mounds. Surely you're not being squeamish about going back to Slagfid's Ban, are you, Leifr?' His tone grew bantering as he saw Leifr's expression darkening and turning sour.

'Stealing that gold was a mistake,' Leifr said. 'What if those jotuns decide to come after it? Or worse yet, what if Thurid finds out?'

'You're a Scipling, with all manner of weaknesses. Thurid will understand. Hogni and Horgull will be back in about two days. That doesn't leave us much time.'

'Time enough to put that gold back where it belongs,' Leifr said.

'Put it back?' Starkad's eyes rounded with horror. 'I'm not going to put it back. I mean to steal more, all I can get my hands on. Don't worry about Hogni and Horgull. We can hide the gold and wait for spring. And I got you through the wards once, so I can do it again – although I did discover that he's changed the ward on the sixth gate. Distrustful, isn't he?'

'Starkad, you interfering lummox, maybe he suspects something. Doesn't it matter at all to you that you'll spend the rest of your life being known as a barrow robber? And what about the curses that might follow barrow gold?'

'If any angry draugar wants to follow me, they'd better know how to swim, because I intend to get off this island and find a place where people enjoy life. I won't care what they say in Hraedsla-dalur about me, because I'll be many, many miles away. And you'll be away from Skarpsey, too. You'd be a fool to turn your back on that gold, Leifr. I can get you through my brother's wards. I know how he makes them, I've broken them often enough. Think of that gold, Leifr, just waiting for the taking. Perhaps you could buy your freedom from Djofull's geas, if we steal enough.'

'All the gold in the world won't break Djofull's geas,' Leifr said. 'Djofull must know about Slagfid's treasure. After the Flayer is dead, he's going to take it all and he won't be satisfied with only part of it.'

'That's Fangelsi gold!' Starkad flared. 'He's not going to have one piece of it as long as I live to defend it! It's going to be mine – except for the part I'll share with you for helping me and being my friend. You'll be as rich as a jarl, Leifr, if we can get that gold.'

'I'm not at all sure I want it,' Leifr said. 'As soon as you've got something worth having, your enemies covet it. If we leave the Flayer alone, so Djofull can't get to the gold, his geas will probably kill us. If we kill the Flayer, Djofull will take the gold and probably kill us. So the only solution is to kill the Flayer, take the gold, hide it someplace else, and spend the rest of our lives fleeing from Djofull.'

'It sounds all right to me,' Starkad said. 'It means you'll

have to take me with you when you leave. Nothing could please me more than getting away from Hogni and Horgull. But Ermingerd – what will become of her?'

'This is a mad scheme,' Leifr said wearily. 'We'll have to think about it. As Hogni is so fond of saying, there will be consequences for every action.'

'But Hogni and Horgull will be back in two days,' Starkad protested.

'They'll have to leave again before the winter's out,' Leifr answered grimly. 'We'll watch for our opportunity.'

When it was nearly dark they ended their work and started to return to the house and its dubious comforts, but Raudbjorn stood like a wall beside the path, gazing alertly toward Skeragil. The troll-hounds crouched around his feet, growling.

'The Flayer!' Starkad said, but Raudbjorn slowly shook his head, rumbling uneasily.

'Blue light,' he said, nodding toward the ruins and the tower. 'Barrow light. Draugar walking tonight.'

As they watched, a blue nimbus crept across the wall of the tower, following the path toward the house. It stopped short where a mossy tricklet of a stream crossed the path, then it moved back toward the ruins.

'It followed us,' Starkad whispered. 'We cleaned our boots in that stream. Leifr, what are we going to do? It's looking for the gold! I hid it up in the ruins! Look how it's drawn toward it!'

'Don't tell anyone,' Leifr said, smothering an angry groan. 'You should have known this might happen, Starkad!'

'Don't blame me,' Starkad answered. 'I'm only the first to take something from Slagfid's cave, and we've got to expect a few difficulties before we can get it all.'

'I don't want any more difficulties of this sort!' Leifr said, starting toward the safety of the house.

Thurid, Syrgja, and Ermingerd also watched from the doorway of the house, with Thurid's alf-light flaring in the cold wind.

245

'This has never happened in my lifetime,' Syrgja said in her carking voice. 'You've disturbed the sleeping dead, wizard, with your prying spells and unwise curiosity.'

'That may be,' Thurid said, 'but that sort of light is usually seen where there is treasure.'

'Not in those ruins,' Syrgja said. 'They've been combed hundreds of times. This is a change and few changes in Fangelsi are for the better. I've learned to beware of anything new and beyond the ordinary order of things. It's always a bad sign when something is different.'

Starkad and Leifr kept quiet that night, instead of reveling in the absence of Hogni and Horgull as they had anticipated. Leifr cleaned and oiled his boots, examining the soles rather anxiously for any trace of barrow dust. Only by the slimmest of chances had he and Starkad avoided tracking barrow dust straight up to the door of the house.

On the next evening the barrow draug appeared again, coming as far as the water, then returning to the ruins. This time, however, it drifted aimlessly instead of hovering over the spot where Starkad had buried his loot. Leifr and Starkad watched it wandering over the hillside, drawing nearer and nearer to Starkad's second hiding place. Finally it halted with a wavering howl of triumph, and spent the night lurking over the cattle pond, unable to touch the water and unable to forsake the submerged gold.

Fortunately Thurid was too preoccupied with his own thoughts to notice any telltale signs of guilt in Leifr and Starkad. Svanlaug, however, seemed suspicious, and Ermingerd's clear eyes dwelt often upon Starkad with a puzzled look. The weight of a guilty secret made Leifr suspect that everyone knew of his misdeeds and was merely waiting for the worst possible moment to accuse him.

Looking up suddenly from his endless study of the contents of the Rhbu satchel, Thurid struck a listening pose, his eyes glazed and unblinking. He thrust his rune sticks and vellums back into his satchel and reached for his cloak hanging near the door.

'Something has breached the wards,' Thurid said sharply, deigning to notice the ordinary mortals who were staring at him in considerable alarm.

'Wait, Thurid,' said Gedvondur's voice, bringing Thurid up short. 'I don't advise your going out there alone.'

'I'm not alone,' Thurid answered in his own voice. 'I've got you. Unless you're not coming. But something has come across Hogni's wards. I'm sure of it. I feel a profound disturbance, a wrongness.'

'So do I,' Gedvondur's voice replied, 'but I won't let you go out there. The dark powers are at their prime peak this near to midwinter. Wait until daylight to investigate this breach.'

Syrgja shuddered and made signs in the air for banishing evil spells. 'I hate it when you talk to yourself!' she said. 'It's demented!'

'I'm not talking to myself,' Gedvondur's voice answered sharply. 'I'm talking to Thurid!'

Thurid hung up his cloak reluctantly, and the distortion of Gedvondur's features vanished from his own. With a portentous sigh, Thurid sat down and gazed broodingly into the fire.

Leifr sat down in the seat next to him and stretched out his feet to the fire, hoping to appear as if he were about to strike up a casual conversation. Svanlaug's attention sharpened instantly, but she was more interested in spying out the healing herbs Syrgja was brewing over the coals for Ketil's poultice.

'What sort of thing has broken through the wards?' Leifr asked in a low tone. 'Day-farer or night-farer? Living or draug?'

Thurid narrowed his eyes. 'It's living,' he said, 'but that's about all I know for certain.'

'How could something come through your wards?' Leifr asked after a pause, relieved that Thurid hadn't detected the draug from the cave. 'I thought you and Hogni had strengthened them past all attack.'

'Our powers and spells fade somewhat when Fantur is at his strongest, unless we keep renewing them,' Thurid said. 'It becomes an exhausting experience, maintaining a border of wards as extensive as Hogni's. We'll have to sacrifice some territory, I fear.'

Leifr gazed into the fire, digesting this bit of unwelcome news. His thoughts strayed back to Dallir, and the long evenings he had spent listening to Thurid haranguing over the mundane affairs of the farm, never dreaming he would eventually find himself in such a situation.

'Do you think it might have been Ljosa following us?' he asked after a moment.

Thurid devoted his attention to finding, stuffing, and lighting his pipe, accompanied by a great deal of distracted muttering, no doubt hoping that Leifr would forget his question if he delayed long enough.

'You don't like to think about Ljosa, do you?' Leifr accused, his temper rising. 'Can't Gedvondur help you figure out how to get her back? Or is he more interested in gold and curses?'

Gedvondur did not deign to reply, busying himself polishing his nails on Thurid's sleeve, but Thurid bestowed a menacing glower upon Leifr. 'Ljosa must wait her turn,' he said. 'I've got all I can do, keeping those wards strong enough to stop the fylgjur-wolves. What an impatient, ungrateful breed you Sciplings are! Do you have any idea where you'd be if not for my unceasing efforts?'

'I couldn't be much worse off,' Leifr retorted and stalked away, aware that everyone in the kitchen was listening to their quarrel with the relish born of winter boredom.

Hogni and Horgull returned from their hay-buying expedition the next day and were apprised of the breach in the wards by Thurid. The three of them departed immediately with the pony sledge and did not return until dusk; their arrival was awaited by an anxious Syrgja. In spite of the atmosphere of dread in the house, no one spoke of the intrusion until the gloomy evening meal was over.

'What creature has come through?' Syrgja demanded. 'Since you've been gone, draugar have started prowling about Slagfid's cursed tower. We'll be lucky to survive this ill-starred winter. It's his ghoul spells and summonings from the past that are disturbing the draugar.' She wagged her head toward Thurid, her fists braced on her hips. 'I hope you're pleased with the trouble you've brought down upon our heads. You should have sent these strangers packing on their way the first day they arrived, but no, you were still curious about Slagfid's curse and Slagfid's treasure. It's the thought of all that gold which keeps you trying, isn't it? Your own foolish greed has brought us to this pass.'

'Hush, aunt,' Hogni replied with a scowl as he noted Svanlaug watching with avid interest. Thurid's attention also was riveted by the mention of gold. 'You talk too much with these strangers listening.'

Syrgja put a hand to her lips, pale and stricken.

'Then the gold is real, and not legend,' Thurid said.

'Do you suddenly find the gold more interesting than the curse?' Hogni sneered. 'Perhaps you've been pretending all along, merely waiting for your chance to get at the gold. I confess, I was fooled. I thought you were a true wizard, searching for the answer to our curse, instead of just another treasure-seeker.'

'I care nothing for that treasure, if it exists,' Thurid retorted.

'Then how do you explain those draugar and blue lights up in the ruins?' Syrgja demanded. 'Something has brought them down out of Slagfid's Ban. Someone has been in that cave and brought out barrow mold on his feet.'

'The Flayer, perhaps,' Starkad suggested with remarkable aplomb.

'Why hasn't it happened before?' Syrgja demanded.

Starkad shrugged. 'He forgot to clean his boots?'

'Starkad!' Hogni snarled. 'Get up into the loft! This is men's conversation!'

Starkad did as he was bidden, his face reddened with shame. Leifr glowered at Hogni, contemptuous of him for his cruelty and arrogance, fearing him for his knowledge, and hating him because he feared him. Although it was wiser to avoid Hogni's attention, Leifr sallied forth with a rash challenge. A brave attack was a good defense for a guilty conscience.

'Are you making an accusation?' he demanded. 'Come out and say it if you are. Are you accusing us of barrow robbing? How do you want to settle it, by notifying your chieftain or between ourselves?'

'I have no desire to trade accusations with you before Jarnvard,' Hogni answered. 'The less said and done about Slagfid's Ban, the better off we'll be. I don't expect anyone to admit they've been in that cave, but whoever it was is standing in this room, and I'll warn him that he'd better not go in there again. Jotun draugar will make the Flayer look tame. We could all be killed if one of those creatures attacks the house.'

Horgull roused himself from his perpetual morose silence long enough to deliver what was for him a lengthy speech. He glared darkly at Syrgja and said, 'None of this would be happening if you weren't opposing nature by holding Ketil here against his will.'

Syrgja blanched and said nothing, holding her head up high in rigid defiance.

Leifr could not resist another goading dig. 'You're a fine one to speak of opposing nature, when you want to get rid of your uncle by exposing him to the jotuns, trolls, and natural elements.'

Hogni rounded upon him with a deadly glint in his eye. 'And what about you, Scipling? You're a blot upon nature, just by being here in this realm where you do not belong. You can't even imagine the forces your presence disturbs, because you know nothing of their existence. A renegade wizard, a straying Dokkalfar, that blood-encrusted Villimadur, those hounds – perhaps all of us are in revolt against our natural places in our respective spheres. Who knows what evil we're about to bring crashing down upon our heads? Such a group of misfits and rebels rends the very fabric of sanity itself!'

He had worked himself into such a fury, pacing up and down and flinging out his hands and causing disturbances with his powers, that Leifr deemed it wise to make a strategic retreat to the main hall to spend the rest of the evening with Raudbjorn. Starkad followed him, and they played a three-man gambling game dear to the heart of Raudbjorn, which was played with the teeth of his dead enemies.

Near midnight Leifr and Starkad ended their game and looked out on the starlit night. The ruins stood starkly in the barren moonlight, shaped into unearthly forms and shadows. The blue light of the draug still flickered steadily over the next place where Starkad had hidden his small cache of loot, the same granary used for locking up Ketil. Starkad looked at Leifr hopefully, waiting for him to speak.

'I don't have any ideas yet,' Leifr said gruffly, 'and you see what your idea has gotten us into. If we take any more of that treasure, we're going to be fighting draugar for it, and everyone else is going to be angry – especially the draugar.'

'You've got that sword,' Starkad said. 'It will kill draugar, and anything else it touches.'

'I can't expect to kill every obstacle in my path,' Leifr replied in exasperation. 'Perhaps I once thought I could, but not after spending this long in the Alfar realm. A man must use his wits part of the time. Now I've got to be doubly on guard, if another threat has crossed the wards.'

After listening to the distant weird howls of the fylgjur-wolves and the hoarse laughter of the trolls, Leifr and Starkad crossed the icy passage to the ruddy warmth of the kitchen. Ermingerd sat in the red glow of the coals on the hearth, waiting for them. She looked at them anxiously, her expression grave.

'Starkad!' she whispered. 'Give it up! We'll never escape from Fangelsi. Don't keep risking your life.'

Starkad stared at her, wide-eyed with surprise and startled guilt.

'Promise me you'll take it back,' she whispered.

'No, I won't,' Starkad said fiercely. 'You should see it, Ermingerd. We found the treasure of Slagfid. There's six fortunes in gold and silver and precious jewels—'

Ermingerd silenced him with a sharp hiss, cocking her head to listen. The Flayer's voice rumbled distantly in the gil behind the granary. 'Listen to that, Starkad. Do you think you're any match for the Flayer? And jotun draugar are walking in Fangelis. Starkad, I warn you – don't disturb the curse any further, or we'll all suffer for it.'

CHAPTER 16

The peaceful and dull winter routine was brought to a decisive end by bringing the jotun gold into the light of day. Daily Starkad moved his plunder, and nightly the draugar found its hiding place. Not only was Leifr's peace of mind transformed to guilty anxiety by the nightly appearances of the accusing draugar, but Ketil seemed determined to prove his ingratitude for his reinstatement into the household. As the draugar became more insistent, the Flayer also became emboldened to prowl and call around the house every night. Ketil became more restless and intractable. He paced lumberingly around the kitchen, treading blindly upon or jolting against anything put in his path. Always he swung his grizzled head toward the door or windows, listening intently for something known only to his fevered consciousness, especially at night. When he began pawing and battering at the doors, Hogni chained him to a rusted ring set in the hearth. Syrgja could not bear to look at him, pacing and groaning like a trapped animal, nor could she tolerate putting him in the storeroom in the passage, where the Flayer might break down the door. She kept herself busy with kitchen tasks long after the usual workday was ended, keeping her eyes averted. Ermingerd tried to sew, but she spent most of her time with her needle idle as she stared at Ketil, her eyes wide with compassion.

Immediately after supper each night, Hogni and Horgull immersed themselves in a chess game, leaving their guests to their own devices for the long winter evening. Raudbjorn and the hounds were the only ones who could make themselves comfortable with Ketil's pacing and

253

animal groans. They retreated to the old hall with the livestock, where the four of them went to sleep in a pile, with Raudbjorn in the middle, twitching when the dogs twitched in their sleep, whining when they whined.

Thurid meditated, sitting like a statue, often with his eyes wide open and unblinking for hours. Nothing seemed to disturb him, and Leifr had the uneasy feeling the essence that was Thurid had absented itself upon more interesting errands, leaving the dross physical bulk behind. Gedvondur's hand with the glittering carbuncle rested on Thurid's chest or shoulder, like some gruesome cloak ornament, coming to life only when Thurid blinked and returned from his travels.

Hogni observed Thurid's efforts with envy barely masked by a thin veneer of disdain. 'You'll have to do better than that to discourage draugar,' he said impatiently after the fifth night of the combined Flayer and draugar visits. 'You need to strike at the source of the jotuns to get rid of them.'

'Indeed? And what might that be?' Thurid inquired.

Hogni looked smug as he shook his head. 'You'll see. I'm going to put a halt to these jotuns, where you can't.'

'Bah! If you could, you would have long ago,' snorted Thurid in contempt.

'It has been done, long ago, several times,' Hogni said with an infuriating smile. 'It works, for a time.'

Svanlaug also eyed Thurid enviously, and amused herself by irritating Syrgja with casual digging remarks or by paying unwonted attention to Starkad's admiring advances. She also drifted around near Leifr, her eyes probing, and uneasily he wondered if she could sense his uneasy guilt. Such a strong and unpleasant emotion could hardly fail to escape the perceptions of the suspicious Hogni, but Hogni gave no outward sign.

The long dark evenings kept Leifr and Starkad occupied with tanning and softening hides, mending tools and weapons, or with a game of their own invention, with

Leifr wishing all the while he were almost anywhere else in Skarpsey. Whenever he glanced up uneasily at Ketil's or Thurid's antics, the glass balls of the game surreptitiously shifted positions on the board, invariably to Starkad's advantage.

Svanlaug also watched Ketil, her eyes narrowed judiciously. One of the boils on his face had ruptured from his continuous pawing and shaking, and oozed a blood-tinged liquid, with a strange dark mass bulging through the hole.

'He's very ill,' Svanlaug said to Syrgja. 'Those poultices aren't enough for a disease like this. I believe there's more than simple disease involved here. I think it's magical in origin.'

Ermingerd's needle hung suspended in midair, her clear gaze raised helplessly toward Syrgja. The older woman bestowed a black, incredulous scowl upon Svanlaug.

'It's the weather here by the sea that makes old bones so miserable,' Syrgja retorted. 'It's nothing magic. You don't understand the life here, so you look for magic to explain away your own ignorance. We take care of our own here, in the way best fit, and we don't want outside advice or interference.' She punctuated her speech with whacks of a great knife on the cutting board as she dealt with an unlucky piece of fresh meat. The Flayer had capriciously broken the neck of a yearling calf and left it.

Svanlaug turned away with a toss of her head. As Leifr watched covertly, Ketil loomed behind Syrgja suddenly, his sunken eyes blazing with a feral light. With one swift scoop of his bandaged hand he snatched the raw meat off the board and shoved it into his mouth. Leifr hastily fastened his eyes upon the game board, shivering.

'You're a pretty poor player,' Starkad informed him, making the move that won him the game. 'What you need is more practice. You must think before you move.'

In the morning, Hogni and Horgull set Starkad to work at dismantling the old dais in the hall and heaping the broken planks and timbers on the sledge. At first light, they harnessed a pony to the load and departed without explanation.

Starkad watched the sledge and its somber riders rumble out of sight into the thick morning fog, the harness bells muffled, as if by wool. Leifr did not like the obstinate set of Starkad's chin, nor the wicked gleam in his fox-colored eyes.

'I think I'm going ranging today,' he announced, with a challenging glance in Syrgja's direction.

'There might be trolls out in this fog,' Syrgja replied. 'You could step off a crag into a crevice. You'd better stay here and see about mending the hall door to keep the Flayer out tonight.'

'No, I'm off,' Starkad said. 'Perhaps I'll see if the high tide has brought in some firewood. On a barren island like Skarpsey, there's nothing more valuable this time of the year than a load of good firewood, and we bought less wood this year from the trader, you recall.' Turning to Leifr, he added, 'Those dogs of yours need a good outing, so why don't you and the Norskur come with me? It would be an honor to have your company.'

Leifr was only too glad to escape the rising tide of his own frustration at his enforced inactivity while Thurid muttered around in the tower. In the honest company of uncomplicated creatures, away from Fangelsi's dark atmosphere, Syrgja's haunted eyes, and Svanlaug's insidious whispers, he felt his thoughts clearing.

His musings ended abruptly when Starkad shunned the seacoast path and headed toward Skera-gil, following the marks of the sledge in the thick frost.

Leifr hesitated. 'Your brothers told everyone to stay away from Skera-gil,' he warned.

'Everyone but themselves?' Starkad questioned. 'What business have they taking a load of wood up Skera-gil, when we can use every piece of it for firewood, or building something needful? Wood is too scarce to waste it. I'm going to see what they're doing with it and why they're being so secretive about it. We know their intentions against Uncle Ketil are evil, so why should we obey what they tell us to do or not do, merely because they can hurt us or because we're afraid of them?'

'Excellent reasons,' Leifr said. 'They're in an enviable position, one which Raudbjorn usually occupies.'

Starkad hitched up his ragged cloak and clapped his hand to his old sword. 'Well, I'm not afraid of them. True hearts need not fear the unscrupled.'

Leifr grunted, 'You've much to learn. Lead on then, we'll see what your unscrupled brothers are doing with that wood.'

Skera-gil in the fog chilled the soul as well as the body. The screaming bird ward remained dark and inoffensive, allowing them to pass. As Leifr plodded along, watching suspiciously, the drifting fog writhed like shapes of men, giants, and horses, all clashing in battle in ghostly silence. Leifr shook his head to clear it of such fanciful notions and startled himself in the muffled quiet with the sound of his own head shaking. Raudbjorn gazed at him anxiously, his small round eyes open wide, and he gripped his halberd with defensive fervor.

From the walls towering above and pressing in from the sides came a feeling of sorrowing gloom. In places where profound events had taken place, such as deaths or battles, Leifr knew that emotions lingered – and frequently the images themselves of what had happened. If dreadful events had taken place here in the past, Skera-gil was the sort of place that would cling to the negative sensations.

At last Leifr called a halt, when the feeling of oppression and despair seemed to rear up before them in a palpable wall. The hounds crouched at his feet, shuddering with growls.

'We can go no further,' Leifr said. 'This place doesn't want us here.' A verifying shiver passed over him, signifying that he had spoken the truth.

'No, we've come this far, and we're going on,' Starkad said grimly, his voice quivering. 'Hogni and Horgull are plotting something, and it won't be good for Uncle Ketil.'

'Starkad, some secrets are best left secret,' Leifr began in exasperation, but Starkad wasn't listening.

The gil had narrowed around them into a rugged, vertical shaft, where scarcely any light penetrated. The fog roiled about in restless curtains, screening the wet black rocks, then revealing glimpses of them through its veils. During one of the brief clear periods, Starkad spied the dim outline of the horse hitched to the sledge, waiting patiently, with his whiskers and eyelashes heavily frost-rimmed. There was no sound but a few leathery creaks as the beast sighed and shifted in its harness. The sledge was loaded with planks and beams taken from the hall at Fangelsi; old, blackened wood, some of it carved and polished, looking sadly out of place. Then came the muffled sounds of hammering. Leifr nudged Starkad warningly as boots crunched in the frost, something dragged, and the sounds diminished.

'Strange weather for building,' he whispered to Starkad. 'As well as a strange place.'

Starkad rose up beside him, bearlike in his hairy-shouldered cloak. 'This is the time to find out what they are keeping from me,' he said. 'I'm no longer a child, I'm going to face them, and find out.'

Raudbjorn groaned softly. 'Brothers might not like to tell right now. Better sneak and see what job they do first, ask questions later. Good thief-taker way.'

'It's not my way,' Starkad declared zealously, taking a step forward. Leifr grabbed his leg and pulled him down as the footsteps of Hogni and Horgull approached them through the fog.

'The child's way is the direct way,' Leifr whispered angrily. 'A man must learn caution first.'

The brothers halted, two looming black forms with faces lost in the gloom. Silently they selected a plank and lifted it together and carried it away into the fog.

Leifr shivered, feeling the portent of gloom and misery, as if a cold hand had touched him. Starkad nudged him insistently, pointing after his brothers and making a motion to follow. Crouching low and moving cautiously, they crept over the intervening jumble of boulders and looked down upon Hogni and Horgull where they worked. The mouth of a cave gaped blacker against the black side of the mountain – a cave which had once possessed a doorframe and a door. All that remained of the door were four massive metal hinges, still bolted to frayed bundles of splinters.

Leifr sniffed at the stench of the cave and backed away, with inner visions of rotting hides and gnawed bones. A thick, dusty barrow smell made his scalp prickle with unease, reminding him of the ancient, lurking memories that drifted through the deserted halls of Bjartur. His experiences had taught him to recognize power and influences when he encountered them.

'Slagfid's Ban!' Starkad whispered urgently, his eyes glowing as he shoved forward for a better view. 'They've found it and they're making a door!'

'There was a door here once before, and someone or something smashed it,' Leifr said uneasily. 'It's going to take more than wood to hold back those draugar and the Flayer. See what your meddling has done, Starkad? If you hadn't stolen those things, the draugar wouldn't have been disturbed, and the cave wouldn't have to be locked up.'

'That means we can't steal any more gold,' Starkad said. 'They probably want it all for themselves. They're afraid we'll get some of it before they do. The greedy cheats! There's enough gold in there for all of us.'

'Maybe it's not the gold they're thinking of,' Leifr said. 'They want to lock us out, or lock something else in. The draugar, perhaps. Or Ketil.'

'You've got them pegged, Leifr,' Starkad said fiercely. 'Next time they'll make sure no one rescues Uncle Ketil. They're going to lock him in, unless we think of something to stop them.'

Raudbjorn groaned and shifted his weight against the rocky earth. 'Too hard to think. Go home to fires and food. Forget about jotuns and draugar and doors.'

They watched awhile longer, until Hogni and Horgull suddenly left their work. They stood a moment, conferring and gazing around so suspiciously that Leifr feared that Hogni knew he was being watched. Nudging Starkad, he persuaded him that they should retreat.

'But the cave and the gold!' Starkad sputtered when it was safe to talk. 'Right here, practically under our noses! If we wait around, we won't be able to get in again! Leifr, I've got to have that gold – at least enough to get Ermingerd away from Fangelsi.'

'Don't worry, we'll get it before they finish the door,' Leifr heard himself assuring Starkad.

'Do you swear it?' Starkad demanded, challenge in his voice. 'You're not just saying that?'

'My word is my bond,' Leifr said haughtily. 'If I didn't mean it, I wouldn't say it.'

Upon further deliberation, he soon began to wish he hadn't said it, but his pride refused to allow him to weasel out of his promise. When they returned to Fangelsi, he looked longingly toward the tower, where Thurid's smoke was boiling out the smoke hole, but he knew that Thurid wouldn't approve of anything that involved going into Skera-gil. If he knew Starkad had helped himself to the jotun's treasure, he would likely fly into a rage and force them to return it instantly, as common sense dictated. Common sense in Leifr's situation, however, was rapidly becoming obfuscated by his growing resolve to break the geas and leave Fangelsi.

The Flayer returned in full fury that night, his approach signalled by the sudden ferocious growling of the hounds across the passage. With crashing and splintering and snarling sounds, the Flayer forced his way into the passage and came clumping toward the kitchen door, where he stopped, breathing with heavy rasping breaths. Syrgja uttered a moan from the wall bed, and Hogni and Horgull arose silently and checked the bars on the doors.

The commotion disturbed Ketil, who had groaned and paced most of the night. He rose up from his bed with a determined rattling of his chain, raising a quavering yell.

The Flayer answered with a savage roar and a mighty crash upon the door panels. Then a deceptively small and meek voice whimpered, 'Come out, brodir! They're locking the door! It will be too late!'

Ketil threw back his head and bellowed, 'Help! Help! I'm murdered! I'm dying! Unlock the door!'

The jotun attacked the kitchen door with a vengeance, crashing into it until the air was filled with dust.

Hogni motioned for Horgull and Starkad to push a heavy chest in front of the door. The Flayer snarled and battered at the door, gradually losing interest, until those inside could hear only his heavy breathing and the straining of Ketil at his chain. Then came a low chuckle in a throaty growling voice that was not the weary whisper of the jotun.

'Halloa, wizard! Are you in there?'

Thurid stepped toward the door, clutching his staff, with Gedvondur gripped around his wrist. 'Who are you?' Thurid demanded. 'I think I recognize you from that filthy tower in the ruins.'

'And I you, trespasser. You will die if you stay here. Get out now.' A blast of icy air seeped under the door, chilling the room with cold and sensations of dread.

'We don't fear you,' Thurid said. 'You're one of the ancient ones, and the old must always give way before the new. I adjure you to give up your secrets before you depart. Tell me the meaning of the spiral and the Convocation of Jotuns.'

Syrgja made a gasping sound behind Thurid, and Hogni made some motion with his hand, but Thurid's attention did not waver from the door. The entity outside uttered a growling sound that might have been evil mirth. 'When you know, it will be too late. You'll be in my power, wizard.'

The Flayer moved away down the passage with his heavy tread, pausing only to give the main hall door a wallop to send the troll-hounds into frenzies of barking.

'We can't hold him off forever,' Hogni said, his face

pale and grim in the guttering lamplight. 'This door can't stand such a beating night after night.'

Thurid gently cleared his throat. 'I thought you had a foolproof plan for getting rid of the jotuns and draugar.'

'It takes time to finish it,' Hogni snapped.

'You're building a door,' Starkad said. 'You're going to lock Uncle Ketil inside Slagfid's Ban! I know, because I saw you, and Leifr and Raudbjorn are my witnesses!'

'Spying always ends in more trouble for those who spy,' Hogni replied with a darkening scowl. 'But you've brought it out into the open now. As the oldest son, I'm the inheritor of Fangelsi and I'll make the decisions for everyone here. Tomorrow night we'll have an end to the destruction and the sleepless nights. Tomorrow we shall lock Ketil in Slagfid's Ban. This is the old way, and it has been done before. There will be no arguing. This is my decision. I only wish I could lock away all your interfering and meddling along with Ketil.'

He looked around the circle of faces for possible challenge, seeing none in sullen Horgull or in bitterly weeping Syrgja. Ermingerd's clear unblinking gaze soon slipped away, downward toward her feet. Thurid motioned Leifr to be silent when he would have stepped forward in defiance, and Leifr could neither move nor speak.

The silent and brooding Horgull suddenly emitted a dire chuckle. 'Comfort yourself with the thought that one day you might be feeding us to the jotuns when we are old. It should cheer you up, little brother.'

'Be silent, you fool!' Syrgja spat. 'Govern your tongue, with strangers and children listening!'

'I'm not a child, aunt!' Starkad exploded.

'It's true, he's not,' Horgull said gloomily. 'He should be told what he wants to know.'

'Silence,' Hogni snapped. 'Your advice is useless.'

'This isn't the way Uncle Ketil used to make decisions, when he was the master here,' muttered Starkad, his chest heaving with fury and grief. 'He was fair. He'd listen to everyone's ideas, at least, before he made decisions. You seem to be in a terrible hurry to be the master of Fangelsi, Hogni. Is that why you want Uncle Ketil out of the way? So you can claim all of Slagfid's gold?'

Starkad hurled his dart and stepped back, noting Hogni's clenching fist.

'You'll spend some time in the granary thinking about your crimes,' Hogni said. 'I've forbidden Skera-gil to you a thousand times, yet you disobeyed.'

Hogni's deadly eye next fell upon his silent guests.

'There is nothing you or anyone can do to change the situation,' he said. 'If you had not interfered so much already the Flayer would not be troubling us for a good many years.'

Thurid gripped his staff. 'My experiments have come nowhere near him, but you've started building a door across his cave. That is the source of his rage, not anything I have done. Unfortunately, I can't speak for Leifr and your younger brother. If you wish to quarrel with Leifr, you are welcome to, but I've washed my hands of anything he does about the Flayer.'

Hogni and Leifr exchanged a mutually hostile stare for a long moment before Hogni's gaze slid away to rest upon Starkad with kindling fury.

'This is your doing!' he snarled. 'Don't let me see your face for at least two days!' Then he whirled on Leifr and Thurid once more. 'Would that I could banish all of you, but you'd likely go to Jarnvard with your complaint. Since there's no help for it, we'll share this house for the rest of the winter, but not without coming to certain terms. No one goes into Skera-gil or Slagfid's Ban for any reason, and no outsider interferes with the personal matters of this family.'

'Fair enough,' Thurid said. 'Just give me some time with that tower before you do such a rash and heartless deed as you are contemplating.'

Syrgja's pleading eyes fastened hopefully upon Hogni and she said, 'Yes, give him more time, nephew.'

263

Hogni's resolve wavered and collapsed after a brief struggle. 'The longer we delay, the worse it will get,' he grumbled, 'but you can have another seven days. After that, the door will be finished and Ketil must surrender to his fate. And we must accept it.'

Ketil halted his restless pacing a moment, watching Hogni intently through his red-rimmed, swollen-looking eyes, as if he were paying close attention to every word. Although Leifr knew his awareness usually wandered freely over the dim ground of past years, Ketil's listening attitude made him uneasy.

Syrgja's proud shoulders sagged. She stood a moment, gazing at Ketil as he struggled bullishly against his restraints, pulling on the chain and using his teeth to tear at the bandages on his hands. When she reached out a soothing hand, he struck it away suspiciously and retreated to the darkest corner he could reach.

'What can be done in seven days?' she asked bitterly.

Thurid lit his pipe and blew clouds of bluish smoke around him as he strode up and down, still dignified, although he was in his night clothes. 'Don't despair just yet, I'm just becoming acquainted with the entity remaining in the tower. I have every reason to believe I can break this spell – if I'm given the time.' His hands trembled with excitement as he talked, and Leifr again noted a thinness about Thurid, as if his experiments had honed him to a razor edge. 'Fantur's power lasts until the spring equinox, then it and your jotuns go into hiding for six months. If Ketil can survive until the Flayer goes to ground for half a year, his disease will also go into abatement, am I correct?'

Hogni considered a moment, then nodded grudgingly.

'But will all that save my poor brother?' Syrgja asked.

'For this winter, at least,' Thurid replied with a portentous glower at Hogni.

In the morning, Hogni seemed more concerned about gathering in the sheep scattered by the Flayer the night before than with disposing of Ketil. After giving Starkad his directions of where to search, he and Horgull departed in the direction of Skera-gil with their tools. Syrgja barred the door, her face a hardened mask.

After a morose breakfast, Thurid retreated into a pile of his vellums, rune wands, and random objects at the kitchen table, where he could keep one eye upon Ketil, with specific orders not to disturb him. He directed Leifr to accompany Starkad, and Raudbjorn elected to accompany Leifr, in spite of the rough walking and the light snow that was falling.

They arrived at the sheepfold on the high meadow to view the Flayer's work of the previous night. The doors had been torn off completely and the frames wrenched from the walls. Inside, the lambing pens were knocked down and three sheep lay with their necks broken.

They had started to patch together the sheepfold as best they could when Ermingerd appeared on the path far below, hurrying and ill-clad for the cold.

Leifr felt the clammy presentiment of bad news. Starkad felt it also. He dropped the broken door with a crash and stood still a moment, as if scenting danger, then dashed down the fell to meet Ermingerd. Leifr and Raudbjorn followed at a less breakneck pace. Starkad came back to give them the news, his expression anxious.

'It's Uncle Ketil,' Starkad said. 'My aunt left him while she went out to look for fjallagross. She meant to be gone only a little while, but something frightened her, and she fell and twisted her ankle. When she returned, Ketil was gone, and the house in a shambles.'

'And Svanlaug and Thurid?' Leifr asked.

'Thurid was in the tower. Svanlaug was hurt. Ketil struck her. She was trying to help him – a different treatment for his sores. It must have released an influence. We've got to hurry. Thurid thought that Ketil cannot get far before we can catch up with him.'

'Is Svanlaug badly hurt?' Leifr asked as they overtook Ermingerd.

'Thurid thinks not. I'm very sorry,' she added, meeting his gaze with her clear gray eyes. 'I did not think there would be any danger, with him chained, but he broke the chain.'

Leifr shook his head, seeing the truth behind the incident all too clearly. Svanlaug had seized her opportunity to attempt some cure of her own on Ketil and had gotten more than she had bargained for.

'Where were you, Ermingerd?' Starkad demanded, and Ermingerd's clear eyes turned away evasively toward the fell separating Fangelsi from Killbeck.

'I went walking,' she said with a faint blush. 'Svanlaug promised to watch him.'

When they returned with haste to the house, they found Svanlaug under the care of Syrgja, with Thurid looking on and offering advice. She was bruised and unconscious, with some of her ribs possibly broken. Syrgja could scarcely hobble along on her twisted foot, but she refused to permit Thurid to examine it or advise her.

'They thought Ketil no longer understood,' Syrgja said with gloomy satisfaction. 'But he heard them and he doesn't want to be locked in the cave. That's why he's done this. Who wouldn't run away at the first chance?'

Leifr thought of Ketil sitting and listening helplessly to his nephews planning his demise. To Thurid he said, 'You shouldn't have left him unwatched.'

Thurid retorted, 'I was gone only moments to fetch something, with Svanlaug and Ermingerd watching him. He seemed to be asleep. I never once suspected that Ketil would do away with himself. Nor did I suspect that Svanlaug would attempt something so foolish.'

'We can track him,' Leifr said, dropping his hand on Kraftig's slender head.

Raudbjorn prowled around the kitchen, garnering malignant glares from Syrgja as he sniffed and scowled suspiciously.

'Strange smell, Leifr,' he rumbled, his face creased into dozens of worried wrinkles. 'Jotun smell.'

'You're imagining it!' Syrgja snapped wrathfully. 'I'm an immaculate housekeeper! I've scoured every inch of

266

that passageway, and no jotun has ever set foot in my kitchen!'

Outside, they found Hogni and Horgull moving the sheep into the main hall for the night. The flock scattered on all sides of the house, tracking up the earth with their strong scent and destroying any of Ketil's footprints with their hundreds of tiny cloven hooves. To worsen matters, the snow was coming down with more purpose now, rapidly covering any faint traces that remained. The hounds anxiously circled the house and the outbuildings with discouraged whines and drooping tails. Starkad stood and called his uncle, his voice muffled by the snow-thickened atmosphere.

'It's just as well,' Horgull said hollowly as he stood and watched. 'It saves us the trouble.'

'We can yet find him today,' Leifr answered with cold challenge in his voice. 'He's not gone far, and the snow isn't too deep for horses.'

'You won't find him, if he doesn't want to be found,' Hogni said unhelpfully and went into the house.

CHAPTER 17

Leifr and Raudbjorn and Starkad saddled horses and spent the rest of the day searching the nearest fells with no result. They rode as far as the sixth gate and saw no trace of Ketil, and the hounds were clearly baffled. The snow was blizzarding by the time they returned to the stables, soaked through and exhausted.

By morning the storm was finished, except for a few drifting flurries and a stiff, howling wind that sculptured drifts around every projection and pierced bones to their marrow. Hogni and Horgull attended to only the most needful of chores outside and returned to immerse themselves in a game of chess. Horgull scowled over the board. Leifr doubted if he ever won a game.

Svanlaug's manner was less than patient as she nursed her sore ribs, keeping to her bed on the sleeping platform for three days, in the darkest corner of the kitchen. She tossed her head in temper and pain, and had no use for anyone's condolences, whether Raudbjorn's bumbling offer to shift her to a warmer position, or Kraftig's long pink tongue slurping across her face. Like a wounded cat, she preferred to vent her frustrations by biting anyone who came near enough. She preferred also to mix her own restoratives secretively, fiercely refusing any help from Thurid or Syrgja.

'I'll be all right,' she snarled at Syrgja when she tried to tempt her appetite with some broth. Her eyes, brilliant with fever and shrunken from lack of nourishment, flashed over the broth with contempt. 'I don't feel like eating anything. The smell sickens me. Take it away and feed it to the pigs.'

Syrgja departed with the broth, muttering furiously. Leifr kept well away, only too glad to abandon Svanlaug to her solitary suffering. At least she would not bother Hogni with her spying for a while, and apparently her own treatment was working, since her strength was returning.

Ermingerd alone braved Svanlaug's temper, soothing her rages with her calm temperament. Svanlaug eventually consented to swallow the required broths and infusions, and by the end of three days a friendship had flowered.

The atmosphere in the kitchen was markedly less hospitable. Each morning Syrgja scowled more gloomily than usual, slapping the platters and dishes onto the table, fearsome and grim in her silent, hard-bitten grief. She glared at Thurid, who was engulfing the table in his mess of rune wands, vellums, and random objects, puffing great clouds of acrid smoke from his pipe. Gedvondur pushed the clutter around, searching for a particular wand. The number of wands had increased greatly since Thurid's ghoul spells had commenced in the tower, as Thurid conjured by night and recorded his findings in runic. Gedvondur ran his fingers over the lines and notches, discarding each with contempt before suddenly seizing upon one. He read it over several times then leaped onto Thurid's wrist so he could speak.

'I've found it!' Gedvondur's voice declared. 'It was the ghoul image where Slagfid's sons slaughtered all the people at Killbeck! Hreidar spoke of the Convocation. I thought he meant invocation of powers. It's that stick there, Thurid. You cut your thumb making it and there's a spot on it.'

'Yes, that's the one,' Thurid said with a chuckle. 'Clever of you, Gedvondur. I wish we had more of you around than just your hand.'

'So do I,' Gedvondur's voice answered. 'One day I intend to take up the matter with Djofull and get my ashes back from him before he uses them to season his soup.'

'I daresay you'd poison him, if he did,' Thurid said.

Syrgja placed her fists on her hips, her eyes blazing with

long-contained fury. 'I thought you promised to keep that hand off my table!' she flared. 'How can I even bear to eat, thinking of that piece of carrion capering around like a live thing, and its evil spirit speaking right out of your lips? Wizard, I warned you once, now I can't bear it any longer! Get that creature out of my house!'

Thurid gazed at her in astonishment. In a cold and civil voice he said, 'No one need throw me out twice. I'm going and I shan't trouble you further with my presence. I shall be found in the tower, if I am wanted.'

'You won't be,' Syrgja snapped.

Ermingerd looked from Syrgja to Thurid in great distress as Thurid stuffed everything back into his satchel and stalked out of the house. By unspoken consensus, Leifr and Starkad put on their boots and reached for their cloaks. Ermingerd picked up a rush basket of scraps for the geese and followed them outside. Raudbjorn and the dogs came out, all yawning and stretching and squinting in the brightness of the fresh snow.

'Go after Thurid! Quick!' she whispered. 'He's going to find something terribly wrong with that tower!'

With Starkad at his heels, Leifr left the house and rushed toward the tower, coming into view in time to hear a bellowing scream and a dull, rumbling explosion. A cloud of mist mingled with a few disturbed bats burst from the slit windows, and the door of the tower burst open with Thurid clinging to it desperately, as if resisting a powerful rebuffing force. The blackness swirled around Thurid in a cloak of ice-cold mist, partially hiding him from view. A windy roaring sound issued from the tower, and vellums and random objects swirled out the doorway in a storm of confusion. Leifr uttered a warning shout, glimpsing Thurid clutching his staff and boldly breasting the dark tide with Gedvondur perched like a small hawk on his upraised wrist.

'Now I know your name!' Gedvondur's voice bellowed triumphantly over the roaring. 'Heldur! You are Heldur!'

In the roiling blackness inside the tower, two red little

270

eyes gleamed, looking down upon Thurid malevolently.

'See what good it does you, wizard!' growled a savage voice, then a mighty arm thrust out the doorway, buffeting Thurid backward and dislodging Gedvondur from his perch on his wrist.

The powerful force knocked Leifr and Starkad off their feet, as helpless as two twigs snatched up by a whirlwind. Raudbjorn staggered backward, trying to stand against the overwhelming force.

Leifr scrambled toward Thurid, who was floundering about in the snow while the force within the tower blasted him with icy torrents of wind and deafening, echoing roars.

'Gedvondur!' Thurid gasped, plowing around in the churned snow. 'He's here somewhere! We've got to find him before Heldur does!'

'We've got to get out of here!' Leifr shouted, pulling on Thurid's arm, but the wizard evaded his grasp, still digging through the snow for the hand.

They all fell to their knees and burrowed through the snow until Raudbjorn suddenly uttered a howl of discovery and held up Gedvondur's hand, pale and stiff. Thurid seized the hand and dashed toward the house.

Thurid flung the hand on the table and bellowed, 'Fetch me some warm water! I need some restoratives, at once!'

Gedvondur's hand was blue and stiff, seemingly dead. Syrgja fell back from the table, making signs in the air, sputtering, 'What manner of evil is this! I want nothing to do with you! You're a necromancer, with your dead hands and draugar!'

Svanlaug eagerly leaped forward as Thurid began flinging pouches and vials and little boxes from his satchel.

'Take a pinch from the two pouches and mix it with two pinches from the red box and three from the green and infuse it with water and six drops from the blue vial!' Thurid bellowed, plowing frantically among his rune wands until he found the one he wanted. He chanted the words as fast as he could, interrupting himself now and

271

then to add more directions to Svanlaug's concoction.

'What are you going to do with it?' Svanlaug asked. 'He can't drink it, you know.'

'We'll bathe him in it,' Thurid replied shortly, going on with his incantation.

'Why don't you just take the revolting thing out and burn it?' Syrgja muttered with a grimace, making another sign. 'I don't want it in my house!'

Gedvondur's hand gradually revived in its warm bath, and finally signalled weakly by waving one finger. While Syrgja looked on in horror, Thurid picked him up gently and wrapped him in a warm rag like a child's doll. Still muttering efficacious words, Thurid sat down beside the fire, warming the hand further between his own.

'He's very weak,' Thurid said, 'but he's going to live. He took the full brunt of Heldur's attack. He shielded me.'

Leifr asked, 'What or who was Heldur?'

'The Dvergar smith who once lived beneath Fangelsi,' Thurid answered, 'but it wasn't a dwarf I saw in the tower. I was working over a ghoul spell, and I looked over my shoulder, and a jotun was standing there in the shadows. I don't know how long he'd been there, just watching and waiting.' He closed his eyes, suddenly trembling and pale and he scowled with a mighty effort of concentration. 'It's Gedvondur. He's trying to speak.'

'Jotun,' Gedvondur's voice whispered feebly.

'It wasn't a jotun,' Ermingerd said. 'It was Ketil.'

'Uncle Ketil! In the tower?' Starkad gasped. 'We've got to get him out of there! He'll go mad – madder than he already is. Remember Uncle Thorkell! He went in there, too, and when he came out he looked terrible, and—'

'Hush!' Syrgja commanded.

'We've got to get him out!' Starkad insisted.

Ermingerd shook her head. 'No. Don't go back there.'

Starkad pulled away, starting to protest, but Thurid lifted one commmanding hand for silence.

'I agree, for the nonce. It would be folly to challenge

Heldur on his own ground right now. The force we felt could have been Ketil's own fear, pain, or discomfort, magnified by Heldur's power that governs the tower. I felt that Ketil was waiting for something – or someone. His dead brother. Death, perhaps.'

Starkad declared, 'He doesn't know what he's doing. We can't just leave him out there to die alone in the cold and dark, perhaps horribly.'

'Maybe he wants to spare his family pain,' Ermingerd suggested quietly. 'He always was soft that way – before.'

'Tell that to Ketil,' Syrgja replied bitterly. 'He won't come out of that tower, for all your fine words. You promised to save him, wizard. Now how are you going to do it if Heldur won't let you near him?'

Her prediction proved correct. Two days passed, and Ketil did not emerge. Syrgja and Ermingerd took food to the tower, and Syrgja coaxed and pleaded outside the door, but Ketil refused to eat or to come out. When Thurid mustered the courage to approach the tower, the black miasma was still present, along with the implied threat of force to defend the tower from intrusion. As Gedvondur was still debilitated from his first encounter with the tower entity, Thurid declined to challenge the extant forces for the possession of Ketil.

'I am forced to capitulate, for the time being,' Thurid admitted loftily after two attempts were rebuffed. 'I wouldn't want to proceed without the advice of my ally Gedvondur. Heldur's got too much power when he's got a living creature in his grasp.'

Syrgja snorted. 'We know who's got the brains. The hand. What a sorry lot you'd be without him. I wonder how such nithlings came by something so valuable.'

Svanlaug tossed her hair free of its net. 'It's quite simple. We stole Gedvondur's hand from Djofull. I had to cut it from his wrist.'

'You're a coldhearted piece, aren't you?' Syrgja's thin lips curled in contempt.

'No doubt of it,' Svanlaug replied. 'At least as coldhearted

273

as a family who wishes their old uncle to die.'

When Hogni and Horgull returned at twilight, Syrgja launched a tirade against them, urging them to bring Ketil from the tower. Her pleas fell upon deaf ears. In her extremity, she turned to Thurid.

'I spoke over-hasty,' she said stiffly, her gaunt and unlovely features drawn into lines of desperate fear. 'It's the worry that shortens my temper, which never was good at its best. Is there nothing you can do to help Ketil? You're the only one who seems to care about him.'

'Can't you help me?' Thurid asked quietly. 'Tell me what the Convocation is, and about Heldur.'

Syrgja shook her head and clenched her apron in her fists. 'I dare not,' she whispered. 'I cannot.'

'Then what am I to do?' Thurid asked. 'My hands are tied unless I can get into the tower. It's the only place I can read the past and find the answers I need. Unless someone can get Ketil out of that tower, we've lost him and you've lost your chance to break Slagfid's curse, and we've lost our chance to break the geas. Hogni couldn't have done a better job himself of thwarting us.'

'I had nothing to do with it,' Hogni said. 'Ketil went there of his own will – although I can't claim to be disappointed by it. I told you all along you couldn't win here, that you'd break yourself on our curse. Heldur's power is far too strong and clever for you. He's thrown you out of his tower and you're not going to get back in as long as he's got Ketil.'

Unable to abide Hogni's gloating, Leifr went outside to walk up and down. Raudbjorn sat down on a crumbled wall to watch him, his large face creased with the unaccustomed lines of struggling thought, looking as worried and puzzled as Leifr inwardly felt in his attempts to deal with the Alfar realm. He and Raudbjorn, he realized, had many common limitations.

'Storm coming,' Raudbjorn rumbled, sniffing in the direction of Skera-gil. The troll-hounds also pointed their sharp noses skyward and sniffed attentively.

'Then we'd better tend to the livestock before it gets here,' Leifr said. 'You and Starkad take the sheep, I'll take the horses, and we'll all feed the cattle.'

The day darkened early with black clouds roiling over Skera-gil and with unseasonal rumblings of thunder and flashes of greenish lightning. The horses shifted uneasily in their stalls, their eyes white-ringed with alarm, their ears twitching at sounds human ears didn't hear. Leifr stroked Jolfr's nose, attempting to soothe him, but the horse tossed his head restlessly and pawed at his bedding.

The cows ignored the hay that was given them, trampling about restlessly and tossing their heads against their halters with loud, uneasy bellows. Leifr had never liked cows; when they were frightened, he considered them even more stupid and dangerous.

Hogni and Horgull stood in the dooryard watching the sky, with Thurid keeping a disdainful distance from them. Syrgja and Ermingerd huddled in the doorway, gazing at the strange-colored clouds warring over Skera-gil. Thurid's alf-light was blown out straight from the knob of his staff to trail away in flying sparks.

'It's Heldur's powers!' Thurid shouted over the buffeting of the wind. 'Elementals clashing! It's not safe out here!'

Hogni shouted back, 'There's no place safe in Fangelsi, wizard! You should know that by now!'

Inside the house, the screaming of the wind was muffled by the thick walls, but icy drafts came in under the door and through the shuttered window. Once something heavy struck the roof, causing a sifting of dust to fall down from the turves. Leifr and Starkad were in the sleeping loft, lying on their bellies and watching the storm through the tiny eaves' window. In silent wonder, they saw Hogni's sledge carom off the roof and go kiting away in the grip of the wind, twirling aloft like a leaf and coming down almost gently atop the dairy house. The heavy door of the horse barn burst open and was torn off with a rending screech, and cartwheeled to its destruction,

275

blown first one way then another.

The storm lasted all the night, making sleep impossible. After the longest night Leifr could remember enduring, the winds died suddenly, leaving an unnatural stillness. Thurid ventured outside first, lighting up his alf-light with a blazing glare that burned away streamers of clammy mist swirling around the house. Not a shred of light penetrated the thick cover of clouds still boiling overhead, flickering with greenish shivers of lightning.

'Is it over?' Syrgja asked tremulously.

Thurid turned to face all the directions, his hand extended to test the air. He shook his head, scowling and muttering to Gedvondur, who was clamped to his shoulder.

'The wards were breached before,' Thurid intoned, 'and something got past. Now we're seeing the results of it. Heldur is doing his best to rebuff a powerful enemy. It seems they've called a truce for a while.'

'I hear horses,' Starkad interrupted excitedly. 'Maybe Jarnvard's coming to see if we're all right.'

Thurid cupped one hand behind his hear to listen. 'Back into the house!' he commanded fiercely. 'That's not Jarnvard coming! It's Djofull! He broke the wards!'

A darker clump of shadow materialized, moving down the side of the fell at a reckless pace. In the midst of the riders was a familiar sledge, lurching over the rough track behind three horses. With no reduction of speed, the riders and horses descended upon Fangelsi, drawing to a foaming, prancing halt before the door of the house.

Leifr came forward with the sword drawn, and the Dokkalfar riders drew back from the deadly gleaming metal as if they were abundantly familiar with the skill of Leifr and *Endalaus Daudi*.

Djofull stepped down from his vehicle, surrounded by a crackling aura of murky red light.

'Don't think to touch even a hair of my head with that sword,' he warned Leifr. 'I'm done dallying with you, Scipling. I can find another to carry that sword for my cause. Greetings, Thurid. You're not looking very well. Have you spent long hours trying to wrest Heldur's secrets from him? A useless occupation, don't you agree?'

'I've made significant progress,' Thurid retorted. 'With the help of Gedvondur's hand. What are you doing here? Don't you trust us to get what you wanted? We've learned about Slagfid's treasure, and many men better than you have perished in the attempt to get it.'

Djofull waved one hand, a metal claw, in a deprecatory gesture. 'Yes, the gold is very tempting, is it not? However, the gold isn't the entire matter in dispute in Fangelsi. I have a quarrel of long standing with Heldur, sort of a sporting competition, and you know my weakness for taking a sporting gamble, or you wouldn't be here now.'

Leifr answered, 'Yes, we're well acquainted with your idea of sport, from our stay in Ulfskrittinn. What sort of amusement do you plan to find in Fangelsi? Heldur and the Flayer and certain restless draugar should give you enough sport.'

Djofull sneered, 'It's watching you clumsy fools dealing with them that provides the sport. Had you cared to linger awhile longer in Ulfskrittinn, I would have given you some further instructions about the geas I laid against you. Now, to show you I have a little pity, I've come to give you some assistance. Is there anyone else who would be so generous with miscreants such as yourselves?'

'Assistance from you in breaking your own geas?' Thurid snorted in disgust. 'Your help is the last thing we want. We're doing splendidly without it. By spring I shall know all I need to know to break Slagfid's curse, thus destroying the night-farers you sent us to Fangelsi to destroy. With the Flayer gone, you'll no doubt feel free to rob Slagfid's Ban of its treasure, as you have planned all along, and we shall be free to your obligation.'

Djofull pursed his lips and shook his head. 'Don't be so hasty, Thurid. There's more than Slagfid's gold at stake. It's the smith Heldur himself that must be destroyed, and the crystal he's making in the flames of his forge must be given to me.'

Hogni stepped forward at the mention of Heldur. 'This talk of destroying Heldur is ridiculous. He's held the fate of Fangelsi in the palm of his hand since the days of Slagfid. If anyone attempts to challenge him, Heldur will smash him like a fly. As for the gold, you won't get it as long as the Flayer walks.'

'Then let the Scipling do the job he was intended for,' Djofull retorted. 'I'd thought he would have killed that jotun by now. If you'll stop interfering with him, maybe he'll have it done before the Convocation. It would simplify the situation a great deal.'

'Never!' Syrgja sputtered, clutching a walking staff like a weapon. 'No one harms the jotuns! It's one of Heldur's laws and it mustn't be broken!'

'Convenient for Heldur,' Djofull answered. 'The jotuns defend him at his labors inside Slagfid's Ban and protect the treasure. We'll destroy the Flayer first, then we'll pay his forge a visit at Convocation time. You're wasting too much time on this jotun curse, Thurid. The curse will run out after the present generation, and by then there will be nothing here that matters to anyone.'

Thurid smiled a frosty smile, his eyes narrowing. 'But if you intervene now, it'll hardly be sporting, will it? Perhaps you don't trust us to bring the geas to a satisfactory conclusion. Perhaps you could do it better without us.'

'Heldur knows me too well or I would come after him,' said Djofull with mounting impatience. 'I'm warning you to stop dragging your feet, Thurid. It's midwinter already, and what have you accomplished? Exactly nothing by way of getting any nearer to Heldur. I think you're too frightened to do anything but maunder and muddle around in that tower. Forget Heldur's curse and its consequences, and show some courage. I must have that crystal, and I must have it before the spring equinox because I don't want to wait another year for another opportunity.'

278

Thurid folded his arms across his chest, still holding his lighted staff aloft. 'I could progress more speedily if I possessed certain information. Tell me what the Convocation is, and the significance of the number ninety-nine. I want to know more about this crystal also.'

Djofull shook his head angrily. 'You don't need to know anything more than you do already. Just do as I tell you and we'll be ready when the proper time comes.'

Hogni said, 'And I tell you, if you attempt to run at cross purposes to Heldur's curse, we'll all perish in the violence of the consequences.'

'I agree,' Thurid said. 'I've seen enough of Heldur and his curse to know the truth when I hear it. We must proceed with utmost care, picking away at it here and there until we get at the meat of Heldur's spell.'

'The time for caution is passed!' Djofull replied. 'I'm taking command at Fangelsi. You'll all do what I tell you or else I'll show you some real consequences! The first thing I'll do is to push back your puny wards until you can get nowhere near Skera-gil, unless you beg to be forgiven for your insufferable arrogance. You'll be completely cut off in this wretched spot. How long can you last without more firewood? Have you got enough hay to last until spring? Do you have plenty of flour and stockfish?'

'What good will it do you to starve and freeze us to death?' Thurid demanded. 'You'll never get your crystal and the gold, if you do.'

'Thurid, you and the Scipling are not the martyr type,' Djofull answered. 'You won't allow it to happen. Doing anything is better than doing nothing, and what you do will be done to the tune that I pipe or you'll suffer for it. Now I'll give you a short while to move your things out of the house and into one of the barns. I've been looking for a snug place to spend the winter.'

Syrgja pushed past Hogni and Thurid to confront Djofull, with her fists braced on her hips. 'This is my house,' she said in a deadly tone, 'and you're not going to defame it by setting one foot inside it. I was born here. I was given my name under its roof, and I've worked every day of my life since I was tall enough to stir a pot. Only one Dokkalfar in my lifetime has come across its threshold, and I'll not live to see another, so if you wish to take my house, you'll have to kill me where I stand. I invoke every spell and protection woven into these hallowed walls by every descendant of Slagfid to keep out the riders of the dark such as yourselves.'

Djofull's nasty chuckle died on his lips as the runes carved into the doorposts and the frames around the windows suddenly came to glowing life. A faint blue mist oozed from the ancient turf walls and from the roof, enveloping the house with a soft light.

Djofull made a contemptuous sound and signalled to his outriders. 'What do I care for women's spells?' he snorted. 'This house is too close to the firth for my taste anyway. When you've suffered joint-ill as much as I have, you avoid damp places when you can. Keep your house, woman. I think it has an atmosphere as old and evil as you are.' He turned and climbed into his sledge, glaring out at Thurid. 'When you decide to be more reasonable, you can send for me to beg for my help.'

'I never beg,' Thurid replied with icy pride. 'You'll get your crystal, Djofull, but I warn you to stay away.'

'And I never accept warnings,' Djofull snarled, giving a signal to his driver. The sledge and horses lurched away with a mighty whip-cracking and self-important rumbling over the frozen earth, leaving Syrgja standing triumphant in front of her house. The runes and the mist were fading, but Leifr was as loath to approach it as Djofull had been.

'What is it?' he asked Thurid suspiciously, in a low voice. 'Syrgja's no sorceress, is she?'

'No, but sometimes it's merely enough to be female to invoke the most ancient of protection spells,' Thurid answered, his words restrained. 'Women have always been a bane to wizards. They've all got a streak of those old powers, if they get angry enough to bring them out.'

Syrgja led the return to the house, running her hand lovingly over the doorframe and touching Slagfid's sword hanging inside. With almost regal pride, she stoked the fire on her hearth and swept her broom across the floor, although nary a crumb was out of place. Order prevailed in her kitchen, dark and miserly though it might be.

'Tomorrow we'll strengthen our wards,' Hogni said in his customary toneless voice, as if it were the most casual of observations. 'We'd better bring them down somewhat to positions we can hold easier. I hope that dead hand of yours will recover soon enough to be useful to us. If we're going to be besieged, we'll need all the help we can get, from whatever source.'

'We'll go to Killbeck,' Starkad suggested. 'Janvard keeps twenty fighting men. We'll fight Djofull and his Dokkalfar.'

'There's no help to be had from that quarter,' Thurid snapped. 'What do you think Jarnvard could do about Djofull, Ketil, the Flayer, or about anything in Fangelsi? His law is useless!'

'We alone can save ourselves,' Hogni said. His eyes probed the circle of faces around the room. 'Something has weakened our defenses. Some disruption of the spell that binds us. One unclean thing brought into our fortress could be our destruction. We must all think what we have done.'

Silence descended in the kitchen, a frozen, watchful silence into which no one dared venture. Hogni and Horgull retreated into a chess game while they waited for the unnatural darkness to lift, and Syrgja looked grimly into the flour barrel, rolling up her sleeves in preparation for mixing more of her solid, heavy dark bread. Leifr could feel the currents of thought pushing and pulling among the Alfar, their tension revealed by a flashing eye or a clenching fist. Starkad looked too pale and guilty.

Frequently Leifr felt Hogni's eyes upon him. Leifr stared back at him, filled with the clammy realization that Hogni must know about the gold taken from Slagfid's

Ban. He was certain his guilt was written all over his face, and someone with Hogni's skills could probably detect such powerful and unpleasant emotions as guilt.

Leifr stood up to peer out the crack in the window. The darkness was dispersing in lumps of moving shadow, like a dark mist dissolving, instead of fading gradually into daylight as a proper, natural darkness would have done.

'What would be the harm in asking Jarnvard's help?' he asked, turning to confront Thurid and the Grimssons. 'If I could get through the wards and back again with twenty men, it would give Djofull second thoughts about pressing us too far. Djofull's men and fylgjur-wolves can die, if you kill them nine times over. He won't want to lose all of them.'

'I don't think it wise to carry our troubles abroad,' Hogni said, 'but the decision is yours. My wards will let you back in, but I can't say the same for Djofull's, if his are behind mine.'

'I'll try it, at least,' Leifr said.

To conceal his unease and a growing smoldering resolve, Leifr busied himself repairing and oiling his equipment, cutting new laces for his boots, mending his saddle girth, and polishing *Endalaus Daudi*. He could feel all the eyes in the room fixed upon the dull glow of its strange metal. Even the hounds watched him interestedly, trying to decide if these were preparations for the hunt.

In the morning Starkad objected strenuously to being left behind when an outing was in prospect, but Leifr insisted just as strenuously that he remain at home. Starkad followed him despondently to the horse barn, still grumbling about being left.

'Starkad, there's a good reason I want you to stay behind,' Leifr said as soon as they were out of hearing of the house. 'If I can't get back, someone's got to help your uncle Ketil get out of the tower. And in case Djofull's waiting to capture me, I want you to guard *Endalaus Daudi* while I'm gone. It can't fall into Dokkalfar hands.

My old Scipling steel and the hounds will protect me well enough.'

He unslung the sword and its belt and handed it over to Starkad, who stared at it in awe not unmingled with pride.

'I'll guard it with my life,' he said fervently. 'But you will come back, Leifr, and with Jarnvard's help.'

'Take the sword into the house, Starkad. If I'm not back in three days at the most, you'll know I'm not coming back at all.'

As Leifr saddled Jolfr, a ray of pale sun somehow penetrated the cloud cover, falling upon the old wall and slightly warming its mossy stones and a small verge of winter-seared grass left uncovered by the snow. After a moment, a movement attracted his attention. It had been there some time, he realized, but he had ignored it in his occupation with more serious problems. Now he saw that it was a cat, basking in the pale sun against the wall, a small furry cat the color of smoke, who lifted its head from the washing of one hind foot to gaze at him with amber eyes. Lumps of snow were matted in its fur, as if it had walked a long way through the snow. Even its long fur could not conceal its gaunt sides and bony spine.

Leifr took a step forward, holding his breath, all his other concerns totally fled. The cat eyed him fearlessly, gathering her legs under her in case a quick retreat was called for.

'Ljosa!' Leifr whispered.

Like a shadow the cat leaped onto the wall, paused to look back at him a moment, with reproach, as he thought, then dived into the shadow on the other side. Leifr came around his end of the wall, searching for her. She was not there, nor even one paw print to mar the white snow.

'Ljosa! Come back here, I know it's you,' he called, irritated by her elusive tactics, but he saw no sign of her. After a futile search, he mounted his horse and resumed his journey to Killbeck, taking the rough trail that had brought them to Fangelsi-hofn.

At the top of the fell, however, Leifr felt the familiar brush of unreasoning fear. Halting his horse, he searched the surrounding rocks for the sign, and he found it emblazoned on a cairn. The screaming crow had been stuck over with a spiral sign Leifr had encountered before. It seemed to leap out at him menacingly, the very sight of it filling him with a chilly species of horror. The first place he had seen it was burned into the palm of an old wanderer and tallow renderer known as Gotiskolker. The carbuncle also recognized the sign and sent him a thrill of warning.

Chafing at his limitations, Leifr paced up and down in the snow, advancing on the ward and steeling himself to endure its warning, in the hope that somehow he could become inured to its terror and pass through. Perversely, the longer he suffered contact with its influence, the less of it he could tolerate the next time he challenged it.

Steeling himself for another and final attempt, he rode his horse determinedly toward the cairn at a gallop, hoping he could charge right through the waves of terror and despair. At the usual distance, however, Jolfr braced his legs and slid to a halt, his neck lathered and his eyes rolling in terror. Whirling on his haunches, the horse lunged away, determinedly heading back toward Fangelsi and its safe, warm barn. Leifr brought Jolfr to a snorting halt and gazed at the other side of the fell broodingly, remembering Hogni's warning. Once on the other side, he might never be permitted to return. Now that he was certain Ljosa's fylgja had appeared, he was particularly loath to leave Fangelsi-hofn.

Slowly he rode back toward Fangelsi, taking the longest possible way around the boundary of the wards. By the end of the day he discovered that Hogni's limits had narrowed, and Djofull had reinforced his side with spiral signs and a well-beaten path made by wolf paws. Hogni's safe ground was confined to the hay meadows and lowlands, forbidding Djofull access to Skera-gil and the fells beyond the sixth gate. On the east was ocean. At the stone gateposts leading into the wild lands of Skera-gil on the west, Hogni's mark halted him. Gazing toward the dark gash that hid Slagfid's Ban, he thought of the gold that lay there, guarded by the jotun, Fangelsi's great secret which Hogni and Horgull were defending and were willing to kill their aging uncle to possess.

CHAPTER 18

Angrily Leifr scanned the horizons of Fangelsi-hofn from the sea all the way around. Even the clouds lowering over the valley reminded him that he was a prisoner here. In defeat, he rode back to Fangelsi-hofn and stabled his horse. He looked around for the gray cat, but she was nowhere in evidence.

When he entered the house, all eyes were raised to him expectantly, except for Hogni; he was lounging at the table with his attention half upon his chess game with Horgull, who sat with his brow furrowed up in concentration.

Leifr dropped his cloak on the sleeping platform and sat down to pull off his boots.

'I didn't go through,' Leifr said resentfully to all of them. 'Djofull's got his marks all over Hogni's, and I had a strong feeling that, once I got out, he wouldn't let me back in. It would be me against Djofull and the fylgjur-wolves outside, and you against the jotuns and Heldur inside.' He yearned to tell Thurid about Ljosa, but Hogni was listening.

'Exactly as I told you,' Hogni said with a grim, satisfied smile. 'But we hold the upper hand as long as we hold Skera-gil.'

Thurid drew deeply upon his pipe as he gazed into the fire and scowled. In a moment he said, 'Don't try to sound as if we're working together, Hogni. I still intend to break Slagfid's curse before the vernal equinox. We've got to get Ketil out of the tower so I can continue. Unless, that is, you've come to your senses and have decided to help by telling me all you know. We can't get to Jarnvard for help against Djofull, nor can we make a complaint about your treatment of Ketil. Time is drawing short, Hogni.'

'The Flayer's demands must be met first,' Hogni said wearily. 'You can't save Ketil from his appointed fate.'

'The only way out of it is to kill the Flayer with *Endalaus Daudi*,' Leifr said, and Starkad nodded emphatically. 'The magic in this sword is more powerful than any enchantment in existence, including Heldur's. What could be more final than absolute and eternal death?'

Hogni eyed Leifr a moment. 'If you try to kill the Flayer with that sword, you may only hasten the natural conclusion to Slagfid's curse. Or you may inflict absolute and eternal death upon yourself and everyone in this house, if its power is turned back upon you – a not unlikely result of tampering with powers beyond your reckoning. As I said before, I have nothing to lose. Perhaps it would be a cleaner end than this.' He made a hopeless gesture to include all of Fangelsi.

'With Djofull's geas, we also have little to lose,' Leifr replied.

Horgull emerged unexpectedly from his self-imposed exile of gloom. 'But much to gain, if you play it properly,' Horgull replied shrewdly. 'You've been given a great weapon, Scipling. Don't let stupidity waste your opportunity. It's not the Flayer or any jotun or draug you should be stalking. The one that should be destroyed is the source of his spell – Heldur. Do that and you will thwart the curse as well as Djofull and his geas.'

'Silence, nephew!' Syrgja commanded, her face alternately paling and flushing. 'How dare you even speak of such things? Are you mad?'

'Yes, we are mad,' Hogni answered for his brother and himself furiously. 'Who could live in Fangelsi with the burdens we bear and not be mad? No one has ever come here with a sword like that, nor have we seen a wizard with three hands. Perhaps it is time to revolt against our fate, aunt!'

'We must stand together, as Slagfid's heirs have always done,' Syrgja answered. 'I can't believe that you would

287

abandon me now, when there are so few years left for the curse to run.'

Hogni sighed hopelessly. His brief insurrection collapsed before the accusing and mournful stare of his aunt. 'There's no use in fighting Heldur,' he said. 'By giving in, at least we don't lose everything.'

'Just Uncle Ketil,' Starkad added in cold fury. When no one rose to his bait, he threw on his cloak and went outside. He floundered through the snow toward the tower, but its forces would not let him approach. At last he returned to the kitchen, wet and miserable, where Ermingerd attempted to console him with a hot drink.

From the surrounding peaks and fells came the weird chorus of wolves howling, filling the night with the ungodly laughter of the rulers of the night. They were much closer, sounding as if they had descended as far as the sixth gate.

For the next several days, Thurid continued to nurse Gedvondur back to health with steamy baths and fragrant oils, while Leifr watched for Ljosa's cat-form. Twice he was rewarded for his vigilance. She kept her distance, watching him distrustfully, no matter how soothingly he called to her.

Thurid snorted at Leifr's revelation, declaring he had seen no gray cat.

'Possibly you are imagining it,' he said to Leifr one evening, in a rare civil humor when Hogni and Horgull were in the barn attending to a calving. 'Often our minds create images from their own worry, guilt, or fear. You feel responsible for what happened to Ljosa.'

Leifr nodded suspiciously. 'I am. The cat is real, and you've got to help her, Thurid. She's followed me halfway across Skarpsey in that pitiful little body. You're the only one left who can help her.'

'Leifr, you Scipling dunderhead, I'm trying to tell you, that cat you see isn't a real cat. It's only an image, a ghost, a shadow that represents Ljosa in your mind—'

'She's real, and you promised to help her. Instead, you

spend all your time out in that cursed tower. You're obsessed with it, completely possessed by that hand.' He gave Gedvondur's hand an injudicious poke where it lay wrapped in a soft wool shawl. Gedvondur's expression surfaced instantly over Thurid's features, with a bellow of outrage. Startled, Syrgja dropped a pan of unskimmed milk and stood glaring across the mess at its perpetrators.

'I curse the day I allowed the lot of you in my house!' she raged.

'The dogs will clean up the milk and be grateful,' Leifr offered in a genuine attempt to placate her.

'Those foul beasts with their troll-breath and blood-stained jaws will never cross my threshold!' Syrgja answered, even more furious than before.

Suddenly the troll-hounds in the main hall howled with the peculiar worried note they reserved for the jotun scent. After a long taut moment of strained listening, Leifr heard a muffled pounding from the direction of the tower. Then Hogni and Horgull burst into the passage outside, barring the door in great haste before entering the kitchen in a hot and breathless condition that indicated a desperate run had been made from the barn.

Hogni gasped, 'It's the Flayer! He's come to the tower for Ketil! He came after us first, then he heard Ketil shouting.'

'Shouting for help?' Syrgja quavered, her eyes reddening with unshed tears. She looked imploringly at her nephews, then turned to Thurid. 'Please help my poor brother, wizard!' she whispered. 'I haven't been kind, but now I beg you, on my knees if you insist – please help Ketil! He doesn't deserve to be torn between Heldur and the Flayer! No man deserves such a fate!'

Thurid rose to his feet with a heroic gleam in his eye, gripping his staff and shoving Gedvondur into his pocket. 'I'll do what I can,' he said. 'I've never yet refused a helpless woman's plea for help!'

'I warn you, wizard, don't interefere,' Hogni replied. 'The penalties will be worse than the curse! I forbid you to leave this house. Let it end now, tonight!'

Thurid exchanged a challenging glare with Hogni and Horgull and strode to the door, throwing his cloak over his shoulders. 'Hang your penalties. I'm going to save him myself. Whatever harm I do by doing it you'd better be ready to counter with spells of your own. Raudbjorn, Leifr, follow me and do as I tell you!'

Starkad leaped to his feet and rushed into the passageway, where the dogs surged eagerly around him.

'May the powers defend us, we are doomed,' Hogni said.

Leifr followed Thurid into the night beyond, with Starkad crowding at his heels despite the remonstrances of his aunt. He saw no sign of the Flayer, but the hounds raced toward the tower without hesitation.

Starkad darted around Thurid and the slow-moving mountain that was Raudbjorn, and rushed ahead. Thurid cursed and followed, wishing he had more light to see by than the sheaves of stars overhead and the thin beams of light from the muffled lantern Starkad carried ahead.

Halfway up the hill Thurid and Leifr stopped, halted by the sounds of wood being bashed to splinters. Each heavy blow was echoed by a growl or grunt from the Flayer. Starkad returned, now less eager to charge away into the unknown. Thurid cautiously led the advance upon the tower. By the time they had reached a hiding place near it, the Flayer had torn the door off its hinges and they saw his huge, dark bulk heaving the door away at least ten paces, uttering groans and animal snarls. Turning, he saw his stalkers and crouched in a warlike stance, eyes and teeth gleaming. In consternation, Leifr measured the size and shape of the jotun. He was almost the size of Ognun, shaped more like a man than a troll, but strangely thickened, like a gnarled tree. His back was humped and his head canted to one side, where the gnarling seemed heavier. For a long moment, Thurid and the jotun measured each other with a deadly scrutiny, while Thurid's staff glowed and trickled a column of smoke.

'So this is your finest art, Heldur,' Thurid said. 'Not lovely to look at, is it? It's been around entirely too long, after seven hundred years of this jotun nonsense. Leifr, don't get too close. You're getting in my way.'

Without warning, he turned the full glare of his alf-light upon the jotun. The creature cringed and squinted, bellowing furiously as it pawed at the light. Then, instead of retreating, he turned and plunged inside the tower, where Ketil was muttering distractedly about taking some sheep to the fair.

Seizing the opportunity, Leifr led a dash to the side of the tower, taking up a position just outside the door, with his sword drawn. Raudbjorn gripped his halberd and waited. Starkad crouched beside him, scarcely breathing.

The Flayer emerged almost immediately, with Ketil slung over his shoulder like a calf. With his enemy looming almost within touching distance, Starkad suddenly lost his nerve. With a yell of defiance, he flung his smothered lantern toward the Flayer and took to his heels, leaving Leifr and Thurid in the unenviable position of confronting the jotun after Starkad set him on fire.

The lantern sprayed flaming oil across the Flayer's massive chest and broke on the rocky ground, releasing a burst of illumination. By its flaring light Leifr saw a tortuously rugged face glowering back at him through the flame, a face so distorted by knots and swellings and crenellations as to make it almost unrecognizable as human. Tiny furious eyes glared through the fissures, and a gash of a mouth opened up in a powerful bellow as Leifr raised the sword menacingly.

The grating voice of Heldur spoke. 'Get away, or you and that sword will be fuel for my forge!'

'I challenge you to face me as you are, Heldur!' Leifr yelled. 'Only a coward hides behind other forms!'

The Flayer lashed out at the sword with one knotted fist the size of a boulder, striking a resounding clang as if indeed the fist were made of stone and not flesh. Sparks showered to the ground and Leifr was jolted back a few paces by the force of the blow and the force of two disparate powers colliding. The sensation was too unpleasant to repeat willingly. The jotun stepped back also, shaking his great encrusted fist and uttering a terrible howl. Before he could take another swing at the jotun, Raudbjorn plunged forward with a bellow of rage, whirling his halberd for a mighty blow.

'Get back!' Thurid panted. 'No weapons, you fools!'

Taking a grip upon his captive, the Flayer began a wary retreat into the darkness, keeping one glittering eye fastened upon Leifr and Raudbjorn. He paused to slap one of the hounds off the back of his knee, then bounded over a shoulder-high wall with astonishing agility for such a malformed creature.

Leifr and Raudbjorn followed the hounds as they dashed for the nearby gate. On the other side of the wall, the jotun staggered over a stretch of rocky earth, where the pebbles rolled under his feet on the flinty ground. Before he could turn to face his pursuers, Leifr slashed at the back of his leg with the sword, again raising a flash of sparks as if he had struck stone. A red-hot gash glowed, fading gradually as the jotun turned and struck out at the menacing sword and the harrying hounds.

'Let the old man go and I'll allow you to escape!' Leifr called over the huffing and growling of the creature. 'This is the sword of endless death. Let it pierce you and you are doomed, Heldur!'

The Flayer glowered at him with red gleaming eyes a moment, and Leifr realized the influence of Heldur had fled.

'Brodir!' the Flayer whimpered, then slowly let Ketil slide from his shoulder to the ground. With a heavy, dragging step the jotun moved away into the night, closely watched by Raudbjorn and the growling dogs. Leifr knelt beside Ketil as Starkad burst through the gate and came clattering through the loose rocks, sliding to a halt beside his uncle.

'Is he alive?' he gasped. 'Is his neck broken? The Flayer

can break the neck of a bull and then carry off the beast entire!'

'A pity we don't have a lantern, or we might see if he is alive or dead,' Thurid replied bitingly. 'Raudbjorn, you carry Ketil and we'll watch out behind in case the Flayer decides to come back for his supper.'

'I didn't mean to run away,' Starkad said. 'I didn't go far. And I did come back. I doubt if anyone has seen the Flayer face-to-face like that and lived to tell of it. You can't blame me for being a little startled, after the tales I've heard about him.'

'He's alive,' Thurid said, as Ketil began snarling and struggling to rise, clubbing Raudbjorn with one fist. He proved so uncooperative that Raudbjorn was forced to carry him to the house on his shoulders.

'We saved Uncle Ketil!' Starkad announced triumphantly the moment they were within shouting distance of the house. 'The Flayer had him thrown over one shoulder, but Leifr and Raudbjorn and I challenged him and drew blood, and he dropped Uncle Ketil.'

'Bring him into the kitchen where it's safe!' Syrgja commanded, sweeping forward from the shadows with sudden energy as they brought Ketil into the light. 'Ermingerd, draw some water and get cloths to bathe him.'

Svanlaug followed Ermingerd, saying determinedly, 'I'll assist you. Many of the healing physician's arts of Ljosalfar and Dokkalfar are the same.'

'No Dokkalfar concoction can result in clean healing,' Syrgja said sharply, but Svanlaug pretended not to hear.

Raudbjorn carried Ketil, still grumbling and protesting, into the kitchen. Ketil groaned and squinted in the lamplight of the kitchen, pawing helplessly with his ragged hands. The bandages had mostly been torn away, revealing raw, swollen clubs that once had been hands, with unkept black nails curling like claws. His face was mottled and red, tightly swollen and tender in several places, as if boils were coming to the surface.

Syrgja pushed Leifr away from his scrutiny of Ketil, mainly by sheer force of her efficiency and her disapproving scowls and glowers. Svanlaug, however, was proof against all Syrgja's efforts to send her away and worked alongside Ermingerd, bandaging and poulticing with a professional skill that soon earned her Syrgja's grudging acceptance.

When Hogni and Horgull returned to the kitchen after securing the tower, Syrgja commenced complaining in an angry undertone. 'That Norskur carried him in here like a sack of grain on his back. It was no wonder Ketil was angry, being mauled about that way by strangers.'

She halted and glared at the strangers in question.

'There was no other way to bring him back,' Leifr said, trying to keep the anger out of his voice. 'The Flayer would not have carried him any more carefully, I assure you. If we had not frightend the jotun away, you certainly would have lost your brother this time.'

Horgull turned his smoldering gaze upon Ketil. 'Better that the jotun had carried him off,' he grunted.

'No!' Syrgja burst out in an anguished cry.

Hogni turned to scrutinize Ketil, who sagged in his chair, dozing heavily, his head with its angry swollen growths sunk upon his chest. His sleep was not an easy one, but filled with grunts and flinches and grumbles. His breathing was like the panting of a dog who sleeps too near to the fire. Once again the chain was fastened around his waist to prevent any irrational charges.

Hogni looked from Leifr to Syrgja. 'This cannot continue,' he said, almost gently.

'We cannot end it,' Syrgja shot back, rising to the challenge with flashing eyes.

'No reason not to,' Horgull grumbled.

'If we keep him out of sight of the strangers,' Syrgja pursued triumphantly, 'he'll be more calm. They upset him, and that's why he wants to leave. We'll put Ketil in the storeroom. It will be cool and dark there.'

Starkad started to rise and protest, but Ermingerd

294

pulled him down on the seat beside her and gave him a warning look that silenced him.

Syrgja unclenched her fists, balled into her apron. 'He'll be more comfortable down there.'

'How long do you think it will work?' Hogni asked.

'Long enough, perhaps,' Syrgja said with a glance toward Thurid.

Hogni motioned Leifr and Raudbjorn toward the shadows in the far end of the room, then approached Ketil cautiously and laid a hand upon his shoulder to awaken him. Ketil awakened instantly at the light touch, as if someone had dropped a hot coal on him. Leaping to his feet, he flailed the air with his arms and howled, staggering blindly to the end of his chain. His eyes were shut tight, and his face twisted up in a grimace of pain. Slowly he turned, rather fearfully, to face the hearth. He pawed in the direction of the low fire burning there, sensing its heat and backing away, shaking his head with worried groans.

Horgull unfastened the chain from his waist while he was thus distracted by the fire. Presently they all heard the sound of a heavy door being bolted, echoing in the vacancy of the great hall.

No longer did silence rule the house; the rooms were filled with the growling and restless pacing of Ketil in the storage room. The nights were disrupted by the bellowing of the Flayer, Ketil's answering rumblings, and the desolate cries of the jotun draugar searching for the stolen barrow gold. In a vengeful humor, the Flayer killed a cow from the shore people's herd and left its remains in the dooryard.

It was always nearly dark by the time Leifr and Starkad had finished their day's labors. As they came around the end of the sheep paddock wall, Kraftig suddenly blocked the way, tipping Leifr over neatly at the knees to sprawl face-first on the ground. An imprecation died on Leifr's lips as a dark bulk hurtled out of the shadows at the same instant, teeth snapping with a chilling staccato click on nothingness overhead. Red eyes blazed with a yelp of frustration, then the troll-hounds rose up in a churning white wave of devastation, pulling down the dark attacker with wild yells of fury. Leifr lurched to his feet and drew his sword, ending the battle when the troll-hounds pinned the fylgjur-wolf to the ground so he could drive the sword through it. With a terrible human shriek the creature blazed a moment like a torch, the wolf spell melting away to the image of the Dokkalfar it concealed; then the Dokkalfar perished in a burst of conflicting powers. Nothing remained but a melting puddle of black ice. Starkad gaped, his eyes huge with awe as he stumbled backward away from the spreading stain.

Lanterns came bobbing from the house, accompanied by shouts from Thurid and Hogni. Leifr brandished his sword, looking around at the multitudes of shifting shadows that could be hiding fylgjur-wolves.

'Get back inside,' he commanded. 'Fylgjur-wolves have come through the wards. There may be more of them.'

Hogni turned his head, listening to the echoes of the wolf's dying shriek. 'Fylgjur-wolves! If that sound is any warning to them, they won't return tonight,' he said grimly. 'The sound of a soul perishing in torment gives anyone pause.' He looked at the sword, still running black and silver with the ichor of the fylgjur-wolf's blood, and shuddered as a sudden presentiment overtook him.

'My wards have been breached again,' he said. 'An influence has taken the upper fell surrounding Skera-gil.'

'This makes one less to worry about,' Leifr replied, stepping around the dark stain. 'If I had my way, fylgjur-wolves and the Flayer would all be driven out or killed. I hate to think my life might depend upon wards that fail so readily. Luckily I can ably defend myself.'

Leifr glared at Hogni accusingly, suspecting that the ward had not let the wolf through by coincidence.

'Your kind is unusually lucky,' Hogni retorted. 'But when your luck runs out, it all runs out at once. I sense a turn in luck ahead for you, Scipling, and it won't be a turn for the better. You could still get out of Fangelsi.'

Leifr glanced toward the tower, where Thurid was smoldering and simmering amid his spells and visions.

'It's not possible until the geas is broken,' he said shortly, letting his temper hide his uneasiness.

A curious and unexpected peace descended upon Fangelsi for the space of four nights. On the morning of the fifth day, Syrgja looked up from her weaving, gazing ahead with unseeing eyes with her shuttle suspended in midair. After a moment she put down her shuttle and rose up from her loom to reach for her outdoors cloak and boots.

'It's old Motsi,' she said. 'I've been summoned. She's dying and I must go to her.'

'Dying?' Starkad looked up from the troll hide he was working into softness. 'Again? This is the third time this year, and last year she was dying six times. If you didn't keep interfering, she might get the job done right. I don't know what keeps those shore people alive in the winter.'

Leifr agreed; he had seen their crude shelters of hides and stacked turf on the salty knolls overlooking the shingle and surf. They were wild, ragged people, and Starkad would have dearly loved to emulate them, if his family had permitted.

Hogni knocked on the window from outside, indicating the sledge waiting in readiness. Leifr glanced around at Ermingerd and the others, but they betrayed no surprise that Hogni should know of his aunt's summons, so he decided not to exhibit further ignorance by asking questions. As Syrgja left, she touched the old sword with her fingertips, as was her habit, but this day the sword dropped from its hook with a resounding clangor. Hastily she restored it to its place, anxiously murmuring a formula under her breath and making some signs in the air to ward off bad luck. Then she hurried outside to climb onto the sledge.

At the far end of the table, Thurid looked up from his perusal of some blackened rune sticks, his eyes fastening

297

upon the sword with sharpening attention. When Leifr turned his head to see what the wizard was staring at so intently, he thought he caught a glimmer of fleeting shadow lingering about the sword. Something beckoned, and Thurid predictably rose to his feet.

'This is a good opportunity for me to examine that sword,' he said, passing his hands around it in all directions as if feeling for a current. 'Don't worry, I shan't hurt it a bit, and it did come down off the wall today of its own volition. I don't believe that was an accident, somehow.'

Taking the sword gingerly in both hands, he carried it with him when he retired to the tower with an eager and somewhat furtive gait.

Having Syrgja and Thurid gone, as well as Hogni and Horgull, was a triple treat. Raudbjorn was asleep in a cool corner of the kitchen and Svanlaug had seized the opportunity to escape from the house. Ermingerd produced some cleaned sheep intestine for the three of them to roast over the fire to puffy, crackling richness. Left to themselves, they soon forgot the woes and cares that usually weighed down their spirits, and their moods quickly waxed festive. Leifr discovered that Ermingerd lost her wan and frightened look when she smiled, and he wished it were not so rare an occurrence with her. With a bittersweet pang, he recalled how she alternately blushed and paled when Jarnvard's name was mentioned, striving heroically to hide her emotions. He wondered what could possibly keep such a likely and handsome pair apart, unless it was the unconscionable obstinacy of Ermingerd's relatives, based perhaps on some foolish prejudice.

The passage door suddenly crashed open and Thurid burst into the kitchen, wearing an expression that boded ill for anyone who crossed him. Raudbjorn awakened instantly, reaching for his halberd and looking around for trouble.

'Leifr!' Thurid commanded, striding up and down in thoughtful distraction. 'I've been reading Slagfid's runes and I need your help. Or Heldur's runes, I should say, since he made that sword for Slagfid. You know the way to Slagfid's cave and more, I suspect. I need the sheath to this sword immediately, and Heldur's hold over Slagfid's heirs will be greatly reduced. Not destroyed, mind you, but by sheathing this sword, we'll weaken Heldur a great deal. Heldur's main position is in the tower, so I must remain here to watch him. Now hasten, before Hogni and Horgull get back. We don't need them complicating a simple barrow robbing.'

Leifr and Starkad gaped at him, startled and guilty.

'It's high time we acted,' Svanlaug's voice interjected from the shadows behind as she breezed into the house without making a sound. 'I'm going with them. You've wasted far too much time and power on Heldur's curse, when the answers are all in that cave.'

'No Dokkalfar witch,' grunted Raudbjorn, thumbing his halberd. 'Just Leifr and Raudbjorn.'

'It's nearly dark,' Ermingerd said, her face pale.

'Darkness is life to a Dokkalfar,' Svanlaug said, freeing her hair to fall down around her shoulders, 'and I've been cooped up here under Syrgja's eyes far too long. If anyone can get you past Djofull and fylgjur-wolves, it has to be me. What magical skills Leifr and Raudbjorn possess could easily be lost in a thimble.'

'As long as I've got *Endalaus Daudi*, I don't need to fear Djofull's wolves or the Flayer,' Leifr interrupted with a glower. 'Supposing I would go into that cave, that is.'

'I know where the sheath is!' Starkad was pulling on his boots already, brushing aside Ermingerd's attempts to protest at his going into Skera-gil. 'Remember how I nearly picked it up last time, Leifr? If only I had trusted my barrow-robbing instincts!'

'Indeed, you could have saved yourselves a trip,' Thurid said. 'Now hasten!'

Inside Skera-gil, the snow eddied and swirled, the wind losing much of the uninterrupted fury possible on the barren fellsides. The lingering cloud of mist pressed down

299

darkly, smelling of mold and damp, and veiling the walls
until all sense of direction would have been lost if not for
the hounds' unfailing noses sniffing and snuffling under
the snow. Leifr, however, was guided by the increasing
and familiar sensation of gathering doom. When he felt
that the terror was almost too great to take another step, he
was suddenly beset with a paralyzing feeling of dread and
incipient failure of their endeavor.

'Hogni's used magic so we can't find the cave again,' he
said, his feet slowing woodenly.

Svanlaug lifted her head, as if scenting something on the
wind, and gestured with her hands.

'A sly one, that Hogni,' she said with a note of
admiration. 'He knows how this cursed place preys upon
the emotions with old memories. It's only a rebuffing
spell, Leifr, and a fading one. You can resist it.'

The sky was still a dull pewter color overhead, but it
was darkening rapidly, as if the darkness were a vile cloud
oozing up from the earth itself. Unerringly, Svanlaug and
the hounds led them to the rocks overlooking Slagfid's
Ban, but at first Leifr could not find the portal. Then he
saw that Hogni and Horgull had finished their work, and
the huge door was closed and barred, sealed with a large
lock.

'The door is locked!' Starkad cried, clenching his fist
and smiting the rock. 'No wonder we haven't seen or
heard the Flayer lately!'

He half fell down the slope to the door and hurled
himself upon the lock. Instantly a dull flash of light
exploded in the gloom, jolting Starkad back several paces.
He uttered a muffled curse, shaking his hands frantically
and squeezing them together, teeth gritted against the
pain.

'Hogni put a ward on that door,' Starkad moaned,
slowly uncurling his scorched fingers one by one. 'I
thought I knew how to break all his wards by now, but
that was a new one. We can't touch that door.'

'The lock,' Svanlaug said. 'Even if we get through the

300

ward-spell, we haven't got the key. Horgull's got it around his neck on a string. I saw it there and wondered what it was for. I never thought about this.'

'Don't worry about the lock,' Leifr said, and Raud-bjorn's vast features creased in a pleased grin. 'Just get rid of the ward.'

'Raudbjorn good with locks,' he rumbled, holding up his two mighty hands, clenched into fists like boulders.

Starkad's voice trembled slightly under the strain of sounding braver than he felt. 'Svanlaug, show us your skill with wards,' he said.

Svanlaug laughed, an eerie sound under their present circumstances. 'Dokkalfar are used to dealing with Ljosal-far wards,' she said scornfully. 'You Ljosalfar are always trying to keep us out of where we must go.'

Svanlaug tossed back her hood, letting the wind and the snow swirl with her tossing hair as if the wildness of the night was a feeling she savored. As she approached the door, the lock glowed a sullen red, and the wood itself lit up with the dull phosphorescence of rotting bog wood. She gestured with her hands, sweeping, powerful move-ments, and she made small signs with one fingertip as she whispered to some source of power which Leifr could only imagine.

Raising her pale hands, Svanlaug explored the air and power currents with her fingers a moment, her head flung back, her eyes hidden in pools of shadow. Then her fluid motions froze suddenly and her body stiffened. Slowly the lurid glowing of the lock and the door faded, concentrat-ing instead into a ball of light that she held in her hands a moment before tossing it away to shatter in a burst of sparks among the boulders, splashing them with leftover traces of the glowing ward-spell. Then with a rush of colder air, the forbidding feelings lurking around the door vanished.

With a satisfied smile she approached the door and placed her hand upon it without fear as she turned and beckoned to the others.

'I have used my skill,' she said. 'Now let this beast use his brute strength.'

Raudbjorn climbed the short slope to the door. He glowered at Svanlaug a moment and shook his shoulders with a powerful rippling movement. Gripping the heavy lock in both hands he twisted it against its staples until wood and metal groaned. In the dim light of the lantern his face also twisted demonically and the cords and veins stood out on his forehead and massive neck. Long past normal human endurance he wrenched against the metal, drawing breath only in tortured gasps that whistled between his teeth.

With a wrenching squeal the lock came free, and Raudbjorn heaved open the door, the old hinges skreeling like herring gulls. The sound echoed down a long shaft, and the fetid breath of the jotun cave, warm and foul, struck them all in their faces.

Starkad advanced to the threshold and peered in as far as the feeble light of his lantern would allow. There was silence within, as if something deep in the heart of the mountain had been awakened by their rude intrusion and lay listening. Svanlaug clearly longed to press forward into the cave, sniffing the smells and fingering the air with her hands.

The echoes died, and they listened. Far below, there came a faint sound, indistinguishable in origin, and a wall of fear seemed to push them backward.

'Flayer,' muttered Raudbjorn, gripping his halberd nervously. The dogs pressing behind his knees growled suspiciously.

'There are things worth having in this place,' Svanlaug muttered, her eyes shining as her nimble fingers explored the air. 'Gold. Jewels. Silver.'

'Don't even think about stealing anything,' Leifr snapped. 'We've already gone that road, and look where it's got us. Raudbjorn, you're our best defense,' Leifr continued. 'You lead the way, I'll guard the rear. We'll let the dogs scout ahead for the Flayer. Starkad, stay behind me.'

At his signal, Kraftig, Farlig, and Frimodig took the lead. As the way descended more sharply and they neared the treasure vault, the hounds slowed their eager pace and began growling suspiciously.

Svanlaug stopped and listened intently. Leifr felt the power radiating from her, fanning his face with a slight cool breeze.

'Something is below,' Svanlaug whispered. 'I think it lives and breathes – not like a draug.'

'It sounds like snoring to me,' Starkad said.

Cautiously they approached the burial chamber. Leifr heard heavy snoring, snorting sounds from within. The doors stood open, revealing the biers and the heaps of gold cups and shields adorning them and the heaps of bone and rag that once had been men. Nothing stirred; it seemed as dead as if dead men truly never walked. As they stood thus peering in at the doors, Starkad seized Leifr's arm and pointed with such a nervous thrill that Leifr clearly received the message in his mind: 'The Flayer!' Starkad pointed to the sledge with the gold harness hames where the Flayer lay stiffly on a bed of rags, bones, and odd bits of twinkling treasure, his huge hands clenched at his sides. He was sound asleep, snoring with his mouth open, his knotted features as fearsome as if he were awake. Leifr tried to draw Starkad away, but Starkad's feet seemed welded to the spot where he stood. Worse yet, Starkad seemed inclined toward the bier where the jotun slept. To Leifr's horror, Starkad took a slow step in that direction, as if pulled by something beyond his power to resist. Leifr hung onto him and pulled, but Starkad continued to advance, hauling Leifr along with him.

For a long moment they both gazed at the sleeping jotun. If anything, he was more terrible asleep than awake and raging; even the peace of sleep appeared contorted and evil on those swollen, scowling jotun features.

'The sheath,' Leifr whispered, and Starkad tore himself away to rummage briefly around Slagfid's bier.

'I've got it,' Starkad's voice said shakily.

'Good. Let's get out of here.'

They left the burial chamber and clambered up to the highest level. Behind them the Flayer uttered a few gruff, querulous calls. When they stopped to catch their breath, they could hear his heavy tread lumbering after them.

Svanlaug halted suddenly with a gasp. Leifr looked up in time to see the gray circle of light slowly eclipsing, vanishing entirely with a distant hollow crash.

Starkad plunged forward with a shout. 'Stop! Wait! There's people in here! Don't shut the door!' In his haste he dropped the lantern, and the oil exploded in a useless, flaming pool. He halted his impetuous rush, his face anguished in the light of the flames, then he hurled himself away with an exasperated curse, stumbling through the darkness toward the door.

Raudbjorn summoned a hidden supply of strength and surged forward, mouthing threats and imprecations upon the heads of whoever had closed the door.

Svanlaug laughed a high, brittle laugh in the darkness somewhere ahead of Leifr. 'We're locked in,' she said, with a sharp edge of hysteria to her voice. 'Hogni and Horgull, no doubt. You certainly fell into their trap, like a stupid Scipling, Leifr Thorljotsson. Old Motsi's summons was obviously a false one, intended to get Syrgja out of the way. Perhaps even Thurid was deceived with the idea of the sheath. We followed the bait in their trap right into Slagfid's Ban. All they had to do was wait until we were inside. The jotun will destroy the evidence of our murder, and it will all appear a perfectly natural end for jotun-hunters.' She laughed again, laughing and wheezing for breath because she could not stop, the sound echoing in the cavern.

'Shut up that laughing,' Leifr snarled, furious with himself. 'We're not dead yet!'

Starkad flung himself upon the door in a frenzy, pounding with his fists, kicking with his feet, until Leifr hurled him backward.

'Save your strength,' he said grimly, turning his head to

listen to the sounds in the tunnel behind them. The dragging footsteps seemed to be hastening to the kill. 'The Flayer will need that sort of thing more than the door does, when he gets here.'

'We can't fight the Flayer!' Svanlaug gasped, with a hysterical chuckle. 'He's going to kill us!'

'Not kill,' Raudbjorn rumbled, unsheathing his halberd from its sling on his back. 'Flayer die.'

'Don't be a fool,' Svanlaug said sharply, regaining her composure quickly. 'We've got to get out. We can't fight and expect all of us to survive. I'll send a summons to Thurid. Come here and make a circle with joined hands. Even you, Norskur. I suppose there's a bit of usable life force in you. Starkad – well, I'll give you a try but you're rather disorderly. Success is often assisted by the most desperate of circumstances. I want all of you to concentrate upon Thurid. Throw out your thoughts to him as if you were calling. Picture him in the tower, with Slagfid's sword beside him on the table.'

Leifr obeyed, but not without misgivings concerning her Dokkalfar magic as she began a rapid, muttered chant.

The Flayer's voice rose in a savage bellow.

'Now there's power!' Svanlaug said, as she gripped Starkad's hand. 'But not enough! Call again!'

The words came into Leifr's mind, and the day that he had heard them from the lips of old Vidskipti, the traveling trader. He knew the hour of need had arrived.

'Komast Undan!' he croaked, and instantly his throat burned fierily, as if the words were too powerful to be spoken by a Scipling. The walls of the cave trembled with a surge of influence, and rocks clattered and clacked as they fell from the ceiling. Svanlaug shrieked as a sudden gust of hot wind struck at them.

CHAPTER 19

Thurid held his hands, the three of them, over Slagfid's sword, and the blackened runes etched there began to gleam like molten silver shining through. Through his eyes Gedvondur perused the runes, slowly deciphering each one in its turn.

Thurid watched in fascination as Gedvondur's hand propelled his own in gestures, while speaking words and names of power from Thurid's mouth that he had never dreamed of speaking. The power surging through his body was like a torrent of pure glacial water streaming from the frozen mass, freed at last. He knew he could call down fire, render himself invisible, transport himself thousands of miles at a spoken word, and confer with the greatest of wizards living and dead, simply by uttering the command.

Suddenly, a force of emotion struck Thurid so forcibly that he staggered back, gasping for wind. The silvery runes vanished in a puff of acrid smoke and the river of power flowing through him was withdrawn. He was abruptly returned to the shadowy kitchen at Fangelsi, where Ermingerd was staring at him with fear in her eyes. Thurid reeled backward and sank into a chair, holding his head in his hands and groaning.

'Thurid, what a duffer you are!' Gedvondur exclaimed aloud, causing Thurid to smite his own brow in an agony of frustration. 'We almost read Slagfid's runes! Once we know what is written there, the curse on Fangelsi is well nigh solved. What is the meaning of this summons?'

Gedvondur's hand scuttled up Thurid's arm to his shoulder and pressed two fingers against his temple. Instantly a picture leaped into Thurid's brain, a picture of

Leifr and Raudbjorn in a dark and menacing place surrounded by writhing shadows. Three of the shadows were Starkad, Raudbjorn, and Svanlaug, but the rest were evil influences leaping and dancing with demonic glee.

Thurid roused himself from his befuddlement with a great snort of wrath, surging to his feet.

'It's Leifr! They're sending for me!' he exclaimed. 'Something has gone wrong! Ermingerd, I must go! Bar the doors and don't be frightened!'

Plucking Gedvondur off his shoulder, he hurled him into his satchel along with a host of other useful objects, snatched up his staff, and charged outside the house. For a moment he stood still, trembling slightly as he searched with all his finer powers for the thin but strong thread of the summons. Striking it suddenly, he plunged out of the tower and away into the driving snow, oblivious of all except the message of distress from his friends.

Gedvondur struggled wrathfully out of the satchel and seized Thurid by the wrist.

'Let me help you!' Gedvondur exclaimed. 'You're going straight into Skera-gil! Can't you feel the influence of Djofull? He's here, you fool! You'd better take a few precautions!'

'There's not time!' Thurid gasped. 'It's almost too late! They can't escape! It's almost upon them!'

'Give me your staff, and hold onto my wrist,' Gedvondur commanded. 'Whatever you do, don't let go, or we'll lose you into the same between place where you lost Ljosa.'

Gedvondur gripped the staff and Thurid gripped Gedvondur's wrist. With a roar of wind and power, Thurid felt himself jerked off his feet and his arm nearly torn from its socket, but nothing except grim death could compel him to release his hold on Gedvondur. The breath was forced out of him completely, and he felt as if his body had been left a long way behind that part of him which was shrieking like a fiery comet through the black walls of Skera-gil.

The door burst into his view suddenly, and he was conscious of a partially successful braking effect before he struck the panels with a thundering crash. An opposing force leaped out to repel him, making his impact twice as painful. Gedvondur sputtered out of sight and sound as he flew out of Thurid's grasp. Thurid struggled to his feet, gasping and bleeding from a gash on his forehead. Facing the door, he saw sinister wisps of murky flame guarding it. The bar thrust through the bent metal loops glowed as if red-hot. Hearing the shouts of Leifr and the others from inside, he returned their shouts with a triumphant roar of attack. Briefly he glimpsed them, standing with hands united, facing the menacing threat looming half-seen in the darkness. With a ferocious yell he shook the blood out of his eyes and made warding-off gestures. Then he seized the glowing bar and wrestled it out of the loops, feeling the terrible heat and smelling the flesh of his hands burning.

He flung the door open with a word of force and illuminated the gullet of the cave with a mighty flaring of alf-light.

'Leifr!' he bellowed, discerning some dark shapes in the billowing waves of light. From somewhere beyond them, the deafening roar of the Flayer sent him staggering back a pace.

'We're all right!' Leifr gasped, pushing Starkad and Svanlaug ahead of him. 'Raudbjorn! Where's Raudbjorn? I'm going back for him!'

He turned to plunge into the cave again, but Thurid seized his cloak, pointing wordlessly ahead. In the white glare of the alf-light, Raudbjorn and the dogs surrounded the lurching form of the Flayer, teasing him away from the others. At Thurid's shout they abandoned their tactics and hastened toward the door. The Flayer came after them, his red, gleaming eyes fastened upon the opening.

Leifr and Starkad crashed shut the door after him and Thurid inserted the molten bar once again, forcing it well into the loops to hold it fast and bending it into an intricate knot. The Flayer pounded on the door with a sound that reverberated down the tunnel and seemed to shake the ancient substance of Skera-gil itself, as if it were a familiar and oft-repeated sound.

Thurid tottered away several paces before looking down at his hands in the pale light of silver sky and falling snow. As he had expected, he saw blackened claws, little more than bones and shreds of charred flesh. Then the pain began to throb, like a distant drum which promised soon to be pounding inside his head.

As he stood there frozenly, Gedvondur wallowed through the snow and grabbed a handful of his cloak to climb up by.

'What rot is this?' Gedvondur demanded upon first contact as Thurid's expression altered to Gedvondur's, twisted into lines of fury and concern.

'Djofull! Landradamadur! Fara burta!' Instantly the hideous claws vanished from Thurid's view, and he found himself gazing at his own fine-boned hands, of which he was always so inordinately proud.

'You weren't deceived by so elementary a trick as that, were you?' Gedvondur demanded with an amused cackle.

'Certainly not!' Thurid flared indignantly. 'I was merely checking to see if my hands had incurred any injury. They're a wizard's most valuable asset, hence my concern.'

'Yes, and lucky is the wizard who has three,' Gedvondur's voice added. 'Leifr! Did you get the sheath?'

Starkad held it up, sparkling darkly with jewels and twisted gold wire. 'We have it,' he said, his voice toneless with exhaustion.

By the time they returned to Fangelsi, the night was made restless by shimmering lightnings and bursts of shouting wind and thunder from beyond Hogni's wards, as if Djofull had been profoundly disturbed. The troll-hounds battled attacking trolls most of their way out of Skera-gil, and Thurid's alf-light raked the cliffs, bringing down trolls in clattering rockfalls. Gedvondur kept up a continuous chatter, interspersed with snatches of odd songs, in reply to the questing howls of the Fylgjur-wolves, daring them to come down to fight. Leifr held *Endalaus Daudi* ready, its pale light glowing in the thick gloom, but Djofull's creatures kept their distance. All Leifr saw of them were a few red eyes shining briefly in the cliffs above before winking away.

Beacon lights were shining from the house. Hogni and Horgull had returned from the shore and were waiting at the first gate with the sledge, peering toward Skera-gil.

'The elements are greatly disturbed,' Hogni said furiously. 'What have you done? What has happened in Skera-gil tonight?'

'Nothing worth retelling,' Leifr snapped. 'Except that we've got the sheath for Slagfid's sword, and your plan for locking Ketil and us in with the Flayer didn't work as you'd hoped.'

Hogni turned to him and stared with manifest unfriend-liness. 'Is that an accusation, Scipling?' he demanded. 'If you were locked in, it was none of my doing. I put the lock on the cave to keep you away from that treasure, and to keep the Flayer away from Fangelsi.'

'Or was it to keep Ketil from escaping from the jotun, once you got the chance to lock him in?' Leifr retorted. 'But tonight you had a different opportunity. You returned after we had left, and once we were inside, you hastened out of hiding and barred the door again.'

'It was not I,' Hogni said.

'Someone did,' Thurid said testily. 'Someone with some magical influence, who didn't want that door opened again. Perhaps it's easier for you to endure your curse than it is to try dissolving it, and easier to hinder those who want to break it. I don't deny we've caused trouble here tonight. Heldur fears what I might do to his scheme.'

'Heldur and I are not alone in wishing to hinder you,' Hogni said, turning to gaze away into the fells for a moment. A lone fylgjur-wolf raised its voice in an eerie, soul-chilling cry unlike that of a wholly animal wolf.

'Djofull wants you to fail in your quest for the night-farers of Fangelsi, perhaps as much as Heldur. He can't allow you to live, once you give him Heldur's crystal.' He chuckled unpleasantly.

'But he hasn't got it yet,' Thurid snapped.

'You're getting too much knowledge and power for either Heldur or Djofull to tolerate,' Hogni said. 'Come, get on the sledge. There's more news waiting for you at Fangelsi.'

As soon as they entered the passage of the house, Leifr knew what had happened. The endless rumbling and bashing and muttering of Ketil was silent, and the door of the storage room stood open as best it could, dangling from one hinge with nearly half of its planks torn off.

Syrgja sat by the fire with her traveling cloak still wrapped around her shoulders. As they all came in, she turned her head to glare with hollow eyes of pain and defeat. The room was a shambles, with furniture overturned and grain and flour scattered over the floor. Ketil had searched out all the food available and eaten it, wasting and trampling a great deal of it.

'Where's Ermingerd?' Starkad demanded in horror. 'Is she all right?'

'I'm here,' said Ermingerd's voice from the other side of the fire, hidden by its glare. 'I'm all right. I climbed into the loft when he started raging around.'

'You left her here alone?' Syrgja accused. 'What were you doing, the lot of you? Fangelsi is about to come down around our ears!'

Thurid strode forward to the table, where Slagfid's sword lay untouched among a heap of rune wands and vellums. Taking up the sword with both hands, he nodded to Starkad and slipped it into its sheath and returned it to the table with a sigh.

'Now then,' he said, 'see how you like that, Heldur.'

Neither Heldur nor Djofull seemed to approve. Wind screamed around the house for the rest of the night and the slit windows of the tower blazed with red light. From the border of wards, the fylgjur-wolves howled demonically.

Leifr was too weary to argue further about who had locked the door, and the warm fire threatened to put him to sleep as swiftly as Djofull's drugged ale. As he sat in the company of the man he suspected had just attemped to kill him, partaking of his fire and shelter and ale, the ironic amusement of the situation made him smile. If not for an inconsequential difference of opinion, Hogni might have been his friend and his stay at Fangelsi entirely pleasant.

The sheathing of Slagfid's sword made no immediate difference in their circumstances that Leifr could see, except that Starkad was locked in the granary for his disobedience. Thurid was violently rebuffed the first time he attempted to re-enter the tower, but on the following day he declared that Heldur's influence had deserted the place. It was scant consolation to Hogni and Horgull, who worried about the consequences of Heldur's expulsion, and to Syrgja, who grieved over Ketil.

After a storm of such fury, there was little hope for Ketil's survival, although Leifr and Raudbjorn took the hounds and searched as near as they could get to Skera-gil. Hogni had moved his wards much nearer the home pastures and fields, leaving the fells to the fylgjur-wolves. Some of these Leifr came upon unaware, and suffered a few violent rebuffs that sent him sprawling in the fresh snow, filled with the nameless dread that refused to be controlled. Looking at Hogni's carrion crow mark and trying to will his fears into control, he knew with certainty that he could never approach and pass such a mark. His reason could tell him it was not so, but his body would not stir a step, convinced the result would be deadly.

Worse yet, Hogni had given up the entire sixth pasture, which had to be crossed if anyone were to get into Skera-gil. Djofull's mark stood next to Hogni's, as if the two of them had agreed upon the gate as a mutual boundary.

Leifr's suspicions of Hogni were fueled by the return of the Flayer two nights later, battering at the sheep fold and carrying off a lamb. Either he had succeeded in smashing down the door in Skera-gil, or someone who could pass the wards had opened the door from the outside to release him. Proving himself an unexpected ally, the Flayer was loath to surrender control of the sixth pasture to the fylgjur-wolves. Almost nightly the sounds of battle drifted down to Fangelsi, and the Flayer raided the barns and folds to carry off two sheep and a calf. As Hogni had predicted, the Flayer left the house alone once Ketil was gone, but Syrgja still grieved.

The jotun draugar had no trouble coming through both sets of wards to skulk about the farm, haunting the ruins where Starkad had hidden his cache of barrow loot. Hogni searched for it several times, but said nothing. Leifr had no doubts that Hogni knew they had stolen something from the cave and would eventually find the proof he was seeking.

Ten days after the escape of Ketil, Syrgja announced that she was out of oil and grease, so Hogni and Horgull hitched up a sledge and loaded it with wood from the hall, planning to trade it to the shore people for stockfish and whale blubber. After spending the night, they would return in the morning.

Svanlaug came out of hiding when they were gone, and Starkad also emerged from his enforced confinement in the granary and was kept under the strict eye of Syrgja.

Thurid took advantage of Hogni's absence and called a conference in the tower. Leifr entered it warily, gazing around in astonishment as he realized its sinister overtones had indeed vanished, leaving behind a harmless old ruin.

Thurid seated himself in the best chair, and Gedvondur perched on his arm, his expression masking Thurid's.

'I have something more to ask of you,' Gedvondur began. 'You performed admirably in getting the sheath of Slagfid's sword, and I'm happy to report that its effects are being felt. Heldur's influence is now confined to Slagfid's Ban and we're much nearer to breaking the curse.'

'But the geas has been almost forgotten,' Leifr interrupted. 'Midwinter is past, and we haven't killed a single night-farer, let alone a jotun.'

'Just remember, Heldur is the source of all this evil,' Gedvondur said. 'By getting him, we end the curse and the geas in one fell swoop. Be patient a little while longer, Leifr, and trust those who know better than you do the workings of powers in this realm. Now I've called you here not only to congratulate you for going into the cave for the sheath, but to make another assignment. I want you to return to Slagfid's Ban and disrupt it as completely as you can. A handful of trinkets has already been brought out, thanks to the avaricious greed of young Starkad, and we've been gratified by the presence of a few minor influences walking about and making blue lights. But there's got to be a major incursion into that treasure vault. I want those jotun draugar stirred to life by the fury of being robbed so they'll start walking. Leifr, how much of that treasure can you and Raudbjorn carry out?'

Leifr reeled a moment from amazement. 'You're telling me to go rob that cave?' he growled suspiciously.

'Yes, Leifr,' Gedvondur replied pleasantly. 'I want to raise such an uproar of jotun daugar as Fangelsi has never seen. Getting them to come here is safer than us going into the cave to visit them. We have the house and the tower for defense, and they are impervious to the wards of both Hogni and Djofull, being dead creatures. All we need is a sizeable lump of their treasure, and we'll be fighting them off every night.'

Raudbjorn groaned miserably and slowly shook his head, looking at Leifr in mute dismay.

'Hogni's not going to approve of this,' Leifr said. 'I can see a glimmer of reason behind it, but he won't.'

'Then we won't ask his opinion,' Svanlaug interjected. 'It's a good idea, Gedvondur.'

'What does Thurid think of it?' Leifr asked, still wary. 'Let me talk to Thurid.'

'Talk away then,' Thurid said impatiently as Gedvondur's features vanished. Thurid's face was worn and pale, lined with sleepless nights and untold horrors the ghoul

314

visions had revealed. 'You Sciplings waste so much time talking and sleeping and eating and worrying, it's a wonder you've managed to infest as much of your realm as you have. You've wanted some action, Leifr; now's your chance. If anyone can bollix up something, I'm sure you can do it. All we're asking is for you to go and do what you've wanted to do all along – rob Slagfid's cave, and be quick about it. We're losing more ground to Djofull every day.'

'What about Djofull's wards?' Leifr asked. 'His are back-to-back with Hogni's.'

Thurid extended a rune wand to Leifr. 'Give this to Starkad. He'll know how to read it.'

'Why Starkad, when I'll be there?' demanded Svanlaug. 'We've got to hurry. Hogni and Horgull are doing their best to seal off Skera-gil. They're furious that you've found the treasure before they did, not that they would grant you any prior claim to it, of course. They'll simply follow your traces to the treasure vault, which the troll-hounds led you to. They've been searching those tunnels for years. They'll kill for it, and they've tried more than once. That fylgjur-wolf getting through was no accident, Leifr. Neither was it an accident that we got locked in that cave. They did it because they want that gold. I don't really believe they want to trade with the shore people. I think they're trying to find the cave.'

'They can have that treasure, every cursed piece of it,' Leifr answered, wanting nothing more than to turn his back upon Fangelsi and its secrets and forget about it as fast as he could. Beneath his angry bluster was a kernel of genuine fear that the web of forces governing Fangelsi would not allow him to leave, as Hogni had warned him. Perhaps it was an oblique way of saying that Hogni intended to kill him to protect the treasure.

'But when we go back to Slagfid's Ben, you're not coming, Svanlaug,' Leifr continued, his mood still suspicious. 'I'll take Raudbjorn and Starkad. I don't want any of your tricks in a place like that.'

'You can trust me!' Svanlaug blazed, tearing off her hair covering furiously. 'Better than either Starkad or Raud-bjorn! Haven't I helped you in the past?'

'Yes, but at the time it didn't seem like help,' Leifr replied. 'I don't want any such risks around jotun draugar. I want to know exactly what's going to happen.'

Svanlaug stalked out of the tower with a nasty oath.

Leifr had to stalk Starkad for several hours before he was able to approach him undetected by Syrgja's gimlet eye. They met at last behind the cow byre, where Starkad was engaged in the never-ending chore of shoveling out. A light of desperation gleamed in Starkad's eye when he turned to return Leifr's greeting.

'Leifr, you're the only chance Ermingerd and I will ever have to get away from this place,' he began feverishly. 'If you don't help us, then we're doomed to grow old and die in Fangelsi. Ermingerd will wither up like Aunt Syrgja. She'll never marry Jarnvard or anyone. As for me, I'll either die trying to get away, or work such as this will be the death of me. But all this withering and dying won't be necessary if only you'll help us get away, before it's too late. Svanlaug is right, my brothers are killers. They'll never let you escape alive, knowing what you know. Hogni has said it often enough – nobody ever escapes from Fangelsi. We're almost out of time, Leifr. This may be our last chance to get the gold and get away.'

Leifr wanted to explain about the geas, the jotuns, and Thurid's apparent entrapment by the curse, but there was no time.

'We're going back to the cave!' he whispered with barely suppressed excitement. For the first time since he had set foot upon Fangelsi soil, events were advancing satisfactorily. He yearned for an opportunity to get his revenge upon Hogni for confining him with those wards. Nor did he much mind stealing something which Hogni and Horgull intended to steal themselves.

Starkad dropped his pitchfork, his petulance instantly forgotten as his old sly grin returned.

'This time we'll take Raudbjorn,' Leifr said. 'If we need him, he can stand up to the Flayer long enough for us to escape.'

'We'll have just a few hours until the Flayer wakes up for his evening fight with the fylgjur-wolves. Think of the weapons waiting for us there. We'll be jarls someday, with such powers. Ordinary mortals don't possess swords and helms made by the Dvergar. They exact a high price sometimes.'

'So do angry daugar,' Leifr added.

'Syrgja's still watching me like a hawk,' Starkad said, 'so I'll come by a different way and meet you at the sixth gate, and she won't be suspicious. Thurid and that hand of his wouldn't like this scheme either, I don't believe.'

'He knows. It was Gedvondur's idea.'

Starkad stopped short. 'That hand? Are you sure you can trust it – or him? You told me it came from Djofull's wrist. And it does have Thurid under its thrall.'

Leifr's own hidden doubts made him short-tempered. 'If you want to stay behind and worry about it, you can, but I'm going back to Slagfid's Ban.'

'Not alone, you're not. You need me to help you get through those wards,' Starkad replied.

Leifr roused Raudbjorn and the dogs from the horse barn, supposedly for a hunting expedition.

Raudbjorn beamed at the prospect of shedding some blood and twanged the sharp edge of his halberd. His happiness did not fade until Leifr had approached the sixth gate at the top of the fell, but not too near. The mere sight of Hogni's screaming bird made Leifr feel ill. Waiting for Starkad to appear, they looked down into the Skera-gil. Then some premonition seized Raudbjorn and he drew his brows together into an apprehensive scowl.

'Leifr not hunting rabbits today,' he growled. 'Hunting big trouble, Raudbjorn thinks.'

'Gold, Raudbjorn. Enough to leave Fangelsi far behind. We'll take Thurid where the Inquisitors can never find him. There's nothing quite like the feeling of having

317

plenty of gold, is there, Raudbjorn?'

Raudbjorn's eyes half closed and he smiled a beatific, enchanted smile. 'Gold keeps stomach full, backside warm, and hay in horse belly. Thief-taker not afraid of man or draug. Where's gold, Leifr?'

'Skera-gil,' Leifr said. 'In Slagfid's Ban. Now are you afraid, thief-taker?'

Raudbjorn swung around for a searching look into Skera-gil. Gripping his halberd he mopped one big paw over his face, leaving behind a grim and scowling visage. 'If Leifr say go, Raudbjorn go,' he rumbled. 'If Leifr say die, Raudbjorn die. Raudbjorn ready to go and die.'

Starkad appeared in a ravine, hurrying alone with eager haste. He grinned at Leifr triumphantly and made a victorious sign with his hands. Leifr gave him Thurid's rune wand, and he read it over several times.

'Now for the ward,' he said, rubbing his fingertips on the rough wool of his cloak as he approached it. He made gestures and recited a list of strange words as he edged nearer. Gingerly he reached out to touch it, and a brilliant spark of energy staggered him back a pace. Leifr winced away, feeling a sinister surge of power rising up threateningly before him. He had a sudden impression of Hogni's presence, very angry and very present, as if Hogni knew their intentions exactly, wherever he was.

'This is a new one,' Starkad said uneasily.

'We'll have to give it up,' Leifr answered, almost relieved. 'He's too clever for us. Don't tamper with it anymore. Something is coming out of it which I'd rather not think about.'

'We can't give up so easily.' Starkad paced up and down in a fever, while Raudbjorn looked on at the proceedings with his mouth ajar in an astonished round aperture.

'Take gate off,' Raudbjorn volunteered, after Starkad had made three more unsuccessful attempts.

'What good would that do?' Starkad retorted impatiently. 'I can't get near enough to it.' He went on with his spells and counter-spells, each time failing with more

318

severe results. Finally the spiral and screaming bird sent him sprawling on his back, and Leifr had to retreat far enough down the mountain that he could no longer see the symbol, even distantly.

Raudbjorn watched patiently, his hands clasping the haft of his halberd. At last he got to his feet, propped his weapon safely against a rock, and advanced upon the gate with his bare hands.

'Thief-taker not afraid,' he said through gritted teeth. 'Thief-taker eats fear!' Bowing his head against the force of the ward he plodded forward determinedly, more slowly with each step as if he were plowing into a stiff wind. Taking a good grip on the top rail, he heaved the gate manfully off its pegs and dragged it to the ravine, where he pitched it down with a crash.

'Bird gone,' he called to Leifr, mopping the sweat from his face. 'Come up now.'

Leifr approached warily. The hovering influence of the ward signs now hung over the ravine. Hogni's boundary line had been broken, and Leifr was free to pass through. He and Starkad both congratulated Raudbjorn, and the dogs wagged their tails delightedly.

As Leifr started forward, a small shape leaped into his path, barring the gate once more. It was a cat, a small gray cat, and Leifr froze in his tracks. He did not doubt it was the same skinny cat with the matted coat he had seen before. It arched its back and hissed at him, its fur standing in a ridge from ears to tail tip. The dogs would see it of course, he thought swiftly, but the dogs trotted through the gate without glancing at the cat. Raudbjorn strode past it without a downward glance, and Starkad stopped and looked back at him in great puzzlement.

'The way is cleared,' he said. 'Is it something else?'

Leifr did not take his eyes off the cat. She arched her back and skittered sidewise at him, either challenging or warning him away. He tore his eyes off her a moment to look toward Skera-gil, and when he glanced back, the cat was gone, and Starkad was looking at him as if he were peculiar.

'You look as if you've seen your own fetch,' he said jokingly. 'You're not frightened, are you? Just think of the gold waiting for us.'

'Think of the freedom from Fangelsi,' Leifr said.

No one spoke until they stood on the ledge overlooking the door to the cave, which stood open, showing much evidence of mighty opposition. Starkad drew in a long breath and slowly expelled it.

'This is for Uncle Ketil as well,' he said. 'He was a lot of trouble, but he didn't deserve to die this way.'

'You'll wait here, Raudbjorn,' Leifr said at the threshold of the cave. 'I don't want that door shut on us a second time.'

As they stepped across the fetid threshold of the cave, a dark bird shape suddenly dived out of the rocks above and vanished into the darkness ahead with a chuckling cry.

'Another bad omen,' Leifr muttered.

'It's only one bird, one man, one of whatever it may be,' Starkad said, busy with the great mass of paraphernalia he carried. He had shovels and bags and lanterns for them both, and some inexplicable lengths of rope and an axe and pick, implements which would have been more suitable for above-ground barrow robbing. In his enthusiasm, Starkad hadn't wanted to leave behind any of the conventional tools of the trade.

With utmost loathing, Leifr again entered Slagfid's Ban. So great was his revulsion that nothing kept him moving forward except Starkad's repeated reminders of the gold that awaited them in the burial vault. Ever he listened for sounds of the Flayer stirring, a shuffling step, a rasping breath in the silence, but all they heard was the steady crunching of their boots. The troll-hounds padded silently at Leifr's heels, ears alert, but no warning growls rumbled in their chests.

When they reached the burial chamber, they hesitated a long moment before hoisting their lanterns and going in.

320

Working as silently and stealthily as possible, they picked the gold cups, buckles, arm rings, and much more from the trash of rotten tapestries and grave clothes. The dust rose in clouds, no matter how careful they were, and they muffled their faces to avoid breathing it.

Before long, in the excitement of violating the forbidden, Leifr was tearing rings off skeletal hands and groping fearlessly for necklaces and arm rings among rib cages and arm bones. Pulling on one especially choice ring with a glittering blue stone, Leifr's eyes suddenly registered on the hollow eye sockets of the corpse he was robbing. The two dark shadows peered at him from a skull that suddenly didn't seem quite right. Knots and crenellations knobbled the surface of the dusty old thing, distorting its shape with extra bone growths which a normal human being, or Alfar, simply did not possess. It made the skull grossly lopsided, and the enlarged jawbones hung down on the sprung rib cage. Leifr's heart stopped beating entirely, except for sickening feeble squirms as he slowly extended his inspection to the hands of the corpse. The arms seemed too long, and the joints were enlarged and crusted with more of the strange bony gnarling that marred the skull. The hands were like tree roots, each joint knotted until the rings were almost sunken, as if in wood that had grown around them.

Leifr dropped the ring he had earlier coveted. Still unbreathing, and now filled with a freezing horror, Leifr sidled away and forced himself to look upon the figure on the next bier. Again most of the flesh was gone, exposing the same gnarled bone growths. Somehow the corpse was longer than a normal Alfar, which usually ran considerably shorter than Leifr. This corpse, however, as nearly as Leifr was able to guess, would have towered over his own head by two feet or more – a veritable giant.

Reaching out, he silently closed a hand on Starkad's shoulder. Starkad shot out of his grasp with a startled, half-muffled shriek, then added a curse under his breath.

'What do you mean, startling me that way?' he growled

beneath the cloth that muffled his nose and mouth. 'You shouldn't play such tricks in a place like this.'

Leifr found his tongue adhering drily to the roof of his mouth. 'Starkad,' he whispered, 'we've got to get out of here, now. At once.'

'What's wrong? The horrors got you?' Starkad chuckled.

'Starkad, these aren't your ancestors. They'll all jotuns. We're robbing jotun graves!' His voice rose to a piercing whisper, almost a whispered shriek.

'Never! This is Slagfid and his sons!' Starkad turned slowly, raising his lantern reluctantly to expose the face of the nearest corpse. After a moment the lantern began to shake alarmingly. Starkad turned to another bier for an inspection of the occupant there, and it was enough to convince him. He jettisoned his barrow-robbing paraphernalia and shouldered his bag of loot, making a clumsy rush for the doorway, scattering bones and rags and remaining treasure as he caromed off one bier and into another in his blind charge. Nothing loosened his grip on the bag, however.

Leifr hesitated a split second over leaving his bag, but in the end he tossed it over his shoulder and ran after Starkad. The moment he entered the dark corridor, Starkad fell back with a howl as something struck him in the face. Leifr glimpsed a black form kiting around the lantern light; then it dived at him. It was scaly and alive, and claws scrabbled for a grip on his arm or shoulder. With a strangled yell he flailed at the creature, driving it off so he could resume his retreat. A burst of light and smoke flared before them, halting even Starkad's bullish headlong retreat.

It was Svanlaug standing there, barring their escape, with a few black feathers swirling around her. She smiled, and her hair rippled like snakes.

'You might have asked me to join your escapade,' she said, moving forward with a gusting of her black cloak. 'What share do I get for not telling Hogni and Horgull? They would relish an excuse such as this for outlawing us

322

all and throwing us out for the fylgjur-wolves, Leifr.'

Leifr let the gold fall to the ground with a heavy clatter
and tinkle of the finer little things. He glared at Starkad,
who gripped his share with dogged resolution.

'We don't have to share with her,' Starkad growled, like
a dog with a bone. 'We did all the work and planning. She
doesn't want to be thrown to the fylgjur-wolves any more
than we do. She won't say anything to my brothers.'

'She's a Dokkalfar,' Leifr said. 'She'd come to some sort
of terms with the fylgjur-wolves.'

'Indeed, I would,' Svanlaug said. 'I'll have Sorkvir's
ashes to bargain with, besides the barrow gold. I think I'll
take half.'

'I think you won't,' Starkad snarled.

Svanlaug shrugged. 'I'm not ungenerous. I'll take a
third. At least this way you'll have some of it left. If I go to
Hogni and Horgull, you won't get any of it.'

Starkad heaved a furious sigh. 'All right, but don't
think to take more. I won't be pushed beyond reasonable
limits, not even by a Dokkalfar witch. This gold belongs
to me and my family, not to you, or jotuns—' His
protective fury wavered as his eyes turned uneasily toward
the burial chamber. 'We'll divide this as soon as we get
outside Slagfid's Ban.'

'We'll divide it now,' Svanlaug said. 'Make haste,
though. I saw the Flayer curled up in his den down below,
and he was sleeping rather lightly.' She pointed into the
darkness extending behind Leifr and Starkad. 'One
scream would awaken him. I daresay he'd be just as
displeased as Hogni and Horgull to see this gold being
spirited away.'

'It's not jotun gold,' Starkad flared, as he upended his
sack to spill out the gold in a glittering flood at his feet.
Unwillingly Leifr followed suit. 'This is Fangelsi gold,
from my ancestors!'

'And all of it stolen on viking raids or extorted as tax or
taken from Dvergar,' Svanlaug replied. 'Every piece of it
is splattered with blood and dishonor. I wonder that you

think you have any more claim upon it than the Flayer. Where are your glorious ancestors, Starkad? They aren't in there.' She tossed her head triumphantly toward the burial chamber. 'Nothing but jotuns.'

'I don't know,' Starkad muttered, kneeling in the shining mass of gold. He divided it hastily into three piles under Svanlaug's sharp eye. Down in the blackness behind them they heard distant snorts and moans, as if the Flayer were awakening and stretching. When they were done, Svanlaug moved aside and they all hurried toward the portal, where Raudbjorn glared at her in amazement.

'No one got by Raudbjorn,' he growled.

'No one but Svanlaug's fylgja form,' Leifr said.

'Many thanks,' she chuckled. 'You've certainly made my life the richer this day, although it's something I never thought I could say of such an unlikely pair. Take care you don't follow me too closely.'

She took her share of the gold and disappeared into the mists of Skera-gil. Leifr and Starkad followed with haste, with Raudbjorn puffing in the rear. By the time they reached the tower, it was nearly dark and the fylgjur-wolves were beginning their nightly squabbles with the trolls.

'This will do nicely,' Thurid said, rubbing his hands in anticipation. 'I'll keep part in the tower to draw them here first.'

'Thurid, what happened to Slagfid and his sons?' Leifr demanded. 'There's nothing but jotun bones in that cave.'

Thurid's eyes suddenly glazed over with thought as an idea struck him. His nostrils flared as he breathed deeply.

'I shall discuss it with Gedvondur,' he said, fastening his cloak and reaching for his staff. 'As soon as you are gone. Hide this part of the gold in the hall and be ready for the draugar. I've got to replace the wards before we lose the fifth pasture.'

Starkad's share was hidden in the old hall at Fangelsi, where Leifr could keep an eye on it as well as on Starkad. What Svanlaug did with her share Leifr did not know or care; the whole business gave him a sick feeling, especially when he considered that he had actually robbed jotuns of their treasure, not merely Alfar remains. How he had allowed Thurid or Gedvondur to lead him so far into the realm of insanity he did not know. Even Ljosa had tried to warn him. Guiltily he remembered the cat at the gate, which he alone had been able to see. Instead of turning back then, he had let his own greed send him rushing into Skera-gil to Slagfid's Ban. It was an inherited flaw, he decided: all his ancestors had been vikings; through their blood, he had acquired his taste for gold and danger.

The night passed without incident. On the next day Hogni and Horgull returned with a load of wood, whale blubber, and a barrel of salted fish and stowed it in the old hall. Leifr watched Hogni narrowly for signs of suspicion, but Hogni said nothing. For a long moment, the Alfar stood gazing around the hall, frowning, then he shrugged and went back to work, as if unable to identify the source of his uneasiness. After nightfall, when they were confined to the house, Leifr found it difficult not to turn his eyes frequently toward Starkad and Svanlaug to see if they appeared as guilty as he felt. Starkad buried his look of guilty triumph with a sulky scowl, pretending to be greatly resentful of the extra duties Syrgja had imposed upon him in the absence of his older brothers. Impassively Svanlaug watched them both, as Leifr was well aware and hoped he did not seem too aware.

CHAPTER 20

That night the full moon rode brazenly through a cloud-wracked sky, casting its fitful light on the silent, frozen world below.

After the evening meal, the occupants of the house sought their usual diversions. Hogni and Horgull removed themselves to a far corner to brood over their chessboard, but Leifr observed Hogni spending more time watching the other occupants of the room than he did in watching his game. Ermingerd and Syrgja sat sewing. Svanlaug was engrossed in her herbs and vellums. Raudbjorn and the hounds were asleep in a great pile near the door, and Starkad and Leifr made themselves enormously busy mending their leathers and saddles and cutting new boot laces. From Starkad's uneasy and hunted expression, Leifr knew he was worried. Leifr thought of Thurid in the tower, waiting over his heap of jotun gold, amidst his flickering lights and roiling clouds and strange, haunted voices from the past.

Starkad raised his head suddenly, listening. In a moment Leifr also heard faint sounds outside, a steady soft scraping in the snow, which squeaked with cold under the weight of footsteps. Syrgja and Ermingerd let their sewing fall to their laps.

'Jotun!' Raudbjorn muttered, awakening at the faintest sound of danger, while the loudest of ordinary sounds failed to make him twitch.

In a moment, something brushed at the outside door at the end of the passage, as might a hand groping for the latch, but this hand clattered and rattled like naked bones. Then a great weight was thrust against it, and the door groaned and shuddered.

Hogni stood up, scowling. 'Something is wrong in this house,' he said with cold certainty.

'More wrong than usual?' Svanlaug queried, not looking up from her pharmacopoeia.

'Yes,' Hogni answered, closing his eyes and testing the air with his hands for influences. 'Heldur is back. The dead are walking. A cold wave of wrath and revenge is breaking over Fangelsi. The elements have never been so restless. I knew something of this nature was coming. Out of ten lambs born this week, four were deformed, two were dead. Heldur holds this land in the palm of his hand. He's going to punish us for disturbing the natural forces of Fangelsi.'

'He's already got Ketil,' Syrgja said, turning a deathly white. 'What more does he want?'

'Aunt, unless we do something to set the elements to order, we'll be overwhelmed by chaos,' Hogni answered.

The draug pounded viciously on the door and tried again to push it open. Frustrated in that ambition, the draug drifted around the house, scratching at the window shutters and calling out in a deceptively feeble voice, 'Mina! Grim! Let me in! It's Gjaldr, your grandsire! Don't leave me out here to die!'

Inside the house, Syrgja and Ermingerd listened, white-faced and taut.

'It seems this family has a tradition of abandoning its elders,' observed Svanlaug. 'That could be the reason for your curse. I wonder how many of your ancestors were abandoned for the jotuns to take? Such deeds do not make for quiet draugar!'

Syrgja lifted a haggard face. 'If there were a better way, we would have done it long ago. Now there is nothing for us except to pay Slagfid's consequences.'

'What did he do to anger Heldur so much against him?' Svanlaug asked.

Syrgja slowly shook her head, her expression grim and unforgiving. 'He started by building his house upon

327

Heldur's land. Then he began to deal with Heldur for powers and riches. He was foolish and greedy. Even when luck smiles upon you, it is dangerous to demand too much. The price becomes too much to bear.'

Leifr shivered in the sudden chill filtering through the room, emanating from the dark passageway. All eyes fastened upon the door as a relentless pounding began again at the outside door.

'Mina! Mina! It's so cold out here!' the draug whispered. 'Let me in, let me in!'

Hogni strode to the door and gave it a rap with his smoking staff. 'Who speaks from beyond the grave and the barriers of death?' he demanded. 'This is the realm of the living. Go back to your bed in Hel, wanderer.'

The draug dealt the door a powerful blow, its voice suddenly the guttural roar of Heldur.

'Thieves! Barrow robbers! Give back what is ours or you won't live long to regret it!'

Starkad and Leifr exchanged a stare of mutual horror.

The air in the room suddenly turned too chill to breathe, and a powerful force pressed down inexorably, making each breath, each movement an agony. The smoldering fire on the hearth dissolved in a cloud of ash and soot, as if crushed by a mighty foot.

From outside the house, footsteps squeaked briskly in the snow and Gedvondur's voice was raised in a shout, speaking words of power. The forces clashed with a ringing sound like crossed swords, then suddenly the oppression was gone, and the draug was gone with it.

In a moment Thurid's voice was heard at the door, followed by a hurried knock. Hogni let him in, glowering as Thurid swept past him to the hearth. Rekindling the flames with a word, Thurid stood and rubbed his hands together briskly over the heat.

'Jotun draugar are on the prowl tonight,' he said. 'Luckily for you I was coming in just then. These doors are getting rather sorry, Hogni.'

'You shouldn't have rebuked it,' Hogni said. 'It'll be

back, loaded with Heldur's vengeance. Give up this dangerous meddling, Thurid. Leave Slagfid's curse to rest undisturbed, or Heldur will destroy you.'

'You saw,' Thurid replied, finding his way to a chair, where he collapsed with a weary groan. 'Gedvondur and I can stand against him.'

Gedvondur added a groan of his own, which turned to a snarl when Svanlaug's fylgja form drooped down from the rafters. 'Not taking any chances, are you, witch?'

Svanlaug glared from Hogni to Thurid. 'Listen to him, Thurid. You're beyond your depth. Fylgjur-wolves are out there in the fells, and jotuns are in here in the valley, and you're doing nothing about it. No wonder the Inquisitors want to divest you of your powers. You're not worthy of calling yourself a wizard, and we're all going to die unless you get us out of this cursed place!'

'Silence, witch,' Thurid said, rising rather shakily and commencing a stately pacing up and down the length of the room, with Gedvondur roosting on his shoulder. 'I am completely unconcerned by the threats and interference of this—' His eyes rolled over Hogni distastefully '—personage. One who is motivated by fear and distrust inevitably manufactures his own downfall. I now have ample material at hand to decipher the riddle of the jotuns, and Slagfid's past crimes.'

'Indeed,' Hogni said, his eyes hard and bright. 'And what have you discovered so far about our curse?'

'I have employed the use of ghoul images to recall past events to a semblance of life,' Thurid said. 'A skilled wizard can summon the lingering images of the past, and this I have done. I have seen Slagfid in all his glory. I have seen the dwarf Heldur, who did everything Slagfid bid him to do, heaping Fangelsi with treasures of his workmanship, and weapons to kill Slagfid's enemies – real or supposed. Slagfid was an honorable man in the beginning, but the gold and the power were his downfall. Heldur cunningly engineered his downfall, leading Slagfid deeper and deeper, until it was Heldur who was master and Slagfid who was slave. The darkest days were the days of Slagfid's sons, who ruled like terrors at Heldur's bidding. And it was all for Heldur's revenge upon the Ljosalfar. His vengeance will continue until ninety and nine of Slagfid's heirs have ruled Fangelsi. But this I suspect you know.'

'That and more,' Hogni said. 'If that's all you know, then you are a long way indeed from breaking our curse.'

'Where do the jotuns come from?' Starkad demanded.

Hogni looked at Thurid expectantly, and Syrgja raised one hand in a gesture of alarm. Thurid shrugged and sighed. 'I don't know that yet. I think they were created to defend Slagfid's treasure mound. Jotuns and gold and Slagfid's heirs are related, but how and why, I can't say. Not yet, but I shall.'

Hogni grinned unpleasantly. 'You may make your escape yet, but once you discover the answer to your last question, you are trapped here forever. Heldur won't allow you to escape – and I must protect Fangelsi's secrets.'

'Fangelsi's secrets have been protected far too long,' Starkad declared. 'I would like to know what it is that's so terrible, besides the jotuns and the treasure. Whatever it is, it hangs over us like a cloud, sucking the life out of us, and nobody will tell me what it is.'

Hogni replied with withering scorn, 'You don't know what you are asking for. Once you have it, you'll wish you didn't. Already you have something which you shouldn't possess, and you see what the consequences are. We may have rebuffed that draug for tonight, but he'll be back, night after night, more angry and more powerful, until he finds what he's looking for. If he destroys us in the process, neither he nor Heldur will feel any regret.'

Leifr seized the first opportunity to corner Thurid in the tower the next day when he was fairly certain Hogni wasn't watching. It wasn't easy; Hogni and his accusing stare seemed to follow him wherever he went. Svanlaug was shadowing him also as he went about his chores.

'Thurid, bringing that gold here was a mistake.' Leifr never felt comfortable in the tower. 'We've got to give it back, or we won't have any future to look forward to!'

Thurid looked up from a pile of random objects which he was studying. 'Mistakes are merely the second-best method of learning,' he said, 'not the end of the world. I'll freely admit that the jotun draugar are more powerful than I'd expected. But I need more time to study them. Every rag and bone of them is imbued with memories. Just inhaling their dust teaches me so much about them.'

'Then why don't you go into Slagfid's Ban and inhale them at close quarters?' Leifr demanded.

'No, no, I couldn't do that,' Thurid replied. 'Not yet. I have too much respect for Heldur to challenge him directly upon his own ground. We have a thin line we must walk, Leifr. If we jar his hold on this land too severely too soon we could lose him and that crystal forever.'

Leifr paced up and down, while Thurid hurled objects against the wall, whether for sport or serious divination Leifr could not guess.

'Thurid, your investigations are taking a dangerous turn,' Leifr tried again. 'Ljosa's cat form tried to stop me from going after that gold. I think she was right. This is worse than the Flayer wanting to take Ketil. What if you pursue Heldur so far down this road that you can't get back? What if—'

'Don't dwell on what might happen,' Thurid interrupted sharply. 'I have enough negative powers to fight against without your adding to the pile. Be patient a little while longer. As soon as we're out of here, we'll find a safe place to hide and I'll begin trying to bring Ljosa back. I can do this, Leifr, but you've got to help me. Keep Hogni from doing something rash. And watch Svanlaug. She's suddenly getting very unstable.'

Leifr sighed. 'She took part of the gold from us.'

'What! And you let her?'

'She threatened to tell Hogni we'd taken it, if we didn't give her a third of it.'

Thurid snorted thoughtfully, then he chuckled rather darkly. 'On her head be her own actions,' he said. 'It's going to keep her busy, I fear.'

It was as Thurid predicted about the jotun draugar and Svanlaug's share of the gold. On the second night they discovered her hiding place in the ruins. Two of them lurked near the gold while another attacked the house, moaning and accusing while it shattered the passage door with its draug strength. Svanlaug next moved the gold to the granary, and that night another jotun draug tried to break down the granary door. Svanlaug moved the gold to the old stables, then to the granary again, and the draugar attacks continued unabated.

Thurid spent long hours in the tower, and Hogni prowled around suspiciously, clearly searching for something, while Starkad and Leifr watched in guilty anticipation.

The lambing season reached its peak in the coldest months of late winter, and everyone in the household worked long freezing hours in the hall to save the lives of the new lambs and ailing ewes. The nightly visits of draugar and the Flayer did nothing to soothe the nerves of the sheep or their attendants. Most often Leifr and Starkad were paired to work the long dark hours of the night, a circumstance which put them on their guard against Hogni's listening and spying, lest they betray themselves or the gold. Svanlaug did almost as much listening and spying on them as she did on Hogni and Horgull, and their suspicion of her was mutual.

In a distant, weird accompaniment to the terror at Fangelsi, the fylgjur-wolves howled in the high fells. After sundown, a profound sense of doom and imprisonment hovered over all the members of the household, guests and hosts alike. They were all prisoners except the Flayer, who came to batter on the doors in fury, departing only when

332

Thurid or Gedvondur's words of power rebuffed him, and then it was in a spirit of tooth-gnashing rage. The rage and fear and suspicion seemed to gather in intensity, building into an atmosphere Leifr found increasingly intolerable. Repeatedly Thurid assured him that the equinox was drawing near and that in a matter of days they would be delivered of Fantur's influence and Djofull would be forced to withdraw into safer Dokkalfar domain.

As the tension mounted, Leifr kept Starkad under his observation, fearing a collapse and a confession of their crime, but Starkad remained steady. His manner was no longer that of the ebullient, unpredictable youth. Starkad's cunning nature showed signs of developing into the deliberate, calculating disposition of a natural srategist.

Svanlaug, however, looked ragged and exhausted from her continuous shifting of the gold. She awaited opportunities to escape from Syrgja's watchful eye, only to realize that Hogni was following her with suspicion of his own.

The jotun draugar appeared shortly after dark, their dark forms lumbering across the snow in an inexorable, determined manner that filled the watchers in the house with dread. Six of them stood in a ragged line, gazing toward the house with the blue fire of their tormented hollow eyes, with the cold wind eddying around their feet. The lone figure of the Flayer advanced, solid and dark, recognizable by his great malformed head canted heavily to one side. He banged on the outer door and shook it, moaning. Then he came around to the one high window where Leifr was watching and clawed at the stout wood bars. The other jotuns circled the house, moaning and whimpering, calling out the names of people who no longer lived there, begging to be let in.

'We're doomed!' Starkad whispered. Everyone gazed at him frozenly, and Syrgja flinched when the Flayer started tearing at the back door to the passage, which had already been torn down and mended so many times that Hogni and Horgull had decided to barricade it shut.

Hogni and Horgull tried with valiant unconcern to

concentrate on their chess game, but it was difficult with draugar plucking at the door lock with skeletal fingers and whimpering through the cracks in the door.

'This cannot go on,' Hogni said at last, rising to his feet and striding to the door into the passage. 'The draugar are enraged against us for something we have done. I feel an influence here. They are angry and vengeful because we have violated the rules governing our existence. The fabric of the Fangelsi curse has been disrupted.'

As he spoke, a cold wind rippled the wall hangings and fanned the fire. Hogni's cold stare came to rest remorselessly upon Syrgja. She shrank back in her chair, her sewing dropping from her hands. 'Another offering must be made.'

'No, not me,' she said pleadingly. 'Not yet. It's not too late. We can wait awhile longer and see if Thurid can break the curse first.'

'We can wait no longer. Someone must be sent out.'

Leifr stepped forward, ignoring Starkad's desperate efforts to signal warningly to him. 'Wait. You can't do such a deed. There's a better way to get rid of them. As you suspected, there's something the jotuns and draugar want at Fangelsi, and it isn't Syrgja.'

Hogni stared at him a moment with a faintly triumphant gleam in his eye. 'It was what I suspected,' he said. 'Perhaps we can bargain with Heldur. He must have either Syrgja or that which you have taken and hidden, in order to restore the natural flow of forces. It will only become more difficult to set things right with the passage of time. The first violation of order must be rectified first.'

'We'll give back the gold we took,' Leifr said, 'but not Syrgja. Enough life has been lost this winter. If the gold isn't enough, we'll have to endure their wrath. It's scarcely a fortnight until equinox, and by then Thurid and Gedvondur will have their answers. We took the gold to help them decipher the jotun curse. Perhaps they have learned enough by now.'

'What a reckless scheme!' Hogni declared furiously.

334

'Disrupting the dead as well as Heldur's spell! How long will it ever take to correct the damage you have all done! My patience is at an end! Tomorrow, that gold must be returned to Slagfid's Ban and no more meddling will be done. If I have to put you out of my boundaries, I will, and Djofull may take you!'

Discomfited by Hogni's threats, everyone in the house stood listening to the roaring of two jotun draugar who seemed determined to tear off the much-mended back door. Syrgja clasped her reddened wrists, standing and wavering a moment in the force of Hogni's arguments.

'I'll go out,' she said. 'Perhaps the jotuns will be satisfied for a short time. Long enough for the wizard to break Heldur's curse.'

'No,' Ermingerd said. 'Let the wizard get rid of the draugar, aunt.'

A heavy barrage on the window interrupted her. While everyone's attention was diverted, wondering if the shutter was designed to tolerate such abuse, Syrgja glided across the room in one swoop and threw the bolts off the door and vanished into the darkness of the passageway before anyone could stop her.

Starkad and Leifr plunged after her, with Raudbjorn in the rear, plowing single-mindedly through the tables and benches and dogs.

Ermingerd came behind with a lamp, casting wild, tilting shadows as she ran, illuminating Syrgja shoving at the bar holding the door. She heaved it aside and the door burst open under the mighty assault of the Flayer's fists. He stood panting a moment in the doorway, as if startled by his unexpected success, and Syrgja stood before him, a straight and fearless gaunt figure.

Raudbjorn shoved her aside and struck the Flayer a powerful blow in the chest. The Flayer lurched back a step, growling furiously, his one eye glaring redly beneath a mass of raw-looking swellings. His hand shot out with cunning speed, dealing Raudbjorn a blow on the side of the head that sent him sprawling. With an amazed expression on his face, Raudbjorn tried to rise to his knees, then collapsed unconscious.

Motioning to Starkad, Leifr plunged at the door and slammed it shut as Starkad was ready to bar it. Then he seized one of Raudbjorn's feet to drag him to the safety of the kitchen.

The outer doors of the hall thundered under a mighty barrage of blows. Shards of broken wood flew, revealing cracks of silver moonlight. The doors heaved inward, bands snapping explosively as the planks gave way.

Hogni darted to the trembling, splintering door and unbarred it. With a crash the door fell inward, nearly ripped from the frame, and a towering figure stood outlined against the pale snow beyond. Lowering his head, the Flayer stepped through the door into the hall with a measured, dragging tread.

Syrgja found her strength and staggered into the passage as the Flayer moved toward the door. The Flayer loomed in the doorway, beckoning ponderously.

'I'll come with you,' Syrgja said. 'I'm not afraid. But you must make these dead ones follow you.'

Svanlaug stepped into the passageway, drawing her cloak around her with a portentous billowing. With a shrill screech, her human form vanished and a dark winged shape hurtled into the hall and dashed against the jotun's face, spitting venom. She circled, screeching and spitting, easily dodging the clumsy blows the jotun aimed at her. The Flayer shook his head and pawed at his eyes where the fylgja creature dived with claws and venom. Then a lucky blow caught the creature and sent it cartwheeling into a corner.

Unable to stand by helplessly, Leifr drew his sword and charged forward, the hounds following with ferocious yells of challenge. Leifr barred them from sweeping into a full-scale and undoubtedly bloody attack. The Flayer stood gnashing his teeth menacingly, long yellow tusks growing at all angles in his malformed mouth. He warned Leifr back with one clublike paw and slowly eased backward out of the door, small secret eyes darting warily from Leifr to Hogni. When he reached the point where he could safely turn his back, he did so and hurried away, with the jotun draugar following him, obviously reluctant.

Raudbjorn hoisted the door back into place so it could be barred for the night. For a moment they all stood angrily confronting each other, with Hogni and Horgull alone on one side against the others, then Hogni turned and strode away into the passage.

Ermingerd slipped silently from the shadows and went to the corner, where Svanlaug lay moaning and cursing under her breath, and extended a hand to help her rise to her feet.

'You see what has happened?' Ermingerd whispered. 'By taking the jotuns' gold, you've stirred up the draugar of past jotuns, and they won't leave us alone until that gold is returned. They won't be satisfied with Uncle Ketil. You've got to do something, before it gets worse.'

'Gold?' Leifr croaked rather feebly, with a scalding rush of guilt. It was painful to think that Ermingerd would forever consider him a barrow robber. He exchanged a startled stare with Svanlaug, who scowled at him furiously.

Ermingerd nodded briefly. 'Of course. I know about everything my brother does. He can hide nothing from me. It wasn't at all wise of any of you.' Turning to Svanlaug she said, 'That was well done, Svanlaug, attacking the Flayer that way. Useless, but a noble gesture nonetheless.'

Svanlaug sizzled with temper, like a mad cat. 'You won't do anything to help yourself, so someone has to make the effort! You need that gold if you're ever going to get away from here! Jarnvard isn't going to wait the rest of his life on the other side of Hogni's wards!'

'You shouldn't care what happens to me,' Ermingerd retorted. 'Nothing can change my fate!'

'You can, if you're not afraid,' Svanlaug replied as she sailed rather crookedly back into the kitchen.

In the kitchen, Syrgja huddled beside the hearth, trembling and wan, looking up only when Thurid rapped at the door. He swept into the kitchen with industrious energy and dropped into a chair beside the hearth and rammed his feet close to the coals.

'I heard the uproar,' he said, his tone guarded. 'I would have come to help you, but I was in the middle of a fascinating scene from Fangelsi's earliest history. I'm getting to feel that I know Slagfid quite well. He wasn't an admirable person, and his sons were worse. I fear they deserved whatever curse Heldur put on them.' He noticed Syrgja sunken in her despair, weeping quietly in the dark. He peered around alertly at the occupants of the room. 'What has happened here tonight? Something's amiss.'

With grim satisfaction Starkad spoke first. 'My aunt thinks it is her turn to go and meet her fate at the hands of the jotuns and draugar. My brother thinks another human offering would quell their appetite for a while.'

'Only to save the rest of us,' Hogni said coldly. 'It is inevitable. The longer we delay it, the worse it becomes. Particularly since something has disturbed those draugar to such an extent, despite my repeated warnings. You have taken advantage of me at every turn, lied, deceived and threatened me. I won't tolerate any more. You've got to get out, all of you, geas or no geas.'

Thurid arose and paced the length of the kitchen, flicking his cloak aside at each turn. Leifr recognized the signs of the wizard's rising temper.

'You couldn't wait just a short while longer?' Thurid demanded of Hogni. 'What would it matter to wait until the equinox, when the forces are neutral? We could hold the jotuns and draugar back until then.'

'You need fail only once, and we're all dead,' Hogni replied. 'You couldn't save Ketil, nor any of us. I can see by the look of you that you know we're doomed, wizard. Heldur has got you trapped. You know too much.'

'I know enough to break this curse, come spring,'

338

Thurid said, 'but not if you keep interfering.'

'Your interfering is causing all the disruption,' Hogni countered. 'You are destroying us as surely as the jotuns and draugar will!'

'Suppose we take back their gold, then,' Thurid conceded. 'All my research will be in vain. You will have come within a hair's breadth of escaping from Slagfid's curse, only to fall back because of your own lack of courage. Djofull will get Heldur's orb, and we will be disposed of once we're of no further use. By all means, take back the gold, if you are able to get into Skera-gil, which I doubt. Will that buy us enough of your goodwill to stay until the equinox, or would you relish tossing us over your boundaries into Djofull's jaws?'

'I don't wish to see anyone die on my property,' Hogni admitted grudgingly.

'Brodir, don't be a fool,' Syrgja said sharply. 'We can't give it up now. You can't surrender them to Djofull now, nor to the Guild Inquisitors in the spring. I forbid it as the ruling matriarch of this house.'

'Very well then,' continued Hogni, 'since my aunt opposes it so vigorously, I won't take any rash action. You'll be safe here at Fangelsi. But wisdom dictates the eventual return of that gold, wizard.'

'No one can go beyond the fifth gate and expect to return,' Syrgja protested.

'The Scipling is wonderfully adept at going into forbidden places,' Hogni said, casting a jaundiced eye in Leifr's direction. 'Perhaps you can find your own way into Slagfid's Ban once again. You've done it often enough to know how to get there blindfolded.'

Leifr ignored Hogni's implication, turning to glare at Thurid in speechless rage. 'Thurid, we risked our lives getting that gold out,' he said. 'We're not going to risk them again by taking it back. Why should we, anyway? Winter is almost over. The curse and the geas are almost destroyed – if we can believe what you say. I say this gold is a fair prize for anyone's taking.'

Turning to Hogni he continued, 'If you knew how often we'd gone there, why didn't you speak up before? Your silence makes you a partner in our crime, if that's what it is. Or did you think you could take the gold more easily from us than from Slagfid's Ban?'

Hogni drew a considering breath. 'You are nothing if not direct, that much I can say for you, utlender. You are an adventuring man, taking your plunder and adventure where you find it. Perhaps it is because you are so brave that you cast covetous eyes upon the possessions of the dead. But I won't touch it. Not so much as one gold coin must leave Slagfid's Ban. You have seen some of the consequences. Nor must word of this treasure pass beyond the limits of Fangelsi-hofn. Thus it is that I demand of you that what is missing from Slagfid's Ban be returned to me immediately, so I can take it back to the cave.'

'I'm not so certain you would want to take it back,' Leifr answered Hogni, struggling to contain his mounting anger. 'You covet that treasure yourself. As soon as Ketil and Syrgja are out of the way, you intend to take it and live like Slagfid himself. If you want your share of the gold, go into Slagfid's Ban and get it yourself, instead of taking what we worked to earn.'

'No one is ever going to call me a barrow robber. I have no desire to possess this cursed gold, but you obviously do desire it. You were there, at least once, and now the draugar are walking. Your guilt is easy to assume. Barrow robbing is a crime almost as shocking as murder.'

'Are you making an accusation? You can't prove it until you find some gold lying around,' Leifr retorted.

'No, but I'll find it. That sly Svanlaug keeps her thoughts well shielded, but you and the thief-taker have few defenses against a bit of prying. Starkad could be forced to reveal it, but you'd do him a kindness by telling me where he's hidden it.'

'Do you think this is the way to ensure my silence about your murdering Ketil?' Leifr demanded hotly. 'I could say you took the gold from the biers with the idea of accusing us of barrow robbing. I could say you've tried to murder us, with that ward which let the fylgjur-wolf slip through, and no one has yet satisfactorily explained who locked us in the cave.'

'Djofull doesn't care one whit for all that,' Hogni snapped.

'Do you want to deal with us, or with Djofull?' Leifr demanded. 'Get rid of us if you think you can, but you'll soon find that Djofull is a far worse houseguest than all of us together. He'll come here for Heldur's crystal. He cares nothing for the fate of this miserable family.'

They glared at each other a long moment, Leifr gripping his sword and Hogni's cloak billowing threateningly.

'Come, come,' Thurid said. 'Enough has been said for one night. We can't keep the gold, and now we can't take it back, thanks to Djofull.'

With a last fiery gesture which thrust Leifr back a pace, Hogni strode away past him and crossed the passage into the main hall. Before Horgull closed the door, Leifr glimpsed him prodding at the hearth stones where Starkad had buried the gold.

In the morning Leifr set out to investigate the upper pastures and Starkad accompanied him. Starkad draped a rope around his shoulders and an assortment of bulging pouches were fastened around his waist. In addition to a rusty sword, he carried a broad double-edged axe and a long knife. So much equipment and weaponry adorning anyone else would have been reassuring, but Leifr could not view Starkad's enthusiastic preparations with anything but misgivings.

As Hogni had predicted, they were unable to approach Skera-gil after the region beyond the fifth gate fell into Djofull's hands. Hogni and Thurid had created a string of powerful wards along the last wall of the fifth pasture to keep Djofull at bay. By night the fylgjur-wolves prowled the sixth and fifth pastures, filling the air with their taunting cries. By day, shrouds of influence veiled the rocky landscape, promising dire consequences if anyone crossed the line. Skera-gil was hidden in a blanket of mist, with only a few black crags showing through.

On the gate, Hogni's carrion crow symbol was crudely slashed with axe marks, and beside it stood Djofull's symbol. It was a spiral, all too familiar to Liefr. The sight of it swamped him with memories of Sorkvir and a pervading sense of unassailable evil. Even Raudbjorn was too spooked to approach it, and the hounds kept their distance, whining uneasily and gazing at Leifr with reproach in their eyes.

'Today it's the fifth gate,' Leifr said with heavy gloom. 'Tomorrow it will be the fourth gate, until we're besieged in that house, waiting to be captured like frightened quail. If Thurid hadn't got himself embroiled in that Heldur spell, we might have been gone from here now.'

'We aren't beaten yet,' Starkad answered grimly. 'If we can only hold off another fifteen days, we'll make it to the equinox. When Fantur falls, the treasure will be ours.'

'How do you know that?' Leifr demanded suspiciously.

'I'm learning,' Starkad said. 'The boy is becoming a man. I possess the Alfar carbuncle, which will tell me everything I need to know about Slagfid's curse. Soon, too. I feel in my blood that the secret is about to be revealed.'

CHAPTER 21

The lambing season was nearly finished, signalling the approaching end of winter. Thurid and Hogni both observed the dawning of each day in the stone circle atop a hill overlooking Fangelsi, noting the progress of the sun toward the heel stone in the center. It was a matter of days until the sun rose directly behind the heel stone, heralding Fantur's fall and the start of spring. The harsh winter weather blustered with ferocious storms and fresh snow, but the days were lengthening and the sun had regained enough strength to begin melting the snow.

Thurid waited for the equinox with barely restrained impatience. His temper frayed easily, and he spent every moment he could in the tower with his spells. His great personal vanity was forgotten, and he looked completely disreputable and shockingly unhealthy, as if he were going far beyond the limits of his endurance. Yet he would hear of no slacking off. Daily he circled the boundary of wards, making certain none of them had given way during the night. By night he stalked the jotun draugar, luring them to the tower with the gold and conjuring them to come with potent summoning spells. Twice he saved himself only by climbing to its top when the draugar smashed his door down. The gold lay in plain view on the table, safely encircled by Thurid's ring of runes scratched in the earth.

To keep some degree of peace with Hogni, Leifr moved the gold from the main hall into the tower. Even Hogni could not deny there was no taking it back now, with Djofull blocking Skera-gil so thoroughly. Nor would Thurid hear of letting the draugar carry it away.

'Once they've got it, they won't come back,' he told Hogni, who had followed the transfer of the gold to the tower to make certain not one ring found its way into someone's pocket. 'I've sampled the dust of nearly all of them now, all except Slagfid himself and his eldest son Hreidar. I know their stories now, and what led them to their destruction. I don't actually need any more information to act upon the curse. Nothing more can be done until the Convocation of Jotuns, when I meet Heldur at last, face-to-face.'

Hogni shivered with horror and made signs behind his back. 'Then you know. You're as doomed as we are, Thurid. You will never leave Fangelsi now.'

'I am doubly burdened, it is true,' Thurid said, holding out his hands to show reddened, swollen joints. 'So you see why nothing must stop me from ending Slagfid's curse. Breaking Djofull's geas is merely one step along the way – a most useful step, since by doing so I will get possession of Heldur's crystal.'

His eyes gleamed at the mention of it. Although Leifr knew it was foolish to ask questions when the answers might ensnare him in Fangelsi forever, he could not forbear.

'What's Heldur's crystal?' he asked. 'I think I have a right to know, if you intend to keep it instead of giving it to Djofull.'

'I do so intend,' Thurid said. 'His geas is only to destroy the night-farers of Fangelsi – the jotuns and the draugar. And Heldur. Once the dirty work is done, he thinks he'll be able to take the crystal, and we'll only be too happy to escape. At this time, he will probably destroy us all. The crystal, however, will save us.'

'Heldur's crystal is an orb of evil influence,' Hogni said. 'You can't possibly wish to possess it, or you'll soon be possessed by the dark side.'

'I beg to differ,' Thurid replied. 'Its influence is powerful, neither good nor evil, but depends upon who holds it. Heldur has been weaving Dvergar powers into it

344

– all the secrets of the earth below the surface. Anyone who possesses that knowledge will be powerful indeed, whether he is day-farer or night-farer. The crystal grew in the head of a dragon, a dragon's carbuncle. Heldur commanded Slagfid and his sons to carve that stone out of the dragon's living skull, and it must be bathed in fire or dragon's blood to use its powers.'

'Where do you plan to get a reliable supply of dragon's blood?' Leifr asked suspiciously.

Thurid snapped his fingers, conjuring a glowing ball of alf-light into the palm of his hand. 'I have plenty of fire. For this very purpose of possessing Heldur's orb was I given the gift of very pure alf-light.'

On the walk back to the house, Hogni broke his morose silence, deigning to speak directly to Leifr for the first time since their quarrel over the treasure.

'He's mad,' Hogni said. 'None of us are going to get out of this alive. Little is lost, I suppose, but once the curse takes that wizard, we'll see horrors here that Slagfid never dreamed of. I daresay there's nothing you can do to reason with him?'

'Nothing at all,' Leifr replied with fatalistic calm. 'I tried to destroy Gedvondur once. It's that hand which governs him, even when you hear him speaking as himself and there's no sign of Gedvondur about him.'

'Why haven't you left by now?' Hogni asked. 'A fighter such as yourself with a sword such as you carry could get through Djofull's wards and wolves.'

'A fighter such as myself doesn't abandon a friend,' Leifr answered. 'Not helpless ones such as Syrgja and Ermingerd. And Ketil. I'm going it live to see the day when I deliver a complaint about his death to your chieftain. I think you opened his door and let him go to his death.'

Hogni sighed and shook his head. 'At one time, I hated the thought of standing trial at the Althing, before all the chieftains and earls of the Four Quarters. But now that I don't believe I'll live to see it, nothing would

345

please me more than to rest my eyes on Thingvellir again, even as a guilty man.'

'You admit to locking us in and letting Ketil out?'

'To one, but not the other,' Hogni replied with a trace of a wry smile. 'I'll leave you to guess which one.'

Out of morbid curiosity, Leifr returned to the tower at dusk, when Thurid usually began his nightly conjurations. It was a beautiful spring dusk, fragrant with thawing earth smells.

'You don't mind if I watch, do you?' he asked. 'I'd like to see Slagfid, or Hreidar as a walking draug.'

Thurid looked inordinately pleased and flattered. 'You've come to see the master perform? I assure you, it'll be a night you'll remember. But you'll have to stand fast and keep calm once I've summoned him here. If you step out of the circle, he'll have power over you and I daresay he'll make the best of his opportunity.'

'I'm not afraid, if that's what you're getting at,' Leifr replied. 'I'm just curious. It's a feeling I get when I'm fairly certain I'm going to be killed soon.'

The setting sun was suddenly blotted from the doorway by a hulking figure, and Leifr's nerves jumped automatically and he reached for his sword. It was only Raudbjorn, craning his neck uneasily to see inside the tower.

'Leifr lead, Raudbjorn follow,' he grunted.

'And I followed Raudbjorn,' Starkad's voice added from the rear. 'What are you doing up here, Leifr? It's almost dark and this is no place to be when Thurid is summoning.'

'I'm going to stay and watch,' Leifr said. 'This may be my last opportunity to see something so interesting.'

'Then I'll stay too,' Starkad volunteered, and Raudbjorn included himself in the offer.

'The robbers of the barrow,' Thurid said as he began to draw a guardian ring around them. 'I couldn't have better bait. The draug should be drawn with hopeless fascination – or a desire for vengeance.'

Thurid next scratched a circle for himself to stand in and lit a pair of braziers, throwing in handfuls of certain substances and speaking certain words, resulting in different colors of flame and smoke.

'Eg kalla saman thu,' he chanted over and over, until Leifr was nearly hypnotized by his voice and intoxicated by the smell of the acrid smoke. He knelt down to steady himself, no longer certain he was curious about the jotun draugar. Starkad's face looked positively green, but it might have been the lurid glare of the braziers.

Suddenly a dim glow appeared between the cracks of the door and something bumped heavily against the panels in a single heavy knock. Raudbjorn and Starkad crouched down, forming a defensive triangle with Leifr at the foremost point.

The creature clawed around for the latch, shaking the handle up and down in growing rage and muttering with almost human frustration. As always, Leifr felt the thrill of helpless, inbred terror of the living for the walking dead. He wanted nothing more than to put a stout door between himself and the draug trying to get in.

'You may enter,' Gedvondur's voice rasped, and the door fell open, revealing a dark mass standing in the opening. A deathly smell drifted into the tower.

The jotun draug shambled to the center of the tower. Leifr had no trouble recognizing him as one of the dead jotuns he had himself plundered on his bier. His massive head was sunk on his chest, as if by its own weight. One misformed hand upraised against the flickering light, the huge creature shuffled a pace nearer, uttering windy gasps through blackened teeth. His raiment was mostly rotted rags, and what flesh he had remaining was cruelly stretched over the knobby accretions that massed over most of his bones. A faint luminescence glowed from within the draug, the merest shadow of his former flesh intersticed with blackened, misshapen bones.

'At last!' breathed Thurid. 'It's either Hreidar or Slagfid himself!' In a commanding voice he addressed the draug, 'Speak, wanderer. Tell me your name you were known by when you walked as a man!'

Facing them, the draug raised one great paw, slowly clenching it into a deadly fist. In a whispering voice, it said, 'I am Hreidar. I've come for my father's gold.'

Thrusting out his staff, with Gedvondur gripping his wrist, Thurid demanded in a thunderous voice, with words that seemed to hang in the air as if written in fire, 'I adjure you, Hreidar, to speak and tell me what I demand to know.'

The draug swung his head slowly from one side to the other. His cavernous eyes were fixed upon the living beings before him. Growling, the jotun turned to face Thurid. In a voice more like the whistling of wind, the creature spoke. 'I seek that which was taken from me. My resting place has been dishonored by thieves. The living have trespassed upon the realm of the dead.'

Thurid sketched some symbols in the air that hung glowing between him and the draug. 'I command you to speak and answer three questions,' he went on relentlessly.

The draug snarled, swatting aside the symbols and lurching forward several more steps toward Thurid.

'You have not the skill,' Hreidar hissed. 'You are on Heldur's earth, and you are in Heldur's power. You must be destroyed!'

'Three questions, Hreidar,' Thurid commanded, hastily producing a burst of alf-light at the end of his staff. 'Tell me where Heldur's forge stands.'

'In the center of the Convocation of Jotuns,' rumbled the draug, raising one ragged paw against the light.

'Tell me when he does his forging.'

'When it is neither spring nor winter, neither day nor night, and the jotuns are neither dead nor alive.'

'How may I destroy Heldur?'

Hreidar swayed on his feet, his blue light flickering with intermittent bright flashes. Thurid muttered to Gedvondur, 'He's balking. I told you he wouldn't answer that question. Heldur's blocking him.'

'Eg skipa!' Gedvondur's voice roared out.

The draug slowly turned in Leifr's direction, his hand still outstretched with a skeletal finger pointing.

'The barrow robber,' Hreidar growled with an intensifying blue glare licking his bones like flames. Whether he spoke in accusation or in answer to the question, Leifr was unsure, but he rose warily from a crouch to his feet, with his hand on the hilt of his sword.

Hreidar shuffled nearer, one shambling step after the other, until he halted at the edge of the ring, jolted by a crackling spark of power. In the blue light streaming from the creature's distorted eye sockets, half-hidden by bony growths, Leifr thought he could see the ghost images of eyes fixed upon him in a tormented stare.

'Free me,' the draug whispered, slowly raising one massive hand again to raise a fiery spark from the ring.

'Not until I'm finished with you,' Thurid answered, although Leifr was certain the draug had spoken to him.

'Free me,' Hreidar repeated.

'Gedvondur!' Thurid ordered in a growing frenzy. 'Do something! We've lost control of him!'

'Don't panic! Wait and see what he does!' Gedvondur answered in a furious growl.

Hreidar sighed a breath that smelled of mold and decay and death. Starkad and Raudbjorn turned away, covering mouth and nose, but Leifr did not think to protect himself. The breath of the grave chilled him to the bone, yet drew him with inexplicable fascination to take a step forward, over the protecting boundary of Thurid's ring.

'Back, Leifr, you fool!' Thurid roared, summoning a mighty gout of alf-light. 'I challenge you, jotun! If any honor remains in your rotten carcass, turn and fight, or I'll cut you down as you stand!'

Slowly the jotun turned his head to survey the source of the challenge. The blue glow brightened until the creature's eyes glared with fury. In one surprisingly quick stride he advanced, one mighty hand outstretched toward Leifr in a grasping motion. Leifr struck at the hand with *Endalaus Daudi*, showering the air with sparks as the

349

sword rang out bright, agonized notes repeatedly as if it were being clashed against stone.

The jotun pressed forward, ignoring Leifr's sword strokes, and Leifr retreated to evade him while Gedvondur and Thurid both shouted at him.

'Not that sword!' Gedvondur roared. 'Get back in the circle, Leifr!'

'Get out of the tower, Leifr!' Thurid yelled, abandoning his own circle and skirmishing at Hreidar's heels with gouts of alf-light. 'Run for your lives! The circle won't save you!'

'Thurid, you great ninny, you'd better get away from him! He's commanded twice already!' Gedvondur retorted, just before abandoning Thurid to his own devices by scurrying up a beam into the high rafters, as a rat on a sinking ship would seek higher ground.

Raudbjorn could be restrained no longer. Unwinding his halberd with a mighty bellow, he plunged forward with a deadly swing at the draug's head. It flung up a fist, blocking the blow and sending a bolt of blinding, crackling force through the haft of the halberd. Raudbjorn spun around, staggering backward, and collapsed in a heap.

With a wild shout Starkad rushed forward to protect Raudbjorn where he lay, lashing the air furiously with Slagfid's sword. Swinging around slowly, Hreidar shuffled ominously toward Starkad and Raudbjorn. A roof timber caught the creature's skull a grinding scrape as he passed beneath it, ripping away a leathery patch of dried skin to reveal the knotted bone beneath. While the draug was momentarily off balance, Starkad darted forward with a triumphant bellow and plunged Slagfid's sword into Hreidar's chest. He stepped back, but Hreidar did not fall as expected. The sword hung there, gleaming whitely in the draug-light.

With a windy rumbling that sounded like a curse, Hreidar raised his fist and struck the offending timber in twain with an explosion of dust and splinters. A large fragment struck the jotun in the chest. Lashing out in response, Hreidar's fist knocked the bracing timber away from the sagging wall. The upper story of the tower uttered a protesting groan. For a moment everyone froze, from Gedvondur clinging to a beam, to Hreidar with his head bullishly lowered. Then the draug struck down another brace and the tower definitely shifted toward its sagging side, voicing a decidedly ominous creaking and cracking sound.

'Get out of here while you can!' Thurid warned Leifr. 'I'll hold him back as long as I'm able!'

'Free me!' repeated the draug for the third time, fixing its terrible tormented eyes upon Leifr.

Leifr gazed frozenly, not hearing Thurid's shouts, hearing only the despairing plea of the draug. Unable to bear the creature's pain, he leaped from behind Raudbjorn and plunged the sword into the jotun's chest as far as the hilt. Yanking it free, he plunged it in again before an icy wave of power knocked him staggering back with a grinding jolt that numbed his arms to the shoulders.

The draug clawed at the sword, while Heldur's voice uttered a terrible shriek of rage and defiance. He took a lurching step forward, but something was going wrong with the draug spell that gave the corpse its semblance of life. The dried flesh and rags and bones shimmered, losing their clarity. Then he began to topple, a section at a time. First the knees gave way with a rocky clatter, then the arms broke away and fell to the floor as the legs continued to wobble and disintegrate, and finally the torso and head collapsed like an avalanche of stone. Indeed, the jotun had turned to stones, and Slagfid's sword clattered among them, coming to rest against *Endalaus Daudi*. A force leaped from the two metals as they touched, and Slagfid's sword blazed hotly a moment and snapped in half.

'Blast!' Thurid muttered in the sudden silence. 'We shouldn't have done that!'

Suddenly a jet of white flame appeared over the stones, gathering in intensity with a rising hissing sound. Before

351

the pillar of flame grew too bright to look at, Leifr thought he saw a form taking shape in the midst of the brilliance. Then with a deafening scream, the white flame shot out the smoke hole in the roof like a geyser, leaving the people blinded and gasping. In the sudden silence, the old tower swayed and sounded a long rumbling warning note.

'Get out, quick!' Gedvondur's voice roared as the hand dropped from the rafters to land on Thurid's head, obscuring one eye. 'It's going to fall!'

'But the gold!' Starkad yelled in protest as Raudbjorn seized him by the neck and plunged toward the doorway.

Leifr shoved them out ahead of him, replying, 'It won't do you any good if you're buried here with it!'

Thurid scuttled around the room, snatching up his most prized objects and stuffing them into his satchel. Leifr tore him away bodily as the first rocks fell and the tower began to collapse in deadly earnest.

The tower fell with a prolonged clatter and rumbling of stones, scattering down the hillside as far as the wall of the horse paddock. When it was finished, nothing remained but a single accusing finger of stone pointing upward; then after a stunned moment, it too collapsed on the heap of fallen stone.

Lanterns came bobbing from the house as Hogni and Horgull approached.

'What has happened?' Hogni demanded, aghast. 'You've destroyed Heldur's tower! What was that unearthly shrieking?'

'A jotun draug was released from Heldur's spell,' Thurid said in a tone of utmost weariness and gloomy satisfaction. 'But now I know all there is to know.'

'But I don't,' Starkad protested. 'Isn't it time I was told?'

'Shut your mouth, Starkad,' Hogni told him. 'The tower leveled, a draug destroyed – this has doomed us as surely as the curse.'

Thurid led the way to the house, where he sat down in a chair and broodingly sank his face into his hands. Silently,

Syrgja brewed tea, strong and fragrant, while Leifr gazed suspiciously from face to face, trying to determine exactly what had happened.

Hogni and Horgull sat and stared vacantly, as if their thoughts were racing down faraway paths. Syrgja too seemed paralyzed, devoid of her usual strong will as she sat and gazed hopelessly at Thurid and her nephews. Svanlaug hovered near the door, her hands busy with the air currents, with occasional small exclamations.

'It's changed!' she remarked. 'For the first time, I feel that this is now Ljosalfar land.'

'How changed?' Starkad demanded, looking from his silent aunt to his brothers. 'What are all of you hiding from me? What's the great secret? All my life you've denied me the truth, and now I think I should know it!'

'Be silent, Starkad!' Syrgja snapped. 'One day perhaps you'll be grateful for this respite!'

Starkad hurled himself away impatiently to stalk up and down the length of the room. Leifr sagged into a chair, closing his eyes and wishing he were elsewhere, anywhere but in Fangelsi-hofn. Looking at Starkad, he guessed that the two of them felt nearly the same – angrily helpless in a world where others held the keys of knowledge.

After the destruction of the tower, Thurid moved his laboratory into the old hall for the last few days of winter. He kept the doors locked and allowed no one to enter, having learned from experience that ordinary mortals could cause dire consequences from meetings with draugar.

The day after the fall of the tower, a last snowstorm blasted Fangelsi with white fury. Warring clouds of sinister influence darkened the sky and veiled Skera-gil as far down as the fourth pasture. Long before natural nightfall, the valley was almost as dark as midnight. Thurid sat hunched before the fire, listening to the storm outside with the troll-hounds curled around his feet to soak up the warmth of the coals. Hogni and Horgull abandoned their chess game, merely to sit and listen to the sounds outside – voices, shouts, the clash of metal, all borne on the shrieking wind. Syrgja moaned and flinched when something went grinding and crashing by.

'There went the bathhouse roof!' she muttered.

Suddenly the wind ceased as if a cork had been put in, and Thurid roused himself from his fiery contemplations, glaring around suspiciously at his companions. Hogni clenched the edge of the table, his face pale and his eyes staring blankly at nothing; then he slumped forward with a hopeless sigh.

'Someone's meddling with the wards on the fourth gate,' Hogni said wearily. 'I can't hold it any longer. It's Djofull, and he's too strong.'

'Let him come in if he dares,' Thurid said, striding after his boots and cloak. 'Come, we're going to meet him. This is no longer Dokkalfar ground.'

'We'll put on a brave show,' Hogni said bitterly, 'but the end is going to be the same.'

Djofull's sledge came rumbling down the pasture road at a breakneck gallop, drawing to a steaming halt at the last wall, where the defenders of the house formed a wary line to greet him with stony silence. Syrgja gripped her distaff, ready again to rebuff the hated Dokkalfar.

Djofull did not dismount from his sledge. He pulled forward his hood to shield his eyes from the glare of Thurid's alf-light.

'Only a few days remain, Thurid,' he barked. 'Are you ready to end this rebellion while there's yet time?'

'I know all I need to know to break Heldur's hold,' Thurid replied. 'The night-farers you sent us to destroy will be gone, and your geas satisfied. If you are wise, you'll be gone also, Djofull.'

'I shall be, as soon as I have the orb,' Djofull replied in a rather conciliatory tone.

'The orb,' Thurid said coldly, 'will be mine.'

'I daresay it won't,' Djofull retorted. 'I need that crystal. I'll duel you for it, and you'll be destroyed.'

'Perhaps we should duel for it now and get it over with,'

Gedvondur's voice suggested truculently.

'There's no time for this quarreling!' Djofull burst out. 'The Inquisitors are on their way! My fylgjur-wolves have seen them at Tagl-vik, only three days by horse from here. If they get here before the Convocation, neither of us will have that orb. I'll keep them out of Fangelsi if you'll swear to give me Heldur's crystal. I'll even help you escape from them.'

'Will you indeed!' Thurid scoffed. 'We shall see, on the first day of spring, how good your promises are.'

'Is that all you have to say?' Djofull demanded. 'Your arrogance is going to suffer a great downfall without me to give you protection! You can't even get into Skera-gil to get to the Convocation of Jotuns unless I withdraw my wards! And that's one thing I won't do until you swear to surrender Heldur's orb!'

'Faugh, Djofull! I'll swear to nothing and surrender nothing! Fara af stad!' Thurid's hand jerked upward to sketch a significant gesture in the air. Djofull ducked and threw up his claw hand in an attempt to protect himself from Thurid's words.

'But thank you for the warning,' Thurid continued. 'I shall be on the lookout for the Inquisitors.'

Djofull shouted to his driver, and the horses lunged forward under the cracking whip. Thurid stood and gazed after the sledge until it had disappeared, then he scratched runes on the ground to seal up the fourth gate again.

'Once more,' Hogni said resignedly, 'I see my folly in taking outlaws as houseguests for the winter. Now I'm likely to be held accountable by the Guild for sheltering a fugitive from their justice. You've surely drawn them here yourself with your own ill-advised summoning.'

'Very likely,' Thurid said curtly. 'Blast them! They'd better not get here before the Convocation of Jotuns. Nothing is going to stop me from being here when Heldur starts firing that crystal. Let the elements combine against me! I will not be stopped!'

As if it had accepted the challenge, the wind began

again, raging straight for two days with driving snow and rain. Thurid struggled diligently up to the observatory at dawn, returning wet and unsatisfied. He buried himself in the old hall, emerging at sundown to march up to the hilltop with a confident gait. He shouted some words that were snatched away by the wind; but by the time he returned to the house, the wind had been banished and the clouds were withdrawing sullenly back into Skera-gil.

During the night, the Flayer returned, full of Heldur's fury. In the morning, Leifr and Starkad went outside to examine the tracks, accompanied by Raudbjorn shuffling sleepily after them, like a bear emerging from hibernation. The troll-hounds frolicked in the snow and leaped over each other's backs, sniffing avidly at the jotun tracks that went round and round the house, stopping and trampling the ground at every door and window. The Flayer had gone to the remains of the tower, circling it twice. The troll-hounds followed the scent avidly, growling and whining. Kraftig halted with one paw upraised, sniffing the air, then he left the established scent and circled through the ruins, head slung low as he searched. Before long he sounded the cry of a scent found, and the other two hounds raced to investigate, leaving Leifr and Starkad to slog after them at a slower pace.

'There's the Flayer's tracks again,' Starkad said and pointed out the dragging trail in the fresh wet snow. 'He's not going toward Skera-gil.'

The hounds stood and waited for Leifr, howling and barking their impatience to show him what they had found. It was a second set of dragging tracks, side by side with those of the Flayer.

'A draug,' Starkad whispered. Then his eyes narrowed in an incredulous frown. He knelt down to look at the tracks more closely. 'Look at the toes on those boots. Long and curling up, like troll head boots. Those draugar didn't wear troll head boots. They had fine ones made of real leather. Only poor people make troll head boots. Who made these tracks, Leifr?'

'Hogni or Horgull, maybe,' Leifr suggested, not liking the sudden fiery resolve kindling in Starkad's eye and stubbornly jutting chin. 'Perhaps one of Djofull's Dokkalfar got through the wards last night.'

'How could he?' Starkad demanded. 'How does the Flayer keep getting through, as if the wards weren't there? Hogni's never been able to keep him out. If these tracks are Hogni's, let's follow them. I suspect we're going to find out that Hogni's been letting the Flayer through all along, just to keep the rest of us frightened!'

Starkad plunged ahead, following the tracks. They crossed the walls into the fourth pasture and proceeded straight toward the barrows. Leifr protested, but Starkad did not appear to be listening. He raised his head slowly and turned to Leifr, a fierce gleam in his eyes.

'The troll tunnel in the fourth pasture,' he announced. 'All the trolls have to come from Skera-gil. Their tunnel must lead straight into it, and the Flayer uses it to get past the wards. We've found the way to get past Djofull for the Convocation.'

'We'd better make sure first,' Leifr said. 'The Flayer might have just hidden here. Let's see if he's inside.'

It was a cold, rainy spring day, but there was no time to wait for better conditions. Cautiously, they followed the tracks up to one of the large barrows which had stood open and vacant for several centuries. A fetid breath issued from the back of the barrow, smelling of trolls and damp earth and decay. The faint breeze also carried a breath of the forbidding terror that pervaded Skera-gil.

'I never went into this one, as a boy,' Starkad whispered. 'Now I know why it always scared me to death.'

At the back of the barrow they found a tunnel, worn to greasy smoothness by generations of trolls passing to and fro. The tunnel was low enough that they had to stoop, and in several places Raudbjorn had to squeeze breathlessly between shoulders of rock, but it was room enough for the Flayer to get through. Their only light was a stub

357

of tallow candle, which Starkad lit with a twist of dry grass wick and a spark from his flint and steel.

They had not gone far when the hounds pricked up their ears and began to growl softly, hanging back near Leifr instead of charging away in their usual joyous abandon when trolls were their quarry. Their unease quickly spread to Leifr and Starkad and they slowed their pace. During a thoughtful pause, when Leifr was about to suggest turning around, they heard a groan up ahead. The candle in Starkad's hand began to shake. Holding it higher, Starkad took a step forward. Its chancy light revealed a movement, and a large heap of something lighter than earth. The heap groaned and tried to ease away into the fissure. Starkad moved closer, drawing his breath in with a sharp gasp.

Ketil crouched there, squinting at the feeble light, vastly altered from his normal appearance. His body appeared bloated, his hands were massively knotted, and his head seemed swollen. To all appearances, he had been beaten and frostbitten and should probably have been dead. As they stood staring in horror and dread, all wondering if perhaps he were a draug, they could see his chest rising and falling with slow breaths.

'Starkad, little systursonur!' croaked Ketil with a rare flash of recognition. 'It's time to milk the cows. What a good lad you are! Next fairing, I promise a colt for you to train.'

Starkad flung off Leifr's restraining grasp and strode forward. 'He lives!' he hissed. 'The Flayer has kept him a prisoner!'

Incredible as it seemed, it was certainly true. Although the mysterious Fangelsi disease had disfigured Ketil to a greater extent without Syrgja's treatments, life with the jotun had not otherwise disagreed with him. They considered the long trek back to Fangelsi, faced by the problem of what to do with Ketil.

'We'll have to carry him back,' Starkad said. 'He's very ill with the disease and look at the condition of his feet.'

His troll's head boots were split, his feet were bloody masses of dirty bandages and strange oozings, and he moaned and tossed his head wretchedly from side to side like a sleeper with a bad dream. His elusive clarity of mind was gone, and he struggled to retreat further into the cave. He seemed his usual surly self, growling and making go-away gestures with his club of a hand.

'Raudbjorn carry.' Raudbjorn knelt down on one knee while they hoisted Ketil onto his shoulders, still moaning and thrashing angrily, but Raudbjorn took a firm grip on him and strode forward with grim resolution.

Once outside the tunnel, Ketil became less cooperative, and they discovered that the weather had taken a similar nasty turn. The driving snow would have made it impossible to find the way home if not for the keen noses of the troll-hounds. Ketil was speedily growing dissatisfied with his rather crude mode of transportation, which probably jolted and ground together the most aching of his bones. He grumbled and threshed around, causing the already-staggering Raudbjorn to stumble along more roughly than before.

'Calm yourself, uncle, we're nearly there,' Starkad said soothingly, patting his uncle to reassure him that he was among family and friends, but Ketil only snarled in response and kicked and squirmed the harder.

Raudbjorn kept his grip and lengthened his stride, but, even in the twilight, Leifr could see his patiently suffering expression. Then in the middle of the second pasture, Ketil managed to bite Raudbjorn's ear, eliciting a pained howl from his burly steed.

'He doesn't know himself or what he's doing,' Starkad said apologetically. 'It's not much farther now, only two more gates.'

Two hayfields and a paddock later they succeeded in reaching the house, where Ermingerd waited beside the door with exclamations of astonishment. Hogni and Horgul also reacted with amazement, leaping to their feet as they staggered into the kitchen, crusted with snow, and dazed with exhaustion. Thurid uttered a peculiar strangled cry, his eyes glaring, and he smote his forehead in dismay. Syrgja rose from her chair, slowly straightening from a hunched-up position as her grief-dulled eyes took in the scene. Her temper returned quickly; she darted a murderous and triumphant glance toward Hogni and Horgull.

'You've failed again, you deceivers!' she cried in a voice hoarse with gloating and rage. 'It's not his time to leave us, and you can't hasten it! You and your false predictions! Bah!'

'We found him hiding in the barrows!' Starkad exclaimed pridefully. 'Imagine him surviving there that long!'

'Yes,' Thurid retorted, 'and how do you think he did it, without help?'

Raudbjorn slumped to his knees, lowering his inert burden from his shoulders. The women of the household flocked around Ketil, peeling away his frozen clothing, and warming him with blankets. Syrgja attempted to force a healing draught between his cold blue lips.

While their attention was thus diverted, Svanlaug heaped an unwonted amount of fuel on the fire and Starkad helped Leifr drag a largely unresponsive Raudbjorn toward its warmth.

The troubles with Ketil were not yet over, after getting him into the house and restoring his senses. Ketil looked around with a bright and feral eye, as if he had no recollection of where he was. They tried to put him into bed, but he slithered off the platform, belted Starkad out of his path with amazing strength, and made a plunge for the doorway, dragging Syrgja and Ermingerd after him.

Leifr saw no alternative; he blocked the doorway and grappled with Ketil, trying to restrain him. With a furious, wordless roar of pure fury, Ketil snared him in a breathtaking bear-hug, lifting him off the floor easily with an enraged growl, his eyes glaring only inches away like a maddened bull's. Just as Leifr's ribs were beginning to creak threateningly, Raudbjorn dived at Ketil's knees, bringing Ketil and Leifr down to the earthen floor with a crash, where the three of them wrestled around and puffed and snarled, shoving the tables and benches helter-skelter and scattering ruin in their wake. Hogni and Horgull attempted to separate the combatants with little success. Above the splinterings and bellowings, Leifr heard Thurid's excited shouts, giving him impossible advice.

Somehow in the fray, Leifr's knife slipped from his belt and skittered across the floor. With one huge paw Ketil pounced on the knife, his eyes gleaming with sudden murderous resolve. Syrgja shrieked in horror. At the sound of his sister's voice, Ketil's hand jerked back from the knife as if it had burned him. Clutching his swollen and oozing hand, he retreated toward his usual corner, bawling wordless threats and shaking his head back and forth in the measured agony of a suffering animal.

Ermingerd made the practical move of swiftly securing the door, while Syrgja collapsed in her chair, her face the color of gray clay. Anxiously, Ermingerd surveyed Leifr as Thurid helped him get to his feet, not without a few painful grunts and cautious explorations of his ribs.

'Are you all right, Leifr?' Ermingerd asked, terror in her eyes. 'I can't believe he would do such a thing, as sick as he's been. He's not himself, that's for certain.'

'I'm fine,' Leifr panted, with a wince at each gasp. He had no desire to upset these two women further, but if there was one thing he was sure of, it was that old Ketil had had every intention of murdering him on the spot. Still reeling from the shock, Leifr sat down in a chair and stared across the room at his ungrateful adversary, who crouched in his corner and stared back at him from under beetling brows.

'It's because you're a stranger,' Syrgja sniffed, recovering quickly from her fright. 'He hates being mauled about by strangers, especially in his own home. I only hope you didn't hurt him.'

'You fools!' Hogni said. 'Look at him! Can't you see what you've done?'

Leifr's feeling of accomplishment suddenly began to trickle away when he became conscious of the frozen atmosphere in the kitchen. Everyone stood still, gazing at Ketil, except Starkad, who was still prancing around in an ecstasy of self-congratulation, not realizing that everyone was ignoring him. Instead of hastening forward with her bandages and remedies, Syrgja took a faltering step backward when Ketil turned his furious eyes upon her, moaning and growling in desperation.

Leifr averted his eyes, not wanting to stare rudely at another's misfortunes, but his initial glimpse was enough to sicken him with horror and revulsion. At first glance, the unfortunate Ketil looked like a not-so-fresh corpse risen from its grave. At second glance, however, Leifr began to see the similarities to the Flayer, and to the jotun draugar. The truth struck him like a bolt between the eyes, with all the accompanying terror and anguish of unavoidable, naked reality. Even Raudbjorn's limited intellect grasped the situation accurately, and he covered his eyes with a groan.

'Why did you bring him back?' Hogni demanded of Starkad, seizing him and forcing him to look at Ketil. 'Look at him, you young fool! Don't you know the answer to the great secret now, at last? Don't you know what we were trying to protect you from, all these years? Look at your uncle, Starkad!'

Ketil squinted in the light of the fire and the lamp, trying to shade his sunken eyes with a clublike hand as he slowly gazed around the room. Moaning, he rose and slowly shuffled toward the door, and no one made a move to stop him. His ferocity was gone now, and his gasping breaths sounded like sobs. Before he vanished into the darkness he lifted one knotted hand in a gesture like a farewell. Syrgja raised a bitter lament, collapsing in his old chair and weeping like a child.

'I don't understand,' Starkad gasped, the color draining

from his face. 'He lookes like a jotun. He can't be a jotun.'

'He *is* a jotun,' Hogni went on grimly, relentlessly. 'While we watched and waited, and you brought him back from his inescapable fate, he was turning into a jotun. Look at us. We are the jotuns yet to come. That is the true nature of the curse Slagfid brought upon us with that sword. The Flayer is your uncle Thorkell. Now it's Ketil's turn to become a jotun. Have you not noticed the signs in our aunt Syrgja? The red swellings, the sore joints? One day it will afflict each one of us. But you, Starkad, must be the last. You are the ninety and ninth heir to Slagfid's curse. There will be no more children born into this family to carry the curse of Slagfid in their blood. You must die here, alone, the last of the jotuns. Thus will end the curse, at long last, with Slagfid's ninety and ninth heir.'

'No! This can't be true!' Starkad looked wildly at Ermingerd. 'Tell me he's lying!'

Ermingerd lifted her eyes, dark with pain and sorrow. 'It is true, Starkad. We are the jotuns.'

'Then it would be better to die now than wait for the curse to begin its slow rot!' Starkad reached for his knife, but Hogni gripped his wrist.

'It was your mother's way to destroy herself, but the curse is not outwitted that way. A draug or a man, it makes no difference to Heldur. The Convocation of Jotuns occurs each spring, when Heldur summons the life forces of all the victims of his curse and whatever jotuns are living, and from their strength he fires his forge in the heart of Skera-gil, forging that ungodly crystal with spells. Tomorrow he calls the Convocation for the hours between sunset and dawn of the first day of spring, just as Fantur is vanishing, when the time stands still, neither spring nor winter, neither day nor dark. Then he closes the way to Slagfid's Ban for another six months. When it opens again, there will be two jotuns, instead of one.'

'I can't live with such knowledge!' Starkad struggled wildly against Hogni and Horgull. 'I'd rather die!'

363

Syrgja quickly moved to the hearth with a handful of dried herbs, which ignited smolderingly, trailing pale yellow smoke. Covering her own mouth and nose, she held the smoking herb in Starkad's face so he inhaled several gasps of the smoke, then she quickly quenched the herb in her apron. Starkad flailed around with lessening ferocity, and finally sank biddably enough onto the sleeping platform, still sobbing wretchedly. Svanlaug, under cover of everyone's mutual reluctance to meet anyone's eye, picked up a shred of the inducing herb and sniffed it curiously.

'Now you know the secret,' Hogni said with a sardonic smile at Leifr and Thurid. 'We are the jotuns yet to come. We are the night-farers Djofull sent you to destroy. We wouldn't put up much of a battle, if you care to finish your job here and now.'

Leifr could only shake his head with an overwhelming mixture of pity and horror.

'Killing you now would do no more good than killing the Flayer or Ketil,' Thurid said gently. 'It's Heldur we have to destroy, and the entire Convocation of Jotuns, all ninety-nine of them, of which you are the last five.'

Hogni smiled mockingly. 'Yes, Heldur. Even Djofull dares not challenge him directly. Do you have that kind of power, Thurid? Or is it merely a reckless desire to die?'

Thurid folded his arms. 'Tomorrow morning we'll find out. What do any of us have to lose?' He tossed his cloak over one shoulder and strode outside, heading for the hall.

The terrible oppression of Fangelsi suddenly struck at Leifr, and he had to get outside for some deep breaths of fresh air. However, looking up at the ceiling of cloud hanging over the valley, he still felt as if he could not draw a free breath. Common sense told him to get out of Fangelsi, if he had to claw his way out and make war against the lowering clouds sealing him in. But the vision of Ermingerd clung in his mind, and Starkad's hopeless battle to rescue her from the dreary captivity of Fangelsi. Now he knew that merely taking Ermingerd away would not ease the burden she shared with her family. Unless the curse was broken, she, too, in her turn, would suffer as Ketil and Thorkell, and all the others who followed Slagfid.

Then he thought of Starkad's happy exuberance turning into the morose gloom of Hogni and Horgull. He shook his head, feeling bowed under the burden of such unavoidable tragedy.

CHAPTER 22

Before dawn, Leifr climbed the hill with Thurid and Hogni to the observatory. The pre-dawn wind whipped at them with a hint of snow as they watched the sun creep over the horizon. It was not quite in line with the hell stone, which stood outside the ring.

'One more day,' Thurid said. 'Heldur begins his forging tonight at the peak of the nameless hours between winter and spring. I must be at the Convocation of Jotuns by sundown. And you?'

Hogni nodded. 'All five of us. We have decided, since we are the last, to end it now. Even young Starkad will come. But are you willing to take such a risk, wizard? No one who goes uncalled ever returns. The few of our ancestors who were over-curious were transformed to jotuns to prevent revealing what they discovered.'

'If I weren't willing, it would mean remaining at Fangelsi and suffering Ketil's fate, since the mark is already on me,' Thurid replied. He turned his haunted, fierce gaze upon Leifr. 'Tomorrow morning, if we haven't returned, you and Raudbjorn must get out of Fangelsi as fast as you can. Djofull's geas will be broken, but he's not going to give up easily. Go to Hefillstad in the South Quarter; I've got some friends there. Look for an old wizard named Gradagur. He taught me when I was a hopeful green youth and sent me to the Guild for the First Examination, where I subsequently disappointed both of us. He'll help you get back to the Scipling realm – here now, don't glare at me like that. This is for your own good.'

Leifr's incredulous and smoldering stare gradually

366

permeated Thurid's layers of preoccupation.

'Thurid, I'm not going to leave you here,' Leifr said. 'Is that the kind of coward you think I am? There's nothing you can do to stop me from going with you to the Convocation of Jotuns. You've seen what *Endalaus Daudi* does to the jotuns. If worse comes to worst, you'll need that sword to get you out of there.'

'You and that sword, against ninety-nine jotuns?' Thurid snorted.

'Ninety-eight. I've destroyed one already.'

'Leifr, I refuse to permit it.'

'If you do, I won't show you how to get into Slagfid's Ban. Djofull won't let you take so much as a single step on the other side of the sixth gate.'

'You wouldn't attempt to threaten me, would you?' Thurid's cloak snapped viciously in a gust of indignation.

'Not as long as you're sensible and allow me to be there to help you.'

Thurid turned to the east and studied Skera-gil. The dark cloud loomed over the ravine, swollen and black-purple, crawling slowly like a crab across the sky over Fangelsi. The region of the sixth pasture was completely obscured by the low-hanging cloud, and the jeering voices of the fylgjur-wolves drifted down to the observatory. Leifr did not doubt that Djofull himself was watching in anticipation as the final hours of his geas approached culmination. Worriedly, Leifr eyed Thurid's tatty appearance and raddled countenance, thinking it was a fragile reed that offered him his only hope of escaping the wrath of Heldur and Djofull.

'You wouldn't dare attempt to withhold such vital information from me,' Thurid declared in the grating voice of Gedvondur, his eyes flashing with menace. Thurid's voice added, 'Sciplings will dare anything, Gedvondur. They have a talent for self-destruction.'

Leifr folded his arms stubbornly. 'I'm sure there will be no need to quarrel, since we'll all be going together,' he said.

'Let him kill himself then,' Gedvondur snapped.

'Never,' Thurid declared just as obdurately.

'While you delay, time runs out,' Leifr said. 'The sooner you change your mind, the shorter the time you'll be in the wrong.'

'What harm can come to him with both of us there?' Gedvondur asked.

With ill grace, Thurid conceded, muttering some remarks about Scipling stubbornness, stupidity, and general intractability, couched in rather uncomplimentary terms.

Starkad was not as boastful as he might have been of their discovery of the tunnel in the fourth pasture. Everyone followed Leifr's lead in the subdued silence that concealed excitement, as in Starkad's case, and fear, which shone in Syrgja's eyes; with Ermingerd, excitement and fear was not unmingled with hope. They traversed the tunnel with the troll-hounds ranging ahead to scour the way of any lingering trolls. As Leifr and Starkad had suspected, the tunnel delivered them into the lower end of Skera-gil.

The gloom and horror of Skera-gil's entire hideous past rose in a formidable cloud of shadows and fearful emotions, as if Heldur were casting up his last defense against them. From the tops of the crags, Djofull's fylgjur-wolves yammered derision from the shadows.

The door into Slagfid's Ban hung open, the lock and bar twisted and cast aside. Syrgja gazed around with a miserable moan on her lips, clasping her hands.

'Is this always the end of it?' she whispered. 'Will I be the next jotun to vanish behind that door?'

'Tomorrow, there will be no sign of this doorway,' Hogni said. 'Not for another six months. Perhaps we'll live to see it reappear. Perhaps this is the last time any of us will look out on the face of Skarpsey.'

Leifr gazed around at the mists and gloom of Skera-gil, fervently hoping this was not to be his last glimpse of the earth, before entering the foul-smelling cave. Thurid lit his alf-light. No one spoke until they reached the treasure room, where Hogni stood gazing a moment, then he whispered, 'So much gold – so much despair.'

Without being bidden, Svanlaug upended the bag she carried, pouring out her stolen loot with a musical clatter. Svanlaug's expression was regretful, but her manner betokened no guilty involvement with the purloined gold. Almost negligently, she shoved it out of sight with her foot, like something she was rather embarrassed by.

They followed Hogni's lead across the burial chamber, trying not to crunch among the scattered bones. Syrgja's breaths came in ragged gasps, but Ermingerd clasped her hand tightly and led her onward with murmured words of encouragement.

Hogni did not spare the biers or the motionless draugar another glance. He pulled aside the tattered tapestries, revealing a door cut in the solid stone. It stood open, leading to a chamber beyond, cluttered with the tools of the smith's trade.

'Heldur's Forge,' Thurid whispered, his eyes firing with the light of challenge as he gazed around.

Hogni nodded his head. 'When the sun reaches equinox, Fantur's position will cause the mountain to close for another six months, with the jotuns inside. We bring our dead to Skera-gil, and Heldur takes them when he requires them for his forge.' He nodded toward a flight of crumbling steps beyond the forge. 'When they live long enough to become jotuns, twice a year they find their own way to Heldur's Forge at Heldur's bidding, for as long as they are able. At the last stage of the curse, there is too much stone in the body for the jotun to move. There are a few who were not yet jotuns who went through that door on their own, but no one has ever witnessed the Convocation of Jotuns and returned to normal mortal life again.'

'Heldur will cease his forging after today,' Thurid said grimly, looking around the dusty forge combatively. 'We will be the first to see the Convocation of Jotuns and live to tell of it.'

369

Thurid was putting on one of his more blatant displays of self-assurance, rustling his cloak like a pair of wings and striding up and down with a masterful attitude, with Gedvondur perched upon his wrist, carbuncle ring sparkling like a hawk's eye. Leifr looked at him narrowly, trying to decide if Thurid was bursting with the overconfidence of Gedvondur's aid, or if it were under-confidence Thurid was worriedly hiding with a blustering front.

Thurid started forward, but Hogni halted him in midstep by raising one hand. He stepped forward, bowing slightly to Thurid and saying, 'I wish to be the first to lay eyes upon the Convocation of Jotuns, since I am Slagfid's heir. Once beyond this room, you shall take command. I feel as if I know this place, so many centuries of dread have bred it into my bones.'

He beckoned Horgull to follow, then Syrgja and Ermingerd and Starkad, followed by Thurid and the others. When Leifr was free of Thurid's obstructing hulk, he found himself standing outdoors, with evening sky overhead and winter-seared earth underfoot. The opening behind him was the narrow door of a barrow mound, crowned with a row of odd-shaped rock cairns. Enough light remained to show him a vast, dark-walled crater rising all around him, with the early stars peering in over its jagged edges. A particularly deep and narrow cleft framed perfectly one bright star, whose light seemed channeled into the crater, casting a swath of faint light through the deepening shadow. Its light fell upon what at first looked to Leifr like the shoulder and arm of a person, but when Leifr looked more suspiciously, he saw a cairn of stone. Beside it stood another, toadstool shaped, with a clump of warty legs supporting it, and beyond it were others. The entire crater was filled with odd little rock formations, pyramids, goblins, gremlins, all heaped up from stone, with none like the next. Their knobs and hollows reminded him fleetingly of faces, or figures, lurking in the half-light. As he was uneasily contemplating the geological oddities of the crater, it struck him that the formations were neatly arranged in concentric rings, spiraling outward from where he stood, over the rounded top of the barrow and outward toward the walls of the crater. Turning slowly, he felt himself to be the center of attention for a vast and silent audience.

'The Ninety and Nine,' Thurid intoned, also sweeping the amphitheater with his stern gaze, with the wind snapping at his cloak. 'And there is the Ninety-Ninth.'

He pointed with his flaring staff to an empty stone seat, which formed the last of the spiral of stone cairns. Beside it were seven other seats, a slight space, then five more empty stone seats, larger than the rest, placed to form the other half of the ring, then the next figure was a squatty block of stone with a conical headpiece, which commenced the spiral procession of stone formations. In the center of the ring of empty seats the earth was blackened, its rocks glassy and distorted from great heat.

'The Convocation of Jotuns,' Hogni said. 'These are all our ancestors. Here the curse began, and here they end, when the curse literally becomes too much to bear. Each of these stone piles represents a lifetime of the agony of knowing what the future is bringing. The essence that lingers provides the fire for Heldur's forging.' Hogni glanced upward at the rim of the crater, where the star gleamed in the shaft. 'We don't have much time,' he said, his voice betraying a sharp edge of anxiety. 'Fantur drops like a stone at sundown and Heldur starts his forging. He fuels his fires with gold and living souls in torment, and it has taken him seven hundred years. What is your plan, wizard?'

'You will take your appointed seats,' Thurid said. 'We're going to hasten the culmination of his forging, and turn it about in a way he won't suspect possible. Syrgja there, as the eldest, then Hogni, Horgull, Ermingerd, and Starkad – the Ninety and Ninth.' He pointed to the last seat, but Starkad folded his arms obdurately and shook his head.

'It's not my seat,' he said, with tightly pent fury. 'I may

be cursed, but I'm no part of this monstrous thing, and I'm not going to touch it.'

Hogni glowered at Starkad, the command shuddering in the air between them. 'Starkad! Sit!' he barked. 'What worse harm can come to you than this you were born with? If the wizard kills us all and we become jotuns now, isn't it better to have the waiting over?'

'If I turn into a jotun, he'll be the first one I come after,' Starkad growled in Thurid's direction, slinking around the last crude seat and tentatively easing one haunch onto it.

Thurid pointed to Raudbjorn, directing him to stand behind Hogni. He placed Leifr behind Horgull, Svanlaug behind Ermingerd, and he stood behind Starkad with an expectant attitude as faint sounds commenced in the barrow. Heavy, dragging footsteps, and laborious groans and grunts signified the approach of the Flayer.

'Now it begins,' Thurid whispered, and Gedvondur scuttled up to his shoulder.

A familiar jotun hulk advanced up the crumbling steps with a heavy, grinding tread and the unmistakable fiery glare of the Flayer's eyes. The less-fiery glare of Ketil followed, and the shambling shapes of two jotuns emerged from the barrow. They moved across the circle, their arms flailing ponderously, as if they fought against a drawing force that compelled them to seat themselves with a grinding and a groaning in the two seats nearest Syrgja. She shrank back in her seat, whispering, 'Ketil? Thorkell? Is it truly my brothers? Can you speak?'

Ketil turned his massive head and moaned in abject misery, and Thorkell raised one swollen paw in faint acknowledgement. It seemed to Leifr that the moan echoed around and around the crater, and rocks grated upon rocks that had been human Alfar flesh at one time. Each succeeding jotun eventually came to this place and took his seat when the burden of the curse was too great for even supernatural strength to drag around, and each jotun relinquished himself to the process of petrification in stone and centuries of imprisonment while the other seats so slowly filled. Now the generations of jotuns were nearly finished, and Thurid had prematurely filled the last seats with fragile, living beings.

The horror and inevitability impressed Starkad to leap out of his seat with a wild, defiant yell, but Thurid seized him by the shoulders and held him there.

'I don't want to turn into a pile of rocks!' Starkad raged. He shook off Thurid's restraining grip and huddled miserably on the last seat. His head snapped up as more sounds came from the barrow, bones scraping and clattering, gold things jingling musically against each other, and the dragging, uneven footsteps that faltered at the stairs.

Six skeleton shapes emerged and hovered a moment around the opening of the barrow, figures clothed in fluttering rags, matted hair, and shreds of leathery flesh peeling away from moldering bone. Through the interstices of ribs and stretched skin glowed an unearthly blue phosphorescence, gleaming through hollowed cheeks and empty eye sockets and twinkling on the gold and jewels still adorning the bony racks that had once been Slagfid and five of his sons. The curse had gnarled their bones with blackened growths and stooped their stances, but it had spared then the final deliverance of turning completely to stone, choosing instead to jerk them from their uneasy grave to preside over the Convocation when Fantur descended. Only the founders of the jotun curse, Slagfid and his sons, had been selected for this additional torment.

Slagfid stood wavering a moment over the empty seat where his missing son should have sat, the one Gedvondur and Leifr had destroyed, then slogged heavily toward his seat, followed by the other five. Sitting down, they faced the living beings opposite, fixing them with their hollow, glowing stares. Even Raudbjorn exuded a fear smell of mingled sweat and dried gore and grease.

'The circle is at last complete,' Thurid whispered, crouching behind Starkad, his alf-light smothered.

'Except for the final player, whom I hope to meet next.'

The wait was not long. The circle of blackened earth began to smoke faintly and an image shimmered in the starlight, taking on more substance by the moment, until a forge and smithy stood complete, with a small fire glowing in the forge. A thick, dark figure stood over the fire, with a craggy face cruelly lit by the firelight and seamed with black wrinkles, scowling over a black object which he held in his sooty hands, turning it over and over intently. Hjaldr's dwarfs of the Grindstone Hall were white dwarfs, who made their way not far from the surface and the light, but this creature, Leifr sensed from the thrilling of the carbuncle, was a creature wholly of the dark and wholly evil. Whether he was a living creature or draug or sorcerous manifestation, Leifr was unable to tell. He sensed an overpowering ancientness in the gnarled form with its huge, seamed hands. Heldur's raiment was an indiscriminate assortment of rags covered with a scorched and blackened leather apron. His clothes, skin, and the strings of matted hair and singed beard were all the same ancient rusty hue.

Heldur placed the black object in the glowing coals, looking up only then to the intruders in his domain. He betrayed no surprise, just slowly surveyed each one in turn, his deep-set eyes flickering in the wizened knot of his face.

Thurid stepped from behind the last seat with a flare of his alf-light and a theatrical swelling of his cloak. Gedvondur rode upon his wrist, bristling with self-importance.

'The Ninety and Nine seats are filled, Heldur,' Thurid said in a voice of power that reverberated against the cliff walls. 'Your curse is at an end, as you yourself foretold.'

'The Ninety and Nine seats are filled,' Heldur rumbled in a voice unaccustomed to speaking, 'but my work is not yet finished. You have achieved nothing, wizard, except to add more fuel to my forge.'

Reaching up, he gave the hanging bellows a pump,

which caused a breath of wind to hiss around and around the spiral of cairns, starting from the outside. By the time it reached the center rings, it glowed as if it flowed through the stones. It passed straight through the living people on the seats and burst into the forge in a gout of flame. The blackened object Heldur held there in his tongs glowed with a faint luminous blue halo for an instant.

'The live ones make Fantur's fire the hotter,' Heldur rumbled, his eyes upon the blue halo and his hand upon the bellows. 'But it will hasten their transformation. They will not leave this place again. I wish only time enough to finish my work.'

He began pumping the bellows with slow, regular beats until the spiral flickered with racing lights. The draugar of Slagfid and his sons swayed and writhed like barren trees in a windstorm. Leifr heard faint windy snatches of ancient conversations and upraised voices rising from the draugar and the stone cairns. Starkad and the others were rigid, unmoving, as the brilliance swept over them. Leifr winced away from the growing heat of the forge, but Thurid stood fast, outlined with a fiery orange halo of his own which seemed to protect him. The orb which Heldur was fashioning glowed with blue fury, too brilliant to gaze upon for long. The gold with which Heldur had kindled his fire melted and burned with a livid light. His powerful long arm pumped the bellows mercilessly, summoning more power and more speed from the stone cairns, and more heat for his unholy forging. Once he had them pumped up to speed, he left them to do their own work and gripped the blue orb with tongs, holding it in the hottest part of the fire.

'I command you to halt this forging!' Thurid shouted over the roar of the flames. 'Your hold over Slagfid's heirs is finished!' He withdrew Slagfid's sword from the folds of his cloak and cast it into the flames with a shower of crackling sparks. It blackened immediately, twisting out of shape and emitting a shrill whistling sound.

Heldur's flinty gaze did not flicker from the orb. His tongs were melting away and he reached for another pair.

'Again I command you to stop!' Thurid bellowed.

Heldur's full attention was upon the orb. Sweat trickled down his swarthy, eroded face in grimy rivulets. The ends of his beard curled and frizzled smokily, but he did not notice.

'This is the third and final warning! Stop this evil misforging or I shall intervene!'

Heldur's response was a curling of his lip into a mocking snarl. The fiery blue of the orb was so intense that it seared the eyes to look at it. Leifr shaded his eyes from its harsh brilliance, which flared upon the distant walls of the crater and obscured the stars in the sky above.

'You have been warned!' Thurid raised his staff and thrust it into the blue-white brilliance of the orb. To Leifr it seemed like hurling a matchstick into a volcano. But the immediate result was a fiery explosion as the bellows blew apart in blackened shreds and flames. Heldur howled in fury, dropping his precious orb. He came at Thurid with his red-hot tongs and Leifr lunged forward with his sword drawn. A towering bulk suddenly loomed up between him and his intended prey as Raudbjorn stepped unbidden from behind Hogni and brandished his halberd under the dwarf's nose. Heldur struck at him furiously with his tongs, which left a sizzling blaze upon Raudbjorn's shield. Raudbjorn fended him off warily and Leifr sidled into a better position.

Thurid held to his staff, thrusting it into the heart of the blue orb, long after it should have burst into flames in his hands. The three hands that clutched the staff were blackened and seared, and the staff itself glowed cherry red. Gritting his teeth in the blazing fury, Thurid battled against the powers of Heldur and Fantur.

'Leifr!' he gasped. 'Leave off that and lend me the strength of that sword! We've got to reverse the spiral! Shove it in and get back!'

Cringing inwardly, Leifr did as he was bidden and

thrust the sword into the blue heart of the flames, feeling the skin on his hands sear. Summoning a mighty word, Thurid sent a wave of power back against the incoming surges of flame. A glow passed from Starkad through the live jotuns and around the ring to Slagfid's seats. The forces collided in one of Slagfid's draug sons, exploding the wraith in a fireball of sparks and charred fragments. A geyser of white flame erupted straight into the air with a pent-up shriek. Determinedly Thurid summoned another surge, a weaker one this time, and the draug next to Thorkell exploded and the white light shrieked upward – uncomfortably near the human links of the chain, which could never withstand such a furious combustion. Again Thurid summoned, repeatedly calling the word. At each collision, the forces exploded and a white light was released from the stone cairn, streaking away into the night sky like a comet.

The Fantur impulses lessened, slowed by Thurid's repeated powerful hammering with the word he spoke. Heldur howled his fury, gnashing his metal teeth in potent rage, flinging his tongs at last straight at Raudbjorn's head, striking him in the eye. With a terrible roar, Raudbjorn went down.

'Now we'll stop this meddling, wizard!' Heldur screamed, his eyes burning like jotun eyes. 'There is an empty place in my spiral, and you shall fill it.'

'Leifr! Take the sword!' Thurid gasped, the sweat trickling down his tortured face in rivers.

Leifr hurled himself over Raudbjorn's bulk to draw *Endalaus Daudi* out of the forge, glowing a molten red and trailing wisps of smoke. He blocked Heldur, whirling his Rhbu sword over his head and bellowing a furious challenge. Heldur whirled, drawing his own broad short sword.

The smith was no swordsman, but centuries of working with metals had made him powerful. When the metals touched, they reverberated with a dissonant scream, hating each other as if they were live things. *Endalaus*

Daudi flashed livid silver, and Heldur's sword gleamed a murderous green, striking howling sparks whenever it clashed with Leifr's.

Leifr spared Thurid an anxious glance to see how he was holding back Fantur's power without the Rhbu sword. Thurid's face twisted as the Fantur forces surged against his, now giving, now gaining in a treacherous pendulum.

'Kill him, Leifr,' Thurid gasped between fiery impulses. 'It's a job Slagfid should have done long ago.'

'Rhbu magic!' Heldur snarled, stepping forward with a sinister winnowing of his sword. 'It can't stop me! This orb will be the mightiest weapon ever forged!'

Heldur lunged forward again, determined to end the battle. Heldur's power would have told early upon Leifr except for the determined fury of *Endalaus Daudi*, which fought with such power of its own that Leifr had his hands full controlling it. Heldur began to recognize the enemy he was standing against and his tactics became even more cunning and desperate, but Leifr pushed him backward inexorably until his back was to the forge.

'Surrender or perish!' Leifr commanded. 'This sword will make an end of you with nothing left over for Hela to claim!'

'Rhbu metal, is it?' Heldur panted between clenched teeth. 'Think to destroy me, do you? Traitors! Pious fools! Thieves of Dvergar knowledge! If I perish, my work perishes with me, and that will never happen!'

With a mad dash of desperate bravado, Heldur hurled himself past Leifr and *Endalaus Daudi*, leaping into the flames of the forge, hurling Thurid backward from his staff. Heldur's hands clawed for the brilliant blue orb, clutching it even as they withered and charred. The dwarf's body dissolved in the fire, crumpling down to a blackened lump. It melted reluctantly, like some obdurate metal, with bright bubblings steaming around the blue orb he had tried to destroy.

Thurid gripped his staff again almost instantly, shouting the summoning word. The forces collided in Slagfid, a

378

mightier explosion than the others. When the white dart of fire escaped from the impact, Leifr had the wild momentary impression of a human form rocketing away.

'The forge is ours!' Thurid bellowed, grinning in savage triumph. 'We've beaten him! See to Raudbjorn! Tell the others to get away from those seats!'

Starkad leaped away with alacrity from the hated jotun seat and snatched Ermingerd to safety. Leifr rebounded from Thurid to Raudbjorn, who rolled on the ground in agony, blinded in his left eye. Svanlaug glided from her retreat and laid her narrow white hands upon Raudbjorn's sweating forehead, calming him while utter mayhem and destruction thundered on all sides.

Leifr looked up to see the lights now spiraling slowly in the opposite direction from which Heldur had started them, drawing power from the forge instead of giving to it. With deadly intensity, each cairn exploded, beginning at the farthest and last which the light touched, releasing the white flame with a deafening shriek, like a geyser erupting from its steamy depths. The flickering impulses slowed as the spiral uncoiled, taking at last the remaining sons of Slagfid, then Thorkell, and Ketil, leaving behind heaps of blackened stone.

Gathering around Thurid at the forge, Hogni and Horgull stood supporting their aunt, with Starkad and Ermingerd numbly gazing across the rubble-filled crater in the sudden silence. The harsh blue light had faded away, and the softer light of spring dawn paled the sky, although the interior of the crater would remain dark until noontime.

Thurid pulled his blackened staff from the dying coals. Gedvondur's hand dropped to the ground, exhausted. Thurid dropped him into his satchel and resumed his examination of his staff. He tapped it on the ground without much hope. Gingerly he peeled away some swollen crackling knobs, and gasped suddenly, his scowl turning incredulous. A glowing blue orb was fused to the end of his staff, set in molten metal streaked with gold. A clawlike smear of metal clutched the orb, as Heldur's hand

379

had attempted to before he perished.

'Heldur's orb,' Hogni observed suspiciously, with his usual canny composure quickly restored. 'You've got new powers you don't dream of in that staff, wizard. I don't know that I'd like to trust it, but it's yours now.'

Thurid anxiously examined the staff from orb to tip. His face was black with soot and his gown burned away, the sleeves gone to the shoulder. 'It doesn't even feel the same, after that bath of fire,' he said. 'It's heavier – and this blue abomination is melded into my Rhbu powers. I hate to think what evils Heldur was weaving into it, and now I'm saddled with it and probably a good deal of the evil in Slagfid's sword. And poor old Raudbjorn blinded, too. There just doesn't seem to be enough affliction to heap upon me, does there? Are you Rhbus satisfied now?' He raised his voice in exasperation as he contemplated the ruin of his clothing, addressing the last question to the uncompromising world in general.

Hogni stepped forward and extended his hand. 'All is forgotten, and all is forgiven, if you are willing to forgive and forget, wizard. We are indebted to you to the last of our days and our children's days. Should you ever require the petty powers that any of us possess, you must send and we will come.'

Ever sentimental, Thurid clasped Hogni's hand warmly, not minding the soot he was grinding into the other's palm. 'It was worth every moment, my dear fellow wizard, although it might have gone easier if you hadn't insisted upon operating at cross purposes to us at every opportunity.'

'It's always difficult to trust a gift from the Rhbus,' Hogni answered with a faint quirking smile. 'Such gifts invariably appear as sorest trials.'

Horgull also presented himself to clasp Thurid's hand and growl his recalcitrant gratitude. 'Aye, a sore trial,' he muttered, but there was a softening of his bitter features as he gazed outward with almost childlike awe upon a world that was suddenly open and inviting.

Syrgja wept and wept, tears that had lodged inside her for many years, and Ermingerd stood sheltering her, as radiant as a sunbeam. Leifr could see that her thoughts had flown far beyond Slagfid's Ban already, as far as Killbeck.

Starkad alone did not seem to share the others' sense of freedom and exultation. He stood broodingly apart, watching the rest of his family carting off the burdens of their despair, begging the others' forgiveness and sharing hopes for the bright future. Even Raudbjorn drew comfort from the gratitude of those flocking around him in tender concern and remorse for his sacrifice, but Starkad turned away from everyone with bitter scowls, refusing to let anyone draw out his poison.

'We've not much time,' Hogni warned sharply, nodding toward the faint pinprick of light in the shaft that was Fantur. 'The door will be closing again, unless Heldur's death and the disturbance we created here destroyed its workings.'

'I wouldn't count upon it,' Thurid said. 'It could continue opening and shutting forever, but if it shuts now it will be half a year before it opens again, if ever, so let's get out. Svanlaug, make an end to your ministrations and let's get Raudbjorn on his feet.'

Raudbjorn grunted, 'One eye a small thing to lose. Plenty of one-eyed thief-takers. Plenty mean, too.'

'None as mean as Raudbjorn,' Leifr added. 'One-eyed or not, you're the finest thief-taker that ever severed a gullet, Raudbjorn.'

Raudbjorn grinned his vast shy smile, clearly embarrassed by such praise, and shouldered his halberd to begin the trek back through the tunnel to Fangelsi.

Thurid cautiously summoned his alf-light, holding the staff out warily and studying the light that responded to his summoning. The staff cast a brighter flare than before, intensified by the blue orb, which glowed with dazzling radiance, as it had in the forge fueled by the life-fires of the captive Alfar.

'It seems normal enough,' Thurid admitted grudgingly. 'It can't be all bad, coming from Alfar the way it has. The underground realm had no fire hot enough for the orb's shaping, so Heldur turned to the stars and Alfar power. Clearly an example of getting beyond one's natural element. Always dangerous and foolhardy.'

'Exactly, and you're just as guilty of overreaching your powers,' Leifr said to him.

'Nonsense,' Thurid snapped with his usual irascibility. 'It's perfectly healthy to go beyond one's limits once in a while. Increases the capacity. Fantur's on the decline; I can afford to tax myself. I suspect your tender concern is more for your own safety and Ljosa's deliverance, both of which lie in my hands, am I right? I assure you, there's plenty more fire where this is coming from, you young Scipling skeptic.'

Leifr smiled in the darkness. Thurid's eyes rested accusingly upon Leifr, but even in the fitful shifting light, Leifr could see that he was too drained to pursue the old argument further, and he had snapped at Leifr as a fond habit. Thurid might have exhausted himself, but he wasn't too tired to lose his temper.

When they emerged from the cave, it was daylight – as much of it as ever reached the bottom of Slagfid's Ban. Leifr and Thurid came out last, and Leifr was suddenly struck with the peculiar stillness of his companions. They fell back to each side and stood dumbfounded. Even Thurid stopped, as if rooted to the spot, while his alf-light sputtered away and died. Gedvondur struggled out of the satchel and dropped to the ground, faithlessly abandoning Thurid to his fate.

It was not Djofull come to claim the orb, as Leifr expected, but the Inquisitors, blocking the only way out.

CHAPTER 23

Fodur dismounted with deliberation from his horse and approached, carrying his staff almost casually in the crook of his arm, but where it would be ready at an instant's notice. He raised his other hand in a greeting salutation, sketching a design in the air.

'Again we meet, Thurid,' he said amiably, as if anxious not to raise Thurid's dander too precipitately.

'Yes, again, and much too soon, in my opinion!' Thurid retorted with a brief fiery flicker of temper, but its sustaining strength did not linger. He was gray-faced with fatigue, almost swaying on his feet. He jammed the staff into the ground to steady himself, flaring at the Inquisitors like a weary fox brought at last to bay.

A concerned frown overspread Fodur's countenance. 'Thurid, what have you been doing to yourself? You look terrible. You've been grasping at things beyond your reach, from the look of you. You're destroying yourself.'

Thurid responded with a rusty chuckle. 'No, I've been destroying jotuns, curses, and black dwarfs.'

'We know, we have seen. We've been watching your career as best we could, despite Hogni's wards.' Fodur shot a keen glance toward Hogni, who stiffened stubbornly under Guild scrutiny. 'Very strong wards, for an uncertified wizard.'

'I did my best to keep you out,' Hogni said with his coldest dignity. 'I'm only a minor practitioner, but what I do, I do well. If I'm guilty of giving safe haven to an outlaw, I'm willing to face the Guild and be punished. As an outlaw, I'll be more free than before Thurid came to Fangelsi-hofn and ended our hereditary curse. If he committed offenses in doing so, then let my punishment be the same as his. A finer wizard never walked.'

Horgull grunted and nodded in approval, and Raudbjorn scowled anxiously from Thurid to Leifr, his fingers twitching on the haft of his halberd.

'We aren't talking of punishments here,' Fodur said. 'We only wish to return Thurid to the Guild to examine his arts and see which ones of them aren't suitable for a Fire Wizard to possess. Our powers must be pure, not a mixed bag of Rhbu, Dvergar, and whatever else one happens to pick up. It's a matter of professional pride – as well as protecting our reputation. If we use the dark powers against the dark side, the day may come when we are no better than our enemies. Earth powers are particularly treacherous. They can trap those who use them. We of the Guild use the powers of stars, fire, and spirit, the influences of the above-ground realm. So far you've done no harm, Thurid – but so far you've been frightfully lucky. There's not a wizard in the Guild who would touch those Rhbu powers, for fear of losing himself.'

'Cowards, all of you,' Thurid growled wearily, his shoulders slumping. 'Are you done with your sermonizing now? I've not had my sleep lately, so let's get on with what you're going to do with me. You came at a good time. I'm too tired to fight today.' He held out his staff in surrender, and Fodur accepted it, not without a flash of trepidation as his eyes fixed upon the blue orb and the metal that fused it.

Fodur motioned, and Einkenni led a horse forward and motioned Thurid to mount, holding the stirrup for him. Thurid looked down at Leifr, who shoved his way forward as near as he dared. Fodur looked at him gently, and Leifr could not move another pace, only stand helplessly against the rising tide of his own rage and panic.

'Thurid! We'll come after you!' Leifr said.

Thurid shook his head. 'Won't do you any good. You'll never get anywhere near the Guildhall. Remember what I said about Gradagur. Djofull isn't going to give up easily.'

'Then what will I do about Ljosa? And what about Gedvondur and the ashes?' The thoughts of Djofull filled Leifr's veins with glacier water.

'Haven't I tried to prepare you?' Thurid responded with a brief flare of his old temper. 'You know what must be done now, Leifr. Go back to your own realm. I'll do what I can for Ljosa. It's not as if I'm going to be drawn and quartered and hung up for the ravens. The worst that can happen is I'll be returned to the Thurid I was before Fridmarr brought the satchel and staff out of Bjartur.' His lips tightened in a faint grimace, and Leifr was pierced with the insight that Thurid would rather die than go back to what he was before, with the knowledge of what he had lost.

'It's for the good of us all,' Fodur said, after mounting his horse, keeping his eyes upon Leifr throughout. 'It's not good to be a wild wizard, Thurid. You'll be much safer and happier when we've brought you into the fold. You won't lose everything, I can almost promise you that.' He lingered behind as the others rode away with Thurid, though he could not possibly have feared an attack from Leifr and Raudbjorn.

Looking at Leifr almost pityingly, he said, 'You should go back to your own realm. You've raised a lot of hackles against you here. I could send you, if you wish it.'

'I don't wish it,' Leifr returned coldly. 'I have work to do here and I won't leave until it's finished.'

'You have no protection,' Fodur said.

'I have enough,' Leifr returned grimly, stepping back and raising his hand in farewell. 'I hope Guild justice is fair justice. If it isn't, we'll meet again on far less friendly terms, wizard.'

'May the gods forbid it,' Fodur replied quietly, and he turned and followed the others.

As Leifr stood watching Thurid being taken away, he felt a tug at his cloak. Looking down he saw a blackened Gedvondur climbing up wearily to drop into his pocket.

He tapped Leifr's wrist in passing, saying, 'They haven't seen the last of me. We'll get Thurid back, one way or another.'

'What can a Scipling, a hand, and a one-eyed thief-taker do against the entire Wizards' Guild?' Leifr demanded bitterly.

They returned to Fangelsi in stunned and weary silence. Thurid's triumph and defeat left Leifr feeling bitter and lost, wondering what the sense in helping other mortals was if the result was punishment.

The only good thing about Thurid's removal by the Inquisitors was the sudden departure of Djofull's wolf-warriors from the surrounding fells. Evidently they had followed Thurid and the orb. Or perhaps they still believed him to be the possessor of Sorkvir's ashes, which reposed in a pouch around Leifr's neck, inside his shirt.

Leifr lost no time in readying for their departure. He found Hefillstad on his map, intending to locate the wizard Gradagur who had taught Thurid as a youth, hoping that he would be willing to direct him to the Guildhall of the Fire Wizards.

Everywhere he turned, he nearly trod upon Starkad, who shadowed Leifr hopefully around Fangelsi as if he didn't dare let him out of his sight, lurking behind walls and corners as if he were working himself up for something. Intuitively, Leifr dreaded it, whatever it was.

Starkad's courage was wound up to its highest point however, and he planted himself firmly in Leifr's path, gazing at him compellingly with his golden eyes. He ignored the troll-hounds' boisterous greetings as they swirled around his legs with waving tails and slurping tongues.

'Leifr, Hogni says you've decided to leave,' he began, as if it were an indictment. 'You're going to the Wizards' Guild to rescue Thurid?'

'Yes,' Leifr answered warily. 'If they attempt to destroy him, I shall certainly do my best to prevent it, or die in the attempt. I owe that much to Ljosa for giving her life for me.'

'Well, I want to go with you. Please,' Starkad added hastily, seeing the growing doubt in Leifr's expression. 'I've always wanted to get away from Fangelsi, and now there's no reason I have to stay, and you'd be there to keep me out of trouble. I won't be a bother. I could even be useful. Three men looks like a lot more than just two, when it comes to a defense against outlaws – or scavengers or Dokkalfar or trolls. It's a dangerous realm to travel in, and the nearer you get to the Guild, the worse it gets. I know some spells, too. Neither you nor Raudbjorn practices magic. You ought to have someone along who can understand it even somewhat. Djofull might still be out there.'

Leifr stopped shaking his head at Starkad's last argument and considered. 'What good would you be against Djofull, if he were waiting for us?'

Starkad shrugged. 'You don't know that I wouldn't be any good. Look how I broke the wards, and I helped rob that cave twice. I'm no longer a coward, Leifr. This might be my only chance to amount to something. Ermingerd and Jarnvard can have the land. I'd rather go anywhere with you, instead of waiting for a better chance.'

'I'll consider it,' Leifr said sternly. 'What makes you think your aunt and your brothers will let you go?'

'They won't need me. Ermingerd is marrying Jarnvard, and he'll be around to help with the work. He'll probably make something out of this place, finally.'

'And you don't want to be here to help?'

'Definitely not. I want to be like you – an adventurer, a warrior, a man of heroic deeds. Or a wizard, perhaps, like Thurid. You could mention to Hogni that you'd like to take me along. I doubt if he'd be sorry to see me go.'

'But Ermingerd would.'

Starkad fell silent, and some of his eagerness diminished. 'Yes, and I'll miss her, too. But I'll be back one day, with all that gold I've promised to bring her.'

Leifr chuckled drily. 'Sensible people don't go looking

for adventures. If you are the sort that things happen to, you'll find that it's not an attribute you want to wish upon someone you care about. Staying here at home would be the safest thing for you, Starkad. But facing some dangers might be the best.'

Starkad beamed and began to prance, shaking Leifr's hand rapturously and already simmering with plans. 'You won't regret it. I'll ask for Hogni's gray pacer. No, I'll beg a horse from Jarnvard. I've made new boots and lacings, knowing I'd be leaving when you did, wherever you were going, and Syrgja's got to give me a new cloak and tunic and breeches, and Hogni's got to lend me his saddle.'

There was no peace after Leifr's imprudent promise. The family discussed it at length; Syrgja was tearful, Ermingerd pale, Hogni and Horgull doubtful. Leifr deemed it discreet to leave the house so they could discuss it freely, so he beckoned to Raudbjorn and went out into the warm spring night. With Raudbjorn, talking was more effort than any possible satisfaction gained by it, so they strolled in amiable silence, broken only by a contented grunt or grumble from somewhere within Raudbjorn's great bulk. The hounds frolicked in the warm moonlight, tumbling over one another's backs in high spirits. A troll coughed somewhere in the direction of Slagfid's Ban, and, at Leifr's signal, the hounds shot away with jubilant howls in search of quarry.

Leifr paused not far from the fallen tower where Thurid had pursued the secret of the jotun curse. Its ruin and emptiness was a desolation in Leifr's heart and he didn't like to dwell upon it. Nothing lingered there now, not even a wisp of evil influence.

Raudbjorn raised his head and sniffed suspiciously, making a warm rumble in his throat. 'Bad smells, Leifr.'

'Probably coming from the trolls in Skera-gil,' Leifr replied. 'Since Djofull and the jotuns are gone, they're getting pretty cocky. Tomorrow we're going after Thurid, Raudbjorn. I don't know what it will take, but we'll get him away from the Inquisitors.'

Raudbjorn grunted, still sniffing and peering about in the darkness with his one good eye.

Fridmarr's carbuncle suddenly felt hot against his chest where it hung next to the pouch of ashes. His outlaw instincts bristled with the sudden dread that had saved his neck from hanging many times before in his viking days. He whirled, drawing the sword, but with a rush they were suddenly all around him, a blur of hairy faces leering in the moonlight. Fylgjur-wolves, not making a sound in their silent, deadly attack. He heard Raudbjorn bellow a warning and the whistle of the halberd before it connected with something with a vicious thud. He slashed at them with the sword, but his motion was curiously slow, as if underwater, and the earth underfoot tilted alarmingly. A set of paws struck him in the back and he staggered forward, reeling as his knees sagged and gave way, as if a mighty hand was crushing him down, pressing the air from his lungs. He had never felt so weak and powerless. The sword clattered out of his grasp, ringing among the rocks on the ground. He collapsed, gasping for breath, as the darkness reddened around him, and his ears were filled with a dizzy roaring. The fylgjur-wolves encircled him, teeth gleaming, savage eyes glaring with blood-lust.

A dark figure thrust aside some of the wolves. With a heavy boot, he rolled Leifr onto his back and bent to peer into his face with a gloating cackle. In spite of the swirling red mists before his eyes, Leifr recognized Djofull, grinning at him in triumph. Djofull pressed the tip of his staff against the base of Leifr's throat, threatening what little air he was able to scrape painfully into his laboring lungs.

'Poor losers shouldn't make wagers,' Leifr croaked.

'True. I'm a very poor loser. You oughtn't have made yourself such an easy target,' Djofull purred. 'Killing you won't be nearly as satisfactory as the geas would have been. However, it will be pleasant to have my possessions returned to me, and certain nuisances eliminated, thanks to the Wizards' Guild. You can't imagine how I've awaited this moment, most particularly since you escaped from the cave, where I locked the door behind you.'

With his false hand, shaped like a pair of murderous claws, he ripped Leifr's shirt to reveal the pouch of ashes, and the carbuncle as well, sparkling in the moonlight. He chuckled, reaching down for the pouch and snapping the thong around Leifr's neck with the knife edge of his hand, then he dropped it into his satchel, keeping his eyes upon Leifr, like a cat playing with a wounded mouse. Then he reached down and grasped the carbuncle with his good hand.

'A poor substitute for the orb,' Djofull said, 'but I'll take it nonetheless to placate the Dokkur Lavardur.'

As his fingers closed around it, a red light suffused Djofull's hand with a smokey sizzle, showing the bones as shadows through the flesh.

Screeching and staggering backward, Djofull dropped the carbuncle, his remaining good hand convulsed with pain. The fylgjur-wolves flattened their ears and cowered back as he raged over his hand in agony. While he was thus distracted, Leifr found he could breathe again, and the spell was lessened enough that he could rise to his knees and reach for his sword, lying forgotten among the stones.

With a final curse Djofull strode away toward his waiting sledge, still shaking his hand and snarling over his shoulder, 'Finish him off, and be quick about it!'

Their first rush was a clumsy charge with the sole object of seeing whose teeth could find Leifr first. He was ready for them, his strength restored; from four lightning blows, four fylgjur-wolves perished in clouds of reeking smoke. As they scrambled to regroup themselves, Leifr retreated toward Raudbjorn, who was wedged between two boulders and slashing at the wolves with his halberd as they came at him.

Leifr whistled for the troll-hounds, who answered with a bugling cry as they swept down a nearby ravine, alerted by the first sounds of the attack on their master. They burst into view on a dead run, not slackening their speed, crashing into the bristling wall of fylgjur-wolves like a single large white missile. Caught between *Endalaus Daudi* and the troll-hounds, the fylgjur-wolves whirled between two deadly enemies while their numbers diminished rapidly with dying shrieks. When less than half their number remained, they turned and fled ignominiously, harried along by the troll-hounds.

Leifr slumped dejectedly, cursing under his breath.

'He got the ashes,' he said, greatly disgusted at himself. 'What a fool I was to think he was gone!'

Raudbjorn shrugged his creaking shoulders with his usual fatalistic calm. 'No matter. We go after ashes and thief. Kill more Dokkalfar wolves. Maybe kill Djofull. Good fight, maybe.' His remaining eye glowed fondly at the prospects.

'No. We help Thurid first.' Leifr whistled for the hounds. Raudbjorn scowled in disapproval.

When they returned to the house, they met Hogni and Horgull hurrying up the path, with Starkad behind them, barely restrained in his battle-fury.

'We heard the wolves!' Starkad blurted. 'It was Djofull, wasn't it? He came back and got through the wards, didn't he? We knew something would go wrong!'

'He got the ashes,' Leifr said heavily.

'Then you'll be going after Djofull,' Starkad said, his eyes wide with excitement.

'No, I'm not going after him yet. My first responsibility is to Thurid. Starkad, you're staying here. None of us may survive, except Gedvondur. He seems to have excellent instincts for self-preservation.'

Starkad opened his mouth to protest, and wisely shut it again, after a warning glower from his brother. He only nodded his head, trying to appear compliant.

'The Guildhall.' Hogni shook his head broodingly. 'You'll be bearding the weasels in their own den. It's going to be dangerous – even for a wizard with carbuncle protection. For a Scipling—' He shook his head. 'We could give you a carbuncle, in the proper way under the skin. A bit painful, perhaps, but worth it. Yet you still refuse?'

Leifr hesitated a moment before nodding curtly. 'I'll manage without it.'

Svanlaug was livid when she heard that Leifr's plans were unchanged. 'You're still going to the Guildhall? Don't be a fool! Every moment is a moment closer to Sorkvir's reincarnation. You've got to go to Djofullhol and stop Djofull.'

'Every moment is a moment closer to Thurid's destruction,' Leifr retorted. 'When the Inquisitors get done with him, he'll be back to teaching children their first runes – if he survives, that is. At the very least, they'll destroy all memory of what he was before or they know he'll go after the powers again. At the very worst, they'll shrug their shoulders and say he didn't survive the purging of the evil earth powers from his system.'

'Thurid has fed you his own fears. He could be wrong about that,' Svanlaug said. 'He has weapons and powers the Guild could use, if they were clever enough to realize it. More than likely, though, they'll destroy Thurid and his powers, and if you walked into their hands looking for Thurid, they'd be glad to divest you of that sword and send you back to the Scipling realm, leaving Gedvondur and me with the problem of dealing with Sorkvir. Even supposing you somehow outwit the Guild and rescue Thurid, it will be too late by then. Sorkvir will be restored to life, and you'll have your bitterest enemy to contend with again. He'll be looking for revenge this time. You'll never get close enough to Djofull for me to get my revenge on him.'

'Is your revenge all you can think about? You want to push us around like pawns for your own purposes. Thurid comes first, then the ashes – or Sorkvir himself. We defeated him once before.'

'The Guild will destroy Thurid and your sword, and possibly you along with it,' Svanlaug retorted angrily.

'Neither of you will be in any condition to challenge anyone ever again. They think they've got enough powers without looking for new ones. If you give yourself over to the Guild you're a worse fool than I'd ever imagined. The only reason they didn't take you along with Thurid is because they're afraid to. I never mentioned it, since Thurid was arrogant enough about his powers, but with only half those ashes, he could be twice as great a wizard as Djofull, who is the Dokkur Lavardur's Grand Wizard. It's treasonous of me even to tell a Scipling, but I don't think you'll do anything about it anyway. You haven't showed much backbone since Thurid was taken.'

'Why should you tell me anything near the truth?' Leifr demanded. 'You're not on the same side as I am.'

'Gedvondur is, and he'll tell you himself we've got to go after Djofull and Sorkvir's ashes if you're going to salvage any of your honor,' Svanlaug answered.

'Gedvondur would like such an opportunity to get his ashes back from Djofull,' Leifr said maliciously. 'Beyond that, he doesn't care. This is all his idea, isn't it?'

Svanlaug lost her reasonable tone and turned spiteful. 'I don't think you've ever trusted him or me completely.'

'I know I haven't,' Leifr said. 'You're a Dokkalfar, and Gedvondur is who knows what. I refuse to take orders from nothing but a hand with a ring on it. Either the both of you do what I tell you to, or we'll part company here and now. The first thing we'll do is save Thurid, then we'll go after the ashes.'

'All right, go your own way, and I'll go mine, and maybe we'll meet again later, if you and Thurid survive the Guild Inquisition. You're throwing away your best opportunity to destroy both Sorkvir and Djofull, Leifr.'

'I'd rather throw that away than my best opportunity to save Thurid,' Leifr retorted. 'If you leave now, we'll be enemies from this moment.'

'For all your threats and bluster, you're frightened to travel without Thurid in our realm. You've done nothing to prove that you're anything more than his shadow.'

393

Svanlaug tossed her head and strode away.

Leifr glared after her, thinking wryly that his wish to prove himself in the Alfar realm certainly had been fulfilled in a manner contrary to his expectations. Gradually he became conscious of a familiar sensation. Turning, he saw Ljosa's fylgja-cat watching him intently from the top of a wall.

'If not for you,' he muttered, 'I'd take Elbegast's rune wand and go back to the Scipling realm.'

The cat showed its gratitude by flattening her ears and hissing at him, then vanishing into the shadows.

In the early morning they discovered that Svanlaug had disappeared, taking her horse sometime in the night without alerting even the wary troll-hounds. Worse yet, Gedvondur was gone, too, and Leifr knew he wouldn't leave except by his own choosing. Gedvondur's defection angered Leifr more than he cared to reveal, but his stony silence and flashing eye were enough to warn even Starkad away. The youth kept his distance, and was not there to bid Leifr farewell as he took his leave from Fangelsi, with the understanding that he would return. Syrgja repeatedly pressed it upon him, more of a stern commandment than an invitation, 'This is your second home, Leifr, and you must come back to us. Fangelsi is in your blood now, and your fate is mixed with ours. We won't rest until we know you have succeeded.'

Leifr promised upon his life and honor and rode away, carrying in his mind the image of Ermingerd smiling after him and waving – a little gray ghost no longer, but a radiantly happy young woman and wife-to-be of the fortunate Jarnvard. If only Svanlaug had possessed a grain of Ermingerd's loyalty, she wouldn't have deserted him. Leifr was certain she had gone to get the ashes for herself. Or perhaps she even intended to throw in her forces with Djofull in a united front against Leifr and Raudbjorn. And Gedvondur's desertion was nothing but self-serving treachery.

'Leifr,' Raudbjorn had been scowling since their

departure, and finally at noonday he spoke. He halted his horse and looked down at Leifr, his remaining eye nearly lost in his worried expression. 'Leifr greatest fighter. Smart like fighting fox. But Leifr made mistake. Raudbjorn advise now.'

'Go ahead,' Leifr said, surprised and curious.

Raudbjorn drew a deep, creaking breath, as if summoning the strength necessary for a major battle. 'Djofull stole Leifr's pride. Honor. Sneak thief shame Leifr. Leifr need to go after Djofull and get back ashes to get back pride. Dokkalfar laugh at man who gets things stolen. Laugh at man who gets rescued from enemies, too. Like baby, too weak to help self. Thurid not pleased to see you.'

Leifr nodded slowly. 'Then you think I'm being Thurid's shadow, too. I should go after Djofull before I go after Thurid, to restore my honor.'

Raudbjorn beamed and nodded, with a huge sigh of relief. 'Honor and fear everything with Dokkalfar. Get Djofull. Teach lesson.'

Reluctantly Leifr had to admit the truth of what Raudbjorn had said, although he saw scant opportunity for defeating Djofull without Thurid. By sundown of their fourth day of travel on Djofull's trail, they had reached the last safe house of the Hraedsla-dalur region, where a solitary old hermit tended his few speckled sheep and occasionally netted fish from the firth. Leifr gave him a token from Hogni to identify himself, and the old hermit wordlessly bid them to stay. He asked no questions, but he did admit that Djofull had passed his house some four days ago, and yes, a solitary woman had gone by without stopping.

'I don't trouble with Dokkalfar, and they don't trouble with me,' he grumbled, his eyes peering warily at Leifr through a hedge of unkempt hair and beard. 'And if you were wise, you wouldn't trouble with them either.'

'I'll be wiser when less is at stake,' Leifr replied grimly.

With the return of the season of sun, the hours of twilight had lengthened until there was very little genuine darkness. Leifr found Raudbjorn and the troll-hounds, well fed on the hermit's dried fish and boiled mutton, taking their ease upon a grassy hilltop while they gazed back upon the way they had come that day.

Leifr dropped to the grass with a grunt beside Raudbjorn, who opened his eye benignly and growled a little by way of greeting.

'Well, how is he doing now?' Leifr asked, nodding toward the rolling fells and rocky valleys behind them.

'Closer now. Catching up soon,' Raudbjorn replied with a chuckle.

In silence they watched the tiny distant figure on horseback plodding determinedly along the edge of the glacier where they had been four or five hours before.

'One thing I must say for Starkad, he's persistent,' Leifr observed with grudging respect. 'I thought he'd give up and go back after the first night on his own with the trolls. He knows this land well.'

'Boy not stupid,' Raudbjorn replied with an amiable grin. 'Needs training, like pup, to make good killer.'

'Then he's yours to train,' Leifr said. 'I've got Djofull to think about.'

Starkad caught up with them at the hermit's hut about four hours before they were ready to start traveling again. Raudbjorn and Leifr were exchanging guard shifts when Starkad rode into the gateyard on his weary horse. The troll-hounds bounded out to greet him delightedly as he dismounted and approached the gate. Peering in between the bars, he said truculently, 'I'm here now, and you didn't have to wait for me – not that you would have anyhow.'

'Yes, you're here now,' Leifr said as he opened the gate to admit the tired horseman, 'but that doesn't mean you're going in the same direction we are. Tomorrow you're going back to Fangelsi where you belong.'

'I'm not going back to Fangelsi,' Starkad retorted, beginning to unsaddle his horse. 'If you won't take me with you, then I'll follow behind where you can't see me.'

'We've been watching you since the first day,' Leifr said. 'In country like Skarpsey, it's easy to see where you were almost a week ago, and where you're going to be next week. You nearly drowned at that first river crossing, didn't you? You should have looked for the markers.'

'I did, and you and Raudbjorn had moved them over to the deep water. That wasn't very decent of you.'

'You'd be better off at Fangelsi.'

'It's for me to decide where I'll be better off, isn't it? If I decide I like Fangelsi better, I'll go back there.'

'We've been trying to persuade you.'

'It won't do you any good. I'm going with you.'

'We'll see about that.'

In the morning, Leifr and Raudbjorn departed quietly, leaving Starkad still sleeping exhaustedly on a pile of hay in the stable. It wasn't until late afternoon when he caught up. His determination to beg, borrow, or steal Jarnvard's horse had rewarded him well; it was a good strong horse that matched Jolfr's long strides for the rest of the day without falling back, in spite of Starkad's pushing him to catch up for four and a half days.

When they made their camp that night, it was their first camp thus far outside a safe house. Leifr chose a spot a short distance from the tracks they had been following, a location which was close to water and afforded an excellent view of both the trail behind and the trail ahead. The troll-hounds sniffed in large circles, searching for their enemies or prey, and discovered nothing more alarming than several hares to bring down.

Starkad worked anxiously at proving his worth, buckling down to his duties with a serious determination that Leifr found greatly promising. Starkad's efforts reminded him of himself, not too many years ago, earnestly trying to prove himself a man on his first voyage with Hrafn Blood-Axe. Obligingly, Leifr and Raudbjorn piled the responsibilities upon Starkad, and when he was done with unsaddling and unloading and grooming and picketing the horses for the night, Raudbjorn commenced his lessons in the art of swordsmanship. Raudbjorn stood placidly waiting behind his shield while Starkad hammered away at him furiously. Then with a few quick and powerful flourishes, Raudbjorn divested Starkad of sword and shield and pinned him to the earth with one great foot, gazing down the length of his sword with benignant amusement. With Raudbjorn, combat was the nearest he would ever come to a spiritual experience, so he took his teaching responsibilities with utmost seriousness. In a world where professional killers were a necessity, Raudbjorn fulfilled his role forthrightly, without guilt or depravity. Thus the travelers passed their evenings learning quiet and efficient methods of killing trolls, Dokkalfar, draugar, witches, and other more rare beings Raudbjorn had the occasion to exterminate. All of this information Starkad soaked up eagerly, with curiosity left over for hundreds of questions.

During the day Raudbjorn enlivened Starkad's existence with surprise attacks and ambushes, until Starkad learned to sense danger in the air, like a wild animal.

Of Svanlaug they saw nothing, and heard nothing from the few travelers they encountered on the roads. Leifr formed the conclusion that she had joined Djofull's entourage with great ease, forgiven or unproven of her former crimes.

They rode onward in the dawn light, with Djofullhol and the Fire Wizards' Guildhall awaiting them somewhere ahead, shrouded in centuries of mystery and dangers yet unrealized, in the everlasting struggle between light and darkness, night and day, and frost and flame.

THE END

THE ELVES AND THE OTTERSKIN
by Elizabeth H. Boyer

Ivarr had been sold to the witch Birna. But now Birna was dead, slain by the evil sorcerer Lorimer. Ivarr was stranded in the land of the elves. His only chance to return to his own realm was to become a hero for a group of outcast, incompetent elves and a wizard of doubtful qualifications.

As he discovered, being a hero was a little difficult. First he had to seek out a magic sword concealed somewhere in the land of the fire giants. Then, to seize a horde of gold, he must somehow find and destroy a terrible dragon. And, finally, he would have to overcome the power of Lorimer and an army of dark elves.

Ivarr knew nothing about being a hero, and the more he heard, the less he liked the idea. But a hero he'd be – or else!

0 552 12759 0

A SELECTED LIST OF FANTASY TITLES
AVAILABLE FROM CORGI BOOKS

THE PRICES SHOWN BELOW WERE CORRECT AT THE TIME OF GOING TO PRESS.
HOWEVER TRANSWORLD PUBLISHERS RESERVE THE RIGHT TO SHOW NEW
RETAIL PRICES ON COVERS WHICH MAY DIFFER FROM THOSE PREVIOUSLY
ADVERTISED IN THE TEXT OR ELSEWHERE.

☐ 12759 0	THE ELVES AND THE OTTERSKIN		Elizabeth H. Boyer	£2.99
☐ 12758 2	THE SWORD AND THE SATCHEL		Elizabeth H. Boyer	£2.99
☐ 12760 4	THE THRALL AND THE DRAGON'S HEART		Elizabeth H. Boyer	£2.99
☐ 12761 2	THE WIZARD AND THE WARLORD		Elizabeth H. Boyer	£2.95
☐ 12566 0	THE WIZARDS AND THE WARRIORS		Hugh Cook	£3.99
☐ 13130 X	THE WORDSMITHS AND THE WARGUILD		Hugh Cook	£2.99
☐ 13131 8	THE WOMEN AND THE WARLORDS		Hugh Cook	£3.99
☐ 13327 2	THE WALRUS AND THE WARLORDS		Hugh Cook	£3.95
☐ 13439 2	THE WICKED AND THE WITLESS		Hugh Cook	£3.99
☐ 13017 6	MALLOREON 1: GUARDIANS OF THE WEST		David Eddings	£3.99
☐ 13018 4	MALLOREON 2: KING OF THE MURGOS		David Eddings	£3.99
☐ 13019 2	MALLOREON 3: DEMON LORD OF KARANDA		David Eddings	£3.99
☐ 12284 X	BOOK ONE OF THE BELGARIAD: PAWN OF PROPHECY			
			David Eddings	£2.99
☐ 12348 X	BOOK TWO OF THE BELGARIAD: QUEEN OF SORCERY			
			David Eddings	£2.99
☐ 12382 X	BOOK THREE OF THE BELGARIAD: MAGICIAN'S GAMBIT			
			David Eddings	£3.50
☐ 12435 4	BOOK FOUR OF THE BELGARIAD: CASTLE OF WIZARDRY			
			David Eddings	£2.99
☐ 12447 8	BOOK FIVE OF THE BELGARIAD: ENCHANTERS' END GAME			
			David Eddings	£3.99
☐ 13101 6	SERVANTS OF ARK 1: THE FIRST NAMED		Jonathan Wylie	£3.50
☐ 13134 2	SERVANTS OF ARK 2: THE CENTRE OF THE CIRCLE		Jonathan Wylie	£2.99
☐ 13161 5	SERVANTS OF ARK 3: THE MAGE-BORN CHILD		Jonathan Wylie	£3.50
☐ 13416 3	THE UNBALANCED EARTH 1: DREAMS OF STONE		Jonathan Wylie	£2.99
☐ 13417 1	THE UNBALANCED EARTH 2: THE LIGHTLESS KINGDOM			
			Jonathan Wylie	£2.99
☐ 13418 X	THE UNBALANCED EARTH 3: THE AGE OF CHAOS		Jonathan Wylie	£3.50

*All Corgi/Bantam Books are available at your bookshop or newsagent, or can be ordered from the
following address:*

Corgi/Bantam Books,
Cash Sales Department,
P.O. Box 11, Falmouth, Cornwall TR10 9EN

Please send a cheque or postal order (no currency) and allow 80p for postage and packing for the
first book plus 20p for each additional book ordered up to a maximum charge of £2.00 in UK.

B.F.P.O. customers please allow 80p for the first book and 20p for each additional book.

Overseas customers, including Eire, please allow £1.50 for postage and packing for the first book,
£1.00 for the second book, and 30p for each subsequent title ordered.